Wakefield Press

The Kangaroo Islanders

Rick Hosking was born in the Flinders Ranges, raised in the mallee and on the west coast of South Australia and educated at Flinders and Adelaide universities. He taught English, Australian Studies and Creative Writing at the Sturt College of Advanced Education and then at Flinders University. He is particularly interested in South Australian (literary) history and representations of contact and conflict between Indigenous people and European settlers in the colonial period. He is co-author (with Rob Foster and Amanda Nettelbeck) of the prize-winning *Fatal Collisions: The South Australian Frontier and the Violence of Memory* (Wakefield Press, 2001).

The Kangaroo Islanders

A story of South Australia
before colonisation 1823

W.A. Cawthorne

Edited and introduced by
RICK HOSKING

Wakefield
Press

Wakefield Press
16 Rose Street
Mile End
South Australia 5031
www.wakefieldpress.com.au

First published 2020

Introduction and Notes copyright © Rick Hosking, 2020

Cover designed by Liz Nicholson, Wakefield Press
Edited by Penelope Curtin
Text designed and typeset by Wakefield Press

ISBN 978 1 86254 655 4

A catalogue record for this
book is available from the
National Library of Australia

Wakefield Press thanks
Coriole Vineyards for
continued support

Contents

Introduction

The Kangaroo Islanders is the first book written about Kangaroo Island. In common with many Australian novels from the colonial period it is an historical novel, in this case written before any official or more orthodox history of the South Australian colony had appeared. It was probably written in the mid-1850s and published in serial form a decade later, in a Melbourne magazine. The writer was an Adelaide schoolteacher named William Anderson Cawthorne; he made a number of trips to the island in the 1850s, when his father, Captain William Cook Cawthorne, was the not only the first head keeper at the Sturt Lighthouse at Cape Willoughby but also *de-facto* Protector of Aborigines, charged with issuing rations to the small and mostly itinerant population of Aboriginal people living on the island.

The Kangaroo Islanders is a remarkable and colourful book, representing life on the island in the period 1802–1836, that fascinating interregnum when the southern coastline of Australia was far better known than the interior, when entrepreneurial young men sailed from Sydney and Hobarton in search of seal colonies and useful products like salt, establishing hunting camps on the offshore islands along the southern main. It has been calculated that as many as 500 non-Indigenous people visited Kangaroo Island in this period, with much smaller numbers remaining for more than one winter sealing season and only a handful settling down.

How did Cawthorne learn about this 'prehistory', life before settlement, about these 'Robinson Crusoes' (as he calls them in his novel) living 'beyond the pale'? He had access to some written records:

Matthew Flinders' journal, one or two government reports, a memoir or two. His main source, however, were stories, reminiscences and memories – oral history. While visiting his father on Kangaroo Island Cawthorne heard anecdotes, yarns, hearsay and gossip about the roaring days, not only from his father who had been a whaler and sealer himself, but also from the handful of old sealers still resident on the island and living in and around Hog Bay, today's Penneshaw. He probably met and chatted with such individuals as Nathaniel Walles Thomas, William Walker, George 'Fireball' Bates and William Wilkins, some of whom are named in his travel writings and who also appear in his novel – with their names changed.

Cawthorne was also able to talk with some of the Indigenous women with whom these men lived on KI, including the Palawa (Tasmanian) women 'Old Bet' and 'Bumblefoot' (her real name Maggerlede, who just happened to be Truganini's sister); both women appear in the novel with the European names they carried in the 1850s. From his various informants he heard stories about the sealers conducting what he calls 'Sabine expeditions' on the mainland, forcibly abducting Indigenous women from coastal camps in Tasmania, Victoria and South Australia.

Cawthorne turned these stories into an extraordinary novel, representing the oral history of the time before the official settlement of the South Australian colony. He tells the story of a 'Captain Meredith'; the novel concludes with his murder on the (mainland) beach at Normanville. George Meredith Junior was a real person, the eldest son of one of the richest and most powerful free settlers in Van Diemen's Land, a young man killed just weeks before the first immigrant ships arrived in 1836 – not in 1823, as the novel's title claims. At the time, Meredith was living with Maggerlede, and it may well be that he was murdered by a jealous rival for her affections. In the novel, however, he is murdered by Kaurna warriors who mistakenly assume Meredith intends to steal women from their camp. Stories that circulated in the colony in the early days about the murder of 'poor Meredith' (and of other similar incidents like the death of Captain Collet Barker at the Murray Mouth in 1831) played a considerable part in fixing in the communal memory the idea that Aboriginal people were not to be trusted, that they acted irrationally, that they were inexplicably violent;

such stories told through the early decades after settlement helped soothe European consciences uneasy about Aboriginal dispossession and disadvantage.

The Kangaroo Islanders is also a remarkable novel for its representation of life beyond the pale, for showing how Indigenous and non-Indigenous people lived and worked together in the early years when there was considerable give and take between the two groups, if only on remote offshore islands. The novel shows these Crusoes learning to live, work and (usually) survive along the southern coast by drawing on the knowledges of their Indigenous companions; the novel shows them adopting and adapting their ways of hunting, foraging and gathering, creating interlocking experiences that helped a handful of first comers learn how to settle down. *The Kangaroo Islanders* is one of the few colonial novels we have that represents in fleeting glimpses some of the improvisational and interactive encounters between the colonisers and the colonised on the edges of the island continent. What happened on Kangaroo Island offered a fragment of opportunity, a creative alternative to the more routine colonial encounters that would follow.

Rick Hosking, Adelaide

Measurements

Imperial	Metric
Length & Distance	
1 inch	2.54 centimetres
1 foot	30.48 centimetres
1 yard	0.91 metres
1 fathom	1.83 metres
1 mile	1.61 kilometres
1 nautical mile	1.852 kilometres
1 league	5.89 kilometres
Speed	
1 knot = 1 nautical mile per hour	1.852 kilometres per hour
Volume	
1 gallon	4.55 litres
1 bushel	36.37 litres
Area	
1 acre	0.405 ha
Mass	
1 ounce	28.3 grams
1 pound weight	454 grams
1 ton	1.02 tonnes
Temperature	
$5/9 \times (°F - 32)$	°C
°F	$9/5°C + 32$

£1 = 240 pence (240d) = 20 shillings (20/–). In 1966, when Australia adopted metric currency, £1 was equivalent to $2.

The Kangaroo Islanders

W.A. Cawthorne

Introductory

On the southern seaboard of the vast continent of Australia, and nearly midway between the two extremes of the east and west coasts, there are two remarkable gulfs penetrating the land to a distance of two hundred miles, and dividing the great colony of South Australia into two unequal portions.

The gulfs lie parallel to each other, and, besides being the only indentations of any magnitude, except the Gulf of Carpentaria, in the whole seacoast of Australia – some 7,000 miles – they make a strong resemblance to each other. Both trend northwards, the eastern shores of both present, half way, extensive sand flats of immense area, while their western shores are bolder, with deeper water and finer harbours. The larger, Spencer Gulf, is double the length and breadth of the smaller, Gulf St. Vincent, being 200 miles by 100, whereas the latter is 100 miles by 50. The French exploring expedition that unexpectedly met Flinders in the Bay now called, from that circumstance, Encounter Bay, named these gulfs Josephine and Napoleon.[1] The peninsula that divides them is some 25 miles broad, and is of similar shape to that of Italy. The heads of both the gulfs consist of large mangrove swamps, and for half their length the eastern shores have no definite coast-line, but an extended, ill-defined, and exceedingly irregular margin of mangrove swamp from a quarter of a mile to five miles in breadth. Through this swamp, meander to apparently interminable distances deep water channels, which, shaded by the thick foliage of the mangrove, present scenes of unsurpassed exotic beauty.

At the entrance to the smaller gulf – the most easterly of the two, and on the eastern shores of which the capital of the province is now situated – lies a large and most interesting island, named Kangaroo Island[2] in 1802[3] by Captain Flinders, from the numbers of that animal observed on its shores.[4] It is nearly 120 miles long, and has an average breadth of from 30 to 50 miles, and a uniform coastline for at least two-thirds of its entire seaboard, of bold, perpendicular cliffs that chill the heart of the mariner in calm or storm.[5] A landing place in 30 miles is about the average accommodation, and even then landing is frequently negotiated with extreme difficulty. The island, in a singular manner, is divided into two unequal portions, and so nearly is the one part severed from the other that barely half-a-mile of sand separates the Southern Ocean from the placid waters of a great lagoon[6] that alternately narrows and widens until it reaches the broad waters of its northern boundary, Gulf St. Vincent. The scenery surrounding the shores of this noble inland bay, and its singular termination in the broad expanse of a fine lagoon dotted with small islands, is singularly wild and romantic. In the islets of the lagoon, for countless ages, the pelican and black swan have found a home, as well as a burial place. Masses of pelican bones bear ample testimony to this fact, for it seems that to the still waters of this land-locked lake the pelican has ever turned his head in his last hours, to die in the home of his birth. This trait in the pelican character, as well as the locality we are describing, has been immortalised by the poet Montgomery in his poem, 'The Island.'[7]

The surface of the land is undulating, and is covered with a dense and interminable scrub, exceeding all other scrubs known on the mainland in its closeness and thorny character.[8] As the danger of being lost on an inland route is very great, owing to the extreme scarcity of fresh water, the only mode of progress from place to place is by whaleboat.[9] In the entire island all the water that can be found is what is known as 'land-soaks,' at or near the coast sandhills.[10] In the deep gullies inland there are many rich patches of soil, but the country is for the most part sandy and sterile.[11] The land, though apparently poor, still nourishes a most luxurious growth of variegated shrubs and trees, the favourite and peculiar habitat of the wallaby and kangaroo. Indeed, it may be said that, at the time of its discovery, the whole island was nothing more nor less than a huge wallaby and kangaroo preserve, being totally uninhabited by human beings.[12] The herds of kangaroo were almost incredibly large, and it was for this reason that runaway convicts[13] from Van Diemen's Land and Sydney regarded it as a kind of paradise.[14] It possessed abundance of game, and produced good salt in its lagoons, so that it became of sufficient importance to induce whalers and sealers to call once a year and exchange brandy, tobacco, etc., for the produce of the land.[15]

The coasts of the island and the neighbouring islands abounded in seals, a source of emolument, however, which only served to add to the violence and cruelty of the annual or bi-annual orgies of the Islanders. Thus situated with an impenetrable land of scrub, and a coast surrounded by dangers, the Islanders regarded themselves as in a fortress, and defied any power that could be brought against them.[16] Living beyond the pale[17] of law, they had no other tie to bind them than the necessity for self-preservation.[18] Fearing neither man nor God, they cared little for their present life, and felt not the remotest interest in the life to come, except so far as stray scraps of religious sayings and opinions might add point to a coarse jest, or piquancy to the usual blasphemy of the hour.

Yet amidst this utter abandonment they exhibited traits of heroism, and even of disinterested action. From the very necessity of their position, it was found advisable to bind themselves together in twos and threes, mates, as they termed themselves, and their mutual fidelity was not easily shaken. Such is the brief outline of the Islanders and their home, which, in a measure, will afford a key to the following story, and prepare the reader for a tale that belongs more to the old times of the bold buccaneers[19] than to a period so comparatively recent as that which opens with the events of the next chapter.

Chapter 2

An Australian Morn. –
Captain Meredith. –
Mr. Ratlin. –
The Rescued Sailor.

In the year 1823,[20] many years before the founders of the model colony of South Australia had begun to rack their brains to invent a system of colonisation that should combine all the excellencies of the ancient Greek plan,[21] all the vigour of the old Raleigh scheme,[22] and all the unity of the 'Vaterland' expatriation,[23] long before this period a brig might have been observed quietly anchored in the calm and beautiful waters of Antechamber Bay,[24] Kangaroo Island. Every spar and every rope was reflected with strict fidelity in the still water, and her hull merged so evenly into the reflection beneath that it was difficult to distinguish where the one began and the other ended. Fishes, as they darted out beneath the keel, sparkled for a moment like fiery diamonds, and vanished as quickly as they slid into the deep black shade of the vessel.

It was early morn, and such a morn as only Australia can boast, a clear, pellucid morn with not a cloud to mar the sky, not the faintest mist, nor any visible thing to blemish the unrivalled beauty of the early day. Looking up into the heavens the eye could perceive unfathomable depths; gazing upon the land, could realise its uttermost distances; and, scanning the sea beneath, could see as in a looking glass. There, at the very bottom, on a floor of pure white sand, the hungry shark was rising and falling or pausing as he watched the huge ship darkening his pathway.[25] There, again, was the ill-shapen 'stingerree,'[26] flapping its huge sides, as a bird does its wings when, hastening on some furtive expedition, it is driven like a small cloud across the expanse of heaven, or with marvellous deception covering itself with the sand until invisible to all eyes. There were the voracious schnapper[27] in countless numbers, moving rapidly along in all the glory of purple and gold in their search for new marine pastures. The supernatural clearness of the atmosphere caused the neighbouring highlands, the distant capes, and the range of mountains in the vicinity of what is now called Cape Jervis,[28] to appear singularly close. On the black rocks, black as ink, that lined some parts of the bay, sat a mass of wild sea fowl, contrastingly white.[29] A little higher up, on another ledge of jutting rocks sat another group of white birds, and higher still a third. In the calm morning, though so far off, their solemn chattering, their spiteful pecking, their clamorous disputing, could be distinctly heard, tipping, tripping, and modulating with the gentle swell of the sea. Anon one of them would rise in order to visit some more favourite spot, and, clattering and spattering upon the water with outstretched wings, would leave behind, straight as the flight of an arrow, an agitated pathway, gradually melting to the finest line; or one would slyly pounce upon an unwary fish, and enjoy the whole relish without a squabble with his brethren as to the lion's share. High in the air could be seen a line of birds, with very long necks and very short bodies, but with flight even and swift. They were black swans[30] making a beeline across the straits to the lakes and islands of the Lower Murray. Over the island could be seen several hundreds of unwieldy pelican[31] flying in their peculiar way, and marking on the blue expanse as far as the eye could follow, the singular outline of the letter 'W.' They were winging their way to the seat of the primeval haunts of their race – the inland lagoons of the island.

On the deck of the brig paced a seaman of a stamp superior to the majority of his class. He had a peculiar expression of face, large and quick eyes, a good forehead, a countenance that betokened energy of purpose, great self-reliance, and acute perception. He was highly adventurous, and, like Lord Byron, who bathed in the very spot in which Shelley was drowned 'to see how it would feel,'[32] he dared the very things before which others had quailed. He could divine intuitively the character of men, and thus gained a strong influence over his lawless set. Although not a strong man, he was lithe and nimble. Added to his strongly marked individuality, to the intrepidity that led him to perform deeds undreamt of by others, and to the strangeness that made him follow the wild and romantic life he had voluntarily adopted, was a deep-seated melancholy, a tone of mind only to be found in the higher races of man, from which are drawn the poet, the painter, and the patriot. Apart from the peril and excitement of his daily life, his spirit would commune in silence with the mystery of Creation. Herein was to be found the apparent anomaly of the man, choosing, as he did, an irregular life that called into full play the qualities of daring and recklessness, yet finding in the solitariness of the midnight watch, the anxiety of the storm, the ever present mystery of the sky, and the loneliness of uninhabited lands, something that ministered to a religious mood, a mood as essential to his mental well-being as food for the nourishment of his body. In the calm of lonely, unnamed bays and islands his spiritual nature found the satisfaction that was denied him amidst the busy throngs of the city, or the worshippers of fashionable Sabbath routine. Often he would spend a moody hour in some sylvan nook, in some out of the way corner of totally unknown land, musing on the mystery of Creation. He would always manage that, at least on Sundays, his vessel should be anchored in some snug cove, in order that he might pursue on shore his Sabbath meditations unobserved. Had he been endowed with a little more of this 'melancholic passion,' he would have been a fit devotee in the convents of Athens,[33] or the fortified retreats of 'Araby the Blest'[34]; with a degree less he would have been a first-class rascal. As it was, he had enough good to prevent him from becoming thoroughly bad, and enough evil to belie the good and cause his actions to appear eccentric. The sailors, who did not understand him, said, 'He's a bit cranky.' His friends shrugged their shoulders, and expressed their pity or their ignorance in the words, 'strange man.' But those who understood him pronounced an altogether different verdict. Such was Captain Meredith.[35]

As the man, so was his vessel – not a rope out of order, not a spar but was in its proper place. All the running gear was hauled taut, the slack neatly coiled down in flemish coils,[36] all the yards squared, and the whole trim of the craft betokened a controlling mind that delighted in neatness and the fitness of all things. If he had a falling in this matter, it was with regard to the right-angled position of the yards. To him they were scarcely ever mathematically correct, and nothing short of this pleased him.

The captain, after a close survey of the shore, half muttered aloud, 'I see nothing of the boat,' which circumstance seemed somewhat to annoy him. Shutting up his telescope, he lightly ran along the deck and skipped agilely along the bowsprit to the uppermost point. There, standing erect on that slippery spot, he cast his eye aloft.

'A haul on the starboard maintopsail lift there!' he sang out.

'Aye, aye, sir,' sang out three or four hands as they growled to each other, 'What on earth does he want squaring the yards for, when there's no one for to see them, aye Bill?'

'Oh, it's for the ourang-outangs[37] ashore there, I s'pose.'

'Belay there!'

'Topgallant lift – so – steady – belay!'

With the sure foot of a cat he nimbly stepped from his insecure perch, and, reaching the foot of the fore mast, looked straight up to the truck.[38]

'Golly, Jim, if Sam drops his tar brush from the cross-trees on the skipper's mug – ha! ha! Ha! I say, tip Sam a wink,' but before the joke could be carried out they were ordered to the braces, for having squared the yards to a right angle with the masts, it was next necessary to get them in the same plane with each other.

'Port foretopsail brace a bit!' 'Topgallant brace a bit!' 'Belay!' sung out the captain; then, jumping into a boat, he shipped an oar, and quietly sculled out to a position some 100 yards ahead, and in a direct line of the vessel and its masts, so that by his advanced distance he might have the better chance of observing the angles of all the yards and ropes, each to each, and the whole as an entirety.

From this position, the vessel looming up against the clear background of the sky, appeared a beautiful complex geometrical problem, a series of isosceles, equilateral, and scalene triangles, whose parts were made up of ropes and spars, one of the most intricate puzzles of human ingenuity, but, to the practised eye of the seamen, one of the simplest imaginable.

'Mainyard there!' shouted out the skipper; 'a haul on the port main-brace – so there – belay!' 'A haul on the starboard vang!' 'Peak halyards a bit,' 'belay!' In fact, line A was not homologous with line B, nor C with D; hence the pulling and hauling, a particularity that certainly was highly commendable in a harbour, but did appear absurdly superfluous in the wild and unknown waters of Kangaroo Island. Having satisfied himself upon the trim of his craft, he leisurely sculled back, scrutinizing at the same time all the minor details of the brig, the buoy, the stunsail booms, and any ropes that might be straggling overboard, fastened the boat to the main chains, and sprang on deck, and again surveyed the shore for the boat he so anxiously expected. At the same time eight bells rang, out clear and plaintively from the ship's forecastle, sounding wide and far over the still expanse, and the steward announced breakfast.

The captain put down his telescope with impatience, implying distinctly enough his mortification that time had so quickly fled, leaving nearly half his crew still unaccountably absent ashore. However, there was no help for it at present, and he descended the companion-stairs to breakfast.

'Mr. Ratlin,[39] what have you for breakfast?' said the captain to the chief mate as he took his chair at the table, where already the first officer was snugly ensconsed, impatiently waiting for the signal to fall to. Next to managing a ship, well he could manage his meals well – in fact, his appetite was his best chronometer on board ship; he could almost work his longitude by it, so regular were its demands.[40] He could anticipate meal times with a wonderful and laughable accuracy.

'Curried schnapper, broiled barracouta, and mutton-birds,[41] which the sooner we commence upon the better we shall preserve their flavour.' Saying this, he looked significantly to the captain, and pointed with a kind of flourish to the three dishes at once, as much as to say, 'of which ———"

'Oh,' said the captain, taking the hint, 'I'll take barracouta; it's the finest flavoured fish that swims, at least to my taste.'[42]

'Were you ever at the Cape?'[43] asked the mate.

'Yes, many times.'

'Well, that's the place for fish, every variety, and so cheap, and such rum ways of preparing it by the slams, it makes one's mouth water to think of *Engelede fisch*.'[44]

'Ah! I dare say it does,' dryly remarked the captain.

'Yes, for a skilling – that is, twopence farthing – you can get a blow-out,' continued the mate, as he spitted a mutton-bird onto his plate.

'However, Mr. Ratlin, leaving your reminiscences on fish for a moment, and turning to present troubles, what do you think has become of the boat's crew? Away since yesterday afternoon, and had positive orders to be on board last night,' rejoined the captain.

'Drunk!' replied the mate sententiously, at the same time putting down his second cup of coffee empty and making a kind of miserable pun upon the word as applied both to the cup and the subject under discussion.

'Where could they get the grog from? Not a drop went ashore yesterday, I am positive.'

'Get it from? why, lor bless you, didn't you know of the Sydney schooner[45] that called here last week, and I'll wager they are all lying drunk in the scrub at this moment.'[46]

'Hang 'em,' growled the captain, as he cracked a biscuit[47] across his knee, 'here we are stuck, with no wind and no sailors, and if it comes on to blow from the N.W. we shall be in a pretty mess.'[48]

'I tell you what it is,' resumed the captain, after a long pause, during which the mate made up for leeway, in sundry tit-bits on the table, for the time caring little for the boat's crew, whether drunk or sober, eaten up or drowned, lost in the scrub, or run away. 'I tell you what,' said the captain, 'our men have never been the same since we picked up that blackguard, Long Bill, off the islands;[49] they have been all adrift.'

'Of course they have,' replied the mate; 'and had you taken my advice you'd left Long Bill alone.'[50]

'What! let him starve on a rock?'[51]

'Yes. I tell you what it is, captain, you are too soft; that fellow is a villain, a runaway Vandemonian;[52] his story of starving is all gammon.[53] I'd bet ten chaws o' tobacco to one it was a planned scheme, his pals were handy, and he has just persuaded you to take him for his own ends; take my advice, and give him the slip.'

'Oh! nonsense, Ratlin, you have a down upon the fellow; keep your weather eye open, and all will be right.'

'If I had not done so,' remarked the mate somewhat sarcastically, 'the night you took the fellow off you would have never seen daylight again, or I either.'

'Oh! pooh, pooh! it was a rock you mistook for a boat.'

'And pray will you say it was a mistake of mine, when I found the fellow with a lantern and his cap behind it standing on the shank of the anchor? Wasn't that a signal for the blackguards close under the rocks?' asked the mate, with some warmth.

'Why – yes,' stammered the captain, 'that *did* look suspicious, and therefore I hauled up.'

'Yes; and if we don't mind that fellow will have the old brig on the rocks[54] yet with his kind offers to pilot[55] us on this wild coast.'

'Well, well, we shall see. Let's be up, and if we don't see the boat, then send the gig ashore, and you must ferret them out by hook or by crook.'[56]

'Aye, aye!' muttered the mate, as he ascended the companion-way; 'and if I don't give that fellow the slip, I'll eat 'possum[57] for a month.'

Chapter 3

The Hot Wind. –
The Lost Boat.

Upon reaching the deck, cat's-paws[58] of wind were visible here and there, scarring the smooth face of the sea; but little other sign of a breeze was abroad. The sun shot down his fervid rays, and the mirage already danced its mystic mazes out and away in the straits – now called Backstairs Passage[59] – commingling with the heave of the waters, and causing the most deceptive and singular phenomena that can well be seen; now sinking the distant capes till barely visible, then elevating and distorting their outline, till it became a difficult matter to retain one's belief that the land was the same as that seen a couple of hours before.

'Signs of hot weather, captain!' remarked the mate, 'and a roaring hot Norther! I always noticed this was the case in my last trip here – though that's many years ago – these Northers give little warning, but come down powerfully strong.[60] On the mainland, the wind is as hot as from an oven; when it sweeps over a gum tree, the leaves fall down in a shower; they are burnt with the heat. I'd advise you to slip and run well under the land, so as to bring the west horn of the Bay[61] nearer to the nor'ard of us; there is good shelter close under the land – close enough to enable you to scrape the barnacles off the ship's bottom, and ride quite snug just outside the surf.'

'I hardly like your advice, to run the brig slap up in that nook. How shall we get out again if a shift of wind comes from the S.E.?'

'Oh! as the night falls the wind dies out,' replied the mate, 'and we can run back off this point.'

'Very well, get the anchor up and let us be off,' said the captain.

The vessel soon glided through the glassy, yet singularly perturbed waters. Far and wide – right away to the middle of the passage – the waters heaved and blinked and swirled, sank and rose, and here and there danced in gigantic riplets; now bearing the appearance of a mirrored repose, anon assuming the smooth, swollen, glistening of mighty blisters, scalded, as it were, by some fiery blast. Headland and cape and distant mountains, all partook of the mystic forms of some supernatural change. Behind the distant panorama to the northward, a bright glow of red-hot air defined the sharp outline of the break between earth and heaven. All nature seemed troubled, as if it were a living sentient being, instinctively cowering before the dread outpouring of the northern gale – the withering blasts of the terrible hot wind. Higher and higher grew the reddening arch; puffs of contrary and circular currents flew hither and thither; fish leapt from the surface of the water; the vessel moved in an unsteady manner; the sea-birds darted tip and down, seaward and landward, and remained not a minute in one place; the distant patches of tall scrub on the island, ever and anon, shook their heads violently, and then lapsed into immobility. The mirage gambolled abroad in its wild career, revelling in its mad pranks with rock and wave – with a dash sinking the boldest promontory, then lifting up from obscurity the tiniest stone, commingling sky, earth, and sea in a fluid phantasmagoria, and shaping, altering, renewing dissolving, and distorting everything within the range of vision. Now great belts of ripples, miles in extent, barred the ocean in alternate stripes,[62] in mirror-like bands, like a sea of quicksilver relieved by deep scarifications of indigo blue. A distant, though faint roar, came booming seaward; another and a quicker reverberation ran along the cliffs; quicker still and louder came a third thundering over the main. Very thin, but peculiarly distinct, could now be seen on the extreme verge of the horizon a line of the deepest hue, advancing with rapid strides down the gulf, while a continued hum and a deep moaning[63] preceded it.

'There's the norther,' sung out the mate; 'it will soon be down upon us.'

'Get a few more fathoms of cable up,' said the captain, 'it looks an ugly customer; we must not be caught napping.'

The line came on, now visible in all its fury, a strange wall of tossing, scudding waves rolling over the placid sea, roaring louder and louder, and eating up, as it were, every secondary movement of the mighty waters, scattering the illusory appearances of the air, and absorbing them into its own grand march of power and might. Louder grew the tumult beyond, yet in and around the vessel the water reflected every angle and point of the hull. The bobstay rose and fell, and met another bobstay in the water beneath, and the figure-head, with its scimitar, nearly struck another figure-head with its scimitar below, and the cabin-boy, looking out of the stern windows, saw his own image, and wondered whether his mother would think he had grown. Another vessel, with all its parts and appurtenances complete, was moving along beneath the other, and as the one rolled with the in-shore swell, so the other rolled, bowing to each other in friendly recognition, keel to keel, mast to mast, and rope to rope.

The hot wind swept on in its fury, and as the word was given to let go the anchor, the blast struck the brig with full force and felled her to the very sea, boring her gunwale beneath the waves, and madly wrenching every rope, straining every spar, and trying the vessel to the very last verge of endurance. Had the first gust not abated, neither wood nor iron, however cunningly put together, could have borne that frightful tussle with the giant wind of the North; as it was, she gradu-ally came head to wind, the yards were braced sharp up, more cable paid out, and the vessel was prepared, for some dozen hours, to do battle with the storm and fury of a scorching hot wind, comparatively secure from the favouring shelter of the neighbouring coast, within four hundred yards of which she now lay snugly anchored.

'That's a stiff'ner!' remarked the captain; 'but we are all safe here. It might as well have spared our jib and topgallant sail; it's worse than a Sydney brickfielder,[64] confound it!'

'It's dreadfully hot!' said the mate. 'By heavens, we melt like the pitch and tar of the deck. Here, boy, bring me a white jacket![65] It will never do, captain, to go ashore now; we shall be fried alive, or get lost in the scrub, and there'll be old Harry[66] to pay, and not a drop of water to drink.'

'Very well,' replied the captain; 'it is hot. When the rascals get sober they'll come off; but any rate, give them a couple of shots, and hoist a whiff;[67] perhaps that will wake them up.'

This was accordingly done; but, though closely watching every bush and brake, and the white sea beach, nothing was seen – man, bird, nor beast – none daring to venture out in that terrible heat. Nothing was heard, save the roar of the hot blasts of wind and the confused jumble of waves on the rocky reefs.

'I say, Tom,' said one of the foremastmen, 'isn't this as hot as that place the parsons are always preaching about? I remember being in a shepherd's hut, when the cove outs with his frying-pan, claps in his bacon, sticks it in the sun, and fries his rashers for three of us, with nothing else but the blessed sun, and not a stick of fire – sort o' heavenly food, you know.[68] Well, it *was* hot that day; when you lifted the rug that hung over the bunk millions of blow-flies was crawling all about; they couldn't stand the heat nohow.'

'Avast there, Bill! lay your yarn on it as thick as the hawser, but don't make it as big as the mainmast.'

'Hold on, you green 'un. What I'm telling yer, I can take my affy-davy on; well, 'pon my soul, there was a deep well near the hut, when yer looked down ye'd see all up the sides every sort of bird – magpies, crows, parrots, all sorts, holding on for life. The poor devils was seeking a bit of cool; and more than this, a great school of martins[69] and them there sort boarded us right slap bang in the hut. Well, the shepherd and me and another chap bolts clean out – do yer see we was taken all aback, so we cut. Well, we gie the birds the hut, and we sits down here and there under a gum tree. Well, I has a pannikin o' water boiling hot for to drink, I'm blessed if the little birds didn't jump on my castor,[70] arms, and flippers; I never seed nor tell of sot a thing afore.

'What for, Bill,' said Tom.

'For to drink, you lubber. Do ye see there was no water, and they fall down and die all about, and then some twigs the pannikin, and down they jumps and drinks it all up. The shepherd and me caught lots o' birds that day with our hands.'

'I say, Bill, did yer put any salt on their tails?'

'Yes, Jack, we did, and cotched a fine bird.'

'What was that?'

'Vy, a laughing-jackass.'

'Ha! ha! ha!' roared all, 'that slewed yer, Dick.'

'Forrard there,' shouted the mate, 'and pump some water on the decks to cool 'em a bit.'

'Aye, aye, sir!'

Near the wheel, and as well under the bulwarks as he could stow himself, squatted the mate, half dead with the heat.

'Mr. Ratlin,' sang out the captain, who, with spy-glass in hand, was leaning over the taffrail, alternately watching the beach and the gale, 'I wish you would just step here and see if you can make out the boat. It was left, you know, near that sand hummock, but it's gone now.'

The mate tried to rise, but in vain. The pitch of the decks had melted with the great heat, and fixed him to the planks. He tugged and pulled, and at last succeeded, but it was at the expense of his clothes. 'Well, I be hanged,' he exclaimed, as he dived down to his cabin.

A roar of laughter from the captain, the steward, and the cabin-boy followed him; but, as the mate was in no humour to be joked with, the cabin-boy and the steward had to stand clear all the remainder of the day.

'What do you think has become of the boat?' sang out the captain down the skylight, really alarmed for the safety of his whaleboat that had been visible in the early morning as a black speck on the sandy beach.

'Melted,' roared out the mate below, who was too much taken up with his own discomforts to care for ought else.

'I wish Long Bill, the boat, and the hot wind fifty fathoms in *Hacklebarney*,'[71] growled the mate.

'I think the tide has washed her away,' continued the captain.

'More likely they have stowed her away in the bushes,' rumbled the mate, 'they are up to all sorts of devilries in this pirate's nest.'[72]

'Well, then, Mr. Ratlin, you had better be getting ready and go ashore as soon as the gale drops and find the boat.'

'Aye, aye, sir.'

Leaving the vessel for awhile, let us follow the doings of the boat that had caused all this anxiety, and whose absence was so inexplicable.

Chapter 4

The Cruise Ashore. –
Long Bill. – Snakes. –
Old Sam.

'Shove off,' sang out Mr. Handspike,[73] the second mate.

'Mind,' said the captain, 'and be back as soon as possible; and as you don't know whom you may meet with, keep your powder dry.[74] You understand me? Keep your weather eye open.'[75]

'All right,' said the mate, 'and if you hear any firing, why don't forget us, that's all.'

These precautions were not altogether unnecessary, when the unprincipled character of the men they had to deal with is taken into account. Mysterious disappearances had from time to time taken place, as were well known to the one or two traders that came to the island;[76] and although the dense nature of the scrub was such as to lend a touch of probability to the usual explanation of 'lost in the bush', still an uneasy impression was left on the mind that there was peculiar danger in landing on the island.

'Here you, Long Bill, tell us how to steer, for I know nothing about this blessed island; it seems to me a wild-looking sort of a hole.'

'Aye, aye, sir!' said Long Bill, as he gave his dirty opossum-skin cap[77] a pull to starboard, and ran his eye over the distant sandhills to note a slight indenture that served the Islanders as a landmark for the best beaching place on the coast;[78] for, although the bay was smooth, yet there was a nasty ground swell,[79] and at times a stupendous ocean swell set in round the point now known as Cape Willoughby,[80] which made it oft a matter of great peril to launch or beach anything.

Briefly indicating the spot to the second mate, Bill resumed his oar, and by his vigorous strokes put all the other men on their mettle.

'Pull away, ye sons of guns,[81] pull!' sung out Bill, 'and let's see what sort of stuff ye're made of.'

'You're in a hurry to get ashore,' growled the bowman, as he in vain endeavoured to prevent the boat being altogether pulled round by Long Bill.

'Why yer see he has four beautiful black gins a-crying for him in the scrub there away,' remarked the stroke oar, 'and in course he is pulling like mad for to see the wives of his bussum.'

'Easy, Bill easy,' said the mate, as Long Bill in a flurry nearly caught a crab,[82] and sent the water flying over the stern sheets, giving the second mate a good wetting.

'Honour bright, Long Bill, how many wives have you got just now?' asked one of the men.

'Three now, but four a while gone; but all hands are going to get some more soon; then, I'm —— if I don't get six, like old Porkey.'[83]

'Well, I'm blessed,' said all hands.

'When I gets back to Wapping, I'll tell the Bishop of Lunnun,' said the bowman.

Long Bill was a remarkable fellow in his way, that is to say he was a remarkable scamp. He ranked high in daring, blackguardism and utter lawlessness. Of tall stature and powerful build, stupid in intellect, he had the brute force and instinct of the animal man, allied with some portions of his superior intelligence, but unredeemed by a single trait of his nobler and higher nature. If he killed a man or so, it was not from a particular delight in blood; if he stole, not from a desire exactly to steal; if he betrayed his closest mate or a friend, it was not from a love to act thus; but his whole life was an expression of lawlessness. He had no self-respect, and all his actions could be explained by this utter self-abandonment. In a word, he was the chief of blackguards; even his associates put no faith in him, beyond the hour. Long Bill was a rogue among rogues; he was tolerated for his invaluable aid in being ever ready to be the leader of any daring, treacherous or foul game. Amongst the drunken he was the most drunken; amongst brawlers the most unscrupulous, using not only the fist but the knife. He was dreaded and hated by all, but still they could scarcely do without him. At present we will not further describe him, but let his character develop itself as the story proceeds.

The commission of the second mate was simply to procure the assistance of some of the islanders to get a cargo of salt from the great lagoons in the middle of the island, and to trade for wallaby and kangaroo skins;[84] and it was a matter of astonishment that this visit to the shore should have been rendered necessary, as the custom of the Islanders was to come off in their boats as soon as a vessel dropped anchor. Their not having done so rather led Captain Meredith to suppose that they had moved away, in accordance with their erratic habits; but Long Bill was so positive that he had seen smoke far inland, and had offered to go and see, that the boat was sent ashore to hunt them up.

'Keep her off a bit,' sang out Long Bill; 'now give her stern to it. That's it!' The boat rose upon a huge green surf, spun in on its crest at the rate of thirty miles an hour, and was beached at the very top of high-water mark as easily as if carried in the arms. It was highly exciting, that grand sweep in the midst of the boiling soap-suds of the wave and the deafening din of the mad career of the giant roller; the sand was churned up and flew ahead and around, and left large streaks between the timbers of the boat. The smallest deviation from the 'dead on' course[85] and the boat would have been toppled over and over, and every man swept up, like so many corks, to be sucked back with the undertow to inevitable death.

'Beautiful! beautiful!' sang out the mate, as, all jumping out, and with a few tugs placing the boat high, dry and safe above high-water mark, they prepared themselves for their inland expedition.

'Come, look alive, mates,' said Bill, as he eyed with suspicious glances the manner in which the crew were adjusting their pistols, 'we have no robbers here.'

'Maybe you have *hourang houtangs*, Master Bill,' said Jim. 'I was told that hereabouts them sorts o' animals was seen with big woolly heads.'[86]

'Avast, Jim,' said another, 'them sort of critters scud about the Inges, the Dyaks, and those covies.'[87]

'But I say, Bill,' sung out a third tar, 'a mate of mine told me a year gone or so, that chaps in these islands smelt like foxes.'[88]

'Go it, Bob. I've seen and smelt 'em, for all the world like Robinson Crusoes and Fridays.[89] Look out, and you will smell 'em, too.'

'I say, Bill, why do you smell like foxes?'

'Do I smell like a fox, you lubbers?' sang out Bill in no pleasant humour; but the truth was Bill had taken care to leave his wallaby skin clothes behind.

'No, of course not, and good reason, too, you've got precious little of any sort of clothes.'

'But,' persisted one of the speakers, 'if ye haven't hourang houtangs you have bunyips[90] and boomer kangaroos[91] as high as the mainmast, haven't yer?'

'Go to ———; heave ahead, and stick together, or you'll be lost in the scrub, and then you will be saying we rubbed you out, and be ——— to you.

'We'll keep an eye on you,' said the mate, significantly. The party now set off in Indian file, Long Bill leading, and the mate bringing up the rear.

'I tell you what, Mister Bill, your infernal garden here has more thorns than roses. Golly, there goes another bit. All my clothes'll be gone soon,' exclaimed Jim, as he tried to disentangle his jacket from the dreadful Kangaroo Island thorn, one of the most terrible and impervious thorn bushes in the continent of Australia.[92]

'Look out, there aft!' sang out Long Bill, who gave a kind of half jump, 'there's a black snake[93] just under this log.'

'Well, I be hanged, that's cool,' replied all hands.

'I shan't go a step further.'

'Nor me.'

'Nor me.'

'Nor me.'

'Bah! go on,' said the mate.

'Well, here goes then,' and away they all cut, each giving a long jump over the log, which probably had no more effect on the snake beneath than a lot of kangaroos flying over. Sweltering for a mile through the heavy scrub of prickly acacia,[94] clothes torn, and hands bleeding, they, suddenly emerged on, and ascended a short, sharp series of low hills, whose rocky ridges ran cross-ways with the path they were travelling.

'Oh, curse this country! Gad, it's as bad as walking end on, on top of a wall with glass,' said the mate.

'Oh!' growled another, as he tripped up and lay sprawling on the hard rocks.

'Broached to?'

'Aye, Jim, sarves yer right for grinning at me,' said Bob.

'Where the ———— are yer taking us to?' bellowed out the rest, very cross and very sore. 'Who can walk on these glass bottles?'

'Half a mile more,' replied Bill, 'and we'll come to anchor; they are only feather pillows.'

'Pillows be ————' growled the whole crew.

'By the holy, if yer don't .we'll 'bout ship, and send yer to your father, Old Nick.'

'I say, Bob, wouldn't "old square-yards" like to be here digging these ere stones? There look at that, now, isn't it splendacious, like a fine piece of green glass.[95] I'll bone that.[96] Why, you old sea-horse, don't yer see there are plenty of all sorts hereabouts? Put your specks on and look at that, and that; but none of your tricks, if the skipper gets wind of it he'll stick in this snake-trap a week, and I tell ye, I don't half like them hourang outangs, and black lubras.'[97]

The party now descended to a flat as beautiful as the neighbouring hills had been rough and rugged. A small track pursued its devious course through a magnificent patch of splendid grass waist high, which bordered a calm sheet of water hemmed in by tall and graceful trees, a variety of the gum, known on the island by the name of 'narrow leaf,'[98] and the reach of water was fringed with gigantic specimens of the tea-tree,[99] whose singular white and ragged bark hung in deep festoons to the water's edge. The change of scene was so sudden and so pleasant, that it affected everyone.

'Now we'll find their shake down,'[100] said one. 'Here's a place for a cabbage garden,' said another.[101]

'My eye, Tom, look here, see there's a mob of black swans, sailing about for all the world as if they were at home.'

'I say, Jack, why don't yer get a gin, and come and spend your honeymoon here? And – Snakes!' roared out Long Bill; away rushed the fellows, right and left, and, of course, met the snake full in the face. Up reared his snakeship in pure self-defence, down tumbled a couple, one against the other, both singing out for help, and cursing their eyes and limbs, Long Bill, the mate, the captain, and everything above the earth and under the earth.

Long Bill ran up. He exclaimed angrily, 'What a row you kick up, you great lubbers, about a snake; wait till you see them as thick as a stunsail boom, nicely coiled up in bed, with yer catawauling over a eight-footer.'

'Back your topsail,'[102] sung out one and all, 'we don't go a step further in this cursed snake hole. Hallo! there goes another; hear him through the grass, a regular gallinipper;[103] look out, all hands, yer chawed up if he grabs yer.' This determination was not altogether unreasonable, for as many as one hundred and fifty large deadly black snakes, from four to ten and twelve feet long, have been killed in one season, in a space not exceeding half-a-dozen acres, and the locality where Bill had brought them was remarkably abundant in these venomous reptiles.[104]

To make matters worse, as one of the seamen was hastening along, he unfortunately blundered on top of another snake, but most probably the very one that had already caused so much alarm. The snake, of course, being thus attacked, very naturally returned the compliment, and striking with his head, fixed his fangs firmly in the loose canvas trousers of the sailor, who thereupon dashed right away among his friends calling upon everybody for help. Happily for the man, the habits of the snake are such that, when once fixed on its prey, it does not repeat the bite, but remains fastened until the victim drops or it is itself torn off.[105] Rushing round the sailor, his mates soon killed the snake, and relieved the poor fellow from an overwhelming horror that was partly ludicrous and partly serious.

High words followed this misadventure. All hands were for returning at once to the ship, yet the mate, who was with them in this respect, had some hesitation in doing so, and therefore urged Long Bill in no polite terms to tell them how far they really had yet to go.

While they were wrangling and making the woods resound with their fierce altercation, a man might have been seen quietly seated on the top of a boulder of quartz rock within a couple of hundred feet just over their heads, concealed by a deep screen of bushes on a point of a hill that projected sharply into the small glade below, where the angry seamen were standing. In fact, if the truth must be told, he had dogged their steps from the first moment of their landing; he had seen them leave the brig from a celebrated spot well known to the lawless crew that squatted in this particular part of the island, and known amongst them as the 'look out,'[106] he had kept near them all the way up to where they now were, and had enjoyed their perplexities in his own peculiar manner, and when the last row took place had calmly sat down to see it out without being observed. This man was as singular a specimen of humanity of the Kangaroo Island species as could be found.[107] His outward appearance was exceedingly strange. He was naturally a man of large build,[108] and hairy, so much so, that it was at times difficult to distinguish his natural hair from the hair of the skins he wore as clothes; he was a veritable Esau;[109] he was clad in leggings made of wallaby skins, a waistcoat of skins, and a cap of wild cat skins[110] – he was his own tailor, and, of course, the fit was not nice to a shade – his arms and neck were bare; he had no underlinen, for the simple reason that the nearest shop was some 1,000 miles away, and then it might not be convenient if one could call and buy, with a peering constable watching one at every step, as if he had some suspicions of having once seen the gentleman purchaser.[111] Hence it was better to wear skin clothes without linen than certain other clothes with linen, and absurdly marked with broad A's.[112] Well, the fit was not the best, but the odour of the suit was marvellous. It was this that gave the Islanders their unenviable notoriety. Many years afterwards, before a grave committee of Parliament, a gentleman was examined who gave it in evidence 'that they stank like foxes.'[113]

Old Sam eyed the party below cautiously and carefully. Long habits of suspicion engendered by the wild life he led with some of the worst specimens of vagabonds had made this necessary. This habit, indeed, was of the utmost importance to him in the thousand and one instances of sudden and imminent peril. 'Well,' said old Sam to himself, 'Long Bill will stick some on 'em yet if they don't mind; I'll just give them a bit of a diwarsion,' so saying he quietly slid down, and parting a bush or two stood in their midst.

'Hourang! Houtang! by all that's good,' exclaimed all hands, as they uneasily bobbed about, and felt for their pistols. Sam looked on and said nothing; in fact, he enjoyed the consternation that his unwonted and outrageous dress occasioned.[114] Folding his bare and hairy arms on a rude walking-stick that he, like all the Islanders, carried as a protection against snakes, he calmly surveyed the whole group, while they in return stood gazing in a stupefied fashion at him.

'Yer have been praying a bit,' said old Sam, in a slow but distinct utterance.[115] In the language of old Sam 'praying' meant cursing and swearing; he never swore, he always 'prayed.' He used to say, 'My father was a Quaker, and them folks never swears, but allers prays; so I prays, and never swears. I am a powerful saint o' praying; so I just come to lend a hand, for I can do a little in that line myself. But hadn't you better go ahead, Bill, and let them gemmen have something to scoff?'

'What have yer got to eat here?' said Jim.

'Snakes,' said old Sam. 'We roasts them. Now, then, here we are, this is my crib,[116] that's Bill's and that's Porky's.[117]

Chapter 5

The Islanders and their Homes. – A Row. – Caught in a Trap.

Such a scene now presented itself that not only took the mate's party by surprise, but was of a character that excited their curiosity to the utmost. In all their experience they had never seen such singular domestic arrangements.

The huts were built of wattle filled in with clay, their roofs a thatch of broom.[118] On the whole they were tolerably comfortable. About a dozen[119] black women were busily employed in preparing and attending to the preservation of kangaroo and wallaby skins.[120] A host of half-caste children of all ages were wandering about, some busy and some playing.[121] There was an air about the whole place that irresistibly conveyed to the mind an impression of gazing at a mode of life unheard of. The wild scenery, the howling dogs,[122] the rough desperadoes, without shoes or hat, clad in skins, their hair on their heads burnt to the colour of hay and matted and tangled to the last degree; the black native women, some quite naked, others dressed like the men, talking and screaming in their savage and unrestrained manner; the uncouth appearance of the swarm of naked children, and the absence of all the usual adjuncts of even the rudest civilised life, formed the strangest picture, unparalleled in the most barbarous tribes of man, or the poorest sections of civilised communities.

The place smacked of the freebooter and the outlaw; the very scent of the locality suggested the lair of the wild beast.[123] The resemblance was complete, and the stories of ourang-outangs capturing women and making them slaves and drudges seemed to be fully realised.[124]

On the party from the ship emerging from the scrub and exposing themselves to full view at the foot of the slope that led to the huts, the native women rose up with one accord, uttered a plaintive wail of warning, and retired to the huts and to the surrounding bushes exclaiming in their native language in tones of anguish, 'Oh! more white devils.' At the same time a legion of dogs came yelling towards the newcomers. A battle royal followed, and many a dog went limping away, receiving the most cruel blows before they would desist from their fierce attack.

'I like this place uncommon,' said Jim, 'first snakes, and then dogs. Look at my trousers?'

'Aye, look at that,' said another, showing, an ugly wound. 'And what's a matter with Jack? Why is he on his beam ends?'[125]

'Oh, he got capsized, and nearly broke his leg.'

'I say,' exclaimed the mate, 'what sort of a place do you call this, Mr. Robinson Crusoe?'

'Why, we calls this ere place a menagerie,' replied old Sam with a leer.[126] 'Ain't we got a fine lot? Can yer see them all? There goes our hourang houtangs,' pointing to the native women that were hiding and peeping behind the trees and bushes. 'There is our wallabies and piccaninnies, parrots and pigs, snakes and kangaroos, dogs and guanos.'

'It must cost you a deal to feed all this lot.'

'No mister, not a bit on it, yer jist wrong there; they feeds us. We are the lords o' creation[127] here away: we eats and we drinks, and we cusses and we fights, and we sleeps, and we do jist what we likes, and the women and the dogs hunts for us;[128] and when they sings out and plays old sodger, and won't work, we ties 'em up, and wollops 'em,[129] and so we lives in a kind of earthly paradise, every man equal to another, and nobody to find fault with his neighbour.'

'You are a rum lot,' said the mate, and, in an undertone, 'an infernal set of blackguards.'

'Yes,' said old Sam, 'we are a rum lot, an unkimmon rum lot, and as for being an infernal set o' blackguards, as you was saying, well I s'pose we is. Yes, we is an infernal set o' blackguards,' soliloquised old Sam, muttering to himself as he strode along towards his hut. Then, turning suddenly round he paused, and tapping the mate on the shoulder said in his usual slow tone,[130] 'I tell yer what, Mr. Mate, when yer comes to our country yer must keep a civil tongue in your head, for we gemmen gets fits now and again.'

'Fits!' exclaimed the mate.

'Yes,' said Sam, 'rale fits! we first prays, then runs a muck as they do in Borneo;[131] then we don't know we does, we strikes right and left, and allers use our knives,' saying which he drew out his knife and gazed at it admiringly, turning it hither and thither in a scientific way, in a manner that showed he was deeply familiar with its use, as well as its abuse.

By this time they had approached the huts; the party divided, and some went into old Sam's hut, some into Long Bill's and some into Porky's, each hut being separated from the other a short distance.

'I'm blessed if I know a man from a woman here,' exclaimed the mate in bewilderment, as he surveyed a lot of the Islanders.

'How's that, Sam? You are all dressed alike – skin breeches for man, the same for woman, skin jackets for one and skin jackets for the other!'[132]

'Why, in course! we has no shops here, so we can't buy bonnets and them toggery, nor stockings, nor boots; we makes our black ladies dress like we, and they're not pertikler. How long do yer think now a pair of petticoats would last in this ere land?'

'Not long,' said the mate, looking at his own clothes already torn with only the experience of one trip.

'I tell yer,' said Sam, 'jist five minutes. No, no, petticoats won't do; but here's something to, scoff, every man helps hisself; pitch in, mate.' One of the black women – one of old Sam's wives, brought in a large lump of fat pork, another a number of wallaby tails, and another a lot of potatoes.

'We never eats bread here.'[133]

'Why?' said the mate.

'Cause yer see we has no mills, no ploughs, and no corn, nor never had none, and I s'pose we never shall. We got taters a year gone, and glad we was; for ten years I never seed nothing else but wallaby and kangaroo, never eats nothing else, never knows nothing else, that's why we is so hairy. Lor bliss yer, I feels I gets more and more like a kangaroo. We lives like a kangaroo, we eats like 'em, we bites and hugs like 'em, and rips, uses our toes, and jumps like 'em, and when

I slips my cable, I believe I shall go sky-larking o'er this ere scrub a boomer.'

Though this was said in a half-joking style, yet it could be distinctly seen that the idea was no new one just started, or suggested by the accidental subject of conversation, though Sam was a most dreadful scoffer at all religion, or at least at the little he knew and recognised as religion. He had his superstitions strongly and irrevocably fixed, and one was the belief in the doctrine of the metamorphosis,[134] one of the earliest and most natural to the human mind under all circumstances of race and climate, and associated as he had been from his youth, with aboriginal thoughts and opinions, enshrined as they are in the fullest degree in this belief.

'Well, Sam,' said the mate, 'my business is to get a lot of you to come and load us with salt, and then we'll come back and buy your skins.'

'Werry perlite; but do yer see we are just now laying a strand,[135] parbuckling[136] a little bit o' fun. We can't go,' said Sam, shaking his head, and then adding, after a long pause, 'if you hadn't hove in sight, we should have been there.'

'Where?' said the mate.

'On the mainland to get some more black empresses. We wants more terribly bad; can't do half the work. Yer see, old Worley[137] got six, Porky has got six, so we is going to haul the seine.[138] No, we can't go with yer this trip.'

The mate looked incredulous.

'What are yer staring at,' mildly remarked Sam. 'Will yer jine us in the spree, and grab two or three for your own property?'

'So you catch them,' at last struck in the mate. 'Catch them like kangaroos.'

'Jist so,' says Sam, 'only more ticklish; catch 'em like fish in a net. Just so, but not so many in a haul. Like bandicoots[139] in a snare. Jist so, but they is harder to hold.[140] Yes,' continued Sam; 'we traps 'em like wallaby; we circumwents 'em.'

'Well, I'm blessed,' said the mate, as he drew a long breath, and involuntarily turned round and gazed at a couple of black women standing at the hut door.

Sam noticed this, and highly amused at the mate's greenness, remarked by way of moral, 'Live and larn, mate; live and larn and as for the manner o' catching 'em, which seems to stick in yer gizzard, tell me, mister, how in arth are we to git 'em otherwise?' Saying this, Sam brought down his fist heavily on the table by way of climax, and gave the mate a prolonged stare.

Mr. Handspike was unable to suggest a better mode, so he wisely deferred the matter, and at once struck up a fresh topic. 'Well, I must top my boom,[141] and make for the boat. Where are all the chaps?' and rising he proceeded to Long Bill's hut, where he found all hands half drunk, and Long Bill leading them in chorus – 'I don't care a d———m what the chief mate says; I don't care what the captain says; Hah! Hoorah! Fol de rol de ray!'[142]

'Belay there,' sung out the mate, 'and shape a course for the boat.'

'I will go ashore, and I shall go ashore to see the old commodore – Hah Hoorah! Fol de rol de ray!' roared out all hands, not heeding the mate.

'Cuss me!' sung out Bill, 'we are going to have a free and easy night of it, and if you, Mr. Mate, comes here parlyvouing, why hang me, I'll rip yer up!' So saying, Long Bill seized one of the sailor's tarpaulin hats[143] in his left hand by way of shield, drew a long ugly knife with his right, and made a half-bound to clear the way. 'Come on, you white nigger, I'll cram this down your gills.' The mate moved slightly on one side, drew his pistol, looked to the pruning, and cocked it. The half-drunken mob rose up, too, and instinctively cocked their pistols, to the infinite danger of friend and foe.

The native women, who had been silent spectators all this while, or acting slaves to their white lords,[144] gave an unearthly yell that foreboded no good, and soon brought to the spot old Porky, Sam, and others who knew well the sign of alarm.

'Hilloo,' said Sam, as he burst in among the combatants, 'going to have a bit of play are yer? Well, just wait awhile, and I'll jine yer.'

'I wants none o' your help,' bawled out Long Bill, 'so just steer clear.'

'Whether yer does or does not.' calmly replied Sam, 'I'll lend a hand,' not saying however, which side he would espouse.

'I'll give in if the mate will leave us alone,' argued Long Bill, 'we are going to make a night on it, so stand clear, and no more yarning.'

'That's it mate,' said Porky, 'here's enough licker for all hands – put up your pop-guns and fall to, and ——'

'Come along men,' said the mate, 'come along to the boat.'

'Go to yer mother; go to old Nick,' shouted all hands in defiant voices, 'let the brig go to Jericho.[145] We sleeps ashore to-night like gemmen.'

'It's no use,' said Sam to the mate, turning away, 'you can't launch the boat yersell, besides I told the women to go down and haul her into the creek.'[146]

'The devil you have,' said the mate, 'this is a strange place. I suppose we are all prisoners.'

'Hold on a bit, mate, yer a stranger in these parts, and we are pooty set o' boys. We cuts up rough wery quick, and we cuts up smooth; so mind yer soundings.'

'It's like your cursed impudence, Mr. Robinson Crusoe, to touch that boat at all!'

'Ha! ha! ha! imperance in Kangaroo Island! Wal that chokes me; will yer hail some peelers, and give us in charge?[147] Wal, wal, but I forgive yer, yer knows no better. I took the boat in the creek, 'cause yer are so cussed wise, and leaves it so that the surf call smash it to pieces; we keeps our boats in the creek; but here we are, so come to an anchor. I say, Bet,[148] give us some baccy,' continued Sam, as they entered his hut.

'But why,' replied the mate, more and more astonished at Sam, at his reasoning, and his own strange position, 'why don't yer go and drink with the chaps? they have got plenty of grog.'

'I never drinks,' said Sam in a subdued voice.

'Never drinks!'

'No, I never drinks. I wish all the drink was in the sea. Once – a long time gone – I drank like ——'[149]

'You are a queer un,' said the mate.

'Yes,' replied Sam, 'I am a queer un, but I never drinks now.'

'Then you did once,' but Sam made no reply. It was quite apparent he did not like the topic; there was a mystery about it that made him uneasy – rude and apparently callous as he was – utterly unmodified by the contact of civilisation, and recognising no other moral obligations than the strongest arm and the stoutest heart. No giant rock on his island home was firmer in his determination when once resolved upon. Leading a life freed from all moral and social control, and surrounded by every form of unbridled license, old Sam exhibited the wonderful virtue of an absolutely sober man.

After a transitory feeling of surprise, and even of involuntary respect at the singular oddity that sat before him, the mate began fully to realise the powerless position he was in, absolutely imprisoned with a set that, for aught he knew, might cut his throat at any moment for any whim or caprice.

'Dash my buttons,' he exclaimed, jumping up and pacing up and down, 'I'm caught in a trap; infernal scoundrels. What'll the skipper say? Hang the lazy dogs.'

'That's right, mate,' said Sam, 'pray away; I allers does. I find it does me good. I know'd a parson aboard a man-o'-war;[150] he used to swear by hissell across the taffrail.[151] One day I cotched him. "It does me good, Sam; it does me good, Sam," says he, and he dives below. I allers follows his example.'

'None of your yarns,' replied the mate; 'come along with me and a couple of women and launch the boat.'

Sam shook his head slowly, and laughed quietly. 'I say, Bet, will yer go down and shove the boat out of the creek.'

'No! No!' screamed Bet, horrified at the idea, 'too much dark, plenty debil, debil.'

'Do yer see,' observed Sam, 'these critters will never go about in the dark; they are sartin the air is chock-o-block full of devils.[152] When they walks at night, they takes a fire stick to keep the devils off, but they never moves more than a hundred yards.[153] No, no, mate, sit down and have a smoke; the women are right, too many devils about.'

'White devils,' remarked the mate bitterly, who could by no means reconcile himself to his forced position of inaction; but there was no remedy, and in no pleasant mood he ultimately consented to the night ashore.

Long Bill's Scheme. –
The Mate Lost in the Bush. –
All Start for the Beach. –
The Plot.

The morning came hot and close, particularly so in the dense scrub, where the huts of the Islanders stood.[154] The drunkards of the previous night were still asleep. During the revelries the native women had taken the precaution to steal away the pistols of the sailors, and throw them in a heap under a tree, knowing from unhappy experience that in these orgies they frequently were the chief sufferers.[155] As the dawn broke Long Bill was up, and in deep conference with a couple of other Islanders who had arrived from some expedition several hours before.

'Well,' said Long Bill, I couldn't do it no how; they were too sharp for me.'

'It was a ——— near squeak,' said one.

'All right, my lads, we will cook 'em yet.' There's a whole boat's load asleep now,' pointing to his hut.

The truth was, it had been a plot between Mr. Long Bill and his two brothers, on their sighting the brig a couple of days before, to make for a certain islet, and to pretend he was in distress, and so arrange the matter as to wreck the vessel – a scheme very likely to succeed, and of a highly profitable character to all concerned – a plot that had been successful on more occasions than one. In fact, it was one of the *legitimate* sources of income, according to the political and social constitution of the empire of Kangaroo Island.[156] They appointed themselves 'general receivers of wrecks,' and were frequently called upon to exercise their office and peculiar functions to the benefit of all concerned. They were a magnificent coast-guard – ever watchful and vigilant. It was singular how frequently they would kindly pilot a ship out of danger of reef and current, and yet by some unlucky chance, make shipwreck of the very object their solicitude. Slanderous tongues would have it that it was designed, a part of their living and of their annual receipts; but the self-appointed pilots of Kangaroo Island could prove by infallible charts, drawn with their fingers on the sand, how it was the skipper's fault.

'The skipper would stand on. I tells him to come about, but he wouldn't. We gets into the tide rips, we heaves about, we wears ship,[157] and then bumps we go on the pint.' Plain and convincing as this statement was, the ship's crew would have it it was just the other way. 'The pilot would stand on, wouldn't heave about, etc., etc.' There was also a curious coincidence of the boats of the Islanders being ready to save life; just popping out of some nook or cove just at the precise moment required. The pious would call it providential, but the wicked shook their wicked heads, and had grave doubts as to the miraculous part of the business.

'How is it,' said one exasperated and unfortunate captain, 'that your boats are always handy when craft go ashore?'

'Oh, they are allers hanging about craw-fishing, do yer see,' was the reply.[158]

'Twas most marvellous some were always craw-fishing, when others were always piloting!'

Mr. Handspike rose from his bed of wallaby skins in no enviable mood. He was determined to be off at once. Come what might, off he'd go with them or without them, so he proceeded straight to where his boat's crew was located. He found them mostly asleep and those awake very sulky, very saucy, and little inclined to make way for the beach.

'Come lads, turn out, and let's be off. The skipper will be in a pretty pucker when we get on board.'

'The skipper be hanged,' growled Jim, 'who the dickens is going to haul and pull through this here "plains o' promise"[159] in this hot weather?'

'Bear a hand', said the mate. Reluctantly they rose up and mustered themselves in a dogged and unwilling spirit, in a state nearer mutiny than obedience. Crawling as far as old Sam's hut, they collected together, ready to follow the leader.

The heat by this time had become frightful. Hemmed in by tall and dense trees, not a breath of air stirred the smallest leaf. Nature seemed in a trance, every leaf, every blade hung listlessly. The birds hopped from one branch to another without a note – merely to find a cooler spot; even the savage dogs didn't care to move and attack the strangers, but lay sprawling about with legs distended and lolling tongues.

'Take it easy, mates,' remarked Sam as they came up, 'we is going to have a regular buster; if yer can't see yer will feel bime-bye rale sheets o' flame; there's plenty o' time, and ———'

'No more jawing,' said the mate in no gentle voice, 'come along and show us the way to the boats; every minute it's getting worse.'

'In course it is, and yer 'spect me to melt all my tallow out for yer brig? No, no, mister, we is never in a hurry here,' and then, sitting deliberately down on a log of wood in an attitude that denoted a fixed determination to take it easy, he added, 'none o' your promenades for the likes of me this morning.'

'Well done, Robinson Crusoe,' struck in several voices. The mate was aghast. By this time Long Bill and others had arrived.

'You'll come with us,' said the mate, addressing Long Bill.

'No, mister, it's too hot,' and he threw himself full length on the ground.

'You'll go,' sharply spoke the mate, turning to old Porky.

Porky shook his head slowly, and said he was going to have a sleep, as the naughty boys, pointing to the sailors, had kept him awake all night.

'Well, if none of you will go, you set of lazy rascals, I'll go by myself, hail the brig, and if I don't square yards with you, my pretty lads,' shaking his fist at the sailors, 'my name isn't Handspike.' Saying this, he dashed right off, not heeding the various remonstrances addressed to him about the heat, no water, getting lost, snakes, etc.

After he had gone some time, old Sam remarked, 'He thinks it all plain sailing. Wal, give 'em plenty of line, and he'll jam hisself some- where; we'll send the women arter him bime-by.'

The morning wore on, a raging, burning, blast swept over the land; the trees shed their leaves at every fiery squall that sent its withering breath to kill, burn, and destroy; the singing locust, the very child of heat, ceased its song; bird and beast sought refuge from the dread atmosphere; the very snakes lay extended about the margins of the salt lagoons; and so enervated became man and dog, and Black and White, that to lie in a shady spot, and to sip water nearly hot, became the only effort that Nature seemed able to accomplish. Poor Handspike during the while was struggling between life and death in the hopeless scrub of the island. When he dashed away, full of wrath and revenge, he was too angry to reflect and to arrange a course for the beach, which he might have done, though with but a bare chance of ever reaching it.

After penetrating a thick belt of dense tea-tree, whose stems were interlaced and entangled, he suddenly found himself on the muddy margin of a great salt lagoon, of which previously he had not the remotest notion, so hidden was it from view. Cursing his ill luck, he tried to force his way towards a point that he thought indicated the head of the lagoon by climbing up, clambering over, and, for considerable distances at a time, crawling under the confused mass of the densest tea-tree that surrounded the lagoon, growing in, and lying on, the soft, oozy mud, in all stages of growth and decay. It was a primeval forest, the home of the deadly black snake, the tarantula, the scorpion, and the centipede, and bitterly did he regret his obstinacy. His progress was retarded to the last degree of endurance. He would take long 'spells' at a time, pondering how it was possible to get either through, under, above, below, around, or over the next bunch of tea-tree before him, until he gradually forgot the purpose of his going to the beach. The dreadful mud beneath that sucked him fast, the snakes that and hissed about his legs, the horrible thirst he was beginning to experience, and the hopeless position in which he was, absorbed all other thoughts and considerations but the one overpowering wish to save himself from what appeared to be fast approaching – inevitable death. With a gigantic struggle he succeeded in extricating his legs from the dire mud, and breaking and scrambling, he burst through some 100 feet of thicket, and suddenly plumped on to what appeared the sweetest spot under heaven. In a small bend of the lake the line of tea-tree had retreated, and the space was covered with the most vivid green of the samphire plant.[160] How refreshing to his sight was that cool, green, semi-transparent verdure! How crisply it crushed under his feet, suggesting the pleasant ideas of frost and ice. He plucked handfuls, and devoured it eagerly. Bitter and saline as the juice was, it, in a slight degree, refreshed him. Utterly prostrated, lie threw himself down and gazed away over the reach of waters before him, so beautifully clear, but so horribly bitter – the Dead Sea itself was not salter or more forbidding.

Not far from him sat some half-dozen black swans, which were apparently enjoying themselves – for of all happy creatures on earth, ducks and swans must be the happiest. Should it be burning hot they live in cool water; should it rain, it is just the weather they revel in. Near them were two or three rocky islets, on which for ages they had reared their little ones.[161] With outstretched neck they were peering and listening to the intrusion of the mate, and giving vent to their surprise by repeated notes of a musical tone. Beyond these was the irregular outline of the lagoon, showing a densely fringed shore of the horrid tea-tree. Glancing round, he found himself shut in by an impervious hedge – a vegetable wall of the thickest growth. To go forward seemed impossible, and to retreat by the way he came was beyond his strength. He thought of wading and swimming over the lake to the nearest point, making the islets his resting places. Happily, he ultimately decided otherwise. Had he gone, his fossilized bones would have been the subject of the deepest speculation in future ages as an incontestable proof of the preadamite theory of the human race.[162]

The mate crawled under the deepest shade he could find, and not being particularly afflicted with nerves, commenced in true sailor style to curse island and ship, old Sam and the sailors, the hot day and himself. At times he would jump up and shout with all his might, but it was of no use, as he was to leeward of the huts instead of to wind-ward, and all the reply he got was the musical notes of his not distant companions, the black swans, for they were too wise to take fright and fly about in that burning blast. At length the mate found that shouting only exhausted himself, and made him more unfit to bear his perilous position. Desisting with an oath, he threw himself down, utterly over-come. The rustling of leaves and cracking of dead boughs, and the occasional note of the black swans, startled and harassed him. At times he thought he heard someone breaking through the horrid thicket; the islets became brigs and ships sailing towards him; the black swans, boats racing to be first to relieve him. So his reeling senses excited his poor brain till a merciful exhaustion threw him into a trance of total unconsciousness.

It was an hour or so before this when, as Sam was amusing himself in the shade of the hut with his numerous dogs, he sang out to one of the native women, 'Here, Bumblefoot'[163] – for such was her name – 'go and fetch in that lubber of a mate; you'll soon find him.' Without a word of reply Bumblefoot went off like a hound. 'I thinks he's got enough on it,' mumbled Sam, as he chuckled to himself, and then went on talking to his dogs.

The woman soon found the direction the mate had taken, and she laughed heartily at the idea of his going direct inland to find the beach. Taking a wide circuit, and judging from time and the rate of progress the mate could make, she determined to strike the lagoon at a point where she would at once find whether the mate had passed, and so save herself a word of toil, a point no other than the identical little bay where the mate was then actually lying! Carefully wading round this point, she knew at once he was not beyond, she had headed him. A few steps further, and she all but stumbled over the poor fellow, who was sitting and gazing at the ships that never came, and the boats ever racing but never getting nearer.

Bumblefoot gave the mate a shake, but noticing his wild stare she quickly took a large bunch of grass, and wetting it well, she put in on his head, to his great relief. He looked at her, but kept pointing to the islets.

'They are all anchored,' he cried despairingly, 'and the boats, too.'

'Come long,' said Bumblefoot, 'boat bime-by.' Retracing her steps, she halted by the way, and from a little native well, supplied the mate with sweet, fresh water, sat him down in the shade, and kept applying grass pads soaked in cold water to his head. The mate recovered his consciousness, and thought that Bumblefoot, though a black gin, with a halt in her leg, kindly bestowed upon her by her white lord and husband, as pretty a creature he had ever seen.[164] Holding on by her arm, she led him through a shady but devious footpath straight to the huts.

'Wal,' said Sam, 'yer look as if all the bounce was taken out of yer, anyhow, mister.'

'Cocoa-nut too tin, lauty sun knock 'im down,' said Bumblefoot by way of explanation.[165]

'I see,' said Sam. 'Cheer up, mate, and here, "Pussy" – another black lady[166] – bring that kangaroo tail soup.[167] Now, mate, stow some of this stick-o'-yer-ribs[168] under hatches.'

'Water, water,' cried the mate.

'And here, you bale away cold water on his nob; we'll soon set yer up all a-taunt-o;[169] but I hopes yer will be werry pertickler arter this how yer goes toddling about in this garden o' ours, which is summet like oursels, werry poorty in some places, and werry ugly in t'other.'[170]

Not very long after this a gun boomed over the island.

'Hello!' cried all hands, 'there she spouts! And there's another!'[171]

'The brig's a firing, and saying why the devil don't yer come,' said Sam.

'They'll shove off next,' said Long Bill, 'so we had better start for the beach. Come, mates, let's have a parting glass.'

But Long Bill had an eye to business. It was by no means his wish that the party should get on board, for his scheme was to retain the men ashore under any pretence by getting them drunk, or getting them lost. So he ordered two or three of his black women to go along with them, and so to manage that at least a couple of sailors should be lost in the bush, which would, of course, cause further delay, reduce the hands on board the brig, and then if a stiff south-easter came to blow – a prevailing wind at that season of the year[172] – the chances were the vessel would be driven ashore. Knowing well that Captain Meredith would despatch another boat as soon as the wind fell, to search for the mate's party, he had sent a couple of women to keep a look-out from the sandhill, with instructions that as soon as they saw a boat put off, they were to walk about the beach to decoy it away from the spot where he had landed the second mate, with the ulterior intention of drawing the men inland, and then abandoning them for the night. Old Sam, though no party to the plot, had, through the usual impulsive habits of a roving life, inadvertently helped the scheme, and the hot day had been exceedingly favourable, not that Sam would have cared much either way, whether the brig went ashore or not. If it had suited his whim and he had known it, he would have probably aided it with all his cunning but as he really knew nothing about it, his waywardness accidentally dove-tailed nicely into Long Bill's plan.

The parting cup was drunk, and the whole party, headed by Sam, and brought up by Long Bill, assisted by a couple of other Islanders, started off to the beach.

Chapter 7

Mr. Ratlin Goes Ashore in Search of the Lost Boat. – His Adventures.

The hot wind had worn its fury out, and all Nature seemed relieved from the oppressive heat of the great gale. On board the ship Captain Meredith was waiting impatiently for the moment when he could with safety despatch a second boat in search of the first.

'Now, Mr. Ratlin,' said the captain, 'just get under weigh[173] as soon as you like, and rouse those lazy rascals out of the scrub.' The mate moved away, and gave the necessary orders to get the boat ready. 'Ah! there they are at last,' exclaimed the captain, as he ran his glass over the beach for the five hundredth time. 'I see one, two, look!' handing the glass to the mate, who thereupon intently watched the distant figures for some minutes.

'They are none of our crew,' said Mr. Ratlin, 'they are either blacks or some of the islanders. If they are our chaps, why don't they stand on for the brig? What are they doing so far down the bay? I rather suspect some stratagem.'

'Well,' said the captain, 'I think we have got among the enchanted islands;[174] however, top your boom,[175] and do your best.'

There was still a heavy jumble of a sea left from the norther. The mate did not half like his mission. He had had some slight acquaintance with the Islanders, and knew what slippery customers they were, how utterly beyond all consistent course of action, wayward, sullen, cunning, and unmanageable, difficult to please and dangerous to offend; but his duty was plain, and he set himself manfully to work, though not in the most pleasant mood. He was cross with the absent men, with Mister Bill, with the hot weather, and, coming nearer home, with the boat, and the manner in which the men pulled, though that was unavoidable, as the sea was abeam, and kept unpleasantly, washing over the gunwale and soaking the mate and the men on the weather side to the skin. The boat was steered straight for the two figures on the beach as seen from the brig, but when within a quarter of a mile they vanished.

'Ah!' said the mate, 'I thought as much. Did you notice, Bob,' addressing one of the men, 'the spot where those men or women or animals last stood?'

'Yes, sir! a little ahead of that heavy lump of black seaweed. Give way, lads, and see if we can't catch 'em whatever they are.'

Carefully feeling his way, the mate at last found a spot where he thought he might with little danger beach the boat, and when just in the act of doing so a black head popped up behind the sandhills, and gave a prolonged coo-e-e[176] that was distinctly heard by the boat's crew, though in the midst of the rush and roar of broken water. The boat was not landed so scientifically as when Long Bill beached the second mate's boat; in fact, it is well known that sailors are very indifferent boatmen. They handle a boat, as they do a ship, which is entirely wrong. They are too slow; too methodical, and too unobservant of the small things that are life and death to boats.[177] Mr. Ratlin found his boat half swamped, but setting to with a will, they soon put it beyond the water's reach.

'Now, men,' said the mate, 'this island is fully of smart tricks; they are up to anything, so safe bind, safe find,[178] Take these oars, two of them down that way, and two the other way, and just bury them, and do it neatly, for these imps of Satan[179] ashore, if they come down, they will take away the oars and jam us hard and fast.' A practical joke of the kind alluded to by the mate, a joke that might entail in the long run the most serious consequences, was one of the sweetest bits of pleasure that occasionally fell to the lot of the Islanders to enjoy. A freak of this kind, with all its perplexing difficulties, would afford ample scope for endless rows between all hands. Should a ship get lost because the crew could not get off at the proper time to assist her – well, so much the better, the joke would be a profitable one; should it end in blows – well, that was the real bone and sinew of a good lark; and should they wish to revenge an insult, or following the example of the great potentates of the earth to pick a quarrel, no subject was so fruitful of dissension as tampering with the boats of the vessels that visited them. A crew adrift and ashore, and the boat rendered useless on the beach, was an advantage not to be lightly esteemed, and one which gave the enemy nine point points of the law – viz., possession. It was an artful dodge[180] continually resorted to. Had the Islanders done wrong, the crew were virtually prisoners, and could be held as hostages till terms of peace were established, So simple a remedy as knocking a hole in the bottom of the boat or carrying away the oars was continually resorted to for a three-fold purpose – for a lark, for revenge, or for war. Mr. Ratlin had had some previous experience of this sort of scheming, and he therefore wisely buried his oars. He certainly could have stationed a hand to watch the boat, but he wanted every man to assist him in capturing the truant crew.

The long shades of the sandhills began to fleck the white beach, and to warn the first mate of the necessity of haste. Climbing up the steep wall of sand, he cast his eye over one of the most forbidding prospects to be imagined. Looking inland as far as he could see, a broad valley stretched away to some higher ground. On the right and left were massive hills, intersected with ugly-looking, deep gullies.[181] Over the whole, and spread evenly as a carpet, was a dense, impervious scrub, rendered doubly solid and repulsive by the dark shadows that were fast accumulating in heavy belts and streaks, in broad masses and abrupt breaks. In that impervious and inhospitable region lay the Islanders' homes and the lost crew. Mr. Ratlin gave an audible grunt as he surveyed the scene.

'Well, I'd rather face a north-wester off the Cape, or a typhoon than that,' remarked the mate to one of the men, pointing to the frowning scrub. 'If we get lost there our goose is cooked.'

The mate's metaphors, whenever he indulged in them, were always culinary (invariably related to the kitchen and to cookery).

While the small party of seamen were pondering for a minute before they made a dash into the uninviting bush, two native women, lying prone on the ground, might have been noticed behind a clump of bushes within a few yards of the sailors, watching them with the intent and stealthy gaze of the cat. With the habits of their race they were passing signs from one to the other, indicating their wishes or their fears precisely as when they hunted the game of the forest. Not a twig was broken, not a leaf moved. Though armies of ants were to crawl over them, no impatience would betray their presence. Neither snake, nor centipede, nor scorpion could disturb their purpose. As the sailors descended the native women rose, and hastily conferred. 'To the gullies,' they whispered and slid away with the rapidity of snakes, disappearing from sight.

Now the gullies lay inland and away from the huts of the Islanders, and were frightful rocky chasms covered with treacherous scrub, and forming a region of interminable difficulties. Once lost in them, the chances were you would never extricate yourself. None but the most experienced Islanders went there; and only the black women were able to thread the glens and scrub of that dire district.

As the mate's party tore through the scrub they soon became separated, each angrily insisting that his way was the best, while the mate besought them to keep together. 'We are "done brown,"' said he, pathetically, as he involuntarily associated the state of a joint and their probable condition, 'if we don't keep together.'

Instead of walking in Indian file, they would slightly straggle; a back slap in the face from a branch would make one dodge round, another would be deluded by the appearance of a favourable break, a third would explore a route on his own account. It soon happened that they could not see each other, but kept still pretty near by mutual shouting, and in this manner they toiled on, in the direction of the last coo-e-ee they had heard.

Pausing to wipe his brow, the mate remarked to one of the men near him, 'We can't be far from where we heard those coo-e-es!'

At the same instant a prolonged coo-e-ee rose upon the evening air, quite from the direction in which they were travelling. Scarcely had it died down when another pierced the sky.

'We'll grab 'em soon,' said Bob, 'a little more to the westward, and we'll find their moorings.'

'To the eastward, yer mean,' replied another, 'yer lost to a dead sartinty if yer go westward.'

Collecting themselves together at the positive injunctions of the mate, they all made a fresh start to the eastward, a direction cunningly contrived by the sly scouts sent by Long Bill to mislead them. Night had now nearly set in. Mr. Ratlin and his men were quite separated, though still keeping up communication by occasional shouting, and so mutually trusting in one of the worst fallacies in bush travelling. The ground became more rough, and the men widened the distance between them more and more. At last the shouting became quicker and more alarming, and gradually fainter, and every effort made to re-unite the party only made matters worse. One or two fell into deep creeks, another wandered towards the beach, and the mate still heard the distant cooing of the decoying blacks, so adroitly managed that it led directly to the terrible country of the gullies.

'Never mind,' thought the mate, 'I hear their coo-e-es and the bark of a dog; I must soon get there, and then I'll send some one to pick up these lubbers that have strayed away.'

The young moon cast her feeble rays over the wild sea of scrub. There was a great calm, and Nature seemed in a profound repose. The mate climbed a rough tree, and leant over a dead limb – as on a topsail yard – to obtain a look-out. The scene that met his gaze was grand and solemn. His stout heart quailed as he gradually comprehended the extraordinary position he was in. He listened in vain for the shouting of his men, now lost in the great wilderness below. Nought but the piercing shriek of the curlew[182] rent the desolation, with the whistling note of the opossum,[183] and the melancholy wooing of the mawpawk.[184] Oft had he looked upon the warring elements of wind and water on the mighty ocean, but there was something inconceivably horrible in that profound, immoveable, and silent waste, in the towering heights rising in successive steps, and clothed with the densest mantle of black scrub, that barred his vision on every side. He descended the tree bewildered. The blacks that had thus far misled him now left, feeling assured that, go which way he would, he was lost for the night. The mate made a desperate effort to recover the beach. Once there he would be safe; within the sound of the breakers he was at home; but in the impenetrable thickets of the island he felt he was impotent and unable to cope with the difficulty. The ground began to rise, and ugly, loose stones impeded his progress and reduced his pace to that of a snail's but still on he went struggling and stumbling, tearing the boughs asunder, wriggling his body through narrow passes. A huge mass of thick bush fairly brought him to a standstill. There appeared no escape but to go through it, over it, or under it. The moon had set, and the bright stars afforded too illusory a light to assist him out of his difficulty. He thought he heard the distant reverberations of the surf, and he felt nerved from this faint strengthening of the only hope that now sustained him. Cheered by this, like another Mungo Park,[185] sustained by the thought that clung around the flower of the desert, he made a bold attempt to push his way to the sea. Scarcely had he gone a dozen paces, than in the twinkling of an eye he felt himself crashing through endless bushes to endless depths below! As he rapidly descended, the leafy canopy closed over him and excluded the stars and light. Down, down he went, bouncing against some hard substance, then rolling over smaller bushes; then sliding, now head first, then feet, accompanied by an avalanche of stones, sticks, gravel, and sand until at last he found himself jammed in a dry water-course, hurt, and utterly stupid. In fact, he had fallen down one of the innumerable gullies that intersected the hilly country he had wandered into, and which gave no warning of their existence, their edges being covered with thick scrub, and in parts reaching across the chasm.

We leave Mr. Ratlin in his unpleasant predicament and follow the fortunes of the first party that was left proceeding to the beach under the guidance of Old Sam and Bill.

Chapter 8

The First Party Reach the Beach. – The Invisible Boathouse. – Sam's Anecdote. – The Pull on Board. – The Shark's Fin.

'Mind how yer place yer feet, mate,' said Sam, as he threaded his way carefully through a miry flat covered with a crust of salt. 'We has no bridges here, and if there was, why I'd soon clear out; no! no! I doesn't like yer bridges, and yer streets, and yer fences, and yer gaols, and yer perlice; all wery well for loafers that can't take care of theirselves; but not for the likes o' me.'[186]

Long Bill, having been joined by one of the native women despatched by him to decoy the party that belonged to Mr. Ratlin's boat, and being told how well that plot was progressing, abandoned his present design of dropping one or two of the crew on their march to the beach – in truth he rather expedited their progress. He selected the shortest cuts, and managed matters so well that they soon heard the welcome fall and rush of the breakers.

'My eye, isn't that purty?' said Jim.

'What's purty?' said Bill.

'Why, you old stingaree, can't yer hear the swell thundering on the beach? And it's a fortnight gone since we heard it last!'

'Avast, Jim; it's just nuffing more nor less than forty-eight hours. If yer go on lying in that style, why yer will sink the brig, and send us all to Davy Jones's Locker.'[187]

'But wasn't every hour as long as the middle watch in a calm night?' replied Jim. 'Then yer see it comes about that a fellow feels like a fortnight in two days. This is a onnatural life, yer knows, and onnatural hours, and days, and weeks. Did yer ever hear tell on a lot of fellows having six black wives apiece? This is a queer land, I can't keep a log[188] no-how! Here, Jack, give us a chaw.'[189]

The party now mounted a sandhill that commanded a view of the bay and the beach. On one side was a fine creek, on the other the sea.

'Where's the boat?' shouted the mate.

'In the creek,' said Long Bill.

'Come, none of your gammon; there's nothing on the creek but a duck or so.'

Like all Australian creeks and, we might add, rivers, there was a great bar in front, several hundred yards in extent of dry sand, and looking up and along the reach of inland water, nought was visible but a couple of ibis[190] sitting upon a protruding branch of a dead stump, a duck just clattering round the distant bend, and a heavy fringe of bushes sweeping the surface of the water in isolated patches. Deeply hidden, and cunningly arranged under one of these patches lay no less than three boats. A man might have travelled up and down the creek the whole day and never discovered them, so admirably were they secured from observation.

'I s'pose we've to stop ashore 'nother night, aye?'

Not heeding the remark, Old Sam beckoned to one of his wives to fetch out the invisible boat. Wading for some considerable distance, she suddenly parted the bushes and disappeared. The seamen thought she had fallen, and was drowning, and were for rendering immediate assistance; but while they were wrangling the boat glided out almost beneath their feet, and the black woman walking alongside, and heading for the bar.

'Well, I'm blowed!' cried all hands.

'Yes, this is the land o' wonders,[191] and we is the chaps that works 'em,' chimed in old Sam, relishing their surprise amazingly; 'that sort o' boathouse is wery convenient, ain't it, Bill? We uses it for all sort o' things. Once a skipper gee us too much jaw, so we hooks his boat in here; down he comes, can't find his boat, then he prays a bit. "May be," says I, "the sea have washed the boat away." He sets to work to find the boat; he hunts all day, and was wery perlite to us, and we helps him; bime-bye he comes down here, and there's the boat all right and snug, jist where he lefts her. "May be," says I, "the sea has washed her up?" The skipper looks queer[192] like, and gives me a squint, and pulls like mad to get on board, ups anchor, and I'd never seed him since.'

The mate and his party were soon afloat, and as they receded from the beach the men began involuntarily to have a feeling of fear for the land they had just left, and its uncouth inhabitants, nor was this feeling in the least degree lessened as they gazed on the figure of Old Sam standing on the beach, with the gloom of evening settling round him, his hairy dress, his hairy face, arms, and legs, his bare feet and bare head, with a great mass of tangled hair, that waved about in the night breeze. In all this there was something peculiarly wild, weird, and devilish. Everything that had been said and done during their short sojourn on the island had been strange and eccentric, and had left an uneasy impression on their minds, a vague and mysterious feeling of dread. A little of the supernatural came by degrees to be associated with their late boat companions, and to superstitious sailors the idea was natural and orthodox.

'Did yer twig how that old rascal chuckled when we could not find the boat? Isn't he a regular hourang – Long Bill is nuffing to him. And all those black gins corroboreeing at nights, singing and yarning in their gibberish, and the yeller imps skipping about the fires; but worser and worser, that old Robinson Crusoe never drinks a drop o' grog. When we gets three sheets in the wind he was sober as a judge, that's the worsest of all. I likes Long Bill; he can drink like a fish, which I holds is natural like.'

Conversing in this style they soon left the land behind them, which now in the faint light of the young moon assumed an unnatural degree of height and boldness, and cast a deep and over-hanging shade on the sea – in fact, so deceptive was the appearance that the land seemed advancing on the sea, the intervening space being absorbed and confused, and it appeared as if the great protuberant hills were toppling over their heads. In the still air of the night, the shrill melancholic wail of the bittern[193] rose loud and long, and startled the seamen in the boat.

The poor second mate seemed very ill. He scarcely spoke, and as he reclined against the side, his head rolled to and fro with the motion of the waves, and the moon lit up fitfully a face that seemed nearer akin to death than to life. The men became silent. They were oppressed, they felt over-awed, they knew not why exactly; but a gale of wind, a storm, anything would have been a relief. That terrible calmness, with that strange land frowning on them seemed unendurable. Then a new horror was added to their superstitious fear, for right in the boat's wake a triangular black patch could be discerned ever and anon flickering in the moonbeams, and keeping an exact intervening space between itself and the stern of the boat. The sailors knew it well; it was the fin of a shark,[194] and to them a sure warning of some one's death. They shook their heads and glanced at the poor mate. To them his fate was sealed, and they cursed that ominous fin that never swerved to the right nor left, neither retired nor advanced, the fell harbinger of the watery grave. They wanted but this to fill the measure of their fears. The spell was on them, and they pulled in silence and in trepidation, with a dying man in the boat, and death in their wake. In the darkness they had got beyond the brig, but happily the still night had carried the echoes of their oars to the vessel.

'Boat a-hoy!' came faintly over the waters, and guided by this pleasant sound they soon found themselves alongside, though the fin had never left them for an instant.

'Is that you, Mr. Ratlin?' said Captain Meredith.

'No, sir, it's Mr. Handspike's boat.'

'And where's Mr. Ratlin?'

'Don't know, sir; we never seed him, knows nothing about him.'

'Good heavens!' ejaculated the captain, 'and why doesn't the mate speak?'

'Oh! He's very ill, we'll get him up directly; easy, Bill, easy easy there.'

'Now, take him below,' said the captain, 'and come one of you aft, and tell me what's kept you away like this. What's the matter with the second mate, where's Ratlin, and why didn't you see, him?'

'Hold on, sir,' said the carpenter, 'and I'll tell yer all about it.'

'Bear a hand, then, and none of your backing and filling, but a straightforward yarn.'

The carpenter told him all, and left Captain Meredith in a state of rage, fear, and curiosity. He wouldn't believe half he heard; he visited the second mate, but he was too ill to talk; he walked the deck for hours, and then retired, determined to go ashore himself the very next morning.

Mr. Ratlin Survives the Night. –
Reaches the Beach. –
Jack Straw Saves Him. –
Goes on Board.

'Out of the frying-pan into the fire,' was the first exclamation Mr. Ratlin made after he recovered consciousness at the bottom of the dry bed of the deep ravine into which he had been so unceremoniously precipitated. 'The ruling passion strong in death'[195] – the kitchen was not forgotten, though he had just escaped the narrowest chance of becoming food for worms. A schoolmaster in the final hour of life, called for a slate and pencil, and as the film of death closed his eyes he added up an imaginary sum but the total was never recorded, nor the difference found, as the king of terrors solved the problem himself. An undertaker, on the last night of his life, chalked his own funeral procession on a piece of board. 'In that carriage,' gasped the dying man, speaking to his friend at his bedside, and tremblingly pointing to it, 'you must ride'; and it was so! As a man fell mortally wounded by the accidental discharge of his gun, he exclaimed. 'God save the King, I'm shot.' It was his habitual expression, and it ushered him from this earthly kingdom to the other. So with the unfortunate mate, his mind intuitively reverted to kitchen experiences. A great danger befalling the body immediately recalled a similar terror to the nervous system, when the omelette fell into the fire, or the ragout was upset. There is but one step from the sublime to the ridiculous.

If falling a hundred feet clown the sides of a scrubby and rocky creek startle the body, so did the destruction of the good things of this life shock the appetising and sensitive epigastrium; this parallelism, though the circumstances were so diverse, necessitated the inevitable associations, and caused the man in danger of death to give vent to his sufferings in apostrophes to the kitchen and the frying-pan.

Poor Mr. Ratlin felt dreadfully astray; he did not know what to do; the place he was in was pitchy dark; all kinds of queer noises were around him. If he went down the chasm he knew not where it would lead him; if he went up, it was equally dangerous.

'What a mess I have got into,' he soliloquised. 'What a stew they'll be in when no boat returns. What a pickle those scamps of blacks have got me in! But it's no use growling, so here goes!'

After a very long struggle the mate found himself somewhere on the top of a hill, in the midst of a plateau covered with short broom – a most delightful change from the trying bush, stones, and ravines that had hitherto barred his way. The moon had set and the night air breathed sadly through the mournful broom bushes. The mate paused, partly to rest himself, and partly to recover the balance of his mind, which had undergone a severe trial in the events of the past few hours. He rapidly reviewed the singular circumstances that brought him there. Above all, to be deceived by blacks whom he had ever regarded, in whatever part of the world he might be, as no very distant relations of the Evil One. His pious grandmother and nurse had told him that the devil was black; all European theology confirmed the popular opinion; and although he had for years been in daily contact with Lascars,[196] Kroomen,[197] Malabars,[198] Malays, Chinese, and Manilla men, Kanyokas,[199] and Mozambiquers, still the belief of his childhood clung to him, and now in the peculiar position in which he stood he regarded himself more than ever the victim in some way or other of his Satanic majesty. As fire has always been considered an exorcism against man's mortal enemy, he fumbled for his flint and steel; but, alas! he had lost them! He felt proportionately depressed as the hope of the aid that fire afforded was thus miserably destroyed. Unable to go onward without the risk of another fall, he sat down, determined to await the blessed light of day.

Ye gentlemen of England, who sit at home at ease, contrast your own comfortable position with that of the poor wanderer seated on the lonely heights of an outlandish island, a dreary and weird waste of interminable scrub, around him the moaning and shrieking of strange night creatures, varied with the sounds of moving animals – now creeping, dashing, or leaping in every direction unseen – through palpably present to the ear. In vain the mate strove to pierce the gloom, to mark his invisible enemies, to defend himself if needs must be, or to allay his fears; fervently did he wish for the dawn of day. At last it came, so faint, however, that nightlight and, daylight were scarcely distinguishable. With it also came a change of wind, which wafted to his ear the pleasant sound of the distant hum of surf.

'I can hold out another twelve hours,' thought the mate, 'then surely I ought to reach the sea'; but a horrible thought struck him – 'suppose I am near the south shore instead of the north, how am I to get back? If it's the wrong shore, I'm a lost man.' The fear was not an idle one – many had been lost there, and though all the cunning of the Islanders, were brought to bear, they had never been found.[200]

In a desponding mood the mate followed the distant roar of the measured swell. On the top of a great ridge he faintly beheld the sea. On he struggled through tangled masses of wild vine, creepers, prickly scrub, and lofty Narrow leaf, till he found himself on the edge of high sandy limestone cliffs, at the foot of which lay a broad white beach, but to the farthest limits that his eyes could scan seaward neither boat nor brig was visible. His heart sank as he sat down and gazed upon the cheerless ocean. However, the pangs of hunger admonished him of the desirability of getting a breakfast, so with infinite labour he descended the cliffs, and had the comfort to find on the rocks quantities of huge periwinkles.[201] Gathering a hatful of these, with two stones he commenced cracking them, and in some measure satisfied the cravings of hunger.

While so occupied, a figure so grotesquely attired that it would be difficult to affirm it man or woman, human or monster, angel or fiend, with a black face and shaggy hair, a wallet[202] behind, and a spear in the right hand, suddenly advanced from a neighbouring ravine. On seeing the mate it as quickly withdrew, and intently surveyed the stranger through the cracks of a fretted limestone rock. The figure soon reappeared, and threw a stone at a cluster of seafowl by way of introduction to the mate, who startled by the noise, jumped up and stood face to face with this strange apparition.

'You are one of the Islanders!' said the mate half doubtingly, as he surveyed the grim figure before him.

'Yes, I is; and my name is Jack Straw,[203] at your service; but what are you doing here?'

'After some of your fellows,' replied the mate in no pleasant tone, 'kept a boat's crew ashore for two days, and then getting me lost in this infernal scrub last night, where I nearly broke my neck a dozen times, you want to know what I am doing here? Well, you are pretty cool, Mr. Jack Straw; I should think you could answer that question better than I!'

'I knows nuffing about your boat's crew, and your brig, and your wandering about snaring wallabies. I comes south; I bushed it about five miles there-away last night, and this morning I sees you. I knows nuffing what you are yabbering about, mate. I came down here to see Old Sam, and if yer will toddle, why I'll show yer the course.'

Gladly Mr. Ratlin followed the odd creature before him, and on rising on one of the great hills he had the inexpressible pleasure of seeing in the distance the brig. A long pull and a strong pull through the scrub brought them to that point of the beach where the boat had been left the previous night, and no sooner had they reached there than they saw coming down the coast a large straggling party, which proved to be the lost men of the previous night with some of the Islanders, including Old Sam. The mate searched the locker of the boat, and, finding a biscuit and a bit of salt beef, he sat down and did justice to the fare.[204]

Mutual recriminations followed between the sailors and the mate, each accusing the other of purposely going the wrong way, as is always the case when a party divides and gets lost.

'It seems to me,' remarked Old Sam, 'that yer the cleverest lot that I ever seed at playing hide-and-go-seek; we gets one party on board, then another starts and has a game, and now we is just here a whole heap of us to beat up yer tracks, and the women are all away to the south to catch yer there, but yer saved our wind? Where did yer pick him up, Jack?'

'Just inside the Rocky Point where the creek opens out. He never sees me, but I spies him, and brings him on.'

'Wal,' says Sam, addressing the mate, 'yer had some sense in yer yet to make for the beach. We've lost lots of green 'uns in the island and they allers dies in the scrub, where now and agen we finds their bones.'

Mr. Ratlin said little but ate much, and while all the party were preparing to go on board, one of them saw a flash of a gun from the brig, and directly after a whiff[205] was hoisted.

'They twigs us,' said one, 'and more than that, a boat's coming ashore.'

'We'll have a lark[206] to-day,' said Jack Straw, 'got any grog in the huts?'

'Yes, a toothful. Easy, my lads,' said Porky, 'sit down, and let's wait for the skipper – for I'm blowed but that's the skipper – and we'll have a cask o' brandy, or we'll sink.'

'Steady, yer old opossum,' said Sam, we's got plenty o' skins, deal wid 'im, and get as much drink as 'll keep yer drunk for a week; but leave the skipper to me; if I likes him I'll take care on 'im, and if I don't likes 'im, why'll gee 'im to you; is that fair, Porky?'

Porky gave a significant wink, and the bargain was kept as if it had been signed, sealed, and delivered.

By this time the boat had been launched, and very soon the two boats met midway between ship and beach, and after a conference the brig's boat headed for the shore, while the mate's proceeded on board.

Chapter 10

Captain Meredith Lands. –
Georgy, alias Doctor Parson. –
How Sam Lost His Bible. –
The Native Oven.

'I say, Bill, did yer twig how that sulky mate planted the oars? I'll be down on 'im yet for that,' remarked Porky, 'they forgets their manners, and they forgets where they is? Next time that lubber comes here I'll be even wid 'im, he'll look a long time afore he finds his oars when I grabs 'em.'

'That's right,' chimed in Jack Straw, 'I had a jolly lark some two years gone down westward. You see I gets a slant[207] and plants the oars. "The —— black gals has got the oars!" swears the crew. I sits down and looks on. "Gee me a bottle of rum," says I, "and I'll look for 'em, for I knows the women's devilries." "Done," said the man; so I hunts about and in the a'ternoon I finds 'em. Ha! ha! ha!'

'The best way is to knock a hole in the bottom, then yer has a chance of the boat,' remarked another, 'or get one of the women to swim off and cut the painter, then it drifts natural like on the rocks, and it's ours.'

'Yes,' said Sam, 'bekase we is Custom-house hofficers hereaway, and seizes everything that comes ashore, and takes care on it for the Hemprors of Kangaroo Island.'

A loud laugh followed this remark, as the idea tickled their fancy and some who had no boats wished to confiscate a boat that very night, for boats were valuable articles to the Islanders. Without them they could not live, they could not seal, nor get to the mainland on Sabine expeditions;[208] hence, if anything under the sun ranked high in the estimation of an Islander, it was his whaleboat. As they lead [sic] the life of a sealer one-half of the year, and that of a hunter the other,[209] the boat became elevated to the highest dignity in the appreciation of the Islanders – 'Love me, love my boat.' Any harm done to it was equivalent to a personal injury, and the honour of the boat was as precious in the eyes of the Islanders as the fair fame of 'ladye love.' The boat was not regarded as a mere convenience, as a coach or gig, a something that has its turn and is done with. It was more than this. It was his 'all in all,' the very type of his life, a sharer in all his dangers, a companion in all his exploits, noble or ignoble. In many a midnight hour in the wild, wild sea, it was his only chance against death, and, thus identified with all the perilous associations of life, his boat became regarded by the Islander with even human affection. With his boat he was a king, a master of all things; without it, a prisoner and a lost being. To estimate the value of a boat, put a man on a lonely rock, and then ask him what he would give for a boat? And this was the everyday experience of the Islanders, and not an exceptional peril. And hence the value they attached to boats was something that verged on the passionate, more than the value to the Arab of his horse.[210]

By this time Captain Meredith was within a short distance of the beach. Though inclined to have a regular 'row,' still, when he saw so numerous a group on the shore, he thought it would be foolhardy to provoke a lot of gentlemen so singularly attired and of so wayward a temper. However, he pulled boldly in, and catching the surf just at the nick of time, very neatly landed himself at the very edge of the highest wash of the wave. He could not have done a better thing to ingratiate himself in the good opinion of the Islanders.[211] To them, a neat handling of the oar, beaching a boat without a drop of water, steering in heavy weather when running without shipping seas, were as the elegant turning of a sentence to a literary man, a sweet smile to a poet, a brilliant touch to a painter.

A dozen willing hands soon placed Captain Meredith's boat under the sandhills.

'Yer have done this thing afore,' said Sam half shyly, not knowing exactly what to say under the circumstances in which all parties were placed, for, strange as it may appear, with all his dare-devilry of character Old Sam had a remarkable degree of shyness.

'Yes, I have,' replied the captain, 'and you chaps seem remarkably clever in hauling boats up, but confoundedly stupid in shoving them off.'

'What do yer mean?' said Jack Straw and one or two others. 'Yer must not be saucy here, you got all yer boats, and that's all yer want, isn't it?'

'But I want to know why you kept my boat's crew ashore all this while?'

'We answers no questions, but if yer want to fight, pick your man and we'll give yer fair play.'

'Belay there,' said Long Bill, 'the captain took me off the rocks; I shall stand by him.'

'Yer better preach us a sarmon, Bill,' said Porky. 'How many more on yer had yer mother? I like yer more and more the longer I lives.'

'Will yer come up to my hut?' said Old Sam, addressing the captain, 'then I'll tell yer all about it.'

'No, no; I merely want to buy your skins, [212] and get half-a-dozen of you to go salt-gathering in the salt lagoons; I have plenty of rum and tobacco.'

'Can't yer wait for a week or so?' said Sam; 'we can't go now, we is going over to the main on pertikler business. If yer'll come up and scoff a bit, I'll tell yer the whole game.'

Curiosity prompted the captain to comply, and so proceeding, attended by several of the men, after a sharp walk arrived at the huts.

'You are the oddest devils I have ever seen,' said Captain Meredith to Old Sam, as he stood at the hut surveying their domestic arrangements.

'There's no devils in the island,' said Sam, 'they lives only war there is books and fellows to yarn about 'em, and draws their pay for the sarvice.'

The captain gave Sam a scrutinising glance. The hidden sarcasm of his speech pleased him, and he found there was a fellow-feeling, a congeniality of sentiment. Outwardly so different, there was between them mentally a close similarity.

'Humph? No pay, no devils, you think?'

'In course. Now do yer see I has lived here a powerful number of years, and I never seed a devil, and I'll tell yer what, I has seen things done here and lent a hand mysell, too, that'd please ten thousand devils, but they never comes; they never says, "Well done, my boys," and that's onnateral, onfatherly-like. It's only in civilised parts that devils lives, hang about churches and preaching shops; but I never seed one in the scrub.'

'Hullo, Georgy!'[213] abruptly exclaimed Sam, addressing a man that had suddenly come out of the neighbouring scrub, carrying a heavy wallet and surrounded by a dozen dogs.

He came rather languidly along. He was tattered and torn in the few skin garments he wore, for or in the matter of dress, even in the Kangaroo Island sense of that word, he was extremely careless. Bare-headed, bare-footed, and nearly naked to his waist, he presented a singular spectacle of humanity; but on a closer inspection a bright eye, a well-developed head, and a good chest betokened a good physical and mental nature. He had not the size nor capacity of Sam,[214] but he had a finer perception of the beautiful in Nature, the goodness of moral beauty, and always held the doctrine of the ever-presence of God. Odd these qualities may sound in one who lived the life of a Kangaroo Islander, in whom high tone was considered to consist of drunkenness in the extreme degree, whenever the chance offered, and other miscellaneous adjuncts, such as a little wrecking, stabbing, and black-hunting. And here let me ask, in what way were these gentlemen of Kangaroo Island more immoral than the gentlemen and ladies of the days of Pope Leo X, or the ladies and gentlemen of the times of Louis the Grand, or those of our own nation in the days of Charles II? Murder, rapine, and debauchery were characteristics of those periods, and to such an extent as to cast the wild life of the Islanders into utter shade. Among his mates, Georgy was known by the nickname of the Parson or the Doctor, which is a seaman's term for cook, for he combined these two, shall we say tastes, in an eminent degree. He was perpetually arguing, moralising, and speechifying on religious questions; yet, the truth must be told, he was a miserable sinner, not in the sense in which that phrase is used by Bond Street gentlemen sitting in velvet cushions in cathedral churches, but a real downright sinner of the old Jewish type,[215] and no one was more conscious of his deep errors than himself. He had a kindly disposition that would not hurt a fly, but when the rum was in the wit was out, and woe betide the man that offended him. His next peculiarity was his love of cookery.[216] The French would have styled him a genius; he had a talent for it, he could make wonderful dishes. Give him anything, save stones, and he'd contrive a dish. He acknowledged also that he [would] eat everything; he had no prejudices. Ant eggs, iguanos,[217] lizards, choice parts of snakes, were absolutely delicacies, and he had a way of turning them to account in culinary art that astonished everyone. In a word, his only amusement or relaxation was 'inventing something new,' not in the Athenian sense, but the Roman.[218] It was the custom of the Islanders to select some one as a 'mate,'[219] sharing and faring in all things equally, a relationship rendered necessary in the lawless state of the place and highly convenient in carrying out their pursuits. Old Sam was Georgy's mate, and was the first was fond of a good meal, but a bad hand in cooking one, Georgy was of no mean consideration. On the other hand, as Georgy lacked the powerful will of Old Sam, there was a mutual accommodation. In a scrimmage Old Sam was to be preferred, but as a companion, Georgy. He was fertile in all resources that pertained to the enjoyments, limited as they were, of a Kangaroo Island life. He had in a measure the gift of language, and could yarn away to the amusement of his comrades. Sam, on the contrary, was an old sceptic, was taciturn, and had a rude, philosophical way of regarding things. He was fond of pondering over the why and the wherefore of the singular phenomena of the vegetable and animal life around him, and with his scant knowledge, his mind had drifted towards pantheism, whereas his mate, Georgy, with a flagrant inconsistency, had the highest reverence for revealed religion, with the greatest practical disregard for its precepts.

'Has yer got anything extra to-day, Georgy? or if yer has will yer turn to and cook us summut out o' yourn cookery book. The skipper will scoff a bit with us bime by.'

'All right, my hearties; but I must have a smoke first. I nearly got beat yesterday, it was so hot I fried a piece of iguano on a stone without fire. Golly it was hot! But what's the brig doing here?'

'Ah! that's just the point,' said Captain Meredith, 'I want you and others to come and help me to get a few tons of salt in American River.'[220]

'Have you got any rum?' asked Georgy.

'Belay!' bellowed out Sam, 'yer allers arter the rum bottle. I wish all the rum was salt water.'

'And I wish,' said Georgy, 'all the sea was rum.' Saying this, he turned away, and calling some of the black women proceeded to cook a Kangaroo Island dinner.

Captain Meredith stood gazing in silent amazement at the scene before him, and his old habit of reflecting on what he saw furnished ample food for thought. Here a parcel of wild men coming from all parts of the earth, of different countries, whose past history was a mystery, cast together by the fortuitous circumstances of shipwreck, sealing and absconding, associated in twos and threes, with half-a-dozen black women a-piece for wives, leading a wild and lawless life, and this mode of existence voluntarily adopted and preferred. It was a problem of a most puzzling nature.

'Do you know what day this is, Sam?' said the captain.

'I don't know, but I thinks I heard one o' your men say summut ab'ut Monday. Perhaps it's Thursday. Yer see we keeps no days nor weeks, nor months, nor nuffing. It blows just as hard on Sundays as on Mondays, and it's just as hot one day as t'other; so we does what Nature does. We makes no difference.'

'Was you ever in a church?'

'Yes, once; and that's a long time gone. I walks in, in Sydney, you know. Well, I'm blowed every chap didn't clap his eyes on me, the parson and the whole crew turns their heads and looks at me, so I waits a bit, and I gets a slant, and out I goes devilish quicker than I gets in. No, I can't abear a church.'

'Did you ever read your Bible?'

'Why doesn't yer ask first if we has a Bible?' I have never seed one for many a year, and now I forget all my larning; but yer see I had one, but I lost it all through a ghost! a ghost! yes, a raal live ghost! Yer see, I was trying to spell a bit o' Bible. I had been very wicked, so I thinks a turn or two at the Bible ud do me good, so I sits down for a raal twister. It was bright moonlight. I hears something; I looks up, and there I sees a live ghost. I looks, I jumps up, I coo-e-es, but nuffing would do. The ghost goes straight on end; I gets queer, I pitches the Bible at it and bolts, and I never found it since.'

'You don't believe in devils, but you believe in ghosts. Well, that's funny.'

'Maybe; but what I sees I believes.'

Captain Meredith and Sam were sitting on a large log of wood outside the hut, four or five black children were playing with the innumerable dogs of the place, Georgy a little way off down on his knees blowing two or three small fires, and in intervals dealing out a cuff or a blow to his assistant cooks.

'Mind those ant eggs, you black crow.'

He would warn one, a slap to another would rouse his attention to the cooking of a fine iguano, while a word of praise would fall to the lot of Black Bet for her solicitude in the matter of roasting a wild dog. It was done after the native fashion in the native oven – a hole dug in the earth, well heated with fire, and partly filled with stones.[221] These removed and with gum leaves arranged, upon which the animal is placed covered with leaves and hot stones and earth, and the oven is completed, and the roast is turned out with every juice preserved and every particle done.

Chapter 11

A Kangaroo Island Dinner. – Baked Wild Dog. – Roasted Iguano. – Ant Eggs. – Wakeries, etc. – Proposed Visit to the Main.

'I smells grub;[222] come, let's go in and stow summut under hatches,' said Sam to the captain.

They found the doctor carefully disposing of the hind leg of a wild dog, the fragrant odours of which were irresistible. Juicy, sweet, and short; such were its characteristics.[223]

'Try a bit of dog, captain?' said Georgy; 'it's a young 'un and wery tender. Veal is nuffing to it.'

With a wooden platter and his own jack-knife, and fingers for forks, the captain tackled the 'dog' and pronounced it delicious.

'What are those things?' said the captain.

'They're ant eggs,'[224] said the doctor, 'and wery nice they is, too. Try some, and call 'em rice, if yer a bit faint-hearted. I eats everything; for, as I reads (for yer see I can read), in the Bible, it says everything was good – that means for to eat – and I knows this much, more nice things are thrown to the dogs or never looked on than there is that people eats. Now, take those ant eggs.' Saying this, he carefully, and with a piece of bark for a spoon, took a good mouthful. 'How sweet they is! How they melts on the tongue! Nuffing like 'em. Many's the time Sam there and me has a good blow-out of them same ant eggs, and we gets fatter arter a week's speel at 'em; don't we, Sam?'

'Yes, yer cannibal; but yer manages to give me the addled ones, and swears they're fresh laid.'

'No, no, Sam, yer is too greedy, and yer eats the little ants wid 'em; that's what makes 'em mouldy-like. Lor bless yer, they're like for all the world "caroway cumforts."[225] Ah! I see, captain, yer doesn't mouth 'em right well. Will yer try one o' them roasted iguanos? and stop, let me give yer a little fat.'

'What fat is it?' inquired the captain, 'it looks rather dark; but still – ' tasting a bit – 'it's very fine.'

'Why, that's wallaby fat. Ah!' said Sam, 'sometimes Georgy almost cries about wallaby fat, 'cause, he says, if the cooks in England only could get a slant of it they'd give him a fortin.'[226]

'Yes,' said the doctor. 'Lor, bless yer, it beats, all the fats holler – lard or suet. It's splendid. I once made a pie on board ship with wallaby fat, and the chaps nearly kills theirselves with eating.'

'Try a little bit o' wegetable?' said Sam; 'we eats it raw; yer can call it turnips, or horse-radish; yer'll find it purty fair.'

'It's a queer-looking vegetable,' remarked Captain Meredith, 'very white and crisp, slightly gummy, and in small flakes.'

'Bite it, captain,' said the doctor, 'there now, good, isn't it, and sweet?'

'Yes, certainly; something like cocoanut. What's it?'

'Well, yer would guess a long time, skipper, afore yer'd guess what that is. I tell yer it's the heart of the grass tree![227] Yer chops all the leaves away and gees it a smart rap, and the heart jumps out beautiful; yer can live upon it by the week.[228] And what can yer do,' said Sam, slyly, putting a large piece of wallaby meat down, and looking Georgy full in the face, 'upon "wakeries?"[229] Ah! How long does yer say a man can live on them things?'

'Why, I suppose, Sam, yer could live for ever; for yer a reg'lar pig at wakeries. I never seed the likes o' yer.'

'What are wakeries?' remarked Captain Meredith.

'Them's them,' said the doctor, pointing to a heap of brown screwed-up pieces of fat, gristle, or meat of the thickness of a finger, and about two inches long; 'and them's them,' pointing his finger to another lot of living, wriggling, furrowed grubs, nearly milk-white or creamy in colour, and to the touch soft as marrow and hairy, though not a caterpillar, still having a strong resemblance, but thicker and with a hard head.

'And this is the way we eats 'em,' said Sam, as he grasped a fist-full of live wakeries or grubs, and commenced eating them one after the other with the greatest relish.

The captain looked astonished, though, as a sailor, he was not in the least squeamish.

'Yes,' said the doctor, interpreting the skipper's looks, 'yer think it now queer-like t' eat them things raw and all alive-o,[230] don't yer? But yer eats oysters all alive-o! and where's the difference? And perrywinks? And if a thing is to be judged by its vartue, why all the blue skins on the main[231] gets fat like porpoises when the wakeries there comes on, and they travels everywhere here for to get them. I like wakeries, live wakeries, you know, better than anything,' and the doctor stuffed his mouth full of the delectable delicacies, and the visitor had nothing else to do but look on and wonder.

Sam pointed to the roasted dainties. 'Try them,' said he.

The captain took a couple, felt them, bit them, tasted them, and declared he had never eaten anything so delicious. There was a motley taste in them, with something of the flavour of the finest brain and marrow united; they were decidedly, in the matter of physical taste, bewitching. From a couple the captain took a handful.

'Yer's like all the rest,' said Sam. 'I never seed a man that onct began to scoff wakeries but he never knowed when to leave off; but take my advice, leave the cooked ones and try the live 'uns; they're the rale rations, and this is a splendid lot o' fat 'uns, so lively, too. Now, isn't it curious?' taking a large, live, wriggling grub between his fingers, 'that this here bit o' worm is the soffest possible,' giving it a squeeze, 'and he lives on the hardest wood[232] in the land? Soft as a bit o' marrow in a bone, but yer'll find 'em half-way in the hardest gum tree. The blacks has a long thin stick with a hook in the end, and they puts it down and hooks 'em out like yer do perrywinks, only these gum tree perry winks is half a yard in.'[233]

'Yes, that's curious, to be sure,' observed the captain, 'but hard or soft, hairy or smooth, whether they are grubs, caterpillars, or worms, they are splendid. I only wish Mr. Ratlin was here, and he'd clear decks for yer in a trice.'

'Who's that?' said the doctor.

'The first mate,' said Sam. 'He came ashore last night, and goes away and catches wallaby all night, I s'pose. I wonder he didn't break his neck; just pick this here bit o' guano. It's beautiful roasted; nobody can keep the juices in like Georgy.'

The captain took the morsel; it was the hindleg. The meat was whiter than chicken, deliciously flavoured. The skin, of course, was peeled off, being somewhat corrugated and scaly. He pronounced it exquisite.

Georgy was highly delighted. His small blue eyes twinkled. He relished two things – the goodly fare before him, and the captain's appreciation.

'What's that?' asked the skipper, pointing to a couple of round masses of apparently very fat ham lying on some green leaves instead of dishes.

'Ah, now,' said Sam, 'yer'll never guess that grub; we calls 'em "porkies."[234] It's a rummy critter; he lives, yer see, in a sandy country and eats ant eggs. He's full o' quills, and he lays eggs and hatches 'em hisself in his pouch; he stows hisself all day under ground, and o' nights he comes out; but we tracks 'em and digs 'em up as yer do taters. Try a bit, captain?'

'Why the fat is two inches thick, and the colour of boiled ham-fat. However. I'll taste the beast – um! pretty good, but too greasy; I like iguano best.'

'Nuffing like wakeries – live wakeries, I means.'

'Yes,' said the doctor, 'live wakeries, they is good. What wouldn't a Frenchman give for 'em? I tell yer all the kings on earth would be arter 'em when onct they got their bearing. I reads somewhere the Emperoor o' Rame sending for oysters to England;[235] perhaps the King of England will send a seventy-four[236] out hereaway for some barrels o' wakeries.'

'Clew up[237],' said Sam, 'and let's hear what the captain wants us for.'

'I want you,' said Captain Meredith, 'to load with salt in the lagoon, and after that I'll buy your skins – seal, kangaroo, or wallaby, whatever have.'

'Well,' said Sam, ''s'pose it'll do arter we've been on the main. Yer see we're going to catch as many black women as we can grab.'[238]

'And is that the way you chaps get all those black women I see here now?'

'Yes; we cotched 'em all, and rare game it is, too; isn't it, Georgy?'

'Yes,' said Georgy, 'and ain't they sly? Kangaroo, wild duck, porkies, is nuffing to 'em, the black skins! I don't think the Government of Sydney would like to know this.'

'Well,' said Sam, 'perhaps the Governor will tell us how we is to get 'em.'[239]

'And I reads,' chimed in the doctor, 'that it was allers the way to steal women in old times; so we is living in the old times of Australia like, and maybe the time may come when all this land hereaway may be chock-a-block wid settlers, and then they'll yarn about the "old times" and us. Islanders grabbing black women for wives. Ha! ha! ha!'

'Avast, Georgy!' exclaimed Sam quite seriously, 'if these darned settlers squat down and build their towns and preaching shops, I shall top my boom and be off. I can't abear a lot o' fellows with their rights o' this and their rights o' that, and their perlice, and their darbies. I hates 'em.'[240]

'Very likely,' remarked the captain, 'that this country will become settled. I suppose there is a bit of good land inland.'

'Yes, splendid,' began the doctor.[241]

'Belay there,' sang out Old Sam, jumping up and thumping the rude table with his fist. 'Tell him nuffing,' roared he, 'tell him nuffing, or he'll tell the Government of Sydney, and then the darned surveying ships will be poking their jib-booms in every hole, and our country will be sold in bits as big as a seal-skin. No, no, Georgy, that big river will bring 'em down soon enuf. Don't yer for to go and tell 'em all yer and me knows.'[242]

'What river?' anxiously inquired Captain Meredith; but both were silent.[243]

'It's nuffing, nuffing,' they remarked at last.

Little did the skipper think the big river alluded to was the now famous River Murray, with its steamboats and its towns, villages, and sheep stations on its banks; but the Islanders had been in the habit, for years, of visiting its banks for the various purposes of "wife-hunting," "visiting the tribes," or lending a hand in the tribal fights that take place invariably on grand annual occasions.[244] As the Islanders on all occasions evinced the greatest dread at the prospect of a regular settlement, either on the main or on the island, it was impossible for Captain Meredith to obtain any further information of the appearance of the country on the main, so he turned to another subject, upon which they were not so scrupulous as to the information they imparted.

'I should think it's sometimes a precious hard job to catch them blacks.'[245]

'Yes, it is; for the women are so cussed stupid, they thinks we catch 'em to eat 'em! They wouldn't mind stopping wid us; but they don't like for we to eat 'em. Last season we goes over and we meets the blacks. Where's my lubra? where's my picaninny? they shouts. We tells 'em they're all right on the island. They says we lies, and we eat em up; in course we can't take 'em back to see their grannies; they'd bolt, nuffing would hold 'em, would they, Georgy?'[246]

Georgy wagged his head and grinned at the idea of holding any o' these black critters, good gals as they were; but they was worser than eels iled.

'Well,' said the captain, 'I hope you will let me go with you and see the sport.'

'No, no,' said Sam, 'we can't allows that – it would shake yer narves – yer see they is rather wild, and jump about like mad. But, arter all, they does just the same when their own chaps cotches them.'

'What is yer laffing about, yer old Stingeray?' suddenly remarked Sam as he noticed the doctor in a convulsion of laughter.

'Why,' gasped he, 'I was just 'memb'ring how "Pussy," when we cotched her, rolled down the hill, and went plop into the water-hole, and you fell in arter her, and there was the devil to pay – fighting like cats! ha! ha! ha! – that's why we calls her "Pussy," captain, 'cause she's so fierce and scratches terrible bad.'[247]

'Look at that,' said Sam, baring his arm, and showing a tremendous scar, 'that's the way they bites – took the piece clean out – cuss 'em.'

'But we never knocks 'em on the head,' said the doctor; 'that's the way the black chaps do on the main; they skulks about and sees a woman digging roots may be – they rushes up and gees them a knock with a wirri,[248] and then drags 'em along half drunk like. Ah! but "Pussy" is a good gal – she has speret, more than two others – and the other gals stand clear when she gits her flying jib set.'

'I should like to go very much,' said the captain.

'It can't be – yer would tell lots o' lies about us, and then get us into trouble with Sydney[249] – no, no, let us alone, and we lets yer alone, every man to his station and cook to the fore sheet; yer knows, captain. When we is done, and cotched a few or so, we'll lend a hand, and get yer a cargo o' salt; yer had better stand away to the westward, and pick up a few of our chaps on the islands, they has plenty o' skins by this time.'[250]

The captain thought this the best advice also. It would be useless to force himself into their proposed attempt on the main, so he determined to go on board and be off the very next morning.

'Well,' said the skipper, 'I must be off, the sun is nearly set.' Georgy and Sam led the way, and were soon upon the beach.

'We'll give yer a call to-morrow morning,' said Sam, as they turned slowly away and disappeared behind the sandhills.

'It'll never do,' said Georgy, 'to let that covey go wid us a gal-hunting.'

'In course not,' gruffly replied Sam, 'if he comes any o' his tricks, why we'll sarve him out; we'll gee 'im to the blacks. We'll stand no nonsense, and they'll bowse 'im up taut.'[251]

Chapter 12

Night. – The Native Women. –
Missionaries. –
The Pull out of the Creek. –
The Midnight Squall.

The night settled down clear and starlight. The transparency of the atmosphere was wonderful, and the magnificent splendours of the starry host exceeded belief. A gaze fixed for a short time on the heavenly bodies became absorbing, and as new glories burst to view, and the eye adapted itself to the effulgence of the scene, the grand panorama of the sky assumed phases of surpassing beauty undreamt of in colder latitudes. Captain Meredith reclined against the taffrail[252] of the ship, and mused on star and constellation; Mr. Ratlin paced the deck slowly, and scanned from time to time the dark ocean and the darker masses of land that lay around him; the poor second mate, Mr. Handspike, sat on the combings of the main hatch, with a sailor attending him. The hallucination of the sunstroke had not yet passed away.

'I see them coming; they are racing ashore,' he muttered.

'What's racing ashore?' said Jim.

'The boats; they are coming to fetch me. I can't get out of this cussed scrub, and the men are all drunk and won't go on board.'

The images of that terrible morning were still uppermost in the poor mate's brain. Then relapsing into a desponding mood, he kept repeating in a despairing tone, that even affected the sailor, 'They're all moored, they're all moored.'

The anchor watch, two men, were pacing up and down the forecastle, four steps one way and four steps the other, the extreme limits of their march.

'I heard the skipper say,' remarked Bill, 'that these Islanders are off to the main tomorrow to catch black women! Isn't that purty, now? I should like to go wid 'em, for to see the fun. Well, this is a rummy place; everything is topsy-turvy!'[253]

'I don't like 'em,' replied his companion. 'I don't like these Robinson Crusoes, with their skin breeches, and smelling like foxes;[254] six wives a-piece, and eating all manner o' things. How did they get here?'

'Well, you axes them next time you seed 'em; you'll have a chance tomorrow.'

On shore and huddled together in a wurley[255] or native hut, sat some half-dozen black women, with their half-caste children, talking to each other in a low plaintive voice in their native tongue.[256]

'How big Yuru looks,'[257] remarked one, as she gazed on the Milky Way; 'what a long river that must be; the old men say it is a river, and that Yuru lives in it. I wish I was over there, where it comes out of the mountains; I would then swim down and get to my own country';[258] and unable to control the thoughts that came rushing into her mind of her lost home, she broke forth in a loud wail, a monotone of lamentations, for the aborigines *sing* for all purposes – to cure disease, for joy, to soothe pain, to express sorrow, to assuage the wrath of sorcerers, and to lament for the dead. For what civilised man flees to priest or doctor the native resorts to song; to them it is a universal remedy for sin and sorrow, and for all the diversified experience of life. The expedient is simple and as efficacious as the more costly and varied helps, spiritual, pharmaceutical, and ritual, of their white brethren. The cure follows, and the afflicted, white or black, is restored.

Let us not quarrel with each other. Music is all potent;[259] man walks up to the cannon's mouth at the beat of the drum; music restored religion in the dark ages, when man and his preaching had become the dry bones of the whited sepulchre. Music ushered in the morn of creation, and it is to conclude the end of all things. Orpheus would never have gained Eurydice but for his lyre;[260] so music, barbarous or civilised, works miracles; faith and imagination are the true rulers of humanity.

Another of the native women pointed out to two or three children the group of stars known to whites as the constellation Pleiades. 'Those,' said she, 'are boys; one day they were digging roots on the hills, and the moon saw them, and loved them, and took them up where you see them now.'[261]

'What are they doing?' said one of the children. 'Digging roots in the heavenly plains.'[262]

'They are going to-morrow across the water to catch some of our people,' remarked Bet to Sally.[263]

'Ah! exclaimed every one in a subdued breath. 'May they be cursed! May their kidney fat be taken![264] May the sorcerers turn them into trees,[265] and may they be smitten with the sacred girdle[266] and the tuft of eagle feathers!'[267]

Uttering these curses in an undertone, they then in one accord sang a low kind of dirge which, like all savage music, was set in the minor key, that extraordinary key that pervades all barbarous races, and is so generally absent from the music of civilised men.

'What the deuce are yer kicking up this row for?' said Porky, as he walked off to the wurley, 'come, just hold yer tongues.'

'None o' yer church music,[268] old Bet, said Sam, 'or I'll make you sing to another tune; do you hear me?'

Bet said nothing, but rose up and went away.

'I say, Porky, the women smell a rat, aye! whose a been and split? this caterwauling means summut.'

'Give 'em a tarnation hiding all around,' suggested another, 'that'l keep 'em quiet while we's away; or slit their ears?'

'Yes,' said Porky, 'that might do some good; letting blood is fust rate. I know's it mysell; when I gets drunk, and gets knocked about, it's the bleeding that does me good; I feels all the better arter.'

As cropping the ears was considered a proper legal punishment a few years back in Christian England, so these Islanders, living a few years after their time, had introduced the English practice of cropping ears as one of their recognised modes of punishment amongst the women.[269] Therefore, one ear, no ears, half an ear, or ears slightly cropped, were not uncommon. No doubt the reader will shudder at such inhumanity, duly forgetting that he speaks the same language in which Blackstone justified this identical mode of suffering as highly proper and Christian-like;[270] and even further, could prove by all laws, human and divine, that drowning or burning was the proper course to adopt with wizards and witches. Whatever atrocities the

Islanders committed, they never alluded to this, nor did they cover their barbarities with the respectabilities of ermine and lawn, or the holy associations of religion. They were emphatically men, one equal to another, having a salutary dread of each other, as a difference of opinion would at once be settled to conclusions. They had a rough and ready mode of dealing out justice that cut the Gordion knot of difficulty at once, without the intervention of lawyers and judges, the fist or the knife, and the matter was settled.

The native women having the option of living in the huts of their lords and masters, preferred to reside in their own wurleys.[271] They could not endure the close atmosphere. They asserted that the huts made them ill. Wherever the adjuncts of civilisation, the hut or house, and the multiple clothing of the white have been forced on unwilling aborigines, especially by missionaries, there death comes in, and the native dies. This is the history of all missionary attempts to Christianise the blacks; they won't allow a native man to go to heaven in an opossum rug, to live on this earth in a clothing suited to the climate God has put him in. The picturesque dresses of the South Sea Islanders were ignored, and the poke bonnet and the four-and-ninepenny substituted as the proper dress, according to the Gospel. Cole-scuttle bonnets and the Christian verities were identical; the missionary's wife would not call that one sister that was naked to the waist and dressed in a robe adorned with feathers. So it is with the poor Australians; first clothe them, then kill them, that they may give signs of conversion on their deathbed. Oh! missionary zeal, thou art a cruel ass, with all thy philanthropy. It is difficult to say which is greater, thy benevolence or thy inhumanity.[272]

'Let's be off,' said Sam, addressing some three or four hands that stood waiting about.

A little below their huts, the creek was situated, and parting a deep fringe of tea-tree the party stepped into one of their boats. They were off on a night expedition to catch crawfish, as a part of the provisions for the morrow's adventures on the main. That night's pull down the placid waters of the creek[273] was of transcendental beauty. So faithfully mirrored were the heavens above, that there was no difference between the luminosity of the stars beneath and those above. As the Islanders gave a long stroke and allowed the boat to shoot ahead, it seemed that she was absolutely cleaving the starry host themselves, as if sailing on and through a bed of stars, thrusting them aside with the dip of the oars, or jostling them together, in long ripples, or sending them dancing in pools and eddies. The high and dense tea-tree assisted this wonderful phenomenon, and gathered the rays of night to a focal point, and the boat with its wild crew skimmed o'er that sheet of reflected light as a cloud o'er the face of heaven. They hauled the boat with the help of skids over the dry bar, launched her through the surf, and boldly made for or one of the distant headlands of the island.

'That's a big cloud just creeping over the land,' remarked Georgy, 'look at it, Sam.'

'Aye, it's a squall.' By this time they had killicked their boat – that is, anchored it by a couple of stones – just beneath the beetling crags of a point now known as Cape Willoughby, on which the first lighthouse built by South Australia was erected.[274] It seemed the very acme of peril to anchor a boat within a few yards of the boiling surf that swept up and against that vast mass of rock, and this, too, by night, and there to lie for hours, while they fished for crawfish.[275] A snap of the rope that held them to the stones as anchor would have been death. They were too wary to be indifferent to their position. Oars were laid across, and one man carefully noted by star or dim point of rock, whether their boat forged in with the gigantic swell that rolled in on this point. The night became pitchy dark, a sudden gust blew one of their oars clean overboard and was lost; the lightning played round the headland and the sea rose wild and sent the spray high in the air.

'Cut the darn'd lines,' yelled out Old Sam, 'or we're doomed.'

So all the nets were lost, and before they could well get their oars shipped, a tremendous swell very nearly finished their earthly career; but Sam was at the steer-oar, and the men met the emergency with the strength of giants. The boat flew to meet the next sea before it could gain its head, and though amidst the roar of elements and a darkness almost palpable, instinctively they headed the seas, and ultimately rounded the Cape, reaching the bar of the creek towards three o'clock in the morning with some fifty crawfish, and the loss of their nets, an oar, and several sealskin hats.

Sam was in a terrible humour; the loss of nets and lines was no mean loss. He prayed – in his style – in a way that even cowed his rough companions. He was a frightful swearer, and when put out he became uncontrollable. Woe unto the poor black women that came across him. Then a stab or worse was no common thing. In a sulky humour the Islanders dragged their boat over the dry bars and launched her on the waters of the creek, and after a silent pull in darkness, intensified by the great tea-tree fringe of the creek, they arrived at the embarking place below their huts.

A mass of dogs yelled a welcome, and the first one that sprang on Sam with a sign of joy was savagely greeted with a deep stab that for ever stopped his boisterous mirth. Sam was in no humour for dogs or men.

The Brig Sails, and Tows the Boats of the Islanders. – Anecdote about Georgy. – Hog Bay. – The Islanders Depart.

The midnight squall had not been without its perils to the brig. Mr Ratlin was more disturbed by the suddenness of the great gust than he was when pitched headlong down the stony gully.

The morning after, as frequently on the Australian coasts during these summer squalls, was beautifully serene, with a light, gentle breeze from the S.E.

'They are getting ready,' remarked Captain Meredith to the first officer, as he handed him the glass.

'Yes; two boats, a heap of dogs, and lots of women,' enumerated Mr. Ratlin.

Shortly afterwards the boats were launched, and pulled away for the brig. The two whale boats approached the vessel with a spring and a dash that showed the sinewy strength of those wielding the oars, and as they breasted the waves the water was divided, and the forefront of each boat leapt up, showed itself in full view, and then sank and parted the coming wave as keen as a knife. In the stern sheets of the foremost boat and grasping the steer-oar with a light but firm grip, stood Old Sam, his hair streaming in the wind. With his huge beard, whiskers, and moustachios, and his bare bull neck and hairy arms, his skin waistcoat and breeches, he formed a remarkable figure, a very sea-god of the antipodean type, such as peculiarly fitted the scenes and locality of Kangaroo Island, and the geologic era of Australia; such as the poets of Greece, had they lived in this end of the world instead of the other, would have described and immortalised. In the next boat Long Bill was steersman, with Jack Straw as aide-de-camp. That tall, dare-devil had his long, matted locks streaming in the wind, and an old sailor's shirt barely covering the upper portion of his body. He was violently gesticulating to his crew and throwing his powerful weight on the stroke oar. He wished to overtake Old Sam, and was, in fact, quickly overhauling him. The greatest curiosity, however, was in Sam's boat. In the bow, and pulling the bow oar, was a woman, 'Black Bet,' Sam's favourite wife. She was a Vandemonian (Tasmanian) black, and exceedingly expert as a huntress on land or water. As a fisherwoman or sailoress her abilities were unrivalled. No tree was too tall or too straight for her to climb in her native fashion with a circular coil of rope made of bark;[276] no water was too profound for her to reach the bottom, and the mighty waves that dashed on the smooth rounded granite boulders of the coasts were her gracious horsemen. Incredible as it may appear, she would oft in mere sport swim out to sea, and then, with adroit skill, come in riding on the top of a stupendous foaming roller, and land herself on the slippery rocks safe and sound.[277] The peril of such a feat was extreme, hence Black Bet took a high rank in the estimation of the Islanders and Sam declared he would not take six other black women for Bet. She was invaluable.

The crew on board the brig paused in their work as the boats shot up alongside. Two sailors were on the topsail yard loosing the sail.

'I say, Bill,' said one, 'do yer twig that black gal among 'em?'

'No.'

'Why, the bowman in old Robinson Crusoe's boat. Don't yer see her black curly wool?[278] Well, I'm danged if these coves is not rum 'uns; see how she handles that boat-hook as a nat'ral born sailor.'

'She's jolly fat, too, isn't she?'[279] said the other, 'and blowed if she isn't purty; I likes the wild look o' hern eyes. What say yer, Jim, let us go ashore, and live as they do?'

At this juncture of the conversation Sam was, handing up to the captain a splendid fresh crayfish.

'There, captain,' said he, 'there's a raal nipper for yer.'

Mr. Ratlin in haste tried to take the delicious morsel, but somehow being weighty and exceedingly prickly, it slipped through his hands and fell overboard. Black Bet no sooner saw the accident than, throwing off her scant garments, she dived after the fish! The sailors were amazed at the idea of a person trying to out-swim a fish.

The water was about five fathoms[280] deep, the bottom white sand, and now, most grotesquely magnified by the water, could be seen this singular hunt – every movement was visible. The crayfish doubled, and Black Bet doubled hither and thither. Bet rose to the [surface of the] water, took an enormous gulp of air, and down she went the second time. The crayfish made for the shore, Bet after him. He then tried to hide himself in the sand. That was a fatal mistake;[281] Bet seized him by his large feelers, and triumphantly bore him back to the ship.

The crew of the brig could not resist bursting out into a hearty cheer, as Bet climbed over the bow of the boat, and put on her man's dress. She smiled in recognition, and then lapsed into her quiet habit and demeanour.

'There now,' said Sam, addressing the mob of heads leaning over the bulwarks fore and aft; 'can yer show me the white woman that had do it? not one o' them, from the empresses right away forrard till yer get to chimbley sweeps. The raal black skin for me; I wouldn't take six lubras of the main there for one of these Vandiemans.'[282]

Sam was proud of his wife,[283] and she had so appropriately proved her high talent, in the Kangaroo Island sense, for to row, to fish, to swim, to fight, to endure, to devise, these were Kangaroo Island abilities, the proofs of genius, the steps of rank, the very LL.D.'s and M.A.'s of their social status. After all, of what merit are the graces of civilisation? They are only relative. It is most unphilosophical to attribute merit to the polish of polite society, for beyond its sphere it is useless. Place a civilised lady on Kangaroo Island, and she be an absolute nonentity – nay, further, she would be a hindrance.[284] The very thing that elevated her in the one case would be her curse in the other. No, Sam was right. Black Bet pulling the bow oar, was the talented, educated, and, in relation to her sisters, the refined lady of the peculiar society of her adopted home.

As this is a narrative of fact to a very large extent, it may be here mentioned that many years after, when her island home had become known to throngs of vessels that passed and re-passed from the colony of South Australia to Port Phillip, a vessel was wrecked, and the crew and passengers got on the shore, on a wild part of the coast.[285] They were nearly famished for water, and this same Black Bet, now an old woman, became the means of their rescue, leading them to a native well, and guiding them to a place of safety.

'When I saw her figure,' feelingly remarked one of the passengers, 'coming over the sandhills, and we all rushed up to her, and she, in her quiet but still active manner led us to the native well, I could almost have worshipped her!'

Black Bet is dead now, and she lies in a spot in a small clearing of the scrub on the hillside that overlooks the very inlet of the great lagoon,[286] where poor Handspike lost himself, and received the sun stroke that nearly killed him, as described in the early part of this tale.

'Where are you bound for?' asked another of the hands recognising Sam.

'Fishing,' replied one of the Islanders.

'What kind of fish?'

'Black fish,' said the Doctor, *alias* Georgy, 'and wery fine fish they is, too.'

'He means black women,' explained a man standing next to the interrogator, who seemed 'green' on the whole matter.

'Will yer give us a tow out about half-way across the straits, and then we'll cast off, and stand up the Gulf?' asked Sam.

'Oh! yes.'

So the boats were duly towed astern – 'Black Bet' in the one, and Long Bill in the other – the crews of both boats going on board for a yarn with the men. The brig was soon under all her canvas, and as she felt the gentle S.E. breeze, she gracefully bent to the pressure on her canvas, and slipped away over the short, white-crested seas, at the rate of knots. Mr. Ratlin paced the port side of the quarter-deck highly satisfied, and could not help remarking that she went through it as smooth as grease. This allusion to culinary matters made him turn white with fear, as he suddenly recollected that he had not given special instruction to the cook about that splendid crayfish. Soon his head was in the galley, and his anxiety relieved.

'So you are off at last,' said Captain Meredith to Sam.

'Yes, we is, and we should have been back again but for yerself.'

'Well, now, how many do yer think you will catch?'

'We has been wery unlucky of late, haven't us,' said Sam, addressing his mate, Georgy.

'Wery,' replied the Doctor, 'one o' the best jumped overboard arter all our trouble, and got on the rocks, and then the blacks comes down, and so we loses her.'

'That was all your'n fault,' said Sam, 'yer will be su cussed kind, yer let go her fastenings, and overboard she jumps.'

'Yes, it was my fault, Sam; I was too kind, too tender-hearted like.'

'Then, another time,' continued Sam, 'one o' our chaps gets a spear in his ribs, right in his heart and yer see it was jagged; so he dies, and we pitches him overboard the same arternoon. The last time the blacks nearly finished me. Yer see that,' and Sam showed his brawny arm; 'there's a big cut, and here on my truck, yer can see how the black skins loves me, darn 'em; but I knows the big black nigger that did it; I'll make him sing out; I'll be even with him.'

'Yes,' said Georgy, 'yer can kill 'em by the law, for he's a-going to kill yer, and I knows law enough for that matter.'

'And what's the law,' said Captain Meredith, 'about taking their wives and women?'

'Why the law of nature, in course?'

'The strongest holds the hardest,' replied Georgy, 'I knows when they grabbed me, some time gone, they never let's go.'

'Ah!' said Sam, 'that was a devilish hard time. Yer see, captain, we were arter him and the black imps was a hundred strong; so we were wery cool; they stands just there away on that pint,' pointing to the place now well known as Cape Jervis; 'they was singing out in their lingo, "to come on" and fetch him; we draws in, and they thinks we was for landing, and they scatters a bit. Georgy sees this, bolts straight on end for the boat, for yer see we was laying on and off. The blacks doesn't know what to make of it; then they throws their spears, but we jumps on the rocks, and we gets Georgy, and pulls right away.'[287]

'Georgy,' said Sam turning to him, 'if yer gets cotched again they'll smash yer head for yer for that day's work.'

'In course they will,' replied Georgy.

'But how was he caught?'

'Why, he is so pertickler,' said Sam, 'he was trying for or a better-looking gal than falls to him; so he stops behind a bit waiting for a slant, for we was parlavouing friendly like, do yer see, wid 'em, when Georgy grabs one and makes for the boats; but the blacks was too smart for him, they overhauls him; we rushes in and we fights, but they drives us to the boats, and they takes Georgy.'

By this time the brig had opened the broad waters of the great inlet, now known as Gulf St. Vincent. Kangaroo Island lay on their left. In front was apparently the boundless sea, and on their right a diversified coastline of rock and hill trending sharply to the north.

The Islanders had by this time got into their boats with the exception of Georgy and Sam.

'How does your course lie now?' asked the captain.

'Right away for that pint,' pointing to a place now well known as N.W. Bluff;[288] we 'spects our friends is lying behind that place fishing this time o' the year;[289] yer see, they moves about like the birds in the rain. They is inland in the summer on the coast, but we shall see their fires.'

'And where is the place yer told me I could pick up a chap that'd pilot me long the island?'

'There,' said Georgy, pointing to a bare high slope on Kangaroo Island; 'that's Hog Bay, as we calls it, bekase some pigs got ashore in a wery mysterious way, do yer mind – so we names it Hog Bay.[290] Ha! ha! ha!' and Georgy laughed at some pleasant tricks and cunning dodges that were deeply associated with this singular euphoniously-named bay, which name, strange to say, is still retained until the present time.[291] Hog Bay now forms a pleasant settlement, and boasts of a post-office.[292]

At last Sam stepped over the gangway, and the tow lines were cast off. The brig headed for Hog Bay, with a flowing sheet, while the boats hauled close to the wind and tried to gain the smooth water under the main land.

Captain Meredith leant upon the taffrail, watching the fast retiring boats till they disappeared, and musing upon the singular characters they contained, their singular destination, and their odd choice of life; 'but the riddle is easily explained,' muttered the captain. The love of liberty, of uncontrolled liberty, is one of our strongest instincts, and in proportion as men are of a bold or timid character will this sentiment be overpowering or weak. After all, the sum total of rascality, or whatever it may be called, is no doubt in a far higher ratio in the crowded city than in this odd fellowship on the Island. With his philosophical conclusion, he turned round and commenced squaring the yards, which to his appreciation were never square. Hog Bay soon began to open out, and ere long the brig lay maintopsail to the mast and hove to, waiting to see if any one was there or would come off.

Chapter 14

A Singular Harbour. –
A Stroll Ashore. –
An Islander Joins the Brig. –
Althorpe Islands.

Long and carefully did Captain Meredith scrutinise the shore for signs of any human being, but the waves lipped and splashed over the pointed rocks that lined the little bay, or played leap-frog over the larger masses that as yet had not been worn down by the everlasting wear and tear of wave and tide, as they did in the eternity of the past.

Hog Bay, as it was called, could scarcely be designated a bay. It was simply a small indent in the coast, open to all winds S. of S.W. round the compass to S.E.; hence it afforded no shelter to the strong gales from the N. and N.W., and further, the water was very deep. At five fathoms you could almost pitch a biscuit on shore, but the marvel of the place was a circular indentation with a portal entrance of some ten feet, which afforded a boat harbour of unsurpassed security.[293]

'There's smoke ashore, sir,' said one of the men, indicating at the same time a large column of dense smoke that arose out of the scrub some miles or so inland.

'They see us,' said the first mate, 'that's the way they talk. They make a smoke, and that's just as good as if they said, "We are coming."[294] It's a capital plan, and as good as bunting nearly.'

'I can't make out any boat, though, on the beach,' remarked the captain, 'and it seems to me as if all hands were away. Ah! there I see a figure just clearing the scrub that at lines that bare patch. He has a lot of dogs and is standing dead for the beach.'

Owing to the steep rise of the land from the water's edge, everything could be discerned from the sea with great exactitude.

'I suppose he's alone.'

'Yes, to be sure he is, for he is waving his arm for us to come ashore.'

'All right, my hearty, but I am up to your tricks now. No duplicate humbug of the last place. So, Mr. Ratlin, just get the gig lowered, and I'll go ashore this time; a couple of hands will do.'

As the captain approached the shore, the figure on the land went towards a small opening in the rocks, which, under other circumstances, would never have been noticed.

'Why, what does the fellow mean?' ejaculated the skipper. 'Are we to go in there? Why, we shall stove our boat, and yet there seems no other landing place in this queer little bay.'

The mystery was soon explained, and the boat went through a small portal between the rocks, that had been especially cleared by the Islanders, and, as if by enchantment, the boat glided into a huge pond of silent water. The men looked utterly [a]stonished. Involuntarily they laid on their oars and gazed round them on the singular geographical feature that puzzled them. The basin was perfectly circular, and when inside nothing could be discerned but a lofty wall of earth, rock, and sand. The blue sky shone above, and the noise of the wind was heard overhead, but the waters of Lethe[295] were not more still than this peculiar pool.

'We're at the bottom of a well, Jim,' said one of the sailors to the other, 'like the bottom of a funnel. What a capital place to stow away.'

The captain muttered to himself. 'An extinct crater, I suppose, truly a most remarkable formation.'[296]

By this time the boat had reached the ledge where the water met the steep wall. There was, nevertheless, a small abrupt margin, sufficient for boats to be hauled up for repairs, if necessary.

'Well,' said the captain, as the boat grounded, addressing the man they had all along seen, and who stood ready to receive them. 'Where are your mates?'

'They is inland – gone away to the south coast.'

'Are you alone here?'

'No, I has my dogs.'

'Sam, of Creek Bay,[297] told me I could get a hand here to go along with me to the westward; one that knows the islands well. Can you go?'

'Hold on a bit,' said the man. 'Where's Sam now?'

'On the main.'

'Dang him!' emphatically swore the Islander. 'And where's all the rest of the coves of Creek Bay?'[298]

'I don't know,' said the captain, 'but I towed two boats half way over the straits; they then cast off and stood to the norrard.'

The Islander began to stamp and swear fearfully. He was evidently dreadfully annoyed.

'Come, mate,' said one of the men, 'haul up a bit.'

'You be blowed,' replied the man. They were on the eve of a general row.

'Will you come along with the brig?' asked Captain Meredith.

'I don't know; but if yer likes to hang on till sundown I'll come back and let yer know. I must go away a bit and take them dogs to my black gal and boy,[299] away back in the scrub, and if I comes back to go wid yer I'll make a fire, and yer can come ashore and fetch us,' saying which, this wild man of the woods climbed the steep wall with accelerated step, cursing and swearing, till both his form and his voice died away in the distance.

Captain Meredith had no alternative. To attempt to navigate amongst the islands, and in the manner he intended – sealing on their coast – without a man well versed in all the intricacies of local navigation, would be an act of folly. It was a customary thing for vessels to visit the island, and take one of the Islanders as a pilot,[300] but it seemed that Captain Meredith had unfortunately arrived at a time when these wayward men had other objects in view than that of piloting, hence the vexatious delay, and tergiversation.[301] But there was no remedy, so he determined to take things as they were and do the bidding of the man that had just left. To kill time Captain Meredith left the boat and ascended the precipitous cliffs that embayed the little model of a harbour in which he then was. From the summit he found the land gradually and evenly rising towards the interior. Looking seaward, he commanded a view of the high hill range, stretching to the N. and E, that is now so well known to ten thousand voyagers.[302] That was the mainland, in some of the bays of which the Islanders, on their 'wife-catching expeditions', were no doubt anchored, and carrying out their plots and schemes.

Captain Meredith wandered about enjoying the wild solitude

of the place, and musing on the probable destiny of the great land, the present scene of the exploits of the wild desperadoes that he had lately been mingling with. As he gained the top of a ridge of sandhills, contiguous to the beach, he suddenly surprised some half-dozen naked and native children, in full play, dashing and darting in the surf as it broke and rolled upon the beach. They continued their gambols, laughing in their wild and unrestrained manner, when one of them perceived the stranger. A yell of fear and surprise pierced the air, and the troop dashed off and disappeared in the neighbouring scrub.[303] The captain in vain tried to find the hut the children came from, so gave up the search and returned, finding the boat riding at her grapnel with a slack line, so imperturbably calm was the pond. As the captain stood on the high brink he looked right into the boat as if one were looking down into a well. A loud coo-e-e reverberated, and woke up the two seamen asleep in the boat. As they pulled out of this remark-able boat harbour, they admired the manner in which the narrow entrance had been cleared, just sufficient to admit one boat at a time, a precaution not wholly unneeded, as civil wars at times prevailed in Kangaroo Island, as well as in Great Britain or France. It is a luxury that is peculiarly indulged in by the human race, in contra-distinction to the animal. Mr. Ratlin no sooner saw the boat creep out of the land, than he squared away and picked her up.

'Well,' said the chief mate, 'what luck?'

'I hardly know yet, that darn'd son of a gun did nothing but curse and swear about old Sam, when he heard he was off wife-hunting, but he promised to come down to-night and let me know whether he'd go with us or not; so we must look out for a fire after sundown, and go ashore and pick him up; and if he won't come by fair means he shall by foul.'

'Dinner is ready!' announced the steward, as the captain stood leaning against the binnacle, watching the ship's head.

'You have a fine spread, Mr. Ratlin,' remarked the captain, as he took his seat at the cuddy table – 'black swan, Cape Barren goose,[304] crayfish, and a schnapper but,' looking round the table, 'you have not "wakeries," those delicious grubs that are found in the grass tree and gum tree.'

'No,' replied Mr. Ratlin sorrowfully, 'truly they are delicious beyond comparison. I had no chance to get any. There ought to be no dinner considered complete without wakeries.'

The afternoon slipped away in a splendid sunshine, tempered with a cool breeze, the island on one side and the main on the other completing the panorama. Vast schools of native herring[305] and bream[306] floated on the water, and covered it with a mass of air bubbles. At times the brig moved in a field of living creatures – the surface of the water was literally a moving mass of fish, multitudes on multitudes, and as they slowly passed away they made an audible and strange sound, which, when heard at night, was weird and unearthly. No sooner had darkness set in than a fire shone brightly on the land. The captain took a boat, and with four men made for the shore.

'I'll go wid yer, pervided yer takes my wife here, and when yer comes back lands us about fifty miles to the westward, where I holds out.'[307]

'Done!' said the captain, and the strange man and his black wife stepped into the boat, and all were soon on board.

The brig spun on before the rising south-easter, and before morning dawned the islands, now known as the Althorpe Islands,[308] were on her starboard bow, peaked and only accessible in one small sandy patch. With these islands is associated a terrible tale of horrors, of human suffering and of inhuman barbarity.

Love and its Consequences. – Flash Tom's Yarn about the Althorpe Island Tragedy. – Tom Goes Ashore.

One of the fertile sources of disagreement between the Islanders was the continual practice of certain worthies of intriguing, and decoying the native women from their respective lords. It has already been stated that the society in the independent empire of Kangaroo Island[309] was amenable to no law except that of the boldest and the strongest, and that for mutual protection it was divided into sets of twos and threes with their black women, few or many, as the case might be. Hence arose a popular theory well put into practice, that if a black woman could be decoyed away, stolen, bought, or openly robbed, it was perfectly right to do so. Bloody enormities arose from this cause, and very suspicious accidents occurred that removed for ever the Don Juans, those who distinguished themselves for their amorous propensities. In the Island women were at a premium. While the Governor, *alias* Worley,[310] had his six, another three, or another two, some had none. Hence their wife-thieving desires, their plot-planning, their women intrigues, their rows, and their mysterious disappearances. In fact, as in the history of Pitcairn Island,[311] so in Kangaroo Island, the women formed the great bone of contention, and there is scarcely a feature in the terrible tragedies of the one that cannot be paralleled in the other, but with this difference, which undoubtedly modified or intensified the atrocities of each – in the one, love, jealousy, and murder were active on a spot barely a few acres in extent; in the other, a land half the size of Scotland, covered with a dense vegetation, and affording the most favourable cover for the wiles and schemes, both of the black and the white, for, strange to say, the native women, partly from fear, partly from revenge, and partly from preference, aided and abetted many a desertion, many a capture, and many a murder. Kangaroo Island, at the period we are writing, presented an admirable study for the moralist and the philosopher. The immutable character of the human heart, under the most diverse circumstances, was as clearly portrayed as in the regions of so-called civilisation. The state of society was neither better nor worse than that of the times of Elizabeth, or Catherine of Russia.[312] The only difference was in the language and in the dress – the one used mellifluous words, while noted your fifth rib, the other stabbed you with a blasphemous oath. The first plotted the destruction of the wife of his bosom friend in silk and satin; the other did the same, dressed in skins of wild animals. The custom was the same, though the manner differed. Instead of the dungeon, the castle, the poison, or the hired assassin, there was the lonely cave, the far-off islet, the deep sea, the sharp knife, or the impenetrable scrub.

The brig lay becalmed off the group of barren isles – the Althorpes. The great wall-like coast of Kangaroo Island rose and fell, and vanished into distance on the one side of the straits, and the low land of the main, now known as Yorke's[313] Peninsula, just loomed on the other, while the high-peaked islands cut sharply against the sky, now only some four miles off, as the brig rolled to the swell.

Flash[314] Tom, the Islander, and his black companion sat under the starboard gunwale in moody silence, not far from the forecastle.

'I don't like those islands sucking us in so close,' remarked a seaman, 'I wonder whether there's any anchorage under their lee?'

'Ask this here Robinson Crusoe; he knows, most like.'

'I say, Tom, can yer anchor inside the islands to leeward there?'

'I don't know,' gruffly replied Flash Tom, in no pleasant mood, and prepared himself to take a nap; but his questioners were persevering.

'I have heard,' said one, 'that sometimes you chaps forget a fellow on these islands and then he is left to starve – perhaps this is one on 'em, aye, only some four miles off,' as the brig rolled to the swell.

'Who told yer that yarn?' asked Tom, now quite awake.

'Oh! we hears it about the coast – come now, tell us all about it; we has nothing to do, and I likes a yarn.'

'Well,' says Tom, 'I'll tell yer 'xactly as all I knows on it; but if yer will take my advice yer will not be yarning it wherever yer goes, 'cause our chaps doesn't like it, or maybe yer will find them rather smart, and brace yer sharp up. Now do yer see, it fell on this ways. There was a chap, many years gone now, that was werry sulky, but he was werry handy in getting seal-skins, and when the Hookers[315] come down and we has a spell at rum, and gets drunk a bit, this chap allers keeps away, and chops his skins on the coast; so the skippers dang's him up and down as a close grip, for they couldn't get so much out of him as they gets out of us fools; for when we gets drunk, yer know, we cares nothing for skins; for where they comes from there's plenty more – maybe your skipper is one o' them. I s'pose yer has plenty of rum under hatches.[316] Howsumever, my yarn lies on another tack. Well, this chap has no boat, but has one black woman, and a capital hand she was, too, and all hands wants her, but it was no go – one time I offers all my skins I gets in a year, a big heap, too, for his gal; but no go, he was too much of a Jew for me. I then tries to steal the gal ——'

'Steal the gal, did yer say!' broke in half-a-dozen voices, in amazement at the unconcerned and matter-of-fact way in which Flash Tom mentioned the incident.

'Yes, in course, how was I to get her, my hearties, in any other way, tell me that? Yer does the same in the old country, but yer calls it by another name. Well, I tries and tries, but he was too sharp for me. Then I lays a trap, and coaxes her away, and I don't know how it is, I allers am a better hand in coaxing the gals away than stealing 'em,' and Flash Tom glanced his eye to the native woman sitting near him. He felt proud at the thought of his successes, and possibly the woman behind him was but another trophy. We shall see.

'I s'pose,' said one of the sailors, 'yer what the fine folks calls "a lady-killer".'

'And a fine 'un, too,' said another, 'with yer kangaroo breeches.'

'Oh! yer be blowed,' replied Tom, 'I never killed a woman in my life. I steals 'em and coaxes 'em away, but I never kills 'em. Well, as I was saying, I coaxes the gal away, and she gets wid me one day's spell away from the cove; but somehow he cotches us the next day. The woman screams, and bolts clean away, and he and I has a set-to; we fights like two bull seals; I gets a big dig with his knife, and I gie him the same. So last he crawls away, and I crawls away. I tells him to look out and so we parts. Some time arter we was sealing in a boat down here, just away there where yer now see a lump of wall like, bigger than the t'others,' and Tom pointed out the place in the dim moonlight. 'Well, as we jumps on the rocks, up jumps old "Grip Hard," for that was his name.[317] "Have yer got plenty skins?" says one, cos we knows his run. "Middling," says he. Then some on 'em in the boat 'gins talking a bit, but I never hears a word on it. "Will yer come wid us, we's going furder on to the pint there, and we'll land yer there, if yer likes." Well, he steps in, and we pulls away; perhaps he was tired, being so lonesome like – perhaps he wanted to lead us chaps away from his nest, as a blind like; howsumever, he comes; we gets about a mile away, when we ups lug and runs to these ere islands to the leeward of us. Old "Grip" springs up and says "dang yer, whe'r going to?" "Nuffing, nuffing," says everyone, we likes to have a look at these ere islands; we shall get there to-night, and come back to-morrow.' Well, just as the sun sets we beaches our boat on the biggest one, the high one there. We makes all snug, and we hears plenty of seal all round. Next day we clubs a lot, and fills the boat wid skins, real fur seal.[318] As we shove off, one o' them says, "hallo! my club's ashore." I say, ""Grip Hard," just jump ashore and get it." He goes up the beach, and goes over the sandhill to where our fire was, and then my mates pulls like devils as hard as they could. "Grip Hard" comes on top o' the sandhills and coo-e-es, but we pulls like mad; he coo-e-es and coo-e-es, and runs on the sandhills till he comes to a big pint, and he can't go no furder. My mates swears and cusses, and pulls like mad; I gets skeered, I talks to 'em, I thinks they are larking. I 'spects them 'bout ship; they cusses each other and everything. We ups lug, and the wind north, we runs dead on for Kangaroo Island. I looks back and sees summut on top o' the island, but my mates cusses me for looking back, and we soon lose the islands astern. Next day my mates takes "Grip Hard's" skins, and we never goes to these islands any more, and I does not like 'em at all meeself, though I had no hand in it. They tells me that yer can hear his cooey yet o' nights and early mornings. I doesn't like to look at 'em even now, though it's long years gone.'[319]

'And what did yer do with the lady yer was so particular in love with?'

'Ah! what comes of her?' cried all the listeners.

Tom fidgeted about, but at last said, 'why my mates took the skins, and I took the gal, and now yer knows the whole yarn, strand for strand.'

'And a purty yarn it is, too.'

'Yer have two sorts of sealing hereaways, haven't yer,' asked one of the men, 'and yer calls 'em the "wet knock down" and the "dry knock down," and the yarn yer been telling on us is the last sort.'[320]

But Tom made no sign. He crouched down deeper under the lee of the bulwarks, and it was evident he did not want to talk further about the matter, and, above all, not to be cross-questioned. The sailors rose up, and muttered that he was as deep a villain as the rest, and that they did not believe half what he said. The night wore on, and the tide drew the ship nearer and nearer to the stern and solitary islands, whose peaked and blackened sides now presented mournful associations as the sailors gazed upon them. Flash Tom was asked about the dangers by Mr. Ratlin, about the outlying reefs; but he scarcely replied, so the mate left him with an oath at his obstinacy, and ordered the anchor to be seen to and a boat to be got ready. The turn of the tide rendered these precautions unnecessary, however, the brig gradually drifted away, and as the morning broke the islands with their dread history were many miles away. Soon after a strong southwester came on to blow, and the vessel making no headway, Captain Meredith determined to seek shelter under a low point, now known as Point Marsden.[321]

Flash Tom seemed to revive as the anchor brought the ship up, and as the place was only a few miles from his abode, asked Captain Meredith to let him go ashore, promising to return early next morning.

'Yes, you may go; but I suppose I'll never see you again.'

This, though spoken half-jestingly, was literally fulfilled, but in a manner very different from what was anticipated. Flash Tom never lived to see daylight, and the Althorpe Island tragedy was fearfully revenged in the dread murder of the murderer that very night.

The Murder of Flash Tom.

When Flash Tom left the brig he took with him a couple of good bottles of rum. He and his black woman were soon landed on the white beach at the foot of a dense wall of scrub. The woman, in native fashion, strapped her wallet on her back, and followed her lord and master, walking in Indian file as their figures disappeared in the scrub, the two boatmen remarked that they believed Flash Tom was at the bottom of the whole plot of leaving 'Grip Hard' to die on the island.

'We'll ask the skipper to heave to off them islands, and we'll go ashore and see if we can't find his bones,' said one; 'and a purty way they has of calling this here "the dry knock down."'

'Well, well, I believe all these islands are full of ghosts,' replied the other.' I won't go ashore to look for his bones. I tell yer the fellow is a Jonah,[322] and he'll sink the ship yet. I s'pose all these small islands, particular those out o' the way, has ghosts? We will tell the skipper, and see what he says, but I won't go ashore, be darned if I do.'

Flash Tom arrived at his hut about sundown, and was surprised to find a native woman quietly making a fire, when he had supposed he would have been alone; but he was doubly surprised as he recognised the woman he had left days previously at Hog Bay, the place where he had joined the ship. He was incensed at this unlooked-for *rencontre*;[323] for, the truth must be told, Tom had by threats and coaxing induced the native woman he brought with him in the brig to accompany him to his hut, a place that was remote from the ordinary track of the Islanders, and therefore admirably adapted for his peculiar vocation. He and his legitimate wife had been on a tour of wallaby-hunting for several weeks. Camping at Hog Bay he met the other woman, on a similar errand, but from another quarter. The brig heaving in sight, he at once conceived the plan of giving his number one wife the slip, at least for a few weeks, and commanding her to stay and get as many wallaby skins as she could, and not to return until two moons' time. She, however, knowing his departure in the brig, determined to start for her home that very night, and she was as much astonished as he was when they encountered each other in the manner already described.

Tom commenced swearing dreadfully at Suky.[324] From swearing he commenced beating, and had it not been for Brown Sal,[325] who threatened to take part with Suky, probably Flash Tom's anger might have led him into dire mischief. He having exhausted his strength, both of tongue and muscle, and tired with his long march, consoled himself with rum, and continued drinking, cursing, and rowing with the women for a long time, until the rum got the upper hand, and he fell into a deep, drunken sleep.

Suky kept up, as she had done ever since her beating, a low native wail, that nothing could induce her to cease, though continually threatened by Tom to have her ears cropped off or her body gashed.

It was a bad sign when native women wail in the particular manner she was expressing her grief. A mother will wail the loss of her murdered son in such language, and taunt her kinsmen till they are goarded [sic] to a frenzy, and oft the listening warrior – the next of kin – will jump up, take spear and shield, and dart away, and not return till he shows the kidney fat of his enemy! Suky continued to wail, and Brown Sal joined her; but Tom snored in his drunken sleep. At last the women ceased.

Without preliminary remark, without considering the matter beyond the scope of the hour, without being troubled as to the morality of the action, Suky came at once to the solution of her troubles – 'Let's kill the wretch,' and she passed her hand across her throat. 'He took "Grip Hard" away, and killed him on the island.'

Natives seldom argue; creatures of impulse, they act as they feel.[326] With a knitted brow and face swollen with crying, Suky rose up and motioned to Sal. There was a stern expression of face that peculiarly belongs to the black races of the earth when their feelings are wrought up to the highest endurance, and as Suky stepped past the doorway of the hut, the moon lighted up the face of a demon, and had the whole race of Islanders been before her and in her power she would have cut the throats of each without the slightest compunction. The hatred of the race, arising from the dire wrongs they had suffered, though stilled and suppressed, was never eradicated.

The drunken man was lying down against the side of the hut. There was a scant fire barely glimmering on the hearth. Suky seized Tom and dragged him into the light, and then felt for his knife, which, as a sealer's, was keen and bright. The poor drunken wretch struggled and swore in an incoherent manner, ordering them to let him alone. Anon he was quieter. Accustomed, as all were, to butchering the seal and the kangaroo, they were adepts in the use of the knife.[327] They handled it skillfully. Brown Sal and Suky scarcely spoke; the latter motioned to a bit of rope, with which she tied the hands of her victim. She then motioned to Sal to keep his head down and back, and then without the slightest tremor she cut Tom's throat from ear to ear. The wretch struggled in his dying agony, but the cut was by a skilful hand, and it was fatal. The women rose with a wild yell, and seizing a stick of fire started out into the deep scrub, and stayed not till miles intervened between them and the murdered man.

Very many months elapsed before the Islanders discovered that Tom had been murdered; but as it was an understood thing not to hold inquests in Kangaroo Island, little was said or done, and soon after a great fire swept over that part of the island and consumed both the hut and the murdered remains of Flash Tom.

The tradition of this murder still remains; and one of the deep gullies that debouch on Investigator Straits is still known by the dire appellation of 'Bloody Tom's.'[328]

All savages regard murder no crime, that is to say, if the victim be of another tribe or race; on the contrary, in such a case it is a noble action and something to applaud. Suky and Sal gloried in the deed. They craftily kept the secret from the Islanders, but rejoicingly told it to their sisters. A song of triumph was extemporised on the occasion, and many and many a night the women droned over the camp fire the murder of Flash Tom.

Chapter 17

Native Signals. – Old Conday. – The Interview – The Rape of the Black Sabines.[329] – The Death of Long Bill.

We left Old Sam and Long Bill in their respective boats closed, hauled, and spinning along the coast north of the point now known as Cape Jervis, with smooth water and a brisk breeze. As they passed point after point dense clouds of smoke suddenly arose, and the Islanders cursed and swore as they recognised the well-known native signal of alarm, clearly indicating the blacks were on the alert, had recognised them, and were then actively engaged in warning and arousing the whole surrounding country.

'There goes another,' sung out Sam, 'and right ahead, too, the sarcy devils; but we'll take a woman for every smoke they makes.'

'We shall have hard work, and summun will lose the number of his mess, I thinks,' chimed in the Doctor.

The other boat sheered alongside, and the crews talked the matter over, the warlike preparations of the natives, and the best plans to adopt.

'Rush the niggers,' said Long Bill, 'and run em through the gills and that'll stop their jaw,' and he laughed a loud laugh as he anticipated the fun of skewering the natives with his lance. 'I've done it afore, and it's a purty game, too,' and he took up his gleaming lance[330] and held it to view. 'He'll never talk wid his mammy that gets that into him.'

Unmindful for a moment of his steer-oar, the boat broached to[331], and shipped a tremendous sea that nearly washed the men out. With a powerful effort he brought the boat before the wind, but in so doing he lost his much-prized lance – a lance that had quivered in more than one man's heart, and was a source of dread both to white and black.

Long Bill was in a fearful rage, his oaths were frightful, and the only consolation he could find was the vengeance he would take against the blacks at the very first opportunity that very day.

'Bale, every mother's son of yer, or we shall all go to he – l,' yelled Long Bill, as he tugged at the steer oar to keep the boat end on to the seas.

'That's a purty beginning,' roared out Sam. 'Why didn't yer mind yer weather-helm, yer loplolly[332] boy?'

'You go to ———,' replied Long Bill.

Georgy was exceedingly disconcerted. 'I never likes to sail on Friday in these 'ere love matches, and I don't like anything to go wrong. It's terribly bad for Bill to lose his lance like that. I must look out for squalls to-day.'

'I tell yer what it is,' said Sam to the Doctor, 'we'll try that 'ere bay inside the bluff, the smokes are all that way. I think there's a powerful number there fishing.'

The boats were soon under the lee of that bold headland of rock now known as the N.W. Bluff, which for some 300 or 400 feet rises abruptly from the jetty black waters that lave its cave-worn base. The sea was quite smooth under its gigantic protection. As the wind then blew S.E., the boats slowly slid along within fifty yards of its towering mass. Thousands of birds flew out of the caves at the unwonted visitors, and screamed and swooped round the boats, so near that more than one was knocked down with an oar or a boat-hook. At last the distant little picturesque sandy beach gradually came into view, and the boats took in sail, and pulled the remaining distance. As they approached, the scene became exceedingly beautiful, the valley, the mouth of which formed the bay, was enclosed by high, rolling hills, and the coast presented a broken wall of bold rock. A stream of fresh water issued and ran over the sand, and noisy cockatoos and parrots resounded on every side; the kangaroo grass[333] stood as thick as a hay-field, and as high as a man. Altogether it was a lovely spot, and even now, though denuded of trees, and dotted over with settlers' homes, though the rotund hills are marred with lines of fences, and a jetty stands on the spot where the Islanders were in the habit of landing, still the place is beautiful, and is certainly the most picturesque on the whole coastline of Gulf St. Vincent.[334] The locality is now called Rapid

Bay, so named after the brig that brought out the first surveying party, including the Surveyor-General, Colonel Light.[335] It was the first place at which the surveyors landed.[336]

As the boats were creeping in, and every man keeping a sharp lookout, of a sudden a tremendous roaring, clattering noise was heard almost overhead, and then a huge splash with a thousand smaller ones succeeding.

'Up to their devilries,' remarked Sam, as he shoved his boat further away from the coast, but yer see, they can't 'xactly find our bearings. It's all chance work, but we'll keep furder off, and then perhaps we shall see 'em.'

High above some 500 feet of nearly perpendicular altitude, a small band of natives was visible, evidently preparing to hurl down a huge boulder of stone, but on perceiving the boats they at once desisted, and became invisible.

When the boats arrived just beyond a spear's throw of the beach they killicked. Though not a sound indicated the presence of the natives, nearly fifty were breathlessly watching from the tall kangaroo grass the movements of the Islanders.

'Let's go ashore,' said one of the Islanders. 'They are not here for sartin.'

'If yer goes ashore now,' said Georgy, 'they'll take yer kidney-fat out of yer, just there on top of that ere rise, and we shall have the pleasure o' seeing them doing it, for I spects it's there they is a looking on us circumspectly like.'

'None o' your fine words,' said Sam, 'yer talks like a parson. I circumspects yer'll have a little work in the butchering line today; 'spose we gie 'em a coo-e-e?' and Sam rose up in the stern sheets of the boat and gave them a prolonged coo-e-e that echoed among the hills. Beyond a solitary scream of a cockatoo not a sound followed. A full hour elapsed; the Islanders availed themselves of the opportunity to look up their weapons, and to have their dinner, being fully persuaded that sooner or later the natives would appear. At this juncture a native stepped out on the white beach. He seemed to be unarmed, with the exception of his waddy.

The Doctor started up – 'Why, that's "old Conday"[337] – the greediest old rascal o' the lot. I'll go ashore and have a yarn.'

'Werry good,' said Sam, get 'em to come down friendly like, with their wives and darters, mind; now yer must parbuckle the thing like the infarnal speerit that yer is allers speaking about in the times o' Adam and Eve. We wants a big haul, Georgy, and if yer lays the strand seamanlike yer shall have the pick between my gal and yourn that we catches.'

Long Bill and all the rest were listening to the advice.

'Round 'em up,' said one, 'don't yer forget to tell 'em we has no guns, and they must leave their spears. Bear a hand, or that blue nigger will bolt.'

Georgy was soon ready. It would have scared the natives to have pulled in, so he slipped quietly overboard and swam ashore. As he neared the beach he spoke to old Conday, who immediately recognised him. A yell of delight brought from rock and rise, bush and brake, some fifty warriors, who with a rush soon joined their companion.[338] Georgy rose from the water, and imitating native etiquette, sat down on the sand in silence.[339] Thereupon, the natives squatted, too. Thus both parties continued for at least ten minutes, then Georgy spoke, and explained their visit. They were friends, fishing and hunting up the Gulf. They had plenty to eat – they wanted to come ashore. The whites would leave their guns, and the blacks were to leave their spears. They were to have a grand dinner, to bring down their wives and daughters, and have a great corroboree. This was agreed to, but not without dissent.

'Where's my sister?' asked one; 'why have yer ate her?'[340]

Georgy said it was some other white man that had her, but the last time he saw her she was well and fat.

'You lie!' replied the other, 'you ate her.'

Here old Conday interposed, and the treaty was concluded. Georgy hailed the boats, while some of the natives went to fetch their families camped a mile inland. The boats were cautiously killicked just outside the surf. A grand roasting of fish, wallaby, and kangaroos followed, and as the sun declined some thirty or forty men and women appeared. It was evident several of the warriors were suspicious, and remained away.

It was now quite dark; the fires gleamed up against the black mountains around them, and a corrobboree was performed.[341] Ample opportunity had by this time been given to each man to select his favourite lady.

'When they blows a bit, and has a spell arter the next singing,' said Sam, 'then I gees you the signal, and every man takes his woman. So, look out, and get handy each on yer near yer pertickler sweetheart; and then yer rushes for the boats for yer life. Take it quiet, boys, don't yer flurry yersels, and hug the greasy ladies like a bear, cos they is so slippery.'

Another corrobboree was sung, and the blacks sat down to rest, or rolled about laughing, quite exhausted with their efforts in the dance and song.

'Now,' roared out Sam, with the voice of a bull, and each Islander seized a women, and hurried her to the waves. A wild yell rent the air, burning brands flew through the darkness, waddies hissed in every direction, the warriors threw a shower of spears, but the night was favourable to the enemy. Shrieks, and wails, and shouts rose loud and long, but the Islanders were victors, though but to a limited extent. Amongst them all six women only were caught.

'Lash 'em down to the thwarts,' sung out Georgy.

'Ah!' and a fearful oath escaped Sam's lips, 'there's one lost.' Yes, one of the women leapt overboard and so escaped.[342]

When the light broke next morning, their captives were still wailing their sorrowful song. They found Long Bill leaning heavily against the steer oar.

'What, are yer crying for the gal that jumped overboard last night?' jokingly remarked Sam, as the two boats neared each other for a mutual conference on the state of affairs. But Bill replied not. The early morning light was still faint, and things were misty.

'I say, Bill,' sung out Georgy, 'cheer up'; but Bill never cheered up; his body merely rose and fell as the wave washed the steer oar.

Bill was dead! In the scrimmage of the preceding night a spear had entered that callous heart of his, and he died without a murmur. A little while after he was thrown to the fishes.

High up in a cavern containing a singular stalactite, and only visible from the sea, overlooking the spot where this tragedy happened, is yet to be seen the strong resemblance of the skeleton of a man.[343] It is known to all coasters as 'Bill's Ghost.'

Chapter 18

The Wreck of the Brig. –
The Desertion of a Boat's Crew. –
Captain Meredith Reaches
the Mainland.

'There he is at last!' exclaimed Captain Meredith, as he turned away from a close scrutiny of the beach.

Mr. Ratlin, who had been similarly employed, made no answer.

The captain became impatient; his anxiety had disturbed his vision, so he jumped to a hasty conclusion.

'Don't you see him?' inquired the captain in a tone of annoyance.

'I see something like a man, but I don't believe it is a man; it looks more like a kangaroo.'

'Kangaroo! pshaw!' Captain Meredith resumed his telescope, and after a long look he turned sharply round and said, 'Get the anchor up; I'll not stop another minute. It's some trick of these Islanders. There's no way of securing the unprincipled rascals.'

The brig had her topsails soon sheeted home, and made easy way out of her snug anchorage, light winds prevailing during the whole day. The distant blue outline of the highest land, now known as Mount Lofty,[344] bore N.E. by N. as the sun set in the gorgeous splendour of an Australian day. A smart S.W. breeze sprang up, and the brig bowled along under top-gallant canvas. A little after the middle watch had been called, a curious grating sensation was felt, then a succession of bumps, the vessel rolled in a most awkward and unusual manner, gradually heeling over till her gunwale was under water, and then became immovable. The brig had run ashore.[345]

When daylight broke and the tide was down, they saw right under them a small strip of green bushes and a most extensive sand flat, with rocks jutting out in ugly patches. The spot is the well-known

'Trowbridge Shoals,'[346] where more than one ship has laid her bones.[347]

The green bushes turned out to be the herbage of a tiny sand ridge, about as broad as the brig herself, and perhaps three times her length.

Provisions were soon landed, and a tolerable shelter rigged up between the bushes. Two boats were saved and safely beached on the lee of the tiny island.

Land was visible from nearly all points of the compass, and the nearest coast appeared scarcely four or five miles away. Captain Meredith had hopes of warping his brig off the shoals, but his men, not liking the additional labour, planned a little conspiracy, and accordingly in the dead of night crept into one of the boats at anchor, and stole quietly away, intending to make for Kangaroo Island and become, lawful and obedient subjects of that extensive empire. Many of them had become enamoured of the free and jolly life of the Islanders. All they had to get – a matter, by the way, of not easy accomplishment – were two or three black women and then they were provided for life. They could sleep watch in and watch out. Of wallaby there was plenty, fish also was abundant; and for amusement, as well as profit, there was the exciting pastime of sealing. They had made a capital beginning, having a splendid whaleboat, that first and paramount requisite of an Islander's life.

'Won't the skipper growl when he finds his best boat gone?' remarked one of the hands.

'Let him growl his ears off; he never more sees her again; we has had enuf of squaring yards, so we wants no wages, but we takes the boat.'

When Mr. Ratlin rose early to rouse all hands to make further efforts to move the brig from her stranded position, great was his amazement at the desertion of the men and boat.

'I told you so,' said he to the captain; 'ever since that rascal came on board we took off the rocks, shamming Abraham[348], the crew has never been the same. Here's a pretty mess! and just at the top of spring tides. We'd sure to get the brig off to-night,' and the mate stamped his feet in his vexation.

The captain said nothing. He was beyond talking; but he had a dire feeling of revenge; one day he would square accounts.

'Who's left?' asked the skipper.

'Only poor Handspike and Black Dick[349] and his lubra.'

'Well, we must be off also; it's no use stopping here, so let us rig up the gig and be off. We shall fall in with the Islanders somewhere, and perhaps induce them to come over here, and by the next springs we may get her off.'

'Never,' replied the mate. 'The chaps will never be such fools as to come. They would much prefer seeing her a wreck. No, Captain Meredith, take your last look of her, for you will never see her afloat again.'

The two men paced up and down the little sandy beach as if they were walking the quarterdeck. Gloomy thoughts made them moody and silent. Poor Handspike sat under the lee of a salt bush,[350] mumbling to himself, and gazing seaward, and the two blacks, man and woman, were busying themselves in getting a few things in the boat; but the hot sun killed the little wind that fanned the sea, and a great calm followed.

As night drew in, and the moon rose in her grand glory, Captain Meredith for the last time visited his hapless vessel, and then leaning on the stump of the bowsprit, he indulged in the natural melancholy reflection that the scene and place inspired – the wreck, the desertion of his crew, the tiny island glittering in the moonbeams, the loud booming of the tide as it rippled over the vast shoals, the shriek of the sea-bird, and the lone grandeur of Nature in her moonlit garniture. Before another hour had elapsed the feeble remnant of the wrecked ship was gradually creeping away under the influence of a light breeze.

Poor Handspike, who had never recovered his senses since his fatal sunstroke, was the only one that seemed merry; he alone, in his perverted faculties, saw cause for being glad. From the tenor of his wanderings: he was evidently under the impression that the boats had come and taken him off, out of that dread scrub on the side the lagoon to which all his thoughts perpetually wandered. Bad and strange was the contrast; the madman merry, and the sane man almost mad. Moon and star vanished, and the pink dawn trembled over the high hills that now lay before them. A smart breeze from the S.W. made the boat jump on her course, which was due for the high land ahead.

'What are you going to do, captain?' said Mr. Ratlin.

'Beat up for the island, if we can, or beach the boat on the coast ahead, and wait a slant of wind to get to the southward. But those confounded blacks on the mainland are as thick as ants; we must be careful.'

'If you are afraid to land you can anchor the boat off and stop in her; but I shall go ashore. I don't fear the blacks.'

'You ought to be careful, you know; the Islanders have been of late somewhere hereaway catching women, and you might be mistaken for one of them and speared.'

'Well, if I am? I have lost everything.'

'Don't despair, captain; something may yet turn up.'

The land was soon neared, and a fine opening to a large inland lake was clearly discernible.[351] The boat was headed for so desirable a spot, and very soon she glided out of the tossing, restless sea, and the forlorn crew found themselves in a lake, surrounded by a vast amphitheatre of hills, the spurs of which were clothed in the peculiar foliage of Australia.

Warily the boat's crew camped themselves on a sandspit that stretched out into the lake, and the boat was kept at anchor. All hands but one went to sleep, and that one was Captain Meredith. He reclined under a large bush, and gave way sorrowful musings.

Chapter the Last

The Murder of
Captain Meredith. –
The Last Glimpse of Old Sam.

For three days the party were kept windbound. At last a change, though a deceitful one, occurred, but their impatience was such that Captain Meredith was determined to risk it; so the boat was duly got out, and with a light breeze they sailed away. Towards the afternoon the wind chopped round, and they were compelled to beach the boat, to their chagrin.

It was a different country from the former. The hills retreated from the coastline, though here and there a kind of conical mound was left. On one of these Captain Meredith determined to camp. Several native fires were seen in the distance. At last piles of smoke rose up as if by enchantment on every side. It was clear the natives had discovered their presence, and were using their bush telegraph.

'Lauty blackfellow,' remarked the native of the party, as she pointed out the columns of smoke. 'Me no stop here; me stop in boat.'

'Good advice, too,' said Mr. Ratlin, 'and I would advise all of us to anchor the boat off shore and sleep in her.'

That night the little shipwrecked crew lay in the boat. As the morning came not a native or a smoke was visible. The stillness of death was on the land; the wind died away, and there was every appearance of a terrific hot day.

'I shall go ashore,' said Captain Meredith; 'it's frightful to be grilled to death in the boat; might as well be speared to death on shore,' and he laughed slightly at the alternative. He little thought he would so soon be called upon to accept the dire choice to which he so jokingly alluded.

'Let me see – it's Sunday to-day, is it not?' said the captain.

'Yes, I think it is,' replied Mr. Ratlin, who was sitting on the gunwale of the boat with his legs dangling in the water to cool himself, while both the blacks were rolling about in the sea like two porpoises.

'Well, if it's Sunday and I must do something, I'll take my Bible with me, and do you see that bare knoll with a few bushes?[352] Well, I'll go there, perhaps there may be a light air blowing, and I can easily scamper down if the blacks come on too thick so good-bye for a while.'

The boat was pushed astern, and he jumped into the water, mounted over the sandhills, and duly ensconced himself under the bushes.

While these arrangements were being carried out, two native warriors might have been observed crouching behind a deep mass of scrub that commanded the whole view before them.

'We will kill them all,' whispered one; 'the spears first, then the waddies. Ah! look there! one of them is coming ashore and coming this way.'

'Ah!' grunted his companion, 'don't spear him, he'll cry out. We'll go and talk to him, and knock him down with the kutta.[353] I wish those other white thieves would come ashore. They have two of my sisters. They have stolen your wife. Ah! we will take their kidney fat before the sun sets.'

Two or three hours elapsed. Captain Meredith was deeply immersed in reading one of the Psalms,[354] and occasionally wondering whether they were written for life in Australia, as well as in Syria,[355] and while so pondering he cast his eye round and saw to his amazement two painted and naked warriors.[356] One was barred and ribbed with red stripes, kangaroo teeth dangled from his front hair, a large bunch of emu feathers[357] hung pendant from his neck and down his back, and he grasped a fighting stick of large proportions. He had no shield. The other warrior was dotted all over with red ochre,[358] his hair was steeped in oil, hung in long ringlets, and shone brilliantly, having been powdered with the fine dust of micaceous ironstone. Through his nose was a long white bone, the fibula of the kangaroo. He wore a girdle of human hair. He had no spears in his hands, but slily the cunning rascals held between their big toes a jagged spear each, which, in the deep grass in which they stood, were, of course, invisible. As the Irishman hides his 'blackthorn' up his sleeve, so the native, not to alarm his victim, drags along the ground the fatal spear held firmly in the grasp of the big toe.

Captain Meredith jumped up and faced his foes. They waved their hands towards the boat. He retreated, and when he thought a favourable opportunity occurred, turned his head to shout for help. That moment was fatal. A waddy[359] with an unerring aim struck him with dreadful force on his head, and he reeled and fell to the ground. Quick as lightning a spear passed through his body, and with a groan of infinite anguish Captain Meredith gave up the ghost.

Dead or alive, the natives cared not. Quickly stripping the corpse, they cut an incision in the side, extracted the kidneys and the fat of the unhappy man, and then sped away to the hills to boast of their valour and their exceeding great luck.

As the evening closed in, Mr. Ratlin became anxious at the pro-longed absence of the captain. He went ashore and coo-e-ed till he was hoarse. At last he mustered all his forces, and marched up to the hill where the captain had been during the day. Alas! half way up that conical mound they found the mutilated corpse of their friend and commander.

Horror struck, they stood mutely gazing on the body, then mutely turning to the sea as if for help, they descried, in the midst of their bewilderment, a sail, evidently that of a boat, standing up and past them. Their immediate impulse was to raise a smoke to induce the boat to come in. An hour afterwards the boat stood in. It proved to be Old Sam,[360] the doctor, and two of their wives; they were bound north to visit a tribe of blacks that lived on the plains below Mount Lofty,[361] now so well known as the Adelaide Plains, in the midst of which is situated the city of Adelaide, the capital of South Australia.

'Speared, do yer say,' said Old Sam, when he heard the full story, 'and yer got ashore on the shoals to the westward.'

'Yes, that's the way in this country, we lives pertickler easy, but it's a wery oneasy life to such as yer are, yer are too green, mate; but come along; let's bury the captain like a Christian. I say, doctor, yers allers preaching, now's the time, and the text I gees yer – kill the ——— wretches.'

'Softly, softly,' replied the doctor, it we kills too much, that's how they kills us; it's all our fault.'

'Bah!' said Sam, 'didn't they kill Long Bill and Harry? didn't they spear me, and cotch you? I tell yer, Georgy, by that dead carcase there, I'll kill five for him before I croaks.'

Georgy said nothing, but wagged his head occasionally.

The united party soon stood round the mutilated body.

'They have taken his fat,' quietly remarked Georgy, as he pointed to the horrid wound.

'In course,' replied Sam, 'they likes our fat uncommon, the black devils; but we'll serve 'em out[362] for this day's work.'

The captain was buried as well as it could be done under the circumstances, and Mr. Ratlin read the Psalms, where apparently the captain himself had been reading when murdered. Georgy stood and listened devoutly with his skin hat in his hand.

Old Sam moved silently away, and stood gazing landward, or else carefully noted the shape of the footprints on the soil, muttering the whole time words of dire import.

On the very spot where this tragedy happened, the plough now moves along, and waving cornfields crown the grave of Captain Meredith. Little is this fact known to the settlers of the district, but the conical hill will remain for ever a monument of this murder, another to the long list of those that became sacrifices for the deeply dyed sins of the Kangaroo Islanders.

The spot is near the Yankalilla River and forms now a part of the farm of one of our wealthy colonists.[363]

'We must go back, I s'pose,' said Sam. 'Yer all adrift here, so let's be off.' As the night closes over the scene, so our story draws to an end.

From the sandhills a native warrior is standing gazing o'er the ocean. The sun throws a glare across wave and hill, and then sinks behind a wall of dense cloud and disappears within the deepest shades. Anon, and the sea also becomes swallowed up in advancing blackness.[364]

A speck of white flickers in the thickening gloom – it is the last glimpse of Old Sam – and then it also vanishes for ever.

In the darkness, in the uncertainty, like their lives, wild and weird, so we leave them.

There, on their favourite element, over their vices, over their follies, their heroism and their barbarities, we draw the veil of night, and bid the 'Islanders' and their Island home farewell for ever.

Notes

for *The Kangaroo Islanders*

Chapter 1

1   Matthew Flinders gives the following account: '8 April [1802] ~ Before two in the afternoon we stretched eastward again; and at four, a white rock was reported from aloft to be seen ahead. On approaching nearer, it proved to be a ship standing towards us; and we cleared for action, in case of being attacked. The stranger was a heavy-looking ship, without any top-gallant masts up; and our colours being hoisted, she showed a French ensign, and afterwards an English Jack forward, as we did a white flag. At half past five, the land being then five miles distant to the north-eastward, I hove to; and learned, as the stranger passed to leeward with a free wind, that it was the French national ship *Le Géographe*, under the command of Captain Nicolas Baudin. We veered round as *Le Géographe* was passing, so as to keep our broadside to her, lest the flag of truce should be a deception; and having come to the wind on the other tack, a boat was hoisted out, and I went on board the French ship, which had also hove to.

2   Kangaroo Island has had a number of names. In 1843 the German missionary at Encounter Bay, H.E.A. Meyer, recorded *Kukakungar* as the Ramindjeri name. Norman Tindale claims the Kaurna called the island *Karta*, the word meaning 'lap' or female genitalia and also insists that *Kukakungar* has a similar meaning, suggesting that these were recent names for the island given because women had been abducted and taken there. Norman Tindale and B.G. Maegraith, 'Traces of an extinct Aboriginal population on Kangaroo Island' (*Records of the South Australian Museum* 4: 285). William Cawthorne also records the name *Kukakum* (A558/A4, State Library of South Australia). George Robinson records that the 'Port Lincoln woman' Kalloongoo told him that 'Kangaroo Island is called DIRK.I.YER.TUN.GER.YER.TER; WAT.ER.KER.TER, an island' (N.J.B. Plomley (ed.), *Weep in Silence: A history of the Flinders Island Aboriginal settlement* (with the Flinders Island Journal of George Augustus Robinson 1835–1839,

Hobert: Blubber Head Press, 1987: 445–6). See, however, Rob Amery, 'Kaurna in Tasmania: A case of mistaken identity', *Aboriginal History*, vol. 20, 1996: 24–50, who argues persuasively that DIRK.I.YER.TUN.GER.YER.TER means 'lived on the land'; that is, when Robinson asked Kalloongoo where she was from, she replied 'the mainland', meaning not Kangaroo Island. Amery has demonstrated that Kalloongoo was a Kaurna woman from the Yankalilla district. In 1802 Flinders named it *Kanguroo* Island, while Nicolas Baudin's preference was *Île Borda*, after the mathematician and astronomer Jean-Charles de Borda. Louis-Claude de Saulses de Freycinet called it *Île Decrès* after a French admiral of that name. The American sealing Captain Isaac Pendleton, who spent some months on the island in 1803, called the place 'Baudin's Island', which seems to have been preferred by the sealing and whaling fraternity, with 'Borda's Island' and 'Border's Land' also used until 1836, when Flinders's original name was restored by the colonists, but with changed spelling. See Anthony J. Brown, *Ill-starred Captains: Flinders and Baudin* (Adelaide: Crawford House Publishing, 2000: 333).

3   The question of who were the first Europeans in South Australian waters – and when – is still open. François Thijssen and Pieter Nuyts sailed the *Gulden Zeepaard* to St Francis and St Peter Islands off Ceduna in January 1627, but they turned around and sailed back west across the Bight. Lieutenant Grant on the *Lady Nelson* sailed through Bass Strait in 1800, and may have landed on Kangaroo Island. Perhaps it was Grant who left the enigmatic message cut into the bark of a gum tree seen and described by W.H. Leigh in 1836: 'This is the place for fat meat, 1800'. See W.H. Leigh, *Reconnoitering voyages and travels with adventures in the new colonies of South Australia, during the years 1836, 1837, 1838* (London: Smith, Elder & Co., 1839: 126). Cumpston notes the possibility that an American vessel the *Fairy* may have visited Kangaroo Island on a sealing expedition in 1793. He also devotes a chapter to the British whaler *Elligood* that was in King George's Sound in Western Australia in August 1800 and may have visited Kangaroo Island either in that year or the next. Flinders believed that wreckage he found on King Island in 1802 was from the *Elligood*. See J.S. Cumpston *Kangaroo Island 1800–1836* (3rd edn, Canberra: Roebuck Society, 1986: 3–5).

4   Flinders describes their discoveries of the kangaroo (he spells the word *kanguroo*) as follows: 'Neither smokes, nor other marks of inhabitants had as yet been perceived upon the southern land, although we had passed along seventy miles of its coast. It was too late to go on shore this evening; but every glass in the ship was pointed there, to see what could be discovered. Several black lumps, like rocks, were pretended to have been seen in motion by some of the young gentlemen, which caused the force of their imaginations to be much admired; next morning, however, on going towards the shore, a number of dark-brown kangaroos were seen feeding upon a grass plat by the side of the wood; and our landing gave them

no disturbance. I had with me a double-barrelled gun, fitted with a bayonet, and the gentlemen my companions had muskets. It would be difficult to guess how many kangaroos were seen; but I killed ten, and the rest of the party made up the number to thirty-one, taken on board in the course of the day; the least of them weighing sixty-nine, and the largest one hundred and twenty-five pounds. These kangaroos had much resemblance to the large species found in the forest lands of New South Wales; except that their colour was darker, and they were not wholly destitute of fat.

After this butchery, for the poor animals suffered themselves to be shot in the eyes with small shot, and in some cases to be knocked on the head with sticks, I scrambled with difficulty through the brush wood, and over fallen trees, to reach the higher land with the surveying instruments; but the thickness and height of the wood prevented anything else from being distinguished. There was little doubt, however, that this extensive piece of land was separated from the continent; for the extraordinary tameness of the kangaroos and the presence of seals upon the shore, concurred with the absence of all traces of men to show that it was not inhabited.

The whole ship's company was employed this afternoon, in skinning and cleaning the kangaroos; and a delightful regale they afforded, after four months privation from almost any fresh provisions. Half a hundred weight of heads, fore-quarters, and tails were stewed down into soup for dinner on this and the succeeding days; and as much steaks given, moreover, to both officers and men, as they could consume by day and by night. In gratitude for so seasonable a supply, I named this land Kangaroo Island.' The Kangaroo Island Grey Kangaroo (*Macropus fuliginosus fuliginosus*), an island subspecies of the Western Grey Kangaroo, was hunted in great numbers after 1802. See Robert W. Inns, Peter F. Aitken and John K. Ling, 'Mammals', *Natural History of Kangaroo Island* (eds M.J. Tyler, C.R. Twidale & J.K. Long, Adelaide: Royal Society of South Australia, 1979: 91).

5   G.D. Chapman *Kangaroo Island Shipwrecks* (Canberra: Roebuck Society, 1972) lists the shipwrecks around the shores of the island.

6   Flinders describes Pelican Lagoon as follows: 'On the 4th, I was accompanied by the naturalist in a boat expedition to the head of the large eastern cove of Nepean Bay; intending if possible to ascend a sandy eminence behind it, from which alone there was any hope of obtaining a view into the interior of the island, all the other hills being thickly covered with wood.

The entrance of the piece of water at the head of Nepean Bay is less than half a mile in width, and mostly shallow; but there is a channel sufficiently deep for all boats near the western shore. After turning two low islets near the east point, the water opens out, becomes deeper, and divides into two branches, each of two or three miles long. Boats can go to the head of the southern branch only at high water; the east branch appeared to be accessible at all times; but as a lead and line were neglected to be put into the boat, I had no opportunity of sounding. There are four small islands in the eastern branch; one of them is moderately high and woody, the others are grassy and lower; and upon two of these we found many young pelicans, unable to fly. Flocks of the old birds were sitting upon the beaches of the lagoon, and it appeared that the islands were their breeding places; not only so, but from the number of skeletons and bones there scattered, it should seem that they had for ages been selected for the closing scene of their existence. Certainly none more likely to be free from disturbance of every kind could have been chosen, than these islets in a hidden lagoon of an uninhabited island, situate upon an unknown coast near the antipodes of Europe; nor can anything be more consonant to the feelings, if pelicans have any, than quietly to resign their breath, whilst surrounded by their progeny, and in the same spot where they first drew it. Alas, for the pelicans! Their golden age is past; but it has much exceeded in duration that of man.

I named this piece of water Pelican Lagoon. It is also frequented by flocks of the pied shag, and by some ducks and gulls; and the shoals supplied us with a few oysters . . .'

7   James Montgomery, *The Pelican Island, and Other Poems* (London: Longman, Rees, Orme, Brown, and Green, 1828). His 'Preface' begins: 'The subject of 'The Pelican 'Island' was suggested by a passage in Captain Flinders's Voyage to Terra Australis'.

8   William Giles wrote to George Fife Angas from Kingscote, 6 March 1839 with the following revealing description: Kangaroo Island's 'interior is a vast mass of wood, which costs at least £25 per acre to grub up & clear away, before the Plough & spade can be used at all, from what I can see and hear, there are not five hundred acres in the whole Island, that are not more or less over-run with this deadly Foe to the Farmer & Grazier. I would not go a Mile into this dense mass of Underwood, on any account; the native women lead the Islanders through this bush for many Miles, but no one else would venture into the Interior.' (PRG 174/1/1377, State Library of South Australia).

9   Carroll describes 'Tasmanian whaleboats' as follows: '[they] followed the American pattern, double-ended and up to thirty-five feet long. Five or six feet at the stern was decked to provide storage and offer a firm support for the steersman. The boats had a graceful sheer – that is, their sides dipped smoothly from bow and stern towards the centre – with rowlocks for five or six pulling oars. At the stern, a housing was located for the long steering oar, and a little forward of the boat's centre was a socket for the mast to be stepped when required. . . . Constructed of strong light wood often no more than half an inch in thickness, the boats could be carried by their own crews.' Harry O'May adds that they 'were rigged with a spritsail and jib tanned red with wattle bark. The mainsail was like a tent at night, the sprit used as a pole . . . they carried a

fire-pot for cooking purposes'. They were ballasted with shingles. J.R. Carroll, *Harpoons to Harvest: The story of Charles and John Mills, Pioneers of Port Fairy* (Warrnambool: Warrnambool Institute Press, 1989: 53–4). Harry O'May, *Hobart River Craft* (Hobart: Government Printer, nd: 41).

10   One of the most famous of these soaks is at Hog Bay, Penneshaw, where Baudin's crew found water and left their famous inscription on what is now known as Frenchman's Rock, now covered with a dome. Baudin records the discovery of water there as follows: 'First thing in the morning on the 23rd [13 January 1803], I sent a boat off under the command of Midshipman Baudin. It was to examine the bay in which we had anchored the first time that we sighted this island and in which we had not remained because our anchor would not hold. As this bay is on the East side of the island, he was gone for the whole day, and on his return, I was informed that one could obtain a little water there by sinking wells. The men from the boat had collected some in this way and had found muddy ground under the shore, from which they had got some that was reasonably good'. Peron and Freycinet record that the place was named *Anse des Sources* (quoted Gill 1909: 127). The inscription on the rock reads: 'EXPEDI/TION DE DE/COUVERTE/PARLE COMMEND/ANI BAUDIN/SUR LE GEORAPHE 1803. Another well-known 'land-soak' can be found at Cape Rouge, on the northern side of the Bay of Shoals, which was used by sealers from 1803 onwards and then supplied the South Australian Company settlement at what is now known as Reeves Point, Kingscote, with drinking water between 1836 and 1838. The water was ferried across the bay at a cost of a half penny to one penny per bucket. 'Well Sites . . . Cape Rouge', *Heritage of Kangaroo Island* (Adelaide: Department of Environment and Planning, 1991).

11   Like a number of regions of South Australia, farmers on Kangaroo Island much benefited from post-war research that led to the adding of trace elements to soils deficient in cobalt and copper, the seeding of pastures with various clovers and regular top dressings with superphosphate.

12   In his journal entry for 23 March 1802, Flinders speculates about the possible causes of bushfires on Kangaroo Island, noting that 'there were no inhabitants upon the island, and that the natives of the continent did not visit it, was demonstrated, if not by the want of all signs of such a visit, yet by the tameness of the kangaroo, an animal which, on the continent, resembles the wild deer in timidity'. Baudin also records the tameness of the island kangaroos, noting that members of his crew had reported that they had 'seen such a large number of kangaroos of the big variety that they compared them to flocks of sheep, saying they were no wilder' [6 January 1803].

13   Among the first non-Indigenous visitors to Kangaroo Island were some of the runaway convicts Nicolas Baudin found on board the *Géographe* after leaving King Island for Kangaroo Island. Baudin certainly mentions 'two Englishmen'

sent ashore on Kangaroo Island to hunt kangaroos 'by lying await for them at night, as is their custom', and there are several other references to 'the hunters' (Nicolas Baudin, *The Journal of Post-Captain Nicolas Baudin, commander-in-chief of the corvettes* Geographe *and* Naturaliste – *assigned by order of the government to a voyage of discovery*, trans. Christine Cornell, Adelaide: Libraries Board of SA, 1974: 464). These shadowy figures thus were among the first (temporary?) European residents of South Australia (pers. com. Anthony J. Brown, December 2001). In May 1803 Baudin had written to Governor King naming eight stowaways detected at King Island: Charles Williams, George Viller, John Coleman, James Gibone, Mecquete Donnis, John Cavenaze, James Fline and John Honatré (*Historical Records of Australia*, series I, vol. iv, (Melbourne: Library Committee of the Commonwealth Parliament, 1915: 151). In spite of these beginnings, there is little evidence that the *majority* of the men who lived on Kangaroo Island between 1802 and 1836 were runaway convicts. While a minority were ticket-of-leave men, most were free men with naval, sealing, whaling and other nautical backgrounds. See the sealers' biographies in N.J.B. Plomley, *Friendly Mission: The Tasmanian Journals and Papers of George Augustus Robinson 1829–1834* (Hobart: Tasmanian Historical Research Association, 1966: 1021–1047).

14   In 1854 Captain John Hart recorded some of his experiences as a sealer in a letter to Charles La Trobe, including this influential representation of Islander life: 'These islanders were principally men who had left various sealing vessels when on their homeward voyage, the masters readily agreeing to an arrangement by which they secured for the next season all the skins obtained during their absence. This island-life had a peculiar charm for the sailors, being supplied from the ship with flour, tea, sugar, tobacco, and a few slops, and living generally in pairs on the shore of one of the little bays. They cultivated a small garden to supply them with potatoes, onions, and a small patch of barley for their poultry. They thus led an easy, independent life, as compared with that on board ship. They obtained wives from the mainland; these attended to the wallaby snares, caught fish, and made up the boat's crew when on a sealing excursion to the neighbouring rocks. At Kangaroo Island, there were some sixteen or eighteen of these men. On a certain day, once a year, they assembled from all parts of the island to meet the vessel in Nepean Bay, and dispose of their skins, getting a supply in return for the following year, the only money required being a sovereign or two for making earrings' (*Letters from Victorian Pioneers: being A Series of Papers on the Early Occupation of the Colony, the Aborigines, etc.*, ed. Thomas Bride, Melbourne: Public Library, 1898, new edn ed. C.E. Sayers, Melbourne: William Heinemann, 1969: 52). After a successful career as a whaler, sea captain, pastoralist and businessman, Hart entered parliament, became Chief Secretary, Treasurer and three times Premier of South Australia, and was knighted. In 1864 he was driving a coach

from Port Willunga to Port Elliott when the coach overturned, fatally injuring Reverend Ridgway William Newland, father of the novelist and politician Simpson Newland. Hart himself died in 1873. See Ruediger 1980: 84–5.

15 The following report about the supply of salt from Kangaroo Island appeared in the *Hobart Town Gazette*, 12 June 1826: 'A bay, called the Bay of Shoals on the north coast next to the main, is resorted to by the fishermen on account of a salt lagoon, or sea pool, which, when dried up after the rainy season, is filled with excellent salt to the depth of 5 or 6 inches. Near it is a lake of fresh water, both being situated about 2 miles from the beach, which distance the productions [salt] are carried on the back to the boats.' The Heritage Survey Item Identification Sheet for 'Salt Lagoon' has the following: '. . . the mining and export of salt was one of the earliest industries on the island, with many salt camps erected near salt lakes and lagoons. The site is most likely the "White Lagoon" from which salt was harvested in 1814 by Peter Dillon.' ('Salt Lagoon', Item reference no. 60, *Heritage of Kangaroo Island* 1991.) W.H. Leigh visited this lagoon in May 1837 and described it thus: 'The appearance of this lagoon is one level plain of sand, of a mile or a mile and a half in diameter. The white flaky salt which covers its surface, gives it a desolate and wintry appearance, as if it were covered in snow. From the sun's rays shining upon the crystals, it dazzles the eyes so that it is painful to look upon it. On a dull day one might fancy it was a hoar frost on a meadow at home; but this beautiful vision of the traveller is soon changed, if he raise his eye to its borders, and beheld the melancholy looking gum-trees that skirt it. This lagoon is caused by the oozing of the sea-water, which, being dried by the sun, produces the fine cottony salt and crystals that supply the island. Many vessels, in former times, touch here for the article, which was bartered by a few islanders who resided here – runaway convicts from Botany. Here these men lived their solitary Selkirk life. Their huts still remain by the borders of the lagoon, and the site of their garden was still visible' (Leigh 1839: 102). Ruediger suggests that in 1810 Kangaroo Island salt was worth £50 per ton (Ruediger 1980: 28), while G. Hull, Deputy Assistant Commissary General at Hobart Town, reported to Commissioner J.T. Bigge on 14 March 1820 that a decade later Kangaroo Island salt was worth £10 a ton. The salt was well regarded for curing seal and kangaroo skins. See Cumpston 1986: 57.

16 In 1826 the brig *Duke of York* under the command of Captain Thomas Whyte sailed from Hobart with troops from the 40th Regiment to Bass Strait to apprehend runaway convicts. The *Hobart Town Gazette*, 25 March 1826 reports the return of the *Duke of York* with a number of prisoners arrested on a number of Bass Strait islands. Even though Kangaroo Island is named as 'a constant resort of these unprincipled characters', it is not clear if Captain Whyte sailed as far west as Kangaroo Island. In 1825 Van Diemen's Land was separated from New South Wales and all the

islands of Bass Strait were ceded to the new colony, but Kangaroo Island was not included. It appears from this report that in 1826 some 200 people were living there: 60 women, 40 sealers and 100 children. After taking runaway convicts into custody, numbers of the women and children were taken to the mainland and released. In 1831 Captain George Sutherland wrote an influential (and controversial) report describing his 1819 visit to Kangaroo Island on the brig *Governor Macquarie*. Sutherland mentions the 1826 expedition to arrest runaways and reassert, he claims, the sovereignty of the administration *in Sydney*. He notes that 'when at last some of these marauders were taken off the island, by an expedition from New South Wales, these women were landed on the mainland with their children and dogs to procure a subsistence, not knowing how their own people might treat them, after so long an absence'. See Cumpston 1986: 51; Ruediger 1980: 83.

17   The term 'beyond the pale' means outside the limits, the other side of the fence. The phrase 'fence paling' still preserves a little of this meaning. In Ireland 'the pale' refers to those territories over which the British had jurisdiction after 1547. Cawthorne is not alone in deploying the term. See Stephen Murray-Smith's study of the Straitsmen of Bass Strait, 'Beyond the Pale: The Islander Community of Bass Strait in the 19th Century' (*Tasmanian Historical Research Association*, vol. 20, no. 4, December 1973: 167–200).

18   Perhaps Cawthorne had in mind this paragraph from the *Hobart Town Gazette*, 10 June 1826, which reminds us how remote the south coast of Australia was in the first couple of decades of the nineteenth century: 'It is however, a curse entailed upon the wicked, to be contented in no situation; and these rovers having again set sail, usually follow the coast . . . until they reach Kangaroo Island, in latitude 35 1/2. This Island, nearly 300 miles in circumference, is the *Ultima Thule*.'

19   The phrase 'bold buccaneers' appears as a quotation in the 1865–66 serial version of the novella. It may have been taken from the title of an 1817 poem by Isaac Pocock, 'Robinson Crusoe; or, the Bold Buccaneers'. It is also used in the poem variously called 'The Return of Abdul Abulbul Amir' or 'The Saga Of Abdul Ameer and Ivan Skivar', a popular recitation piece last century and the inspiration for one of the best-known 'dirty ditties' still told in certain disreputable circles today. The phrase also appears in a nautical song 'The Jolly, Jolly Roger'. When removing the inverted commas no doubt the 1926 editor did not wish to draw the reader's attention to the fact that Cawthorne seems to have known a few raunchy songs. The phrase also has another history. Writing to Colonial Secretary Campbell in Sydney, 28 September 1815, the sealing master William Stewart refers to 'banditti of Bush Rangers' inhabiting the islands along the southern coast of Australia (*Historical Records of Australia*, series III, vol. II, Melbourne: Library Committee of the Commonwealth Parliament, 1921: 575). The word 'buccaneer' was originally applied to Europeans living rough

in the West Indies who smoke-cured meat on a *boucan*. In the seventeenth and eighteenth centuries the buccaneers took to sea and preyed on Spanish colonies and shipping in and around the Caribbean.

Chapter 2

20 The murder of Captain George Meredith, which concludes this novel, occurred in 1836, more than decade *after* Cawthorne gave this date to his tale. In the *Observer*, 3 June 1865, Suppl. 1g, 'Our Correspondent in Kangaroo Island' reported from Hog Bay that 'An *Illustrated Melbourne Post* has found its way into the hands of some of our old islanders containing Mr. Cawthorne's story. They think it a queer yarn, but not very complimentary to them. They suggest the dates should be altered.' 1823 is, however, the year when George 'Fireball' Bates arrived on Kangaroo Island. If Cawthorne met Bates on one of his several trips to the island, then perhaps the date fixed itself in his mind. In a chapter he calls 'Sealing reaches its Climax', J.S. Cumpston records many ships visiting in the period 1823–24, including the *Alligator*, *Minerva*, *Water Mole*, *Perseverance*, *Nereus*, *Belinda*, *Eclipse*, *Liberty*, *Samuel* and the *Governor Brisbane*. See Cumpston 1986: 68–75. Carroll notes that the 'summer of 1820–21 . . . saw a final, self-destroying flurry of sealing, "the islands seething with activity". Fifteen to twenty British vessels and about thirty American were working the Islands' (J.R. Carroll, *Harpoons to Harvest: The story of Charles and John Mills, Pioneers of Port Fairy* (Warrnambool: Warrnambool Institute Press, 1989: 44). Cumpston quotes the *Hobart Town Gazette*, 10 December 1824: 'an extraordinary number of small Colonial craft are employed this season at the sealing islands in the Straits, where their enterprise has been rewarded with success unusually flattering' (Cumpston 1986: 74).

21 Cawthorne refers here to the establishment of the many Greek colonies around the shores of the Mediterranean from the ninth to the fifth centuries BC.

22 In 1585 Sir Walter Ralegh sent an expedition to settle what is now North Carolina, which was named Virginia after Queen Elizabeth I, the Virgin Queen. The survivors were taken back to Britain a year later by Sir Francis Drake.

23 Cawthorne may refer here to the large numbers of Germans who left the 'Varterland', most to the United States – some to South Australia – after the collapse of the Märzrevolution (the March Revolution) of 1848. Numbers peaked in 1854 when a quarter of a million Germans migrated. If this reference is to this mass movement of immigrants in that year, then the reference is very topical, in that there is some evidence that Cawthorne drafted his novella in that year.

24 A bay on the north-eastern corner of the island, facing the mainland and 14 km south-east of Penneshaw, named by Matthew Flinders, *Voyage to Terra Australis*, 7 April 1802: 'The small bay where we had anchored is called the Ante-chamber [to Back-Stairs passage]'. The Chapman River enters the sea at Antechamber Bay,

hence its older name, Creek Bay. Nathaniel Walles Thomas lived a mile upstream with Old Bet at a property called 'Freshfields'.

25   There are many comments about the large number of sharks, in the Bay of Shoals in particular. 'But of all fish of this island, the most remarkable is a species of shark, which attains 15 to 20 ft. [French] in length and which is very common in Nepean Bay. Day and night many of these monstrous animals were seen, surrounding the vessel in search of food. One of these formidable sharks having hooked itself, we had to reeve some tackle to haul it on board; it measured 5 metres [15 ft 6 in.], and weighed between 500 and 600 kilos [1100 to 1300 Eng. lbs]. Its hideous jaw was furnished with seven rows of teeth and measured when open, 74 centimetres (23 inches). There were, however, in the water sharks a great deal larger than this one' (quoted Thomas Gill, 'A Cruise in the S.S. "Governor Musgrave", *Proceedings of the Royal Geographical Society of Australasia, South Australian Branch*, Session 1907–8, vol. X, 1909, from vol. II, 'Voyage de Decouvertes aux Terres Australes' of MM. Peron and Freycinet: 133).

26   *Myliobatis australis*, the stingray, which can reach 120 cm and weigh more than 100 kg.

27   *Pagrus auratus*, now spelled snapper, unfortunately declining in numbers and never seen in schools of this size, more's the pity.

28   Named by Flinders, 23 March 1802, after John Jervis, Earl of St Vincent. Baudin named it *Cap de la Secheresse*, or Cape Barren. Freycinet named it *Cap D'Alembert*. The Ramindjeri called it *Parawa*, possibly meaning 'water'. There was a natural small boat harbour there before the present-day ferry terminal was built. See Plate XLV, 'Cape Jervis with Part of Kangaroo Island' for a contemporary illustration of the Cape (George Fife Angas, *Savage Life and Scenes in Australian and New Zealand*, 2 vols. London: Smith, Elder and Co. 1847).

29   Cawthorne probably means the ubiquitous seagull, or silver gull, *Larus novaehollandiae*.

30   *Cygnus atratus*, common in the sheltered waters along the north coast of Kangaroo Island and in Pelican Lagoon.

31   *Pelecanus conspicillatus*, very common on the island, as still to be seen as Cawthorne describes them here.

32   In 1822 Shelley was living with friends at the Bay of Lerici on the Italian Riviera. During a voyage from Leghorn to Lerici, his schooner *Ariel* sank and he drowned 8 July 1822. His body was washed ashore at Viareggio, where, in the presence of his friends Lord Byron and Leigh Hunt, he was cremated on the beach. His heart was given to his wife. Shelley was later buried in Rome.

33   That is, as an associate of the Greek philosopher Plato (c. 427–348 BC).

34   John Milton, *Paradise Lost*, Book IV, line 162: 'Sabean odours from the spicy shore/Of Araby the Blest'.

35 See the Introduction for Meredith's biography.

36 A special method for coiling rope on a deck so that it might run out freely, especially used in whaleboats.

37 The first of a number of references in the novella that present the nineteenth-century racist commonplace that Aboriginal Australians in general (and Tasmanian Aboriginal people in particular) might be seen as the 'missing link' in the evolutionary chain linking *Homo sapiens* with the great apes. See, for example, James Backhouse, *A Narrative of a Visit to the Australian Colonies* (London: Hamilton, Adams and Co., 1843: 165). In another place Cawthorne notes that 'The natives of Adelaide are very hairy, some of them covered from head to foot with tufts of hair an inch long. These tufts are close together especially on the shoulders, breasts, thighs, etc, in the ears as well as outside the hair is often more than an inch long. To see one of these hairy beings in perfect nudity up a tree resembles a large baboon – exactly – nothing can represent a Cape baboon than one of these natives, and especially if they are sitting on their haunches like a monkey' (Cawthorne 1991: 12). Here, however, Cawthorne suggests that from a distance the Islanders (European men and Aboriginal women) cannot be distinguished from each other, implying that the men have been 'detribalised'. See Lyndall Ryan, 'The Extinction of the Tasmanian Aborigines: Myth and reality', *Tasmanian Historical Research Association*, vol. 19, no. 2, June 1972: 61–77.

38 *The Australian Concise Oxford Dictionary* has 'A wooden disc at the top of the mast with holes for halyards'.

39 A nautical term for small lines or ropes fastened across a ship's shrouds like the rungs of a ladder.

40 Cawthorne here refers to the crucial role played by accurate clocks in determining longitude. See Dava Sobel's *Longitude: The true story of a lone genius who solved the greatest scientific problem of his time* (London: Fourth Estate, 1995).

41 The Mutton bird (*Puffinus tenuirostris* or short-tailed shearwater) is Australia's most abundant seabird. In 1798 Matthew Flinders recorded the following description of 'sooty petrels' on the wing one December morning: 'There was a stream from 50 to 80 yards in depth, and of three hundred yards, or more, in breadth; the birds were not scattered but flying as compactly as free movement of their wings seemd to allow; and during a full hour and a half, this stream of petrels continued to pass without interruption, at a rate little inferior to the swiftness of a pigeon. On the lowest computation, I think the number could not have been less than a hundred millions' (*Terra Australis: Matthew Flinders' Great Adventures in the Circumnavigation of Australia*, ed. by Tim Flannery [Melbourne: Text Publishing, 2000]: 23). The mutton bird migrates to southern Australia from the northern Pacific and nests on many islands in Bass Strait and along

the coast of Tasmania. It arrives by the end of September and lays one egg in nests in burrows lined with grass, usually on the same day, 21 November, each year. It is protected in all states except Tasmania, where there is a five-week season for commercial killing of mutton bird chicks, 27 March to 30 April, and a two-week season for recreational killing, supervised by the Tasmanian National Parks and Wildlife Service. The oily stomach contents are used in the making of pharmaceutical products (including a sun-burn lotion), the down collected for sleeping bags, the body fat used as an additive for stock food and the carcases are brined and smoked for eating, the final product something like red herring. See D.L. Serventy, 'Mutton-birding', in *Bass Strait: Australia's last frontier* (rev. edn, Sydney: ABC, 1987): 62–8. See also Mark Howard, 'Archdeacon Thomas Reiby's 1862 missionary voyage to the islands of Bass Strait,' *Tasmanian Historical Research Association Papers & Proceedings*, vol. 38, no. 2, 1991: 80. For two hundred years mutton birding on the Bass Strait islands has been associated with the Palawa people of Tasmania in particular, and traditional methods of catching, salting and drying the birds are still employed. Chappell Island in Bass Strait is where the most densely populated rookeries can still be found, although numbers have much declined since Flinders saw them flying in 1798. In South Australia (where they are protected) mutton birds nest on the Althorpes and on St Francis Island off Ceduna. W.H. Leigh observes in 1838 that 'it requires a desperate stomach to attack such an oily mess' (Leigh 1839: 109).

42 In the booklet containing manuscripts of several poems and a small glossary (A558/A4, State Library of South Australia), Cawthorne defines 'BARACOUTA' as: 'The same as the Snook of the Cape. – a species of Pike and of delicious eating.' No doubt he has in mind *Thyrsites atun*, caught from 'couta boats' for the 'fish'n'chips trade' but overfished by the late twentieth century. Another 'couta-like fish found in southern waters is the snook (*Sphyraena novaehollandiae*), often caught by amateur anglers.

43 Cawthorne spent much of the first decade of his life in the Cape Province, South Africa, before arriving in South Australia. As Cawthorne's diaries reveal, he obviously knew Dutch.

44 In Africaans 'ingele(g)de vis(ch)' is a kind of pickled fish, such as pickled herring: the 1926 book version of the novella misspells the word, which is given as *Engelede* in the 1865 serial version. I am grateful to Peter Mühlhaüsler for this suggestion. Cawthorne may also mean 'English Fillet' or smoked fish, well known on South Australian tables. These days Australian 'English fillet' is mostly sourced from South Africa.

45 *The Australian Concise Oxford Dictionary* has: 'a fore-and-aft rigged ship with two or more masts, the foremast being smaller than the other masts'. The *Oxford English Dictionary* has this version of the word's origins: 'When the first schooner

was being launched (at Gloucester, Mass., about 1713), a bystander exclaimed "Oh, how she scoons!" The builder, Capt. Andrew Robinson, replied, "A schooner let her be!"' '

46   There are many references to this practice. In his eightieth year, George 'Fireball' Bates told an *Advertiser* journalist 'strange stories of his experiences in the old days, when vessels used to call and deal with the Islanders and purchase from them at the expense of £10 or £12 property worth £1000. At various points along the coast the islanders had stores of skins of the seal, the wallaby, and the kangaroo, and the traders who dealt with them made the poor fellows drunk, and kept them so while in all the pride of sobriety they drove uncommonly hard bargains, and sold a needle or two or a few fishhooks for a sealskin worth £3. All these times the sealers had with them native women they had taken from Tasmania, or sometimes they stole a few from the mainland opposite to Kangaroo Island, and Mr Bates states that the traders who visited the island occasionally brought them a Tasmanian lubra for consideration' (*Advertiser*, 20 March 1880, suppl. 1b).

47   Ship's biscuit or hard tack, a kind of dried bread, mass-produced by the bakehouses of the Royal Navy's victualling yards. The normal allowance of biscuit in the navy was one pound for each man per day. See Anne Chotzinoff Grossman and Lisa Grossman Thomas, *Lobscouse and Spotted Dog: Which it's a gastronomic companion to the Aubrey/Maturin novels* (Foreword by Patrick O'Brian, New York: W.W. Norton & Company, 1997: 102–3).

48   Although the north coast of Kangaroo Island is generally sheltered from the prevailing sou-westerly winds, any north-west change can cause anxiety.

49   It may be that Cawthorne has the Irishman Bill Bryan in mind here, a sealer who lived for a number of years on Flinders Island (and possibly St Peter Island off Ceduna). Unlike most of the other Islanders, he does not seem to have arrived in South Australian waters via Van Diemen's Land or the Bass Strait islands: he is not named by G.A. Robinson (in Plomley 1966). Bryan lived with Sally (Sal, or Brown Sal) and Charlotte, both Nauo women from the Port Lincoln area, on Flinders Island, where they established a large garden and ran stock, selling vegetables and fresh meat to passing ships. Ruediger's version of the story notes that there were a number of children. When Bryan Sr died, Sal and Charlotte were taken to Western Australia by 'Black Jack' Williams, Charlotte returning after some time to live with sealers named Manson and Jackson on St Peter Island. Charlotte was the survivor of a whaleboat mishap: she managed to make it to shore and walked to the nearest settlement at Coffin Bay. Charlotte told her rescuers stories of the cruelties of the sealers. Sal seems then to have moved to Kangaroo Island, where she lived variously with Harry Smith and Bob Thompson. See Philip A. Clarke, 'The Aboriginal Presence on Kangaroo Island,

South Australia,' *History in Portraits: Biographies of nineteenth century South Australian Aboriginal people* (eds. Jane Simpson & Louise Hercus, Aboriginal history monograph 6, Sydney: Aboriginal History, 1998: 41) and Cherrie De Leiuen, 'The Power of Gender,' A thesis submitted in partial fulfillment of the BA (Hons) in Archaeology, Flinders University, 1998. Sal may well be a source for the character 'Brown Sal' introduced in Chapter 16 of this text. Bill Brien, the 'human enigma' referred to the Nathaniel Hailes's account, is Bryan's son with Charlotte. Their story seems to have been well known: the earliest account is Nathanial Hailes's, in the *Register*, 6 June 1878, reprinted as 'Bill Brien, a Human Enigma' in *Recollections: Nathaniel Hailes' adventurous life in colonial South Australia* (edited by Allan L. Peters, Adelaide: Wakefield Press, 1998: 129–34), which describes Bill Bryan Jr arriving in Port Lincoln in 1845. Hailes claims that they had lived on Flinders Island, not St Peter, but it is likely that Bryan and his extended family may have lived on more than one island. See also *The Australian*, 8 November 1902.

50   Numbers of sealers carried the nickname 'Long': Robinson records Long Jack Riddle and Long Tom Thomas (Plomley 1966: 1015, 1016).

51   Cawthorne may have based this detail on a story told by Captain John Hart about an Englishman who lived apart from his fellows on Thistle Island in the early 1830s: 'There was another class of men . . . who had escaped from Van Diemen's Land . . . [and who] lived generally on islands apart from the others . . . there was one man who had been unvisited for three years when I saw him on this [1831] trip. This man lay under the suspicion of having murdered his original companions. He had two wives, whose woolly heads clearly showed their Van Diemen's Land origin. Although so long without supplies, he had every comfort about him. A convenient stone house, good garden, small wheat and barley paddocks, with pigs, goats, and poultry, made him quite independent, save for tea and tobacco. He had collected 7,000 wallaby skins of a kind peculiar to this island, very small, fine-furred, and beautifully mottled in colour. I sold these in Sydney for the China market' (Hart 1854: 52).

52   An escaped convict from the penal settlements of Van Diemen's Land, which was renamed Tasmania, 1 January 1856, in an attempt to wipe away the convict stain.

53   An interesting word, believed to be 18th century in origin, meaning pretence, humbug, 'bullshit'; of convict origin. Often used by writers when attempting to represent nineteenth-century Indigenous or working class English.

54   One of the stories that circulated about the Islanders was that they were 'wreckers', although there is little evidence for the practice. While Ruediger records a story about a gang of sealers led by John Williams responsible for murdering an entire ship's crew on the west coast of South Australia (Ruediger 1980: 81), it is more likely Cawthorne heard reports of the loss of the *Britomart*

on Preservation Island in Bass Strait in 1840, which some writers assert was wrecked by a gang of sealers. James Munro was charged but not convicted with the possession of salvaged goods. See Stan Blyth, *The Britomart's Gold and Other Stories* (Prospect, Tas.: S. Blyth, 1990: 17–30).

55   Nat Thomas listed his profession as 'pilot' when applying for work as a light keeper at the Sturt Light, Cape Willoughby. He is also described as a 'pilot' in Captain John Hart's 1836 list of Kangaroo Island residents (Cumpston 1986: 140). Later he worked for Colonel William Light, helping survey the coastline in 1836 (Ruediger 1980: 53–4). In Cawthorne's 1853 travel piece Thomas is quoted as saying he 'went surveying under King', with Phillip Parker King, the 'king' of the Australian coast. No doubt Thomas learned how to use a sextant during his various stints in the Royal Navy and whaling.

56   This phrase may have a nautical meaning. 'Hook' and 'Crook' . . . [are] the names of headlands on either side of a bay north of Waterford, Ireland, referring to a captain's determination to make the haven of the bay in bad weather using one headland or the other as a guide. (http://alt-usage-english.org/excerpts/fxbyhook. html, accessed 11 November 2002).

57   This remark is footnoted in the 1865–66 serial version, with the remark 'The flesh of the opossum is very rank and offensive'. It is the only footnote given, anticipating the footnoting in such later Australian historical novels as Marcus Clarke's *His Natural Life* (1870) and Simpson Newland's *Paving the Way: a Romance of the Australian Bush* (1893).

Chapter 3

58   A breeze or 'puff' rippling across the surface of a calm sea.

59   The name of the passage between Cape Jervis and Kangaroo Island, named by Matthew Flinders as it offered a 'private entrance as it were, to the two gulphs; I named it Back-Stairs Passage. The small bay where we had anchored is called the Ante-chamber'. Flinders, *Voyage to Terra Australis*, 7 April 1802. It was named 'the dirty gutter' in some colonial accounts: see *Register*, 14 September 1895: 5e.

60   Cawthorne describes here a distinctive weather phenomenon in southern Australia: the hot wind from the north in summer that precedes a cooler sou'westerly change. Such weather conditions can be deemed 'red alert' when the threat of bushfire is extreme.

61   Cape Coutts is the headland at the northern end of Antechamber Bay.

62   Flinders noticed this phenomenon while sailing along the west coast of South Australia, naming Streaky Bay accordingly.

63   In a ms. held in the State Library of South Australia, Cawthorne records strange sound effects in the gulf waters: 'On the vast sand flats in the St. Vincent's Gulf – when the tide rises – one of the most singular and unearthly noises may be

heard – on a calm night, caused by the tide – running over these shoals – perhaps an inch requiring probably a couple of hours before it comes to that depth. (A558/A4, State Library of South Australia.)

64   A hot dry wind, usually carrying dust, coming over Brickfield Hill in Sydney. H. Hussey, *Colonial Life and Christian Experience* (Adelaide: Hussey & Gillingham, 1897: 55), calls the brickfielder 'a terror to the citizens of Adelaide in the early days of the Colony [and] generally occurred when a fierce hot wind had been blowing in the early part of the day, followed . . . by a change of wind from the west, just as cool as it had previously been hot.'

65   Nautical garb for hot climates, still worn by navy personnel. See Herman Melville, *White-Jacket; or, The World in a Man-of-War* (London: Richard Bentley, 1850).

66   Synonymous for Hell.

67   *The Shorter Oxford English Dictionary* has 'flag hoisted as a signal' dating from 1693.

68   This story about Australian summers was often told to 'new-chums' and is a stock device in colonial fiction.

69   Probably the common Welcome Swallow, *Hirundo neoxena*.

70   Salt and pepper shakers.

71   The *Shorter Oxford* has 'barney', a small cart used in underground mining. Does this refer to a deep mine somewhere, close enough to Hell? There is a Hacklebarney State Park in Morris County, New Jersey, USA.

72   Cawthorne may be referring here to a famous description of the Islanders in a journal by Major Lockyer, 'Expedition sent from Sydney in 1826 to found a settlement at King George's Sound, W.A.' in which he describes them as 'a complete set of pirates going from island to island along the southern coast of New Holland from Rottnest Island to Bass's Straits, having their chief resort or den at Kangaroo Island, making occasional descents on the main and carry off by force females, and no doubt when resisted carry their point by superior effect of the firearms with which they are armed with [sic], besides which each man has a large knife and a steel along by his side. Being left by vessels on these islands with sometimes a month or two provisions at most and do not call for them again for eight, ten, fourteen months and sometimes longer, from the nauseous food these people make use, and the miserable life they lead, it is no wonder they become actually savages. The great scene of villainy is at Kangaroo Island, where, to use the term of one of them, a great number of graves are to be seen, and where some desperate characters are, many of them runaways from Sydney and Van Dieman's [sic] Land.' Quoted H.P. Moore, 'Notes on the Early Settlers in South Australia Prior to 1836', *Proceedings of the Royal Geographical Society of Australasia, South Australian Branch*, Session 1923–24, vol. XXV, 1925: 125. See also *Australian*, 8 November 1902. By 1836 the Islanders seem to have done something about their public image; John Woodforde, surgeon on board Colonel William Light's *Rapid*,

notes that the colonists 'were given to understand that they were little better than pirates, but were agreeably surprised to find them a civil sort of men'. Diary entry 6 September 1836, 'Abstract of a voyage to South Australia in the surveying brig "Rapid" – Capt. Light – written by John Woodforde, M.R.S. & L.A.H., surgeon of the surveying party, August 19th 1836', (PRG 502/1/2, State Library of South Australia).

Chapter 4

73   The *Shorter Oxford Dictionary* has 'wooden bar, used as a lever or crow, especially on shipboard'.

74   Be prepared, from the days of muzzle-loading weapons, the gunpowder for which was carried in horns or other containers. Damp powder made the weapon useless.

75   Be prepared. Sailors on watch in the days of sail were charged to look to the weather side, into the wind, watching for signs of squalls.

76   In fact many ships traded with the Islanders between 1802 and 1836. J.S. Cumpston lists the names of many vessels and their crews. See J.S. Cumpston *Kangaroo Island 1800–1836* (3rd edn. Canberra: Roebuck Society, 1986).

77   Flinders's crew was the first to make hats from island marsupials: Flinders informed Baudin 'as a proof of the refreshments to be obtained at the large island opposite to it [Cape Jervis], pointed out the kangaroo-skin caps worn by my boat's crew; and told him the name I had affixed to the island in consequence', *Journal*, 8 April 1802.

78   Probably near to the spot where the Chapman River meets the sea.

79   A heavy sea usually caused by a distant storm, or a sea still running after heavy weather.

80   'Named by Matthew Flinders in 7 April 1802 after a village in Lincolnshire, which means 'at the willows". Geoffrey Manning, *Manning's Place Names of South Australia* (Adelaide: the Author, 1990: 336).

81   A British naval expression, originating on the West Indies station, for a bastard, an illegitimate child. On some ships women were allowed on board, and if children were born (the father unknown) then an entry of 'son of a gun' would be made in the ship's log.

82   A false or faulty pull at an oar, when the oar is not dug deep enough below the surface.

83   Cawthorne uses this spelling only once in *The Kangaroo Islanders*; elsewhere it is Porky, which might refer to a 'runaway whaler' called *Pirkey*, a man obviously known to Mary Seymour, the daughter of Nat Thomas and Old Bet. She told Herbert Basedow that (in the 1820s and early 1830s?) Pirkey was living on Kangaroo Island with a number of Aboriginal women who had been stolen from Cape Jervis. 'Quite a number of children are said to have been brought to the

world as a result of this importation, but according to Mrs. Seymour, they either died from natural causes or were knocked on the head directly they were born'. There does not seem to be any other published reference to Pirkey/Porky: he is not named by G.A. Robinson, and does not appear in any of Cumpston's shipping lists. Philip Clarke suggests without evidence that Porky is another name for Henry Wallen, which does not seem likely, given Cawthorne also has a character named 'Governor' Worley. It may be that here Porky is based on Henry 'Fireball' Bates, who Cawthorne probably met in Hog Bay on one of his visits, and who is still remembered for running pigs there. See Herbert Basedow, 'Relic of the lost Tasmanian race – obituary notice of Mary Seymour,' (*Man*, 81, (1914: 161).

84   Even after settlement Kangaroo Island wallaby skins seemed to have enjoyed quite a reputation as high-quality shoe leather. The Islanders made their own versions of colonial ugg boots, no doubt learning from their Indigenous women companions. The skin of a freshly killed wallaby was tied around the foot – fur in – and left on until it dried, after which the moccasin kept the shape of the foot. Wallaby skins were also sewn together using sinews from the animal's tail to form rugs which were very popular among the colonists to sleep or sit on. A rug of 40 skins was worth 40 shillings (*Observer*, 25 September 1844: 6).

85   'Dead on' means holding the boat exactly on line, at right angles to the wave. The word 'dead' is often used in nautical language: 'dead reckoning', 'dead ahead' and so on.

86   Cawthorne here refers to the characteristic hair of the Palawa, the Indigenous people of Tasmania, a signifying detail found in most colonial representations of these people.

87   Incas? The Dyaks are the Indigenous people of Borneo and Sarawak, rumoured in the nineteenth century to be headhunters. 'Covy' is convict slang for cove, fellow or bloke, possibly from the Romany *kova* for thing or person, according to *The Australian Concise Oxford Dictionary*.

88   This suggests that Cawthorne had access to a copy of *Evidence respecting the Soil, Climate and production of the South Coast of Australia*, a document prepared for the committee formed in London for the purpose of establishing a colony in South Australia. Captain George Sutherland of the brig *Governor Macquarie* had visited Kangaroo Island on a salt and seal-skin buying voyage in 1819. In 1831 he reported to the committee about Kangaroo Island in a well-known paragraph about the Islanders: 'There are no harbours on the south side of the Island, but in fine weather a ship may anchor for a few hours in any place along the coast, but must always he ready to slip in case of the appearance of bad weather, It was the case with me at the south-west side of the Island, There are no natives on the Island; several Europeans assembled there; some who have run from ships that traded for salt; others from Sydney and Van Diemen's Land, who were prisoners of the Crown.

These gangs joined after a lapse of time, and became the terror of ships going to the Island for salt, etc., being little better than pirates. They are complete savages, living in bark huts like the natives, not cultivating anything, but living entirely on kangaroos, emus, and small porcupines, and getting spirits and tobacco in barter for the skins which they lay up during the sealing season. They dress in kangaroo skins without linen, and wear sandals made of sealskins. *They smell like foxes*, They have carried their daring acts to extreme, venturing on the mainland in their boats, and seizing on the natives, particularly the women, and keeping them in a state of slavery, cruelly beating them on every trifling occasion; and when at last some of the marauders were taken off the island by an expedition from New South Wales, these women were landed on the main with their children and dogs to procure a subsistence, not knowing how their own people might treat them after a long absence. There are a few even still on the island, whom it would be desirable to have removed, if a permanent settlement were established in the neighbourhood.' Sutherland's report is given in *South Australia Outline of the plan of a proposed colony to be founded on the south coast of Australia, with an account of the soil, climate, rivers &c. with maps 1834* (Hampstead Gardens, SA: Austaprint, 1978: 50–1). My emphasis.

89   The first of many references to Defoe's *Robinson Crusoe* scattered through the novella. Leigh 1839 may well have been a source for Cawthorne's *The Kangaroo Islanders*. One of the first books published about the new colony, it contains a vivid representation of meetings with a number of the Islanders, and the only known visual representation of the Islanders and their 'native wives'. Chapter 13 describes an 'Expedition into the Interior', when Leigh and a friend set off to meet 'Governor Wallen', who is described as 'the august Robinson Crusoe (an excellent personification)' (126) on his '"Island home," his three wives, his two friends – man Fridays, his pigs, his some hundred and odd fowls' (124). In his journal Captain Robert Morgan from the immigrant ship *Duke of York*, also recorded meeting Wallen: 'I saw a man some what like when a boy I have seen Robinson cruso with long hair and beard a stick in his hand and verry little apperil' (Morgan's spelling, 2 August 1836, 'Journal of the *Duke of York*, 25 February 1836 – 10 February 1838', Mitchell Library A270: 36).

90   Mythical water monster, *bunib*, from the Wemba-wemba language from NW Victoria/SW New South Wales. Appended to a manuscript copy of three poems by William Cawthorne held in the State Library of South Australia (A558/A4) are several pages of definitions, including one of the bunyip. See Steve Hemming, 'The Mulgewongk, a Water Monster or "Bunyip" of the Lower Murray River region of South Australia,' *Journal of the Anthropological Society of South Australia*, vol. 23, no. 1, 1985: 11–16. Some believe that seals swimming up rivers along the south coast may have inspired such story-telling.

91   A 'boomer' is a large, mature kangaroo.

92 The Kangaroo Thorn, *Acacia paradoxa*, well known to bushwalkers.

93 Probably the Black Tiger Snake, *Notechis ater niger*, very common on the island, or the Red-bellied Black Snake, *Pseudechis porphyricus*.

94 *Acacia paradoxa* again.

95 Cawthorne seems to be suggesting here that in the future gemstones will be found on Kangaroo Island. If so, this is a very early reference to such deposits, which were not worked until much later in the nineteenth century. Hallack records visiting the gem fields that were situated off the road from Penneshaw to Cape Willoughby, where 'claims are being worked by an Adelaide syndicate for tourmaline, with a possibility of diamonds and other precious stones' (E.H. Hallack, *Kangaroo Island: Adelaide sanatorium, with map and illustrations by 'a native'* (Adelaide: W.K. Thomas, 1905): 8, 42). There seems to be some confusion about when the gems were found, in that E.L. Bates claims that 'Green tourmalines were discovered under a yacka by George Cox in 1906 and proved the genuine article. Great excitement prevailed and many claims were pegged and some good stones procured, but the field soon gave out.' (E.L. Bates, 'History of East End of Kangaroo Island', *Kangaroo Island Past and Present: Being a short history of the oldest settlement in South Australia* (Adelaide: Kingscote Country Women's Association, 1951): 26). Cawthorne was very interested in mineralogy, as his friendship with (and biography of) Johannes Menge indicates. In December 1855, Cawthorne held an exhibition of 200 drawings and watercolours, 'all having a colonial interest attaching to them', together with collections of shells, fossils, minerals and precious stones at his Academy in Victoria Square.

96 To steal, according to the *Australian Concise Oxford Dictionary*. 'Flash' or convict slang.

97 Pejorative term for Indigenous women, possibly from a Tasmanian language, according to *The Australian Concise Oxford Dictionary*.

98 Kangaroo Island narrow-leafed mallee, *Eucalyptus cneorfolia*, common especially on the eastern end of the island.

99 Tea-tree, *Melaleuca acuminata*, very common around salt lakes. Numbers of commentators have described how the Islanders made a tea from the leaves (hence its name). The policeman Alexander Tolmer notes that '[t]hey all use it, by boiling the green leaves. It is not unpleasant, particularly with sugar and milk. It acts medicinally and purifies the blood'; (*Register*, 25 September 1844: 3e).

100 *The Shorter Oxford English Dictionary* has 'a bed made upon straw loosely disposed upon the floor', any makeshift bed.

101 It may be that Cawthorne has in mind his friend Johannes Menge's attempts to grow cabbages at Kingscote. W. H. Leigh describes 'Old Mr. M ——, the geologist, has been most indefatigable in his attempts to cultivate a few culinary vegetables [at Kingscote]. He has enclosed a small plot of sandy land, the best in the neighbourhood, and may be seen, with his German pipe in his mouth, toiling

at it from sunrise until nightfall. He showed me, on the 24th of April [1837], cabbages just sprung up; he shaded them, faddled with them, and went to look at them every hour; and this day, 30th June, they are grown to the enormous height of one inch and three quarters standard measure; so that, if they continue to flourish at the same ratio, they will be fit to be given to the pigs this day in four years!' (Leigh 1839: 113).

102 Slow down, calm down. 'When a sailing ship wishes to "heave to" or stop without using her anchor, the sails on the mainmast were trimmed so that the wind would be on the wrong side, working in opposition to the sails on the other two masts, thus causing the vessel's way to be checked. The manoeuvre was called "backing the main-yard" or "backing the main tops'l."' Stan Hugill, *Shanties from the Seven Seas: Shipboard work-songs and songs used as work-songs from the great days of sail* (London: Routledge & Kegan Paul, 1966): 591).

103 The *Shorter Oxford Dictionary* has early nineteenth century, US, large mosquito.

104 Cawthorne is here quoting figures about annual snake kills collected from his father at the Sturt Light at Cape Willoughby during his Christmas visit of 1853–54, as his travel piece makes clear ('Journal of a Trip to Kangaroo Island', *Observer*, 15 January 1853).

105 Cawthorne seems to have had something of a phobia about snakes, as this fanciful comment suggests.

106 Alex (or Alecs) Lookout, 10 km or so to the north-west of Antechamber Bay, is reputed to have been a whalers' lookout from the days of shore whaling before settlement in 1836. Who 'Alex' was is now not known.

107 There is circumstantial evidence that this character, Old Sam, is loosely based on Nathaniel Walles Thomas, one of the most famous of the Islanders. There are at least five stories about how 'Nat' Thomas arrived on Kangaroo Island: his own version of events as told to Cawthorne suggests that he remained behind on the island after absconding from an un-named sealing vessel. However, the Thomas family memory has Thomas and William Everett arriving in 1827 in a whale boat from Tasmania with two Tasmanian women, Sophie and Little Sal. Nunn quotes B.C. Mollison's Notes on the Thomas family from his ms. 'The Tasmanian Aborigines', which contains the story that Thomas was working as a pilot on the Derwent where he heard stories of 'Ultima Thule', absconding in the boat with James Everett and the women, landing first at Encounter Bay and then later settling at Antechamber Bay. See Jean M. Nunn, *This Southern Land: Kangaroo Island* (Kingswood, SA: the Author, 1989: 39). In an interview in the *Advertiser*, 27 December 1886, George 'Fireball' Bates claimed Thomas jumped ship in 1830 from the *Mary*, a vessel sent from Sydney to search for the Sturt expedition.

108 Nathaniel Thomas was known as a man of great physical strength. Ruediger quotes Harry Bates describing Thomas as an old man in his eighties using one

hand to force an unbroken colt back on its haunches and hold it there. See Ruediger 1980: 54.

109 *The Bible*, Genesis 27: 10–12: 'And Jacob said to Rebekah his mother, Behold, Esau my brother is a hairy man, and I am a smooth man', as we remember from Alan Bennett's vicar in a sketch 'Take a Pew' from *Beyond the Fringe*.

110 An intriguing detail which at first glance might support the belief that feral cats lived on the island before 1836, where they were hunted by an early nineteenth-century Dr John Warmsley. No doubt Cawthorne had the 'native cat' in mind, one of the carnivorous, long-tailed spotted marsupials of the genus *Dasyurus*, possibly *D. viverrinus* or *D. maculatus*, both extinct on the island today. Leigh describes shooting one of these animals that had been raiding their poultry: 'a large wild-cat, half as large again as the domestic one. He had a head resembling the tiger, amazingly long fangs, and was spotted upon a brown ground with raw umber, with a large bushy tail, resembling, in some degree, the lion's, having the bush at the end: though not a very large animal, it must inflict a frearful bite, as its incisive teeth were an inch long. They are very numerous [on Kangaroo Island]. On the last visit he paid us, he slew five fine chickens. Like the fox, he kills more than he wants, and sucks their blood. The fowls appear to be aware of his approach, as chanticleer and his harem crow most lustily – an unusual thing, unless they are disturbed' (Leigh 1839: 96–7).

111 The implication is, of course, that Old Sam is a runaway convict. There is no evidence that Thomas was ever a convict.

112 The mark of the convict, the 'broad arrow'.

113 See note 88.

114 Cawthorne may be referring here to a number of anecdotes about the impression Nat Thomas and other Islanders made on the colonists when they arrived on Kangaroo Island in 1836. 'One evening in September [1836] . . . Nat Thomas made his appearance in their camp, which was the pitched at Hog Bay River, and excitedly told his mate that a large ship crowded with people had anchored off Kingscote in Nepean Bay. This was the *John Pirie*, having on board the first instalment of the South Australian Company's immigrants. The next day at dawn Bates with his mate, three native women, and several dogs started off to welcome the newcomers, but were received with shouts of alarm and a general stampede of men, women, and children up the cliff from the beach. The two islanders – clothed in opossum skin shirts, and with coats, trousers, and boots made of the skin on the red kangaroo – were mistaken for savage inhabitants of the new country.' (*Advertiser* 27 December 1886: 6f). In a letter to the *Advertiser* (27 December 1886, 6f), Henry Alford also recalls the colonists' alarm when the Islanders (one of them Nat Thomas) appeared in their midst in their animal skin clothing and with their wives in tow. Mary Thomas also met Thomas later in 1836, recording this

impression in her diary: 'a resident on the Island many years but his appearance, I thought, was more like that of a savage than an Englishman. This man by some mischance fell overboard and as the tide was running strongly at the time, he was carried some distance from the vessel before assistance could be rendered, and although he could swim well enough, he was watched with considerable anxiety, on account of the sharks, which were known to be numerous – an oar, however, was thrown to him, on which he got astride, till the Boat reached him, and when he came again on the deck, he shook himself, as a dog does when just out of water and took no more notice of the matter'. (*The Diary and Letters of Mary Thomas 1836–1866*, ed. Evan Kyffin Thomas, Adelaide: Thomas, 1925: 45).

115 The speech of some of the Islanders attracted the attention of the colonists in 1836. Captain Robert Morgan noted that 'Governor' Wallen's companion, William Day, 'appeared to be a rough sailor though left of sea and had bing on the island about   years and had become quite natified his voice appeard to have lost his mother tongue as regards voice' (Morgan's spelling, 2 August 1836, 'Journal of the *Duke of York*, 25 February 1836–10 February 1838', Mitchell Library A270: 36).

116 *The Shorter Oxford Dictionary* has 'Thieves' slang. A dwelling-house . . . berth'.

117 From here on Cawthorne spells the name 'Porky'.

Chapter 5

118 W.H. Leigh records the following details about 'Governor' Henry Wallen's 'farm-house' on the Three Wells [Cygnet] River inland from Kingscote: 'we reached the wigwam . . . a square some ten feet long by five, the sides resembling the letter A, composed of the bark of a tree; the little fence in front of the same size as the interior, to "keep all vexatious intruders away," and render it snug.' Wallen's farm on the Cygnet River was later taken over by the South Australian Company and Wallen 'became a ruined outcast, and a wandering drunkard' (Leigh 1839: 123–4). A remarkable photograph is now held in the Penneshaw Maritime and Folk Museum on Kangaroo Island, representing a woman with six dogs in front of a wurlie. She is believed to be Mary Seymour, Betty Thomas's daughter. I am grateful to Keryn James for bringing this photograph to my attention.

119 The figure of a dozen Cawthorne uses here has some historical interest, in that it is clear that between 1802 and 1836 there were many Aboriginal women resident on Kangaroo Island, numbers of them originating from Tasmania. The true figures are impossible to calculate, but given that estimates of 500 Europeans have been made, then it is likely that as many as hundreds of Aboriginal women spent time on the island in the three decades in question.

120 Alexander Tolmer records the following about the mode of catching the wallaby: 'They get a new piece of canvass, with the threads of which they make a set of strings eighteen inches long, with a noose. The set is three hundred, being

the number required to make a profit. The wallabys [sic] have numerous established pathways through the scrub, in every part of the island, and across these the snares are placed, so that when the wallaby springs along the path, it is almost sure to be caught. These nooses the black women visit about day-break, and generally return loaded about nine or ten o'clock. Their masters skin the wallabys: the skins are then extended on sticks till they dry, and are afterwards put up in bundles, fifty in each . . . These [skins] are worth sixpence each in Adelaide [in 1844 and] . . . suit admirably for upper-leathers of shoes . . . They are also made into rugs and coats, by the Islanders, with sinews drawn from the tail of the wallaby. A rug of forty skins is worth forty shillings' (Alexander Tolmer, *Register*, 25 September 1844: 3e). In many early accounts the word is given as 'wallaba'.

121 This tiny glimpse of the children of the Islanders and their women is all too brief. Cawthorne may have met or heard about such characters as 'Black Harry' Wallen, son of 'Governor' Henry Wallen, who is mentioned as 'a native of Kangaroo Island' and a cabin-boy in 1839 on the *William* bound for Hobart in a vignette in H. Hussey's *Colonial Life and Christian Experience* (Adelaide: Hussey and Gillingham, 1897: 36–8). Harry Wallen was educated in Hobart and later went to sea as a whaler. He is named 'Henry Whalley' as a pall-bearer at the funeral of his ship-mate from the *Runnymede*, William Lanney (or Lanne, the last so-called 'full-blood' male Tasmanian), in Hobart in March 1869. Whalley died in the shipwreck of the *Bencleugh* at Macquarie Island in August 1877. See the appropriate years of B.C. Mollison & Coral Everitt, *A Chronology of Events Affecting Tasmanian Aboriginal People since Contact by Whites* (Hobart: University of Tasmania, 1977). See also Lyndall Ryan, *The Aboriginal Tasmanians* (2nd edn., Sydney: Allen & Unwin, 1996: 214–217), especially the appalling story of the desecration of Lanney's grave and the stealing of his body. Nathaniel Thomas and Old Bet had three children, the second of whom, Mary, Cawthorne obviously knew. Alexander Tolmer also met Mary, her brother and her sister in 1844, describing them as 'three very interesting little children, who combine the intelligence of the white with the activity of the native' (Alexander Tolmer, *Southern Australian*, 24 September 1844: 2c). The first child was born in 1830, a son, Lorne, also known as Sam. He joined a whaler at Antechamber Bay when he was 14, wrote to his family from Liverpool and was last heard of sailing for China. He never returned to the island. The second child was Mary Seymour, her birth at Wilson's River 13 September 1833 recorded in a birthday book now in the possession of the Golder family, direct descendents. Mary died 9 September 1913. The third child's name was Jenny, born 1839, who married Thomas Simpson, postmaster at Hog Bay. Norman Tindale interviewed Mary's son, the 80-year-old Joseph Seymour, in 1937, discovering that the family continued to use 'Hobart Town language' into the third generation, some fragments still surviving in 1937. See

Norman B. Tindale, 'Tasmanian Aborigines on Kangaroo Island, South Australia', *Records of the South Australian Museum*, vol. VI, 1937: 36. See also Basedow 1914: 161–2 and Rebe Taylor, *Unearthed: The Aboriginal Tasmanians of Kangaroo Island* (Adelaide: Wakefield Press, 2002), especially the section 'The Descendants'.

122 Dogs played a crucial role in the hunting of wallabies in the island economy. While details are scanty, it appears that these dogs were a mixed breed, with greyhound, staghound and wolfhound predominating. By 1860, decades after settlement, the two Aboriginal women still living on Kangaroo Island travelled the interior of the island with packs of dogs for company: 'They are very seldom seen by any of the white residents, as they are afraid to come near the settlements, having a large pack of dogs (14) with them. Should the lame black woman [Bumblefoot Sal] die first, what a horrid and miserable death the poor blind one [Suke] may expect' (*Observer*, 26 May 1860: 8b).

123 It is this combination of lifestyle qualities that fascinated the early arrivals. On the one hand there is the following disapproving and censorious report, published in the *Hobart Town Gazette*, 10 June 1826: '[Carrying water] as well as every other labour is performed by the native women whom these unprincipled men carry off from the main, and compel to hunt, work, and fish, and do every other menial service, while they themselves sit on the beach and smoke, drink, and sleep by turns, occasionally, perhaps, arousing to kill a young seal which is basking on the sunny beach. This food, though far from palatable, is all that their indolence will in general allow them to procure, and they sometimes salt it down for future store. It is much to be lamented that so debased a specimen of the Christian race as these men should be the first to give an impression to the natives [on the mainland], who are there very numerous and of a superior class to those here and in Sydney . . . When the fishing season for seals is over, these men, with the native women and their offspring, amounting to about 40, retire into a valley in the interior of the island, where they have a garden and some huts. One man called Abyssinia ['Abyssinia Jack', John Anderson] has led this life for fourteen years. Are then these men, thus strangers to religion, strangers to principle, among who rapine of every kind, and even murder is not infrequent, are they to be suffered to debase human nature? They are at present supported and encouraged by the Colonial vessels that visit them for the purpose of bartering their skins for rum. Many of them are armed, and in a short time it will not be safe even for a large vessel to go among them' (quoted Cumpston 1986: 85).

124 This remark makes sense of the earlier references to Hourang Houtangs. Cawthorne refers here to a popular belief (a nineteenth-century urban legend) that the ourang-outangs from what was then called Borneo in the East Indies abducted women. Edgar Allen Poe's 'The Murders in the Rue Morgue' (1841) contains such a representation of an ourang-outang.

125 At the end of his resources.

126 Reasonable circumstantial evidence that Old Sam is based on Nat Thomas. For
Cawthorne's impressions of first visiting Nat Thomas's farm 'Freshfields', see his
'Journal of a Trip to Kangaroo Island', (*Observer*, 15 January 1853). A number of
visitors to 'Freshfields' at Creek or Antechamber Bay recorded similar reactions.
Alexander Tolmer describes visiting in 1844 'an excellent farm, a good house
and dairy. He [Thomas] has a herd of 300 goats, and a great number of fowls'
(*Register*, 25 September 1844: 3d).

127 Probably originally from *Genesis*, suggesting the place of human beings in the
great chain of being. The phrase is often used ironically about Victorian men, and
about the empire-builders in particular.

128 See Keryn James, 'Wife or Slave? Australian Sealing Slavery,' in *Alas, for the
Pelicans! Flinders, Baudin and Beyond. Essays and Poems*, eds. Anne Chittleborough,
Gillian Dooley, Brenda Glover and Rick Hosking (Adelaide: Wakefield Press,
2002: 175–85). James argues that the Indigenous women on Kangaroo Island
in this period were (with one or two exceptions) treated little better than slaves.
Plomley 1966 makes it very clear that Robinson, the main source for much
of our information about the sealers, their women and their lifestyles in the
early decades of the nineteenth century, also regarded the women as the sealers'
chattels. Many dozens of them were bought and sold in the period 1800–40,
moving from man to man, island to island across southern Australia. However,
other commentators have argued recently that the women's possession of bush
and fishing skills meant that many of them were very highly valued by the men,
some (like Old Bet) enjoying a degree of both respect and independence that
makes the label 'slave' inappropriate. Cawthorne's representation of Old Bet in
particular in this novella clearly supports this more recent view.

129 Cawthorne suggests here that the Islanders were violent and they regularly
beat their Aboriginal companions, a detail in the novella supported by George
Robinson's views in his journals. Captain Robert Morgan records the following
telling anecdote that speaks volumes about the Islanders' attitudes to their
women: 'Mr. Stephens invited them [Wallen and Day] to come with their wives
to see him on Sunday and have a religious service but says the men to introduce
our wives was to be like introducing a dog to your presence' (2 August 1836,
'Journal of the *Duke of York*, 25 February 1836 – 10 February 1838', Mitchell
Library A270: 36).

130 Again, circumstantial evidence that Old Sam is based on Nathaniel Thomas,
whom Cawthorne represents as deliberate and slow-speaking in a letter to the
Register, 15 September 1856: 3d.

131 From the Malay *amok*, to rush about in a frenzy.

132 This suggests Cawthorne may have had access to W.H. Leigh's *Reconnoitering
voyages and travels with adventures in the new colonies of South Australia, during the*

years 1836, 1837, 1838 (London: Smith, Elder & Co., 1839: 104), which contains the only visual representation of the Islanders, an illustration that hardly distinguishes between men and women.

133 Most visitors to Kangaroo Island between 1802 and 1836 report that numbers of the Islanders grew small winter crops of wheat and barley. In 1836 an anonymous colonist recently arrived at the South Australian Company camp at Kingscote accompanied a couple of other men on a walk upstream along the banks of the 'Three Wells River' (now the Cygnet) to Henry Wallen's farm. The 'Governor' welcomed his guests with a leg of pork and 'some remarkably nice home-baked bread'. After they had eaten, 'Mr. W. begged we would excuse him while he laid down a "damper"; this is what they called their bread before it is baked, which they make in the following manner: – They mix some flour in a tub, and after well kneading it sprinkle some flour upon a cloth and form the dough into the shape of a cheese, about four inches thick and eight in diameter. Some dry flour is them rubbed over it, and it is ready for baking. The ashes of the wood fire are afterwards removed and the place made suitable to the size of the loaf; it is then put in and the ashes covered over it, where it remains for about an hour, when it is done. The ashes are then brushed off, and the loaf is as clean as if baked in an oven, and although no yeast is used it is sufficiently light' (quoted Moore 1925: 97).

134 The 1865–66 serial version has 'metempsychosis' here, the idea that after death the soul 'migrates' to a different body, perhaps even to a different species. It seems Cawthorne's Rigby's editor in 1926 decided 'metamorphosis' was actually what the writer meant.

135 The lay of rope describes the manner in which the wires in a strand or the strands in a rope are helically laid, or the distance measured parallel to the axis of the rope (or strand) in which a strand (or wire) makes one complete helical convolution about the core (or centre). In this connection, the lay is also referred to as 'lay length' or 'pitch.' Here a nautical expression, meaning to prepare. (http://www. hanford.gov/docs/rl9236/rl9236a.htm, accessed 25 May 2002).

136 'PARBUCKLE, a contrivance used by sailors to *lower* a cask or bale from any height, as the top of a wharf or key, into a boat or lighter, which lies along-side, being chiefly employed where there is no crane or tackle. It is formed by fastening the *bight* of a rope to a post, or ring, upon the wharf, and thence pulling the two parts of the rope under the two quarters of the cast, and bringing them back again over it; so that when the two lower parts remain firmly attached to the post, the two upper parts are gradually slackened together, and the barrel, or bale, suffered to roll easily downward to that place where it is received below. This method is also frequently used by masons, in lifting up or letting down large stones, when they are employed in building; and from them it has probably been adopted by seamen' (William Falconer's *Dictionary of the Marine*, https://www.gutenberg.org/

files/57705/57705-h/57705-h.htm, accessed 29 May 2019). Here the sense is to raise, bring up, organise.

137 'Governor' Henry Wallen. Cawthorne also uses this spelling in his 1853 travel piece, 'Journal of a Trip to Kangaroo Island' (*Observer*, 15 January 1853: 3d).

138 That is, drag the net.

139 The Short-nosed Bandicoot *Isoodon obesulus* is found on Kangaroo Island but rarely seen.

140 Perhaps Cawthorne had heard some of the stories about how naked Aboriginal men might be physically restrained. Tolmer records the following revealing detail about how the *male* suspects were controlled, in Alexander Tolmer, *Reminiscences of an Adventurous and Chequered Career at Home and at the Antipodes* (2 vols, London: Sampson Low, Marston, Searle, & Rivington, 1882): 'Then quickly, at a given signal we simultaneously rushed into the wurleys, each trooper seizing and firmly holding a black-fellow, which is no easy matter in his state of nudity, when he is as slippery as an eel, and is all the while yelling, struggling, and biting as a savage only can. If the captor is experienced, however, by adroitly adopting a peculiar but indescribable knack, the difficulty is much diminished (vol. 2: 101). John Wrathall Bull was obviously familiar with this method of restraining Aboriginal suspects, for he alludes discreetly to the practice seemingly pioneered by O'Halloran and Tolmer: 'I have the advantage of the use of the diary of Major O'Halloran during the time he was out in the Port Lincoln district to endeavour to *catch and hold* [Bull's emphasis] natives, naked and greasy'. (John Wrathal Bull, *Early experiences of life in South Australia and an extended colonial history*, (2nd edn. Adelaide, London: E.S. Wigg & Son; Sampson Low, Marston, Searle & Rivington, 1884: 298).

141 Make a move. *The Oxford English Dictionary* has an entry for 1867, Smyth's *Sailors' Word-Book*, 'to top one's boom' is to start off. This is an earlier usage.

142 Obviously a song. I have not been able to trace it, although the chorus 'Fol de rol de ray' is very similar to a whistling shanty called 'Fol-de-lol-day', an alternative title for 'The Girl in Portland Street', where the 'Fol-de-lol-day' is a whistle. Stan Hugill, *Shanties from the seven seas: shipboard work-songs and songs used as work-songs from the great days of sail*, (London: Routledge & Kegan Paul, 1961: 54). Hugill also notes it was a song often heard in the south of Britain, a tinkers' song.

143 Although Cawthorne usually represents the Islanders wearing hats made of animal skins, here he describes a canvas sailor's hat, 'in Nelson's day worn by both naval and merchant seamen. Shaped like a straw-hat and covered with tarred canvas it was an early form of sou'wester. "Tarpaulins" was a name used for both oilskins and naval seamen' (Hugill 1961: 598).

144 As early as 1815 there were official representations to the Colonial Government in Sydney about the status of Aboriginal women living with sealers to the islands

of the southern coastline. William Stewart wrote to Colonial Secretary Campbell 28 September 1815 that the sealers 'mostly obtain by force and keep as slaves or Negroes, hunting and foraging for them'. See *Historical Records of Australia* Series III, vol. II (Melbourne: Library Committee of the Commonwealth Parliament, 1921: 575). G.A. Robinson's journal records this: 'The aboriginal female Mary informed me that the sealers at the straits carry on a complete system of slavery; that they barter in exchange for women flour and potatoes; that she herself was bought off the black men for a bag of flour and potatoes; that they took her away by force, tied her hands and feet, and put her in the boat; that white man beat black woman with a rope. Fanny, who speaks English well and knows not a word of the aboriginal tongue, said there were fifty women at the straits and plenty of children; that the three women from Brune Island who were coercively taken away by a man named Baker, a man of colour, were at Kangaroo Island. The aboriginal female Fanny states that this slave traffic is very common at the straits, and that the women so bartered or sold are subjected to every hardship which their merciless tyrants can think of and that from the time their slavery commences they are habituated to all the fatiguing drudgery which their profitable trade imposes. Surely this is the African slave trade in miniature, and the voice of reason as well as humanity loudly calls for its abolition. This information is further confirmed by the man Baker, who was himself a sealer in Bass's Straits and had for a considerable length of time cohabited with the female Fanny. He was transported from Launceston to Hobart Town on a charge of having forcibly taken away three native women from Brune Island; but the charges not having been proved he was dismissed, although there was little doubt as to his guilt.' Elsewhere Robinson noted 17 November 1830 that: 'These miscreants the sealers ought to be forthwith removed. It is a disgrace that those wretched men should have been suffered so long to exist. To abolish the slave trade the government at home has expended millions; and that it should exist in this her colony is certainly improper and disgraceful. These men put the government at defiance' (Plomley 1966: 82, 279).

145 'And Jesus answering said, A certain man went down from Jerusalem to Jericho, and fell among thieves, which stripped him of his raiment, and wounded him, and departed, leaving him half dead' (*Bible*, Luke 10:30).

146 At Antechamber Bay (or Creek Bay as it was known to the Islanders) there is usually a considerable sand bar at the mouth of the Chapman River, necessitating quite a haul to move a five-tonne whaleboat into the security of the creek, which in the earlynineteenth century was navigable upstream for about a kilometre or so. Cawthorne certainly knew this: see his description of hauling Nat Thomas's boat over the sand in his 'Journal of a Trip to Kangaroo Island', (*Observer*, 15 January 1853: 3d – e).

147 He means 'will you call the police, and have us arrested?' 'Peelers' were originally

nicknames for members of the Irish constabulary, founded by Sir Robert Peel 1812–18, and later came to be used for English policemen.

148 Betty Thomas, variously known as Polecat, Old Bet and Black Bet, is perhaps the best-known of all the Tasmanian Indigenous women taken to Kangaroo Island. See the Introduction for more information about her.

149 Ruediger records an island legend that 'Governor' Henry Wallen was (for some time at least) a teetotaller – not Nat Thomas, whom I think Old Sam is based upon. This suggests that Cawthorne probably drew on stories told about a number of individuals when constructing individual characters in his novella. It seems Wallen took to the bottle in later life, and died in the Gresham Hotel in Adelaide, 21 May 1856, aged 71 years (Ruediger 1980: 43–5). There may also be a personal note here. As a young man Cawthorne was a strict teetotaller, and a member of various Temperance societies in Adelaide, although it seems form the evidence of travel pieces written later in the 1850s and 1860s he did drink occasionally, No doubt his motivation was disgust at his father's alcoholism, culminating in his father's sacking in 1862 as head light keeper at the Sturt Light, Cape Willoughby, for (among other things) being drunk on duty.

150 More circumstantial evidence that Old Sam is based on Nathaniel Thomas, who told Cawthorne he had run away to sea 'during the war'.

151 'The rail around the ship's poop, to which a piece of canvas called a weather-cloth was fastened, enabling the officer of the watch to have some sort of a 'lee' (Hugill 1966: 596).

152 If Old Sam is based on Nat Thomas, see an intriguing vignette in Bull's *Early Experiences of Life in South Australia* that reveals something of Nat's understanding of Indigenous culture. The passage represents a search by a party of colonists for missing horses in early 1837. 'Nat, a sealer from the island', led the party south along the coast to what seems to be the mouth of the Onkaparinga River where they came across a camp of people identified by Nat as 'Onkaparinga and Encounter Bay blacks'. He gave the impression to his companions that he was not willing to confront them, explaining that 'the black woman whom he had on the island belonged to one of these tribes, and he was aware that they were not pleased with her absence. He understood a few of their words, but thought it better for him to keep as much out of sight as possible' (Bull 1884: 32–3).

153 The first example in the novel where Cawthorne puts to use his knowledge of Indigenous (notably Kaurna) belief systems, gained from his time spent at the Native Location on the Torrens and elsewhere in the company of Indigenous people. In a note to his *The Legend of Kuperree; or, The Red Kangaroo* (1858), Cawthorne included the following note: 'No native retires to rest without some kind of precaution; their belief is, that evil spirits are busy, in the dark, to kill them. Fire is a sure guardian. The writer once met a native, many miles from his

camp, benighted; he carried a large fire-stick for protection'. For a full account of the ethnographical significance of Cawthorne's diaries and other writings, see Foster 1991.

Chapter 6

154 Cawthorne seems to have had in mind 'Freshfields', Nat Thomas's house at Antechamber Bay. Cawthorne visited this house on a number of occasions while travelling to the Sturt Light to see his father. 'The original four roomed cottage dates from about 1827. Although it was later extended and completely encircled by additions, the dwelling is an extremely rare, intact relic of that period of pre-colonial European contact' (*Heritage of Kangaroo Island* 1991: 8).

155 Cawthorne's reference here to domestic violence is entirely consistent with the anecdotal evidence collected by G.A. Robinson. His journal of 28 May 1831 records the sealer James Munro's stories as follows: 'Said that the greatest and most barbarous cruelties was practised by the sealers at Kangaroo Island towards the black women; that the sealers cut the flesh off the cheek of a black boy and made him eat it; that [the sealer John] Anderson told him that the sealers tied up a black woman to a tree and then cut the flesh off her thigh and cut her ears and made her eat it (this was because she had run away; the cause of their going away from the sealers was on account of the wanton cruelty which had been inflicted upon them); that when they sent the women after kangaroo, if they should happen to return with a small quantity they would tie them up to a tree and flog them, which treatment induced the women to take to the bush' (Plomley 1966: 357).

156 This remark got Cawthorne into some trouble. In the *Observer*, 3 June 1865, Suppl. 1g, 'Our Correspondent in Kangaroo Island' reported from Hog Bay that 'An *Illustrated Melbourne Post* has found its way into the hands of some of our old islanders containing Mr. Cawthorne's story. They think it a queer yarn, but not very complimentary to them. They suggest the dates should be altered. I dare say that when Mr. C. revisits the island he may find hospitality at a premium.'

157 'To "wear" means to pass the stern of the ship through the wind as opposed to "tacking" in which the bows pass through the wind (Hugill 1966: 597).

158 These days crayfishing, or even lobstering.

159 Perhaps Cawthorne had the vexed question of state borders in mind here; if so, he is referring to western Queensland. In 1844 John Stokes was the first European to survey the Gulf country, travelling 80 km inland to discover the 'Plains of Promise', the rich cattle-grazing the savannah between Burketown and Normanton. 'When Queensland separated from New South Wales in 1859, the new colony's western boundary was fixed at 141 degrees east longitude, an extension of South Australia's eastern boundary northwards to the Gulf of

Carpentaria. However, Queensland had its eyes on a potentially rich pastoral area, the 'Plains of Promise' bordering the Albert River, and the prospect of a deep water port at Sweer's Island in the Gulf. The explorer A.C. Gregory proposed that Queensland should push its boundary westward to midway along the shores of the Gulf, and that a new colony, 'Albert', be created to the west, with its capital on the Victoria River. Western Australia would have lost its northwest regions, and South Australia was annoyed at the thought of losing lands just explored by John McDouall Stuart.' If he is referring here to this region of what is now Queensland, then it is likely that this sentence was written in the 1860s rather than 1854. (http:// www.foundingdocs.gov.au/places/qld/qld3i.htm, accessed 1 June 2002).

160 *Halosarcia pergranulata*, very common succulent prostrate plant growing in country affected by salinity.

161 Cawthorne is alluding here again to Matthew Flinders's famous entry about Pelican Lagoon: 'Alas, for the Pelicans! See Note 6.

162 Cawthorne may refer here to the speculation about the human occupation of Kangaroo Island. It was not until the archaeological work of Norman Tindale, Alison Harvey and B.G. Maegraith in the 1920s and 1930s that the first systematic versions of the story of human occupation of the island were published. Cawthorne here refers to the nineteenth-century questioning of the Biblical insistence on Adam as the first man. By the 1850s and 1860s many scientists were examining the Biblical explanation for human origins by turning to archaeological evidence.

163 Bumblefoot Sal or Big Sal is an historical character, known as 'Bumblefoot' because she lost two toes while sleeping too close to a fire; W.H. Leigh insists one of her hands was also deformed from the same accident. A sister of Trukanini, Maggerlede was abducted by the sealer John 'Black' Baker from North Bruny Island, Tasmania, and taken to Kangaroo Island where she lived with a man named Hepthernet [James Everett?]. In 1825 she was taken from King Island to St Paul in the Indian Ocean by James Craig on the *Hunter* with four other Tasmanian women. A year later they were on the Isle of France (Mauritius), returning to Sydney on the *Orpheus* in 1827 before being repatriated to Launceston. According to one source she was back on Kangaroo Island living with William Cooper in 1831. A year or so later she was taken back to the islands of Bass Strait, where she became involved with (or was bought by?) George Meredith, travelling with him and George Brown in a whaleboat from Bass Strait back to Kangaroo Island, where they settled at Middle River. She may have been either a witness or even more directly involved in Meredith's murder in 1836: in 1844 she was named by the policeman Alexander Tolmer as a suspect. She was taken to Adelaide but later released because of insufficient evidence, although some sources claim she admitted her guilt. After 1836 Maggerlede lived with William Cooper when the

latter worked for Colonel William Light: she may have been one of the 'native women' mentioned by Light who cared for his garden at Rapid Bay. She then lived with George Brown when he worked at the whaling station at Encounter Bay, but when he abandoned her she moved back to Kangaroo Island. In her later years she roamed the island with her friend Suke. She died in a gully off to the east from the Middle River in 1874, the blind Suke trying to find her way back to Maggerlede's body by tracking with her feet. The site still called 'Sal's Gully' in the 1950s: her body was never found. In the 1930s Tindale interviewed islanders who remembered her as a 'fine-looking big black … her hair … wonderfully curly … dark skin and woolly hair'. See Leigh 1839: 146; *Observer*, 7 October 1871; 7b; *News*, 19 March 1932; Tindale 1937: 30; Plomley 1966: 246, 336, 981, 1011. Plomley 1966: 246, 336; Norman Tindale, 'Journal of Anthropological Researches on Kangaroo Island, South Australia 1930–1974 and additions', South Australian Museum, AA 338/1/32; See especially Brian Plomley and Kristen Anne Henley, *The Sealers of Bass Strait and the Cape Barren Island Community* (Hobart: Blubber Head Press, 1990: 16–7) and Clarke 1998: 34.

164 Numbers of sources make it clear Maggerlede was crippled by sleeping too close to a fire when drunk. In spite of such injuries, she was well known for her looks. See note 163.

165 Bumblefoot here makes a joke at the mate's expense: his skull is too thin, she says, so the sun can knock him down. The word 'lauty' (used twice in the novel) is meant to signify the English word 'plenty'. In his unpublished diary, his 'Literarium Diarium', entry 21 October 1843, Cawthorne records the words of an unnamed (Kaurna?) man drawing comparisons between Governors Gawler and Grey: 'Cockatoo man (former Governor) very good – long time ago came here – give lanty tuckout (feast) – lanty blanket – Lanty Bullocky (beef) – lanty sheepy (mutton) – lanty very good. This man (the present Governor) no good, give piccannini meat (and here he made a contemptuous face) piccanniny bullocky, piccanniny bread, piccanniny blanket, Gubnor Gay (Grey) no good, gubnor Gay bloody rogue!!' (quoted Foster 1991: 25, 27, 42, where the word is also spelled 'lanty').

166 Puss or Pussy is an historical character, probably a Ngarrindjeri woman from the mainland. George 'Fireball' Bates told the story of her abduction when interviewed by the *Advertiser* in 1886: 'the party of five [islanders] … crossed over to the mainland to undertake this *chasse aux femmes*. They landed at Cape Jervis and walked across country to Lake Alexandrina, having no small difficulty in eluding the natives, who were very numerous. Their method of capturing the women was simple. Waiting until the morning was well advanced, and the men were out hunting, they stole up under cover until close to the camp, when at a signal they rushed forward and secured their prizes before they had time to escape. They made four trips with this object at different times, securing one or two women each time

who, when captured, had their hands tied behind their backs, and were made to walk with the their captors in double quick time back to the boat. They were set at liberty on reaching Hog Bay, where they in most cases proved useful and willing slaves. One girl, whom Bates named "Puss", from her propensity to scratch the face of her owner when in a rage, lived for years afterwards at Hog Bay' (*Advertiser*, 27 December 1886: 6c–e). If Cawthorne did not meet her in person, he probably heard about her from Bates during his Christmas visit in 1852.

167 Colonel William Light, in a letter to the Colonization Commissioners dated 10 September 1836, written at anchor at Rapid Bay, Cape Jervis, notes that 'I have engaged one of the sealers from Kangaroo Island [William Cooper] with his two native wives [Doughboy and Sal], and find them very useful; the women are the hunters, and we have already been the better by their exertions, by the tail and hind quarters of an enormous kangaroo, which is fine food; and to those who are fond of ox-tail soup, I should recommend a trip to South Australia to eat kangaroo-tail soup, which, if made with all the skill that soups in England are, would as far surpass the ox as turtle does the French potage'. *Supplement to the First Report of the Directors of the South Australian Company* (London: William Johnstone, 1837: 23). W.H. Leigh also insists that wallaby tail makes 'a most delicious soup; and though myself no epicure, I must prefer it to oxtail' (Leigh 1839: 83). Here's an updated version of the old recipe, although these days most marsupials are fully protected: skin a kangaroo tail, wash well and joint. Soak the pieces in cold salted water for thirty minutes. Roll the tail pieces in seasoned flour. Then heat some butter and olive oil in a large pan and brown the floured pieces. Remove the tail pieces, and then fry several rashers of bacon, a sliced onion and 3 cloves of garlic until the onion is soft. Spoon out the onion, garlic and bacon and deglaze with a cup of red wine. Return the tail sections and onion, garlic and bacon to the pot. Add 2 sliced carrots, 2 sliced turnips, 2 chopped sticks celery, thyme, a bay leaf or two, sage and parsley, 6 cloves, 1 tablespoon sugar, the zest and juice of a lemon. Cover everything with water or beef stock. Cook gently for at least three hours.

168 The soup will be solid, sustaining fare, which will 'stick in your ribs'.

169 'Fully rigged, as a vessel; with all sails set; set on end or set right. Origin: French, *Autant* as much (as possible). Source: *Websters Dictionary*'. Charles Dickens's *Bleak House* (1852–3), Chapter 13, Esther's Narrative: 'The dear old Crippler!' said Mrs. Badger, shaking her head. 'She was a noble vessel. Trim, ship-shape, all a taunto, as Captain Swosser used to say. You must excuse me if I occasionally introduce a nautical expression; I was quite a sailor once.'

170 This realistic estimate of the diversity and utility of Kangaroo Island landscapes can be compared with these enthusiastic and revealing observations made by the colonist John Morphett in 1836: 'the eye is gratified with the sight of beautifully verdant and secluded valleys, well-watered and finely wooded plains, gently

undulating and rising towards the range of hills in the background. The heart of the emigrant is filled with joy in gazing on this long sought object of his wishes; and should he have travelled, he compares the scene before him with other countries favoured by nature, and rendered more valuable by art; and he feels that the beneficence of the Great Creator of all things has here furnished him with the means of [realizing] his most cherished schemes for worldly [aggrandizement] or personal comfort'. (John Morphett, *South Australia: Latest Information from this colony contained in a letter written by Mr. Morphett dated Nov. 25th, 1836*, (Facsimile editions no. 5, Adelaide: Libraries Board of South Australia: 6).

171 Cawthorne is obviously attempting to suggest the whaling experience of his characters.

172 As it still is, through the early months of summer.

Chapter 7

173 *The Australian Concise Oxford Dictionary* has '18th c. from an erroneous association with weigh anchor'.

174 The Galapagos islands, off Chile, and incidentally where Alexander Selkirk was marooned, the original for Defoe's *Robinson Crusoe*.

175 'Some sails, mainly the fore and aft ones, need a long spar to spread their foot, a boom. When the boom is topped the vessel is ready to start. Also, to die – when a person starts on the long voyage with no return. (http://www.julianstockwin.com/glossary.htm, accessed 30 June 2002).

176 W.H. Leigh records: 'a native word signifying "ahoy!"' (Leigh 1839: 85). The *Australian Concise Oxford Dictionary* notes that word entered English from the Dharuk *guuu-wi* from the earliest years of the settlement at Sydney Cove.

177 Cawthorne speaks here with the authority of personal experience. His diary records a number of close-run things in small boats. See *South Australian*, 1 January 1847, 'Port Gawler', describing a miserable Christmas trip in a dingy that ended ignominiously on the sand flats to the north of Adelaide. In the following year he nearly drowned when knocked overboard by the boom when his boat gybed in a squall off Glenelg. See the diary entry 10 December 1848. The entry 8 January 1854 has 'Just returned from K.Isld. – with my usual luck – nearly got drowned – wife and child with me – besides 3 boarders – & Mrs Fooks – dreadful with thrunderstorms – nearly all wrecked in sight of the Light House – fearful situation . . . right glad to get back.'

178 Proverbial: Thomas Tusser (c. 1515–80) 'Dry sun, dry wind;/Safe bind, safe find', referring to taking care with hanging out the washing in an age where stealing of clothes was commonplace. Shakespeare has 'Fast bind, fast find', *The Merchant of Venice* 2.6. 53, from the proverbial for keeping goods secure so that they might be found quickly.

179 Satan's attendants. Sometimes used for children in the nineteenth century, here used almost as an expletive.

180 From Charles Dickens' *Oliver Twist* (1837), the young thief 'the Artful Dodger', Jack Dawkins, pickpocket in Fagin's gang.

181 Although he does not use the term here, in a booklet containing manuscripts of several poems and a small glossary (A558/A4, State Library of South Australia), Cawthorne records the following definition of 'gulches': 'the sealers in Kangaroo Island call the enormous fissures of the rocky coast – gulches – or GULCHWAYS – a word probably corrupted from the Spanish'.

182 Bush Stone-curlew, *Burhinus magnirostris*. A ground-nesting bird with a very distinctive mournful call, often heard while camping at night on the island. In the 'Notes, ETC.' appended to the second edition of Cawthorne's *The Legend of Kuperree; or, The Red Kangaroo* (Adelaide: Alfred Cawthorne, 1858), Cawthorne notes that the Curlew (or *Kokunya* (Port Lincoln language?) 'is said at times to be inhabited with the spirit of death. If a native dreams of his visitation, he dies.'

183 The brushtail possum: *Trichosurus vulpecula*, abundant on Kangaroo Island and the mainland, now well adapted to living with humans in suburbia. A pest in New Zealand.

184 Appended to a manuscript copy of three poems by William Cawthorne held in the State Library of South Australia (A558/A4) are several pages of definitions, including this one of a 'mawpawk': 'A species of turtle-dove. It is named for the cry – 'Maw Pawk' – sounds very pleasing in a summer's night – in some copse of wood.'

185 Mungo Park (1771–1806), the archetypal colonial adventurer. Born in Scotland, he became ship's surgeon in the merchant marine. He was a friend of Sir Walter Scott and is remembered for having explored the course of the Niger. His *Travels in the Interior of Africa* (1799) is one of the great travel books. He died in Boussa in Africa.

Chapter 8

186 Old Sam's speech is reminiscent of the words of a sailor who was very familiar with South Australian waters: Joseph Conrad, master of the *Otago*, which sailed on a regular run between Liverpool and Port Adelaide in the 1880s. Conrad left the sea in 1894. In *Heart of Darkness* the narrator Marlow interrupts his narrative on one occasion to deliver a reminder to his listeners: 'Here you all are, each moored with two good addresses, like a hulk with two anchors, a butcher round one corner, a policeman round another, excellent appetites, and temperature normal – you hear – normal from year's end to year's end.' (Joseph Conrad, *Heart of Darkness* [1902] http://pd.sparknotes.com/conrad/heartofdarkness, accessed 25 May 2002).

187 The *Shorter Oxford Dictionary* gives 1751 for the first use of this nautical slang for the bottom of the sea.

188 Meaning, this land defies accurate recording, in a ship's logbook.

189 Chewing tobacco.

190 White Ibis, (*Threskiornis aethiopica*), common on Kangaroo Island.

191 A phrase used by Washington Irving in 'Rip Van Winkle', 1820.

192 'Flash' language, convict usage for strange.

193 Hugh Ford lists the Australian Bittern (*Botaurus poiciloptilus*) as a vagrant on Kangaroo Island. See Hugh Ford, 'Birds', in *Natural History of Kangaroo Island*, eds. M.J. Tyler, C.R. Twidale & J.K. Ling (Adelaide: Royal Society of South Australia, 1979: 104).

194 W.A. Deacon, in a 1836 letter to G.F. Angas, describes sharks in the Bay of Shoals '17 [feet] long which come within 20 yards of shore'. (PRG 174/1/467, State Library of South Australia). It seems yarning about the size of sharks was as much feature of colonial life in the 1830s as it is today. Jane Isabella Watts relates one such story with a gustro Baron Munchausen would have been proud of: 'the captain of a whaler, as he was being rowed ashore [at Nepean Bay] came across one of these leviathans of the deep which had the effrontery to seize hold of the boat he was in, shaking and crushing it between his teeth. The party, managing however to escape from its grasp, immediately obtained another, set off in pursuit, and after a fierce struggle the creature was despatched and towed ashore. It was found to measure thirty-five feet in length, and on its head being cut off, so vast was its size that *three full-grown men* stood side by side within its enormous jaws, and the liver produced sixty gallons of oil'. (Jane Isabella Watts, *Family Life in South Australia Fifty-three years ago* Adelaide: W.K. Thomas, 1890: 55).

Chapter 9

195 Much-quoted aphorism, from Alexander Pope's 'An Essay on Man in Four Epistles', Epistle Two, lines 133–8.

196 A term applied to any 'South Asian' sailors, originally Bengali seamen employed by the East India Company.

197 The Kru are a West African people from the Liberian coast, sometimes employed on Royal Navy vessels in the nineteenth century.

198 The Malabar coast is the western coast of south India. The Coromandel coast is the eastern.

199 Usually Kanakas, Pacific Islanders, the word originally from Hawaii.

200 Cawthorne refers here to attempts made by George Bates, Nat Thomas (Old Sam in this novella) and Thomas's wife Bet to find the two passengers missing from the *Africaine*. In October 1836 a party of colonists had left their becalmed ship intending to walk from the western end of Kangaroo Island to Nepean Bay. The group included a surgeon, Dr John Slater, and E.W. Osborne, an apprentice printer, and four others: Fisher, Nantes, Warner and Baggs. They landed at Harvey's

Return and attempted to walk overland to the South Australian Company camp at Kingscote. After an eight-day ordeal, in which they trekked for miles through the scrub, five survived, but Osborne and Slater were left behind by the others somewhere near Murray's Lagoon, too distressed to continue: their remains were not found until much later. Their deaths rocked the small immigrant community, making it apparent that South Australia was not the benign paradise promised by the propagandists for the Company. Mary Thomas describes them as 'ramblers' in her diary! Bet spent 16 days searching for the lost men, following their footsteps to Flour Cask Bay and beyond into stony country near Salt Lake when the tracks disappeared (*Register*, 8 July 1837). She and Nat earned £6/10/- for their efforts. In 1858 skeletal remains were found 20 miles inland from Cape Borda, and further skeleton, a flask and a knife marked 'E.O' were found in 1888. See Alfred Austin Lendon, 'Kangaroo Island: The Tragedy of Dr Slater and Mr Osborne. A Story of Ninety Years Ago.' (*Proceedings of the Royal Geographical Society of Australasia (South Australian Branch)*, vol. XXVI, 1926: 67–84). Cawthorne may also have in mind the death of Joseph Pennington, after whom the bay south of Pelican Lagoon on the south coast is named. Cawthorne names him in a manuscript poem held in the State Library of South Australia (Cawthorne Papers, PRG 489/7): he obviously knew the story of his disappearance. Hallack describes him as 'Associate to the late Chief Justice Hanson' (Hallack 1905: 39). Geoffrey Manning quotes the following account of Pennington's death, 'It was named by Captain Bloomfield Douglas in December 1857 after Joseph Pennington who was lost in the scrub in the vicinity of Prospect Hill (Mount Thisby). 'On 28 December 1855 the steamer *Young Australian* started from Port Adelaide on an excursion to Kangaroo Island, Mr Pennington, Chief Clerk in R.D. Hanson's office, being one of the party. The ship went down American River as far as Rabbit Island. when Messrs Heath, Andrews, R. Stuckey, Prankerd, Carruthers, James [sic] Pennington and F.R. Simpson, took the ship's boat and rowed some distance further on and landed at Mount Tisby [sic], now called Prospect Hill, and walked across to Osmanli Beach. 'After a short time Pennington remained behind on a sandhill. The others, who were on ahead, waved to him thinking he was tired and would wait their return: that was the last ever seen of him. On their return a few hours afterwards, they made a search for him, in vain, on Sunday, Monday and Tuesday, including Buick, a settler on the Island and a native woman. They did find his tracks, but lost them in the sand: the search was continued long after the party returned to Adelaide' (Manning 1990: 245). Hallack records that skeletal remains and buttons were found at White Lagoon years after his disappearance, the buttons used to identify the remains as those of Pennington (Hallack 1905: 40). See also *Observer*, 26 January 1856, Supplement 4f.

201 Periwinkles, *Littorina Turbo undulatus*, small edible marine gastropod (sea snail) found along rocky and reefy shorelines.

202 *The Australian Concise Oxford Dictionary* has 'archaic a bag for carrying food etc. on a journey'.

203 The 1865–66 serial version has 'Shaw' for the first reference, 'Straw' after. William Shaw was an early visitor to Kangaroo Island, sailing on the *Rosetta* in 1816 which took 2000 skins and 50 tons of salt back to Sydney for Jonathan Griffiths. See Cumpston 1986: 42, 43.

204 Charles Napier records the following instructions for preparing salt beef for eating: 'Let it soak in cold water for forty-eight hours, changing the water several times. Then put it into cold water, coming to the boil slowly, and when it boils, throw out the water and again put it into cold water to boil slowly, taking care never to let it boil fast. It should remain at this simmer for as many quarters of an hour as there are pounds of weight in the piece of beef. For ship-use the brisket part is best.' (Charles James Napier, *Colonisation: Particularly in South Australia, with some remarks on Small Farms and Over-Population*, London: 1835; New York: Augustus M. Kelly, 1969: 225).

205 A signal flag.

206 'Flash' language, convict usage for fun.

Chapter 10

207 Get an opportunity, perhaps from the Dutch *slenter* 'knavery', trick', according to *The Australian Concise Oxford Dictionary*.

208 Expeditions to steal Aboriginal women, after the Rape of the Sabine women. The Sabines lived in the central Apennines in ancient Italy. According to the legend, there were no women in Rome when Romulus founded the city, so he asked nearby cities to allow Roman men to choose wives from among their women. When the neighbours refused, Romulus invited them to attend a festival, and during the games, the Romans abducted the young Sabine women.

209 In January 1819, John Bigge was commissioned by the British Government to examine all the laws, regulations and usages of the New South Wales colonies. He conducted a number of hearings in Sydney and Hobart, including several into the sealing industry. On 3 May 1820 he interviewed Captain James Kelly, then Harbour Master at Hobart Town, who gave him many insights into the industry, including the information that sealing was conducted in summer. See Cumpston 1986: 56. Mutton-birding was an autumn activity, while in the winter months the Islanders moved inland to escape the gales and the cold and trapped wallabies. These seasonal patterns follow those of the Indigenous people of the southern Australian coastlines, the 'white sand' peoples.

210 Proverbial. 'The poorest Bedouin has his domesticated steed, which shares with him and his wife and children the shelter of his humble tent, his caresses, and his scanty fare'. (H.D. Richardson, *The Horse*. London, 1852, http://www. geocities.com/Heartland/Estates/3095/ConnTributes51.html, accessed 2 March

2003). The Bedouin believe that the Arab horse was created from a handful of the southern wind.

211 An interesting detail about Meredith, in that the historical character does not seem to have been such a remarkable seaman, losing at least two and possibly three boats. J.S. Cumpston records the wreck of his father's 'beautiful large schooner the *Black Swan* lost off the west coast of King Island' in 1830, and then in 1833 the *Defiance*, lost 'on a sealing voyage fifteen miles below Twofold Bay' (Cumpston 1986: 131). Then there is the mystery of the *Independent*, the Meredith family vessel involved in the raid on Point Nepean in Port Phillip Bay with Meredith aboard, which his gang did not sail on to Kangaroo Island, coasting instead in a whaleboat. Was the *Independent* also wrecked somewhere in Bass Strait in 1834?

212 The early years of sealing must have been very lucrative for all concerned. The American sealing vessel, the *Union*, captained by Captain Pendleton returned to Sydney from Kangaroo Island in 1804 with 12,000 skins. The *Independence*, a 35-ton schooner built on the western shore of American River in 1803 reached Sydney in June 1804 with 14,000 skins that were sold to the merchant Simeon Lord. See Cumpston 1986: 26–9.

213 Did Cawthorne have George 'Fireball' Bates in mind? Or is 'the Doctor' based on George Horman, a sealer named by Basedow in his obituary of Mary Seymour, Nat Thomas's and Old Bet's daughter? It is obvious from the context that Horman's name was known to members of the family. See Basedow 1914: 161–2.

214 This suggestion that 'Georgy' was a small man is circumstantial evidence that he is based on George 'Fireball' Bates, who was 5'4 1/4", 'blue eyes, red hair, a fresh freckled complexion' (*Sydney Gazette*, 3 January 1822).

215 Cawthorne means here the sterner morality of the Old Testament of the Bible.

216 If 'Georgy' is George 'Fireball' Bates, then this is a detail about Bates not recorded in other accounts. Perhaps Cawthorne had enjoyed the experience of eating 'bush tucker' with Bates as well as with Nat Thomas, as his travel pieces make clear.

217 Rosenburg's Goanna, *Varanus rosenburgi*, very common on Kangaroo Island, the largest land predator. The name goanna is a corruption of the Spanish *iguana*, or lizard.

218 Cawthorne may be referring here to the first century Marcus Gavius Apicius, the legendary Roman gourmet who lived at the resort of Minturnae during the reign of Tiberius. Pliny tells us that he invented dishes of flamingos' tongues and mullet livers, and created what we would now call *pâté de foie gras*. He spent so much money on his lavish dinners that when he could not afford to entertain in such style any more, he chose to commit suicide rather than eat ordinary fare. His name is now synonymous with gluttons. (http://www.bbc.co.uk/radio4/history/romanway_recipes2.shtml, accessed 22 December 2002).

219 Cawthorne uses a traditional argument here in suggesting that the origins of Australian mateship lie in the convict origins of the first British settlements on the main.

220 Some Salt Lake salt was scraped by the Islanders from salt lakes to the south-west of Pelican Lagoon, American River, although most of the salt digging seems to have been done at the salt lake near Bay of Shoals. After settlement salt was gathered from Salt Lake, and a small railway built to the Muston Jetty where small boats like the *Kapoola* and *Karacka* took the salt to Adelaide. See Ivy Buick and Bev Willson, 'Growing up at the Salt Lake', *Colours of Kangaroo Island: 100 Stories of the people and places that make up its history* (Penneshaw: Dudley Writers Group, 1996: 32–3). Geoffrey Manning has the following about the naming of American River: 'Officially named by the first settlers on Kangaroo Island from the fact that an American whaler was wrecked there *circa* 1816. The marooned crew built a boat from pine trees, *etc.*, and the structure on which the boat was launched was, according to Mr W.L. Beare who arrived on the *Duke of York* in 1836, still visible at the time. This information recorded by H.C. Talbot probably relates to Captain Pendleton of the *Union* and is, in some respects, in contradiction to what is believed to be the facts . . . On Flinders' charts it is known as Pelican Lagoon . . . Baudin called it *Port Dache*. The town [of American River] was laid out by Ludmilla Hughes in 1927' (Manning 1990: 10). Fanning names American River Union Harbour. See Edmund Fanning, *Voyages and Discoveries in the South Seas 1792–1832* (Salem: Marine Research Society, 1924: 232).

221 In his *Sketch of the Aborigines of South Australia* Cawthorne insists that wild dog is food for 'Burkas', for full-grown men. 'The baking process is as follows: a hole is dug in the ground not very deep, and fire thrown therein, together with a quantity of stones which are to be heated. While this is doing they prepare the game or vegetables. This done, the stones and larger remains of the wood are remov'd, and if a Kangaroo or dead dog is to be stewed they fill its inside with part of the hot stones and leaves and place it in the oven. After proper time the meat is taken out and served up on Gum leaves, each taking his part, but never more than his allotted quantum, the men always take the best portions, and throw the rest to their favourite wives and children if they have been successful in hunting: the women enjoy the bones, which they are fond of breaking into bits and chewing' (Foster 1991: 73). The ground oven is called *kanya-yappa* (C.G. Teichelmann and C.W. Schürmann, *Outlines of a Grammar, Vocabulary, and Phraseology of the Aboriginal Language of South Australia*, Adelaide: the Authors, 1840: 12). The word is also given in a 1842 report: see Robert Foster, 'Two early reports on the Aborigines in South Australia,' *Journal of the Anthropological Society of South Australia* 28.1: 41.

Chapter 11

222 'Flash' language: a word of convict origins.

223 A paraphrase of Thomas Hobbes: 'No arts; no letters; no society; and which is worse of all, continual fear and danger of violent death; and the life of man, solitary, poor, nasty, brutish and short'.

224 W.H. Leigh describes a meeting with 'Governor' Wallen – he calls him 'Robinson Crusoe' – as follows: 'We were overtaken in our march by an Islander and his three black wives, or gins as they are called. He was upon a hunting expedition and having previously set snares in the paths through the woods in which we were travelling he hurried off to examine them. He had been a resident for fifteen years. About these regions we saw innumerable ant hills (termites) of a large size but invariably they were broken open and knocked to pieces, the inhabitants appearing also to be gone. Being surprised at the circumstances I asked Robinson concerning them and he told me we were now upon some of his women's favourite hunting grounds and as they were immoderately fond of ants they had pulled them to pieces to obtain the inhabitants. I afterwards saw them in the act. Taking a large piece of the ant hill they jostled and shook it about till the ants were nearly all out in their hands, then they conveyed the crawling insects in the shape of a ball into their mouths sucking and munching till their hearts content' (Leigh 1839: 129–30).

225 Caraway seed is the dried fruit of *Carum carvi L.*, a tiny white-flowered umbelliferous annual or biennial of the parsley family. The seeds have an aniseedy, minty flavour. The word caraway originated in Caria, a province of Asia Minor. The seeds are used in many European, Moslem and Asian cuisines as a flavouring, a condiment, a seasoning or a digestive. The seeds also look a little like ant eggs.

226 See Cawthorne's travel piece, 'A Christmas Trip', first published *Register* 9, February 1859: 3b–c, in which he also sings the praises of wallaby fat.

227 *Xanthorrhoea tateana*, the grass tree, yakka (or yacca), or blackboy; commonly eaten as a fresh vegetable not only by Indigenous people but by the settlers in the early years of the colony. The word 'yacca' is a borrowing from the Kaurna language (Rob Amery, 'Encoding New Concepts in Old Languages: A case study of Kaurna, the language of the Adelaide Plains', *Australian Aboriginal Studies*, no. 1, 1993: 40). Leigh records that 'the beautiful grass-tree . . . grows to a height of some twenty feet, on a knotty gummy stem; the head is like long coarse grass; I compare the form of the tree, in the distance, to a gigantic umbrella, on a thick post. It is a beautiful sea-green colour; the natives eat the bark, which is a kind of think gum; and, the "Governor" ate the head of it, which he chopped out and boiled; it tasted like endive: it is also used by the natives, but they roast it. (Leigh 1839: 129). Mollison and Everitt 1977 record the earliest harvesting of the yacca from 1806–09, when Joseph Murrell and 'Abyssinia Jack's' gang were engaged

in 'gumming' around Harvey's Return. Since then 'yacca gum' or resin has been collected by 'gummers' and sold locally to Fauldings who used it for medicinal purposes and to make glues. For some time Australian postage stamps used 'gum acacia' for glue. It was also exported for a while to Germany where it was used in explosives and varnish manufacture. E.L. Bates records that struggling farmers earned £3 or £4 a ton; in 1951 it was still being gathered, by then worth £25 ton (Bates 1951: 33). Cawthorne completed a watercolour of the plant, a version of which can be found in the *Illustrated Melbourne Post*, although he is not acknowledged as the artist.

228 According to Norman Tindale's informants, 20 years after this sentence was written about the dietary value of the heart of the *Xanthorrhoea tateana*, Suke (who was almost blind) survived for a week on the heart of a yacca after the death of her companion Big Sal at Middle River in 1874. See Clarke 1998: 35.

229 Cawthorne refers here to what are now more commonly known as witchetty grubs, the large wood-eating larva or pupa of several kinds of moths and beetles. The Kaurna word for similar grubs is *bardy* or *barti*. Cawthorne describes these grubs in his 'Sketch of the Aborigines of South Australia': The Grub of which there is a great variety, is the most repulsive dainty to appearance that can be well imagined; its general size two inches, soft, of a brown and whitish color, and composed of rings. It is however described as possessing a flavor superlatively fine. Great sagacity is displayed by the native in discovering the Grub. When seeking after those which inhabit trees he carefully examines the bark with his Wadna till he finds a hole. Then with the Pileyah [a small plaint stick with a hook at one end which is generally carried in their hair] extracts him precisely as a European would extract a periwinkle. The Grub is eaten raw or roasted; but generally alive' (Foster 1991: 72). Witchetty is derived from *wityu*, the equivalent hooked stick used to extract the grubs from their holes in a tree trunk, so named by the Adnyamathanha people of the Flinders Ranges. 'Wakerie', however, refers to a ground-dwelling grub common along the River Murray. The town of Waikerie is named after the Giant Swift Moth (*Trictenna Argentata*), a food source for the Meru and Barkindji people who dug them from the ground or caught the moth as it flew around their camp fires at night. It is now known more commonly as the Rain Moth because of its habit of emerging from its cocoon in the earth following late autumn rains. (http://www.murray-river.net/regions/waikerie/waikerie.htm, accessed 23 December 2002).

230 The doctor is quoting the famous old Irish folk-song here about Molly Malone who sold shell fish for a living 'In Dublin's fair city'. The song is now sung to support the Irish rugby team.

231 He means the Kaurna and Ngarrindjeri people of the mainland.

232 In the 'Notes, ETC.' appended to the second edition of Cawthorne's *The*

Legend of Kuperree; or, The Red Kangaroo (Adelaide: Alfred Cawthorne, 1858), Cawthorne describes the grubs 'inhabiting gum-trees, grass-sticks, &c.', called *kupe* by the Nauo of southern Eyre peninsula: 'Though the softest of creatures, it penetrates the hardest of woods. Its natural history is little known. When *once* eaten by Europeans it is so relished as never after to be despised. The difficulty lies in the *first* attempt.'

233 Leigh describes the techniques and instruments needed for 'maggot hunting', including a stick with a little fish-bone hook on one end used to insert in the holes in tree trunks and then extract the grub, 'the size of my thumb' (Leigh 1839: 90).

234 The echidna, *Tachyglossus aculeatus multiaculeatus*, the Australian 'porcupine', one of six recognised subspecies and very common on Kangaroo Island.

235 The Romans were so impressed with the oysters from around Colchester they sent slaves to work as oyster-gatherers, the oysters transported back to Rome in barrels of brine. The Roman Emperor Vitellius was said to have eaten a thousand oysters at a single sitting.

236 A 'seventy-four' was a 'third rate' man-of-war carrying 74 guns on two gun decks. At the beginning of the nineteenth century, about a third of the British Navy's ships of the line were seventy-fours, which were noted for their balance of firepower and seaworthiness. Lord Anson first set up the system by which warships were rated in the middle of the eighteenth century. First rate ships carried 100 or more guns; second rate, 84; third rate, 70; fourth rate, 50; fifth rate, 32; and sixth rate 32 guns or less.

237 To draw the lower ends of a sail up to a yard or to the mast ready for furling. Sam means 'get ready', listen.

238 This following revealing observation recorded by Lady Jane Franklin notes the value of the women to the Islanders. She visited Kingscote 15 January 1841; her diary records this fascinating vignette of island life: 'The whole population of Kangaroo Island according to Mr. Woodroffe (South Australian Company agent) is 76, men, women and children, including the sealers with their black wives and mongrel children. These live chiefly in the interior when not engaged in sealing. Their wives who are numerous and whom they interchange are chiefly, if not altogether from V.D.L. We saw one of these women at the settlement (Kingscote). She wore a man's long coat, buttoned down the front. The child had improved features, but more of the mother than the father. It was lighter hued however particularly in face and had curly light, soft hair. The woman said she was from Hobart Town. These black women are essential to men who live chiefly on fishing and hunting. The wallaby which the women are skilful in taking is one of their chief articles of food. Their offspring are very scanty – not above 2 or 3 of the black women of the island have children. The men are of the worst description of character. When they come into town, it is only to get drunk and

make broils. The old man, called Governor Waller in Leigh's South Australia is still living on the island. ('Diary of Lady Franklin', copy held at Kingscote National Trust 'Hope' Museum).

239   The 'Governor' here is Henry Wallen, one of the best-known of the Islanders. W.H. Leigh records his meeting Samuel Stephens, Manager of the South Australian Company, in 1836. 'Mr. S ——— landed with his cargo, when Wallen went to the beach to know who he was. "Who are you?" quoth S ——— to W ———. "I am the governor," says Wallen. "You are no such thing," retorted the enraged S ——— to the astonished islander; "*I* am the governor." – "I tell you I *am*," says Wallen stoutly; and enquired, "Who made you a governor" you a governor? Why you are not even one of King John's men; you don't stand four feet in your stockings.' Stephens was a very small man: an alcoholic and quick to anger. See Leigh 1839: 124.

240   Old Sam's speech here is at odds with reports written to the Colonization Commissioners about the sealers of Kangaroo Island. John Morphett's letter 14 September 1836, quoted in *Supplement to the First Report of the Directors of the South Australian Company* (London: William Johnstone, 1837), mentions that the newly arrived colonists had met six residents and that they were 'intelligent, quiet men . . . I have no doubt we shall find these men of great use, and they have all expressed pleasure at the opportunity of entering into the relations of civilized life' (28–9). Lady Jane Franklin thought otherwise. See Note 238.

241   Circumstantial evidence that 'the Doctor' is based on George 'Fireball' Bates, who spent a considerable period of time living on the mainland. Cawthorne here also alludes to the part played by Islander opinion of the mainland in encouraging Colonel William Light to decide on the present site of Adelaide for the colony's capital.

242   According to Edith Wells, in *Cradle of a Colony* (Kingscote: Island Press, 1978: 35), a *Register* journalist attempting to interview George 'Fireball' Bates, one of the last of the Islanders, but who found it difficult to get him to talk about the days before 1836. However, Bates obviously thought more highly of the *Advertiser*, for he gave a long and very detailed interview which forms the basis of a long piece, 'Old George Bates', in the *Advertiser*, 27 December 1886: 6c–f, describing many incidents with the Aboriginal people of the mainland, including what is called *chasse aux femmes*.

243   Cawthorne's novel is set in 1823, in which year the Murray's mouth was still not known to non-Indigenous people. Matthew Flinders did not see it in 1802, nor Baudin in 1803. In February 1830 Captain Charles Sturt and his party sailed and rowed their whaleboat down the Goolwa channel. They did not actually navigate as far as the Murray mouth, but crossed the coastal dunes and walked east to the mouth. Captain Collet Barker landed at the mouth of the Onkaparinga 17 April 1831, walked overland to Mount Lofty, noted the Port Adelaide inlet, saw the hill which was later to be named after him to the east and then returned to his ship.

He then landed near Cape Jervis and walked overland to the mouth, swimming the Murray and disappearing in the dunes on the southern side 30 April 1831. It was later discovered he was murdered on the Ninety Mile Beach. A. Grenfell Price, in 'The Work of Captain Collet Barker in South Australia' (*Proceedings of the Royal Geographical Society of Australasia, South Australian Branch*, vol. 26, 1926: 52–67), suggests that about 1828 'some of the sealers discovered Lake Alexandrina, and apparently crossed the Mount Lofty Ranges, since they reported it was three days' journey from Cape Jervis' (55). Perhaps one of Cawthorne's sources had told him the lakes and the Murray mouth had been visited by sealers before 1828. George 'Fireball' Bates is not named in Gill's 1906 article, but it is very likely he was the sealer who had deserted from the *Nereus* in c. 1825 and who had lived variously at Thistle Island, Cape Jervis and Kangaroo Island. See Thomas Gill, 'Who Discovered Lake Alexandrina?' (*Proceedings of the Royal Geographical Society of Australasia, South Australian Branch*, vol. 8, 1906: 48–54).

244 Cawthorne's diary 24 December 1842 and 2 November 1843 records two such 'dreadful fights', the first between the Mount Barker and Encounter Bay blacks, the result of which a few deaths and many wounded, and the second between the Encounter Bay and Adelaide people in alliance against the Moorunde and Mount Barker people. Cawthorne also recorded the actions of the police in breaking up a third fight (22 April 1844. Foster 1991: 9–10, 26, 46). Cawthorne wrote to the *Observer*, 24 April 1844 about such native fights.

245 Cawthorne seems not to have heard stories about George Meredith's history of abducting Indigenous women. Meredith was directly involved in the abduction of New Holland women from Point Nepean, Port Phillip and may have been involved in a second raid at Port Lincoln in c. 1835. There is no doubt that Nat Thomas knew such stories about Meredith, in that he showed Cawthorne where he was buried.

246 Note that the Islanders can speak enough of the languages of the main to understand what is said to them. Note too Cawthorne's suggestion that Indigenous people thought that the Europeans were cannibals, an ironic reversal of the more typical view.

247 Cawthorne probably heard a version of this story from George 'Fireball' Bates, who described a raid on the mainland to an *Advertiser* journalist in 1886 as follows: 'the party of five [islanders] . . . crossed over to the mainland to undertake this *chasse aux femmes*. They landed at Cape Jervis and walked across country to Lake Alexandrina, having no small difficulty in eluding the natives, who were very numerous. Their method of capturing the women was simple. Waiting until the morning was well advanced, and the men were out hunting, they stole up under cover until close to the camp, when at a signal they rushed forward and secured their prizes before they had time to escape. They made four trips with this object

at different times, securing one or two women each time who, when captured, had their hands tied behind their backs, and were made to walk with the their captors in double quick time back to the boat. They were set at liberty on reaching Hog Bay, where they in most cases proved useful and willing slaves. One girl, whom Bates named "Puss," from her propensity to scratch the face of her owner when in a rage, lived for years afterwards at Hog Bay'. (*Advertiser*, 27 December 1886: 6c).

248 A spear or stick, often mentioned in Cawthorne's diaries. See Foster 1991: 3.

249 Cawthorne seems here to make oblique reference to the several expeditions sent from Sydney to round up runaway convicts and reassert the New South Wales Governor's power, at least until 1825, when a separate colony was established in Van Diemen's Land. Details are sketchy; it may be that such vessels did not sail beyond the Bass Strait islands as far as 'Ultima Thule', Kangaroo Island. However, local legends persist that some escaped convicts were rounded up and their Indigenous companions returned to Tasmania. According to W.H. Skelton, in a letter in a Sydney paper, *Australian*, 9 March 1826, Captain Thomas Whyte commanded one vessel sent to the straits on a mission to clean up the islands of the southern coast. In his letter Skelton mentions Whyte's voyage, and reprimands those Sydney businessmen who are in business with the Straitsmen for the 'enticement held out to those wretched men to embark in and continue their abandoned way of life' and goes on later to observe how 'injudicious it would be to permit any settlers on these islands and other remote situations except in numbers and with property sufficient to induce Government to protect it by a detachment of military' (quoted Moore 1925: 106.) See also Thomas Willson's remarks in 'Tasmanian Aboriginals', *Observer* 7, October 1871: 7b insisting that 'Captain Duff' took numbers of women back to Tasmania on the *Africaine*. John Duff was master of the *Africaine*, one of the ships that brought immigrants to the colony in 1836, arriving 3 November 1836.

250 The implication is that the Islanders operated as a loose confederation, sending some of their number sealing on the islands to the west. The Althorpes, Thistle, Flinders, Franklin and St Peters islands were all visited by sealers during the first three decades of the nineteenth century, and one or two of them had people living for a number of years. Archaeological work has been done on several of the sites. See Parry Kostoglou and Justin McCarthy, *Whaling and Sealing Sites in South Australia*, Australian Institute for Maritime Archaeology, Special publication no. 6, (Adelaide: State Heritage Branch, Department of Environment and Planning, 1991).

251 Tie him up tight.

Chapter 12

252 The rail around the ship's stern.

253 Cawthorne here uses a very familiar trope about Australia as the Antipodes of Europe.

254 Cawthorne's third reference to Captain Sutherland's Report.

255 From the Kaurna word *warli*, from the Adelaide Plains. In his 'Sketch of the Aborigines of South Australia, Their Manners, Customs, Ceremonies, etc.', Cawthorne has the following: 'Dwellings. These are the most simple probably ever known merely a few branches placed in a semi-circle during the Summer months, under which they lie with a fire in the middle, in the winter season they are made a little more substantial. The sides are then heightened and supported by a few sticks meeting at the top, cover'd with bark, earth, or grass, forming when finished a domicile in the shape of a half dome. When an encampment takes place the 'Warlies' as they are called are generally made close together and in rows. On a moonlight night the many glimmering lights and Spears stuck all around, with now and then a shrill peal of laughter echoing through the forests present a most wild and striking appearance to the eye and car of a casual observer (Foster 1991: 74). In the 'Notes, ETC.' appended to the second edition of Cawthorne's *The Legend of Kuperree; or, The Red Kangaroo*, Cawthorne has the following: 'Native huts, made of the boughs of trees, and in winter strongly constructed, of a dome shape, and capable of holding from six to a dozen persons. Near whaling stations, the ribs of whales are employed as the frame-work, and the divisions filled up with boughs and sea-weed.'

256 Part of the interest in this novella is that Cawthorne represents Indigenous culture with some sympathy and awareness. He tried to learn Kaurna, gave his children Kaurna names and wrote *The Legend of Kuperee* under the influence of the American poet Longfellow, representing a Port Lincoln 'Dreaming'. He was one of the first Australian writers to attempt such a task.

257 In his 'Sketch of the Aborigines of South Australia, Their Manners, Customs, Ceremonies, etc.', Cawthorne asserts that the Aborigines 'consider the firmament with its bodies as a land similar to what they live upon: therefore the Milky Way is a large river, say they, along the banks of which reeds are growing. The dark spots in it are water lagoons in which monsters called 'Yuru' are living. The Magellan clouds are the ashes of a species of paraquets which were assembled there by a constellation and afterwards treacherously roasted.' However, in his public lecture 'Aborigines and their Customs', delivered 15 April 1864, he states that 'To them the visible heavens are great hunting plains, the Milky Way a large stream, in which lives one of their most dreaded monsters, Yura, a black snake, the author of the rite of circumscision. The stars, with sun and moon, have all been men once; the moon was the first to leave the earth and enticed all the others; the Pleiades, are girls gathering roots; and the Orion are boys hunting' (Foster 1991: 77, 90). Gell also records the name: 'Yura, who taught circumcision, was changed into a snake, now inhabiting the milky way'. (John Philip Gell, 'The Vocabulary of the Adelaide Tribe', *Tasmanian Journal of Natural Science*, vol. 1, 1842: 123). Although neither

acknowledges the fact, it is more than likely that their source is Christian Gottlieb Teichelmann, *Aborigines of South Australia, Illustrative and explanatory note of the manners, customs, habits and superstitions of the natives of South Australia* (Adelaide: Committee of the SA Wesleyan Methodist Auxiliary Missionary Society, 1841: 8).

258 Given the uncharacteristic fluency of expression represented here, it seems Cawthorne might have agreed with Teichelmann: 'I must note that, before the execution of their two brothers the Aborigines were more communicative in language than they now are, and it is now very difficult to get a complete phrase out of them, in that they want to keep Europeans in ignorance of their speech and speak broken language to the Europeans, as the Europeans speak broken language to them' (Teichelmann Papers: Letter to the Brothers 4/7/1839/p. 199, Jane Simpson's translation) (Jane Simpson, 'Introduction', *History in Portraits: Biographies of nineteenth century South Australian Aboriginal people* (eds. Jane Simpson & Louise Hercus, Aboriginal history monograph 6, Sydney: Aboriginal History, 1998: 11).

259 The Cawthorne family is now remembered for its contributions to music in South Australia. Cawthorne's eldest son, Charles Witto-Witto Cawthorne (1854–1925), joined his father in the firm Cawthorne & Co., which set up premises in 1884 in the city at the Grenfell Street and Gawler Place corner. Father William retired in 1887, leaving his son Charles to build up what was to become the biggest supplier of sheet music and instruments in Adelaide. In 1911 a prime site in Rundle Street was established, in a building called Cawthorne's. Charles Cawthorne went on to manage orchestras, to work as a musical entrepreneur in Adelaide and to help develop the local musical culture. See the entry for Charles Cawthorne, *Australian Dictionary of Biography*, (Melbourne: Melbourne University Press, 1979, vol. 7: 1891–1939, A – CH: 594–5).

260 Eurydice, a tree nymph, fell in love with Orpheus when she heard him playing his lyre.

261 In his 'Sketch of the Aborigines of South Australia, Their Manners, Customs, Ceremonies, etc.', Cawthorne notes that Aboriginal people 'believe all the celestial bodies formerly living upon the earth, partly as Animals, partly as men, and that they quitted the lower regions in exchange for the higher. Therefore all the names which they apply to the beings on earth they give the celestial bodies, believing them to be obnoxious to their influence, and describing to them malformation of the body and other casualties. The first celestial body that left this earth was the Moon, who is considered a Male, he persuaded all the rest to follow that he might have companions. The Sun is his Wife, who beats him every month till he dies, but in dying (Phoenix like) he revives again. Besides this, he keeps a great number of dogs for hunting, which have two heads but no tail. The Pleiades are Girls gathering roots and other vegetables; Orion, boys hunting: so that Celestial bodies

are believed to obey the same laws as men and animals below.' The association of the Pleiades with a group of *women* is very common in many cultures around the world: the constellation is often called the Seven Sisters. Cawthorne here seems not to have remembered his own essay. Elsewhere in his 'Literarium Diarium', Cawthorne records the Kaurna word for the moon: *Cearkera* (Foster 1991: 6, 77).

262 This is a very interesting moment in the text, in which it is clearly suggested that the children of the relationships between the Islanders and their Indigenous women associated strongly with their mothers, even to the extent of speaking what in this case Cawthorne probably intended to be taken as 'Hobart Town Language'. Even as late as 1837 one of Nat Thomas's grandchildren, the 80-year-old Joseph Seymour, could still remember fragments of the songs sung to him as a child. See Norman B. Tindale, 'Tasmanian Aborigines on Kangaroo Island, South Australia,' *Records of the South Australian Museum* 6 (1937): 36, which also records another un-named grandson's remark that 'the two families at one time used many words which were not understood by other people, but the children had forgotten most of them'.

263 Is this 'Bumblefoot Sal', or another women 'Sally'? Cawthorne uses this name only once, hinting at the much-travelled and well-known Kaurna woman Sally, daughter of Condoy or Conday, also named later in this novella. See Rob Amery, 'Sally and Harry: Insights into early Kaurna contact history,' *History in Portraits: Biographies of nineteenth century South Australian Aboriginal people* eds. Jane Simpson & Louise Hercus, Aboriginal history monograph, 6 (Sydney: Aboriginal History, 1998: 49–87).

264 Cawthorne refers here to stories alleging controversial Aboriginal practice, that of removing the kidneys and kidney ('caul') fat from a victim. Many non-Indigenous commentators asserted that this practice existed. A.W. Howitt asserts that the 'practice of using human fat as a powerful magical ingredient is widely spread over Australia, and consequently the belief is universal that the medicine-men have the power of abstracting it magically from individuals, or also of actually taking it by violence accompanied by magic. This is usually spoken of by the whites as taking "the kidney fat," but it appears to be the caul-fat of the omentum' (A.W. Howitt, *The Native Tribes of South-East Australia*, London: Macmillan, 1904; Facsimile Edition, Canberra: Aboriginal Studies Press, 1996: 367). Robert Bruce, pastoralist and author, insists that in 1852 a man named Robert Richardson was murdered on the Aroona run in the Flinders and his caul fat removed, but police records make it clear there was no such mutilation of the corpse. See Robert Bruce, *Recollections of an Old Squatter* (Adelaide: W.K. Thomas and Co., 1902: 108).

265 In Cawthorne's 'Rough notes on the manners and customs of the natives' *Proceedings of the Royal Geographical Society of Australasia (South Australian Branch*, vol. 23, no. 6, 1926: 29), an essay probably written in 1845, he records 'Last year one individual [*Warrawarra* or sorcerer] transformed himself into a

sheoak when pursued by Europeans'. In a public lecture he gave, 15 April 1864, Cawthorne also observed that 'It was devoutly believed that a certain man was transformed into a sheoak tree, the one that stood a little way above the old Frome Bridge' (Foster 1991: 91). This story is also quoted by John Philip Gell in 'The Vocabulary of the Adelaide Tribe', (*Tasmanian Journal of Natural Science*, vol. 1, 1842: 123). Both are quoting Teichelmann 1841: 10, which is obviously Cawthorne's source, in that he quotes Teichelmann word-perfect.

266 Robert Foster has noticed that a stanza Cawthorne quotes in his 'Sketch of the Aborigines of South Australia' contains a line referring to both the tuft of eagle feathers and the girdle is taken from G.C. Teichelmann and C.W. Schürmann, *Outline of a Grammar, Vocabulary and Phraseology, of the Aboriginal Language of South Australia* (Adelaide: 1840: 73). See Foster 1991: 75. The girdle is called *wilkatja* on p. 72 and *gadlotta* on p. 81.

267 Cawthorne names the tuft of emu feathers *kariwoppa* or *kari-wappa* (Foster: 1991: 47, 81).

268 In his 'Literarium Diarium', 26 April 1844, Cawthorne recorded the following observation: 'But hark! The natives are singing and dancing their wild corroboree. There is something ever soothing in that un[nerving] and ferocious song. Ah! oh' oh' etc Wail on natives, louder, louder, shriller, deeper, lower. Thou art blessed above us no care, no mental misery to afflict thee. Thy house is the earth and thy home a few branches, thy clothing the oppossum's skin and thy only sorrow a hungry belly occasionally. Little does the savage of Australia [know] the many many causes of trouble and pain that the white man suffers and the 100,000 petty grievances he has to endure, of the difficulties he is often placed in by that unknown thing to thee money. Wail on natives. Your day will come, the next generation of black men will be the servants of the next generation of white man. May they be treated with [levity?] Ah! now then, the deep sounds of the "tarpurro" [possum-skin drum], now the shrill voices of the women and children. The men are striking in, the song is increasing, louder yet There! it ends abruptly with a grand "ah!" Silence reigns as usual, not a voice is heard. Blessed are the natives. No care sits upon the brow, dear sorrow upon their heart' (Foster 1991: 47).

269 N.J.B. Plomley records the story told by John Anderson (Abyssinia Jack) to Tasmanian Protector of Aborigines, G.A. Robinson, of a sealer named James Allen who tied a Van Diemen's Land woman called Lar.roon.er to a tree 'at American Wharf Lagoon' (American River? American Beach?). He then slashed her buttocks with his sealer's knife and also cut off part of her ear. This accusation of ear cropping was also levelled against Nat Thomas, Cawthorne's source for many stories about the Islanders. John Anderson also told G.A. Robinson that Thomas had cut off the ears of a seven-year-old 'New Holland' boy, cutting so close to the head that a piece of the cheek was also removed. After lingering

for several weeks the lad died. It is not clear if this boy is the lad called Pra.re mentioned by Robinson; he seems to have been the son of James Allen and Emue. Emue (or Emma) later lived with John Anderson; she was probably of Kaurna or Ramindjeri origin. Anderson handed Emma and her son over to G.A. Robinson on 29 March 1831: Robinson interrogated her at length and recorded a great deal of information about the women living with sealers on Kangaroo Island. In 1836 she was living with James Munro on a Bass Strait island, where it seems she died shortly after (Plomley 1966: 327, 335, 360, 479, 1010, 1016).

270 Sir William Blackstone (1723–80), English jurist and academic. After an unsuccessful legal practice, in 1758 Blackstone he became the first Vinerian professor of law at Oxford, where he inaugurated courses in English law. Blackstone published his lectures as *Commentaries on the Laws of England* (4 vols., 1765–69). Blackstone's book exerted tremendous influence on the legal profession and on the teaching of law in England and in the United States. In his later life Blackstone resumed practice, served in Parliament, was solicitor general to the queen, and was a judge of the Court of Common Pleas. Perhaps Cawthorne had the following paragraph in mind: 'If all these resources fail, the court must pronounce that judgment, which the law hath annexed to the crime, and which hath been constantly mentioned, together with the crime itself, in some or other of the former chapters. Of these some are capital, which extend to the life of the offender, and consist generally in being hanged by the neck till dead; though in very atrocious crimes other circumstances of terror, pain or disgrace are superadded: as, in treasons of all kinds, being drawn or dragged to the place of execution; in high treason affecting the king's person or government, embowelling alive, beheading, and quartering; and in murder, a public dissection. And, in case of any treason committed by a female, the judgment is to be burned alive. But the humanity of the English nation has authorized, by a tacit consent, an almost general mitigation of such part of these judgments as favour of torture or cruelty: a fledge of hurdle being usually allowed to such traitors as are condemned to be drawn; and there being very few instances (and those accidental or by negligence) of any person's being embowelled or burned, till previously deprived of sensation by strangling. Some punishments consist in exile or banishment, by abjuration of the realm, or transportation to the American colonies: others in loss of liberty, by perpetual or temporary imprisonment. Some extend to confiscation, by forfeiture of lands, or moveables, or both, or of the profits of lands for life: others induce a disability, of holding offices or employments, being heirs, executors, and the like. Some, though rarely, occasion a mutilation or dismembering, by cutting off the hand or ears: others fix a lasting stigma on the offender, by flitting the nostrils, or branding in the hand or face. Some are merely pecuniary, by slatted or discretionary fines: and lastly there are others, that consist principally in their ignominy, though most of them are

mixed with some degree of corporal pain; and these are inflicted chiefly for crimes, which arise from indigence, or which render even opulence disgraceful. Such as whipping, hard labour in the house of correction, the pillory, the flocks, and the ducking-stool. Disgusting as this catalogue may seem, it will afford pleasure to an English reader, and do honour to the English law, to compare it with that shocking apparatus of death and torment, to be met with in the criminal codes of almost every other nation in Europe' William Blackstone, *Commentaries of the Laws of England* (A facsimile of the first edition of 1765–1769. vol. IV, Of Public Wrongs, with an Introduction by Thomas A. Green, Chicago & London: The University of Chicago Press, 1979: 370–1).

271 For confirmation of this practice, see a letter dated 10 December 1836, describing a visit to 'Governor' Henry Wallen's farm at Three Wells River, Kangaroo Island: 'We then proceeded to the farmyard, where we beheld pigs, poultry, and everything pertaining to a farm. Here was a house in which lived three black women – two natives of the main and one of Van Dieman's [sic] Land' quoted H.P. Moore, 'Notes on the Early Settlers in South Australia prior to 1836,' (*Proceedings of the Royal Geographical Society of Australasia South Australian Branch*, vol. 25, 1925: 96). George Wilkinson also records a similar observation: 'As to living in the huts built for them, they complied for a short time with the request to do so, but have always quitted these habitations for little *worleys* or shelters of their own, which are soon deserted and others formed. This might be thought an evidence of their wandering and unsettled life, but they have a reason for frequent changes. Ask them why they do not live in such and such a place, where there is a shelter of their own making, and they answer, *"No good that one; too much plenty fleas; no sleep; too much bite 'um black fellow;"* and at the same time they commence scratching their bodies to exemplify their meaning'. See George Blakiston Wilkinson, *South Australia: its advantages and its resources, being a description of that colony and a manual of information for emigrants* (London: John Murray, 1848: 319).

272 In his 'Literarium Diarium', 7 September 1843, Cawthorne records the following: 'I am an enemy to missionaries generally speaking. I believe little what they say, for I know that they write lies. They gull the people at home, they are obliged to do it.'

273 The Chapman River.

274 The building of the Sturt Light commenced in 1849 at Cape Willoughby, and it was finished in 1851. It was constructed of stone quarried from a ravine just to the south of the site – Nat Thomas ('Old Sam' here) worked both as a builder and later as third keeper at the light. Between October 1851 and 16 May 1862 Cawthorne's father, Captain William Cook Cawthorne, was the first head keeper at the Light, earning £100 per annum and later £200. In 1862 the Captain was dismissed from the Service for drunkenness and other offences. He died in 1875 and is buried in Brighton. The lighthouse still stands, and a highlight of a visit to

tourist sites on the island is to take a guided tour with a national park guide. One of the light keeper's cottages there is called 'Cawthorne'.

275 Crayfish, or these days Southern Rock Lobster, *Jasus novæhollanaiæ*. W.H. Leigh complains that 'though good-sized fish, are nothing but shell, and not worth boiling', although in a footnote he does admit that 'they may grow thin after spawning' (Leigh 1839: 134). The man's dreaming.

Chapter 13

276 Cawthorne illustrated the 'native method of tree climbing'. See f. 15, 'Sketches of Aborigines', (PX*A1409 f. 1–2, Mitchell Library).

277 This is an early expression of admiration for body surfing, reinforcing a view that the Palawa women in particular were very much at home in the water.

278 Curly hair is usually given as a signifier of the difference of the Palawa women.

279 Something Cawthorne observed about Bet's daughter, Mary, when he met her just before Christmas 1852.

280 Therefore, 30 feet, or about ten metres. James Backhouse, the Quaker visitor to the Australian colonies in the 1830s, notes that Tasmanian Aboriginal women were skilled divers: 'Some of the women went into the water among the large sea-tangle to take Cray-fish. These women seem quite at home in the water, and frequently immerse their faces to enable them to see objects at the bottom. When they discover the object of their search, they dive, often using the long stems of kelp to enable them to reach the bottom; these they handle as dexterously in descending, as a sailor would a rope, in ascending' (Backhouse 1843: 168). This observation in Backhouse may be a source for Cawthorne.

281 On Cawthorne's part too. Crayfish live on reefs, not over sand.

282 There is some evidence that the Tasmanian women thought themselves superior to the 'New Holland' women also abducted, and thus stuck together. See Basedow 1914: 161. Cawthorne's father's journal from the Sturt Light certainly records the circumstantial detail that even as late as the 1850s Bet and Sal were still keeping company, and other Kangaroo Island sources also describe them as a pair.

283 There are a number of references to Nat Thomas's affection for Old Bet, often represented in such a fashion as to suggest that such emotional attachments between Islanders and their women were rare.

284 James Backhouse recorded a similar perception when he observes that 'the natives of V.D. Land . . . exceeded Europeans in skill, in those things to which their attention had been directed from childhood, just as much as Europeans exceeded them, in the points to which the attention of the former had been turned, under the culture of civilization. There is similar variety of talent and of temper among the Tasmanian Aborigines, to what is to be found among other branches of the

human family; and it would not be more erroneous in one of these people, to look upon an English woman as defective in capacity, because she could neither dive into the deep and bring up cray-fish, nor ascend the lofty gum-trees to catch opossums for her family, than it would be for an English woman to look upon the Tasmanian as defective in capacity, because she could neither sew nor read, nor perform the duties of civil, domestic life. Were the two to change stations, it is not too much to assume, that the untutored native of the woods would much sooner learn to obtain her food, by acquiring the arts of civilization, than the woman from civilized society would, by acquiring the arts belonmging to savage life' (Backhouse 1843: 173–4).

285 Cawthorne here refers to the wreck of the *Osmanli*, which ran up on a reef near Cape Linois in D'Estree Bay about midnight on 23 November 1853 – George Tinline, an acting manager of the Bank of South Australia was on board, so the nearest feature ashore is now known as Point Tinline. As the National Parks' signage tells us on the shore, when the ship struck, Captain Corbett's thumb was split away from his hand with the impact. All of the crew and passengers managed to make it to shore that evening in the ship's boats. W. Leigh, a passenger, completed at least two well-known drawings of the encampment, which are today in the Mitchell Library, Sydney. Four days later Captain Corbett sent one of the boats for help: it stopped at the Sturt Light, where Captain Cawthorne promised to send assistance. The boat then proceeded to Adelaide to report the wreck. In the meantime Captain Cawthorne sent Nat Thomas and Old Bet to assist the stranded passengers and crew: they carried ship's biscuit, flour and some eggs with them. Old Bet then led people to a spring some eight kilometres from the wreck site, a spring still used for stock watering (*Observer*, 3 December 1853). Some contemporarous accounts insist the woman in question was Old Bet's daughter Mary, the first child to be born on Kangaroo Island to a European parent. Given Cawthorne must have heard about the *Osmanli* from his father, it is very likely that this note in his novella proves that it was mother Bet, not daughter Mary. It is something of a coincidence that on the very day of the wreck, 23 November 1853, Captain Cawthorne wrote to the Trinity Board requesting leave of absence in the following January. In the enquiry into the wreck, it was alleged that the Sturt Light was not functioning on the evening in question – or that the glass was dirty and the light thus unable to be seen. See *Register*, 26 July 1853. As it happens, Nat Thomas was on duty that evening. Some time after the wreck Old Bet found some planking from the stern of the *Osmanli* 'with the usual gilt carving and scroll work' and returned to Cape Willoughby tremendously excited by her discovery. See *Register* 15 September 1856: 3d. Cawthorne also wrote about the sinking of the *Golbourn*, which went down just off Cape Willoughby while being towed by the steamer *Melbourne*.

Four died. See his formerly unpublished Ms. 'Lines . . . Loss of *Golbourn* . . . July 1856' (A/558/A4, State Records).

286 The implication of this remark is that Old Bet is buried near Pelican Lagoon, near American River. She is believed to be buried in a cleared paddock on the west side of the road some 100 metres short of where the main road from Penneshaw to Cape Willoughby runs parallel to the Chapman River, about a kilometre from the sea. The site of her burial was kept a secret by the family for many years because they feared desecration of the grave by those seeking 'Tasmanian' skeletal remains. As recently as the 1950s there were still employees at the South Australian Museum writing memoranda about exhuming those remains. There is a large stone monument there now, erected by the Kangaroo Island Pioneers Association and the Department of State Aboriginal Affairs, with a plaque which reads: EARLY SETTLERS IN THIS ARE INCLUDED NAT. THOMAS WHO, WITH HIS TASMANIAN ABORIGINAL WIFE BETTY, ARRIVED ON KANGAROO ISLAND IN 1827 AND FARMED THE AREA AT THE EASTERN END OF ANTECHAMBER BAY UNTIL 1878. THIS COUPLE HAD THREE CHILDREN, A SON AND TWO DAUGHTERS, THE ELDER DAUGHTER, MARY, BORN IN MAY 1833, WAS THE FIRST DOCUMENTED CHILD OF A EUROPEAN BORN IN SOUTH AUSTRALIA. WHILE NOT ALWAYS WELL TREATED, THE ABORIGINAL COMPANIONS OF THE PRE 1836 SETTLERS MADE A SIGNIFICANT CONTRIBUTION TO THE EARLY DEVELOPMENT OF THE ISLAND. SEVERAL WERE BROUGHT FROM TASMANIA AND OTHERS MAINLY FROM NEARBY FLEURIEU PENINSULA. BETTY DIED IN 1878, AND WHILE THE ACTUAL SITE OF HER GRAVE IS UNKNOWN, IT IS BELIEVED TO BE IN THIS VICINITY.

287 This sounds like an anecdote told by George 'Fireball' Bates to an *Advertiser* reporter in 1886. Bates may have also told Cawthorne something like the same story 30 years before when they met at Hog Bay. The *Advertiser* version reads as follows: 'About this time (1830) Bates very foolishly hazarded himself amongst the blacks of Cape Jervis. He had persuaded an old native of that tribe to come over to Hog Bay with his son. The lad died, and Bates accepted the bereaved parents' invitation to go back with him to his tribe. The men would hunt for him, give him wives, and make him a chief among them. Against the wishes and warnings of his comrades Bates went; and was received at a grand corroboree, where he was presumably made a member of the tribe by being thrown on his back, and having all the males jump on his body in succession. At first the natives treated him as one of themselves, although they never let him out of their sight, and appeared suspicious of him; but when the dogs he had brought over were knocked up by hunting, he was left to shift for himself. He fell ill, and the three natives who remained with him – the old

man Condoy, a young girl named Sal, and a boy nicknamed Friday – begrudged him almost any provisions. When he had given up hope and lain down to die in a cave near the shore, he was discovered by his mates, who had crossed over to the mainland to find out what had become of the missing man. As a punishment for their neglect of Bates the three natives mentioned above were carried away into captivity on the Island'. (*Advertiser*, 27 December 1886: 6c–e).

288 Cawthorne refers here to what is known now as Rapid Head, named after the *Rapid*, the surveying brig that brought Colonel William Light to South Australia in 1836. Flinders's name is no longer used.

289 In his 'Literarium Diarium', 15 February 1844, Cawthorne records his intention to travel to Rapid and Encounter Bays with George French Angas. Interestingly, he does not mention sketching or drawing: 'We shall both go on horseback. I shall take a gun and bullets, perhaps shoot a kangaroo, or a blackfellow. I don't care which. I think I should have a better chance at the latter than the former' (Foster 1991: 38). While Cawthorne's image of a fishing scene at Second Valley is not well known (it is in the Mitchell Library – PXB 213 f.10 – a photograph is held in the State Library of South Australia, PRG/489/9/4), Angas produced a much more famous drawing of the same scene, later to be turned into a lithograph, 'Coast Scene near Rapid Bay, Sunset. Natives Fishing with nets, 1844', which is in the Art Gallery of South Australia, 667G53. John Tregenza has this to say of the scene: 'When Angas sketched this scene in 1844 he was sitting on rocks which now lead to the jetty at Second Valley, beside the mouth of the River Parananacooka'. Of the native method of fishing 'at the calm hour of sunset' he writes: 'The mode adopted by the tribes inhabiting the vicinity of Rapid Bay, is nearly similar to that of Europeans; they use a seine [net] about twenty or thirty feet in length, stretched upon sticks placed crosswise at intervals; a couple of men will drag this net amongst the rocks and shallows where fish are most abundant, and, gradually getting it closer as they reach the shore, the fish are secured in the folds of the net, and but few moments elapse before they are laid alive upon the embers of the native fires that are blazing ready before the adjoining huts. The nets are composed of chewed fibres of reeds, rolled upon the thigh, and twisted into cord for the purpose.' The cove remains a popular fishing spot to this day. Unfortunately a number of fishing boat sheds now disfigure the rocky promontory' John Tregenza, *George French Angas: Artist, Traveller and Naturalist 1882–1886*, Adelaide: Art Gallery Board of South Australia, rev. edn., 1982: 47).

290 This assertion suggests that some of the existing names on the Kangaroo Island map have survived from the Islanders' place-naming over the period 1802–36. American River, Harveys Return, Smith Bay and Stokes Bay are such survivals, as is Murray's Lagoon, a corruption of Joseph Murrell's name. Harveys Return was earlier known as Murrell's Landing. After being attacked at Jervis Bay on his

way to Kangaroo Island in October 1805, Joseph Murrell eventually arrived with a sealing gang in 1806, remaining on the island for three years and then returning for a number of later sealing trips.

291 Hog Bay is the name given to the waters where the ferry docks at Penneshaw. The name Hog Bay also survives as the name of a river on the Dudley Peninsula. Baudin mentions leaving pigs ashore on Kangaroo Island, at the spot where his crew found water, on the eastern end of the beach at Penneshaw: 'The 30TH – As the weather was fine on the morning of the 30th [29th – 19 January], I had a rooster and two hens put ashore at the place where the water is collected. On this beach I likewise left a boar and sow to multiply and possibly be of use to future navigators in these regions. During the summer this island will be able to provide good refreshments for ships that want to stop here; and the anchorage seems to me to be sound enough for one to ride securely at it, provided the winds are not strongly from North-East, North or North-West. The sea then is very rough and choppy in it, but one can always set sail easily and return when the bad weather has passed.' On some old maps Hog Bay is named as Freshwater Bay (Hallack 1905: 8). There seems to be another local legend on the island to the effect that Hog Bay earned its name when 'Governor' Henry Wallen moved there after he had lost his farm in 1836 at Cygnet (or Three Wells) River, allowing his pigs to wallow in the spring where Baudin and his men had watered. 'Penneshaw is a composite name, made up of part of the name of Dr. Pennefather, Secretary to Governor Jervois, and Miss Flora Shaw, later Lady Lugard, wife of the Governor of Hong Kong. It was declared a township in 4th January, 1896' (Bates 1951: 32).

292 The postmaster at Hog Bay was Tom Simpson, 'a fair haired man from Lincolnshire', who married Jenny Thomas, the youngest daughter of Nat Thomas and Old Bet. Their eldest son was Nathaniel Thomas Simpson, born 8 December 1860, who became a JP and a member of local government. His brother was Stamford W. or 'Tiger' Simpson who served in the 10th Battalion in the First World War and was responsible for leaving a hat on a corner on the Penneshaw to Kingscote road, now known as Felt Hat Corner. There are a number of anecdotes about 'Tiger' Simpson collected in *Colours of Kangaroo Island: 100 stories of the people and places that make up its history*, including references to his skill on the accordian. He died 21 October 1955, aged 79 years. 'Tiger' Simpson once owned an 1835 Bible inscribed 'George Bates, from S. Stephens, Esq., Kingscote, October 2, 1836' (Bates 1951: 36). The Bible is still in the possession of the Simpson family of Penneshaw (Wells 1978: 33).

Chapter 14

293 Christmas Cove, a few hundred metres to the west of the Penneshaw headland on which stands the hotel, a safe boat haven.

294 Smoke signalling, learned from the Indigenous people of the mainland.

295 A river in Hades, producing forgetfulness of the past.

296 B. Daily et al. describe Christmas Cove as revealing 'smoothed and striated glacial pavements cut on Kanmantoo Group metasediments in the partially exhumed Permian glacial depression', which I take to mean that the cove is glacial in origin, not volcanic (B. Daily, A.R. Milnes, C.R. Twidale and Jennifer A. Bourne, 'Geology and Geomorphology', in *Natural History of Kangaroo Island* eds. M.J. Tyler, C.R. Twidale & J.K. Ling, Adelaide: Royal Society of South Australia, 1979: 26).

297 Conclusive evidence that Sam is based on Nat Thomas, of 'Freshfields', Creek Bay, now Antechamber Bay. The Gilfillan property is called 'Creek Bay' and contains the site of Nat Thomas's house 'Freshfields' which now forms the inner part of the Gilfillan house, the oldest European dwelling in South Australia.

298 A small detail suggesting that Cawthorne did have access to reliable sources of information about the decades before offical settlement in 1836, when a number of Islanders lived at Creek Bay.

299 A tiny fragment of evidence that some Indigenous *men* were also involved in sealing. While Indigenous women (and especially Palawa women) seemed to have been skilled sealers in pre-contact society, the evidence for the involvement of men is scanty, which makes this reference significant. Quoting Ryan 1981, Kostoglou notes that Mannalargenna, a well-known individual from the north-east of Van Diemen's Land, made several sealing voyages. In 1813 when James Kelly took the *Brothers* sealing in Bass Strait there were two Aboriginal men aboard. George Augustus Robinson only refers to one or two in his dairies: a young 'North west of New Holland' boy named Praree lived and worked with John 'Abyssinia Jack' Anderson, but whether he was taken as a worker or as a sexual partner is not clear. See Parry Kostoglou, *Sealing in Tasmania: Historical Research Project A Report for the Parks and Wildlife Service* (Hobart: Department of Environment and Land Management, 1996: 38). Another Indigenous man is mentioned as a member of a sealing gang left on Solander Island for three years, living with his fellow-castaways on 'terms of perfect amity and understanding' (Thomas Dunbadin, *Sailing the World's Edge: Sea Stories from old Sydney*, London: Newnes, [1937]: 119).

300 Several of the Islanders worked as pilots and guides when the South Australia Company vessels arrived in 1836. With his companions Doughboy and Sal, Walker worked for Colonel William Light, not only helping with the surveying but also tending the garden Light established at Rapid Bay. In later life Nat Thomas claimed that he had also worked as a 'chainman' for Colonel Light, no doubt because he had served with Phillip Parker King on the *Bathurst*, which sailed from Sydney May 1821 to chart the north coast of Australia. The *Bathurst* returned to Sydney in 1822 after circumnavigating the continent. See Marsden

Hordern, *King of the Australian Coast: The Work of Phillip Parker King in the Mermaid and Bathurst 1817–1822* (Melbourne: Melbourne University Press, 1997).

301 Equivocation.

302 From the cliffs above Christmas Cove where now stands the Penneshaw Hotel there are remarkable views of Backstairs Passage, Cape Jervis, Rapid Head and away in the distance on a clear day Mount Lofty, the high hill above the city of Adelaide. Flinders too was much taken with this view, naming Mount Lofty from a little to the west of this point.

303 An all-too-brief description of the 'mixed race' children of the Islanders and their women. Given the scene is near Hog Bay, it is tempting to suggest represented here are the children of William Wilkins (sometimes Wilkinson) and Mary Manatto or Minato, who lived in a cottage at the eastern end of Hog Bay above Frenchman's Rock on Section 100, called for many years after 'the Aboriginal'. Ruediger notes that Wilkins and his son both died of pneumonia after sailing to the western end of the island to rescue the crew of the wrecked Finnish barque *Fides*, which went up on the rocks at Snug Cove 22 May 1860. See Ruediger 1980: 100. Cawthorne's father helped organise food and other support for Mary and her children after Wilkins and his son died in October 1860. Eventually the surviving children were moved to Raukkan: Ruediger insists Mary is buried at Hog Bay.

304 *Cereopsis novaehollandiae*, once threatened with extinction but now secure as a species. The geese were re-introduced to Kangaroo Island in the 1920s and 1930s and are now commonly seen.

305 The ubiquitous tommy ruff: *Arripis georgianus*, still abundant and excellent eating.

306 *Acanthopagrus butcheri*. It is hard to imagine vast schools of bream just outside Christmas Cove.

307 More or less 50 miles (80 kilometres) west of present-day Penneshaw is Snelling Beach and Western River Cove, both places where sealers lived at the time the novella is set. George Meredith and his party arrived at Western River Cove and built a hut in February 1834: no other source agrees with Cawthorne's insistence here in this novella that George Meredith was in Kangaroo Island waters as early as 1823. See Cumpston 1986: 132.

308 Manning reports: 'named by Matthew Flinders on 20 March 1802 supposedly after Lord Spencer's eldest son and heir . . . Baudin called them *Archip. De L'est* (Eastern Archipelago) while Freycinet's charts show *Is. Vauban* (Manning 1990: 10).

Chapter 15

309 Perhaps Cawthorne had read reports like those of Captain Hammond (or Hammant) of the *Endeavour*, who called at Kangaroo Island to load salt in 1817. He found 'thirteen Europeans, most or all of whom have gone from these settlements [at Sydney], are living on Kangaroo Island in a curious state of

independence, having nothing to depend on for subsistence but the wild birds that inhabit it' (from the *Sydney Gazette*, 5 April 1817, quoted Cumpston 1986: 107). Nunn notes that the 'notion of "island men" as a group with their own separate identity was accepted and generally used by 1819' (Nunn 1989: 29).

310 'Governor' Henry Wallen, one of the most famous of the Islanders. Wallen lived first at Three Well River, where his farm was, later, after selling the farm for a barrel of rum, wandered around the island according to Leigh. Later he moved to Hog Bay, building a stone hut not far from Frenchman's Rock, near the spring discovered by the French. His pigs wallowing in the mud around the spring are supposed to be one explanation for why Hog Bay is so called. Wallen is buried at Kingscote in the 'old cemetery'.

311 Cawthorne refers here to the history of the mutineers from the *Bounty* who settled on Pitcairn with island women after the mutiny in 1787.

312 Elizabeth I of England (1533–1603) and Catherine the Great of Russia (1729–96).

313 'Named by Matthew Flinders on 30 March 1802. Right Honourable Charles Philip Yorke of the Admiralty. Baudin called it *Cambaceres Peninsula* after Jean Jacques Regis Cambaceres, Duke of Parma' (Manning 1990: 353).

314 The implication of 'Flash' is that he was an old lag, a convict.

315 The *Oxford English Dictionary* has 'a dogger-boat . . . a fishing-boat, so-called from *hoeck*, Dutch for hook', also, 'a one-masted fishing-smack on the Irish coast and south-west of England, similar to a hoy in build'. Here hookers are small coastal vessels sailing out of Hobart for the islands of Bass Strait and beyond to Kangaroo Island, trading rum for seal and wallaby skins, yakka gum, wattle bark and salt. Such vessels were known as Wood Hookers: similar vessels called She Oakers provided Hobart's wood supply. See Harry O'May, *Wooden Hookers of Hobart Town* (Hobart: L.G. Shea, n.d.). See also D.G. O'May, 'Sailing Traders of Southern Tasmania', *Australian and New Zealand Sail Traders* (ed.Garry J. Kerr, Blackwood, SA: Lynton Publications, 1974: 82). I am grateful for Mark Staniforth for making this connection. In the 1950s when I was a child living in Port Lincoln, South Australian whiting fishermen were known as 'hookers', fishing from small sailing craft from ports like Thevenard, Port Pirie and Port Lincoln. The name is still used.

316 Ruediger quotes the following newspaper story about the Sydney and Hobart vessels that came to Kangaroo Island to trade for salt and skins: 'It is said that it was usual to set up a keg of rum upon the deck, directly the anchor was dropped, knock the head out and place plenty of pannikins around. Not a word of business was allowed to be spoken until every visitor had well drunken, and then the captain obtained the most liberal bargains. After the orgie was over the men generally found themselves on shore, with splitting headaches, fevered circulation, a few groceries, perhaps a bottle or so of rum and some tobacco and always a good

supply of twine, with which to makes snares to catch more wallabys, or course the vessel was gone and so were all the skins (Ruediger 1980: 81).

317 This may record a sealer's nickname Cawthorne collected from his informants Nathaniel Thomas and George 'Fireball' Bates, the man's real name lost.

318 Flash Tom means the New Zealand Fur Seal (*Arctocephalus forsteri*) rather than the Australian Sea Lion (*Neophoca cinerea*), both of which are still found on Kangaroo Island: the former at Admiral's Arch and the latter at the world-famous Seal Bay.

319 It is difficult to know if Cawthorne has a specific marooning episode in mind here. Obviously many stories circulated about individuals left on rocky islets and reefs to kill seals and to fend for themselves. George Robinson recorded that following anecdote 18 June 1830: 'The Pyramid [is] a large rock, from the appearance the altitude two hundred and fifty feet . . . I was informed that a man died on this rock who had been left there by a sealing vessel. He was found in a cave and it was supposed he had been dead eighteen months. The spray of the sea had broke over him and he was as it were cured and looked quite fresh. These men are left by the sealing vessels with so many gallons of water, provision &c, and the vessels then go away to the eastern straights, so that if anything happens to the vessel the man on the rock must perish' (Plomley 1966: 177). Perhaps the most graphic of the many stories circulating about marooning is that given in the *Sydney Gazette*, 18 April 1824: 'Mr. Dawson, commander of the *Samuel*, has brought with him this voyage a black native woman with a child two years old. She had been taken by the American ship *General Gates* from Kangaroo Island and left on the South Cape of New Zealand with a gang of sealers. After these men had been there some short time, a horde of savages came upon them and nearly massacred all the party. The poor native, with her little one, took shelter under a rock, till the New Zealanders left the spot. For eight months the mother and the child lived, without fire, on birds and seals. They are yet on board the *Samuel*, and were in good health when rescued by Mr. Dawson from danger' (Quoted Cumpston 1986: 66). A story from South Australian waters is told by John Hart of leaving a man named Bermingham on Baudin Rocks in Guichen Bay to skin and dry the skins of 30 seals killed by the crew of Hart's sealing vessel. See K. Bermingham, *The sixth eleven tales of Robe* (Kingston: J.M. Banks, 1975: 40). See also Hart 1854: 52.

320 Cawthorne is probably referring here to a seal-killing practice adopted by the Islanders and the Aboriginal women who worked for them, recorded in this remarkable description by James Kelly of an episode in 1816: "a Most Singular Mode it is, It is here Described. We gave the Women Each a Club that We had used to Kill Seals" with they went to the Waters Edge and Wet themselves" all over their head and Body as they Said to Prevent the Seals from Smelling them as

they Walked along the Rocks they were Verry Cautious not to go to Windward of them as they Said a Seal Would sooner Belive his Nose than his Eyes" When a Man or Woman Came Near him, the Six Women Walked into The Water two and two and Swam to three Rocks about 50 yards from the Shore Each Rock had about 9 or 10 Seals on it they were all Laying aparently asleep, Two Women went to Each Rock with thair Clubs in hand Each of them Crept Slowly Close up to their Seal and Lay Down with thair Club alongside them Some of the Seals aRose thair heads up to Look at thair New Visitors and Smell them Scratchd themselves and Lay Down again – this Was Done by thair fin or flipper The Women Went Nearly through the Same Motion as the Seal Did by holding up the Left Elbow a little and Scratching themselves with thair Left hands Keeping the Club firm in the Right hand Ready for the attack – the Seals Seemed Verry Cautious" Now and then Lifting up thair heads Looking around Scratching themselves with thair flippers and Laying their heads Down again, the Women went through the Same Motions as Near as possible – after they had been Laying on the Rocks for Nearly an hour the Sea ociationly washing over them and they quite Naked We – Could not tell thair meaning for Remaining So Long all of a Sudden the Women aRose" up on thair Seats thair Clubs up at arms Length – Each Struck a Seal on the Nose Which Killed him, and in an Instant they all Jumped up as if by Magic and Killed one More Each, after giving the the Seals Several Blows on the head and Securing them, they Commenced Loud Laughing and Dancing as if they had gained a great Victory" over the Seals, Each of them Draged a Seal into the Water and Swam with it to the Rock Where we was Standing and then Swam Back to the Rock and Brought one more Each Which made twelve Seals the Skins of Which being worth one pound each in Hobart Town Was not a Bad Begining by the Black Ladies, the Six Women then went to the top of a Small Hill and Made Smoaks to the Natives on the Main that they had been Killing Seals Which was soon answered by Smoaks" on the Beach We Skined the Seals and peged them out to Dry the Women them Commenced – Cooking their Supper Each Cut a Shoulder off a young Seal Weighing three or four pounds and threw them on the fire When they were about Half Done they Commenced Devouring them and Rubing the oil on their Skin Saying they had a Glorious Meal' (James Kelly, 'First Discovery of Port Davey and Macquarie Harbour', *Papers and Proceedings of the Royal Society of Tasmania* 1920: 177–8).

321 The western end of Shoal Bay, named by Flinders, 21 March 1802 after William Marsden, Second Secretary to the Board of the Admiralty, an unlikely anchorage, given the safety provided by the Bay of Shoal just a few kilometres further on to the east (Manning 1990: 195).

Chapter 16

322 A person who brings bad luck.

323 French, meeting.

324 An historical character. known variously as Suke, Sal, Sall, Black Sal, Old Suke, Sook and Sukey. She seems to have been born around around 1800: of the dozens of Tasmanian women who lived on Kangaroo Island, she seems to have lived the longest. Like her friend Sal, she was a familiar figure on Kangaroo Island in the decades after settlement until her death around 1880. There is doubt about Suke's home country, some Kangaroo Island sources claiming she was from Cape Portland in Tasmania. Tindale calls her a Tasmanian, but George Robinson's diaries and journals do not mention any woman of this name. Others believe she was abducted by Meredith's party from Port Lincoln in 1834. In 1844 Alexander Tolmer arrested Suke and her friend 'Bumblefoot' Sal for Meredith's murder but they were released: Tolmer insists she was originally from the Port Lincoln district. In the last years of her life she was blind, living with Sal near the Middle River until her companion died in 1874, the poor woman surviving on the heart of a grass tree for the week it took her to feel her way to a neighbouring homestead to report the death. Suke then moved to the Antechamber Bay district, no doubt to be close to Nat Thomas's daughter Mary Seymour and to the rations distributed from the Sturt Light: there is a reference to her present in Nat Thomas's company in 1877. It seems Suke was uneasy in the company of strangers and even though she was blind, she would often disappear into the bush with her dogs for weeks on end. James cites an 1894 Destitute Board Office Docket 280/1894 that states Suke had not received rations for nearly six years, suggesting that Suke died around 1888. See Clarke 1998: 34–5, citing Tindale 1936–65: 311–313; James 2001: 63, citing Tindale AA 338/1/36 301–307, South Australian Museum.

325 An historical character. See Note 49.

326 Note the use of the 'ethnographic' or the stereotyping present tense: 'all natives are . . .'

327 James Kelly's famous diary records detailed impressions of the hunting skills of Van Diemen's Land women, noting that one sealer named Briggs had travelled from the Bass Strait islands to 'purchase the Young Grown" up Native females to Keep them as their Wives and for Hunting Kangaroos" and Catching Seals, Both for thair Skins they Were Wonderfully Dextrous' (James Kelly, 'First Discovery of Port Davey and Macquarie Harbour', *Papers and Proceedings of the Royal Society of Tasmania for the Year 1920*: 173).

328 Alexander Tolmer refers to a 'Bloody Jack's Bay', which he claims is to the west of Point Marsden, where he says 'there is a nice little stream with a constant supply of fresh water. There is also a valley with twenty or thirty acres of good land nearly clear . . . This place is at present unoccupied, Mr Purcell, the last

resident, having been drowned, and his widow lately returned to the mainland' (*Register*, 25 September 1844: 3d). Ruediger claims that Bloody Jack's is Middle River, and notes that 'It appears the whaler who lay claim to this area, and made his home there seldom spoke, but when he did, his remarks were always prefixed by the great Australian adjective, hence the sobriquet' (Ruediger 1980: 32). Given Middle River is the place where Meredith settled, built a house and established a garden in 1835, Ruediger may record here a local legend about Meredith or about one of the party who lived there with him.

Chapter 17

329   The novelist Simpson Newland, in his *Paving the Way: A romance of the Australian bush* (London: Gay & Bird, 1893) also refers to the Rape of the Sabines. This is an early description of the Encounter Bay whaling station in the novel: 'The station itself nestled at the foot of the ridge that connects the Bluff with the hills which form the background of the bay. Protected from the west and south winds, wooden huts had been built to shelter the rude, bold, often lawless men who hunted the monster of the deep. All honour to these men, who were the first, the very first, pioneers of South Australia! In the long and glorious record of British pioneering they surely should find a place. They paved the way, in some sense, for the miner, the squatter, and the tiller of the soil, who followed to conquer and subdue the land, by conquering and making their own the wealth of the seas. But when we inquire into their relations with the wild aboriginal inhabitants of the new land, the merest instinct of justice compels us to condemn much of their conduct. Almost as lawless and unscrupulous as the old sea-kings of the North, they paid small regard to the rights, matrimonial or other, of the unfortunate people amongst whom they dwelt. Modern editions of the Rape of the Sabines were by no means uncommon, though possibly not on so extensive a scale as the original. Individual instances of disregard of the institutions, customs and feelings of the aborigines, where their women were concerned, were still more frequent. The white man, exiled from the society of the women of his own race, coveted the charms of her dusky sisters; and where, when unrestrained by the wholesome influence of law and order or deterred by the force of public opinion, has "the European learned to control his passions?"' (31).

330   Long Bill's lance was probably similar to those used to kill the huge sea elephants, now rarely seen in Australian coastal waters. James Bonwick quotes M. Peron, the naturalist to the French expedition of 1802 who was the first to describe how the Bass Strait sealers killed the sea elephants which once came ashore on King Island: 'The sealers, with their lances fifteen feet in length, seized the time when the animal raised its left fore fin, and plunged the weapon to the heart. "As soon as they see themselves attacked, they seek to fly. If their retreat is cut off, they are violently agitated; their looks carry the expression of despair; they shed tears. I have myself

seen one of these young females shed them abundantly, whilst one of our sailors, a cruel wicked man, amused himself, every time she opened her mouth, with striking her teeth with the thick end of one of the boat-hooks: this poor animal inspired pity: all its mouth was bloody, and tears ran from its eyes"' (James Bonwick, *The Last of the Tasmanians* London: Sampson, Low, Son & Marston, 1870: 291).

331 Broaching-to: 'To incline suddenly to windward of the ship's course, so as to present her side to the wind, and endanger her oversetting. (http://www. leicesterandleicestershire.com/Nautical_Words_Page2.htm, accessed 21 February 2005).

332 *Loplolly* or *Loblolly boy* has a number of meanings. A young boy serving in the surgeon's quarters of a warship. Here the meaning is seaman who is fit for no other work than to attend the sick and feed them gruel (loblolly).

333 Kangaroo grass, *Themeda triandra*, a tufty fodder grass that grows in spring and summer, the seeds of which can be collected and ground into a flour. It is one of the most widespread of all Australian native grasses, and is often described in the journals of the early explorers and settlers. Today this grass is found on roadsides or in country which is regularly burned. James Backhouse describes walking in the foothills of the Mount Lofty Ranges in November 1837: 'the Kangaroo-grass was up to our elbows, and resembled two years' seed meadows, in England, in thickness; in many places, three tons of hay per acre, might be mown off it' (Backhouse 1843: 511).

334 These days the view from the sea has been affected by the scarring of the coastal scarp caused by BHP's dolomite mining. The dumping of unsightly overburden on the beach and over the cliffs has defaced the dramatic line of cliffs along the coast.

335 The Kaurna name for the location was Tankulrawun. See Tindale 1987: 6.

336 Light employed the Islander William Cooper and two women, Sal and Doughboy to tend a garden he planted at Rapid Bay, describing his first evening ashore there as follows: 'At two, I went on shore, and was enchanted with the appearance of the whole. A fine stream of fresh water ran through the middle of the valley into the sea, and the soil was rich beyond expectation; my hopes were now raised to a pitch I cannot describe. I walked up one of the hills, and was delighted to find, that as far as I could see all around, there was an appearance of fertility, and a total absence of those wastes and barren spots, which the accounts I received in England had led me to expect' (Geoffrey Dutton and David Elder, *Colonel William Light – Founder of a City*, Melbourne: Melbourne University Press, 1991: 163).

337 An historical character, aka Condoy, King Con. His name first appears in the report written by Dr Robert Davis in 1831 describing the circumstances of Captain Collet Barker's disappearance at the Murray Mouth. When looking for Barker, Davis met an Aboriginal woman called Sally whom he took to Kangaroo Island to find George 'Fireball' Bates to assist with the search. They returned to

the mainland and met Condoy, Sally's father, who then interrogated Ngarrindjeri people to determine Barker's fate. Conday is also named by George 'Fireball' Bates as a man from the mainland who with his son 'Friday' accompanied Bates to Hog Bay on Kangaroo Island. When the son died, Bates returned to the mainland with Conday where both men lived with Conday's people for some time. Eventually Bates was found ill in a cave by other Islanders and taken back across Backstairs Passage; Conday, Friday and Sal taken with them as punishment for Bates's treatment. Condoy is also mentioned several times in John Woodforde's Journal, see for example the entry 31 August 1836 (PRG 502/1/2, State Library of South Australia). It is possible Cawthorne learned of Conday through talking with George Bates at Hog Bay. See *Advertiser*, 27 December 1886: 6c; Cumpston 1986: 128; Clarke 1998: 39; Rob Amery, 'Sally and Harry: Insights into early Kaurna contact history', *History in Portraits: Biographies of nineteenth century South Australian Aboriginal people* eds. Jane Simpson & Louise Hercus Aboriginal history monograph 6. (Sydney: Aboriginal History, 1998 49–87).

338 Good evidence again that 'Georgie' is based on George 'Fireball' Bates, who seems to have been on rather better terms with the Kaurna and the Ngarrindjeri than some of his fellow-Islanders. See the long article *Advertiser*, 27 December 1886: 6c–f based on an interview with Bates, then in his eighty-sixth year, which records Bates' particpation in ceremonies and even what is described as his initiation into 'the blacks of Cape Jervis', the Ramindjeri clan of the Ngarrindjeri from Encounter Bay. In comparison, Nat Thomas (Old Sam here) seems to have been nervous and unsure of himself in the company of the 'Onkaparinga and Encounter Bay blacks'. See the revealing episode when Thomas led a group of settlers into country around the Onkaparinga searching for lost horses and then tried to prevent their recognising him as an Islander who had abducted women from their community (Bull 1884: 33).

339 An interesting moment in the novella, suggesting the extent to which the Islanders had taken on the customs and practices of the Aboriginal people of the region, here respecting the protocols about meetings that still exist in some communities today, the 'sit-down' ceremony. Cawthorne's novella gives some support to the view that the Kaurna were affected by contact with the sealers, and vice versa, supporting the views of a number of contemporary historians and anthropologists.

340 Here 'Georgie' is clearly represented as speaking language. A number of the Islanders seem to have been familiar with not only some of the languages of the main, but also of Van Diemen's Land. See the Introduction, which makes the point that many of them were living hybrid lives, heavily influenced by Indigenous manners and customs. Note here too that Cawthorne presents an ironic reversal of the nineteenth-century stereotype of Indigenous cannibalism.

341 In his 'Literarium Diarium', Cawthorne records both hearing and being present at a number of corrobborees at the Native Location on the Torrens River. He

made available to the artist George French Angas, son of one of the colony's founding fathers, a description and water colours of the Kaurna ceremony the Kuri Dance, which Angas later included without full acknowledgement in *Savage Life and Scenes in Australia and New Zealand*: 102–08. Robert Foster includes the relevant pages in Foster 1991: 96–7.

342 This moment gestures to the still-told story about an Indigenous girl abducted to Kangaroo Island who escapes and manages to swim back across Backstairs Passage to the mainland. In some versions she survives, in others she dies in the attempt, but her child survives. Such stories are still told both on Kangaroo Island and in the Ngarrindjeri community. There are dozens of versions of this story: George 'Fireball' Bates told an *Advertiser* journalist about two failed attempts. See *Advertiser*, 27 December 1886: 6e.

343 In his travel piece 'Journal of a Trip to Kangaroo Island', *Observer*, 15 January 1853: 3d, Cawthorne records this description: 'At 5 p.m. reached Rapid Bay, hauled up the boat; in passing the cliffs a very large niche is observable, about 400 or 500 feet high, and in it a huge white stalactite, and of such a form as to resemble a human skeleton: it is a most singular curiosity'.

Chapter 18

344 Named by Matthew Flinders, 23 March 1802, viewed from Kangaroo Head, Kangaroo Island. The hill was climbed by Captain Collet Barker and party, 17 March 1831.

345 Cawthorne may have had in mind the wreck of the *Parsee* on Troubridge Shoal, 17 November 1838. The barque had been sailing from Hobart to Adelaide with 28 passengers, one of whom, Mrs C. Boucher, died in the wreck. The *Rapid* was sent to render assistance, taking the passengers off and landing them on Torrens Island, where sealers had been working, leaving rotting carcases. See C. Bateson, *Australian shipwrecks: including vessels wrecked en route to or from Australia, and some strandings* (vol. 1 Sydney: Reed: 134; and R.T. Sexton, *Shipping Arrivals and Departures South Australia 1627–1850*, (Canberra: Gould Books & Roebuck Society, 1990: 41).

346 'Troubridge Shoal and Point: – In Saint Vincent Gulf were named by Matthew Flinders on 24 March 1802, Admiral Sir Thomas Troubridge, a close friend of Lord Nelson; a baronetcy was bestowed upon him in 1799 for services in the Mediterranean' (Manning 1990: 314). Cawthorne's father, Captain Cawthorne, when applying for the job as head keeper at the Sturt Light, attached to his application a drawing of the Kokskear Light, Gulf of Finland, (probably done by his son), suggesting that something like this structure be erected on the Troubridge Shoal. See State Records, GRG 24/6/1851/1329.

347 Cawthorne may have seen the wreck of the *Sultana* on Troubridge Shoals. Edward Snell recorded this in November 1849: 'At 2 o'clock we came in sight of the [Yorke]

peninsula dividing Spencer's Gulf from Gulf St Vincent – low, scrubby and barren, the coast being a perfectly level line . . . A little to the Eastward . . . we passed the wreck of a large ship apparently of 800 or 1000 tons, lying on Troubridge Shoals. She only had her 3 lower masts, bowsprit and fore yard standing, a sloop was lying about half a mile from her, I suppose rendering assistance, or shifting cargo'. (Tom Griffiths, ed., *The Life and Adventures of Edward Snell, the Illustrated Diary of an Artist, Engineer and Adventurer in the Australian Colonies 1849 to 1859*, North Ryde, NSW: Angus & Robertson, 1988: 42–3).

348 'A person who shams insanity; named for the Abraham ward at Bedlam (a lunatic asylum, named after the Bethlehem ward at the Hospital of St Mary in London). To feigh sickness; to malinger. Hence a malingerer is called, in sailors' cant, 'Sham Abram,' or 'Sham Abraham' . . . The phrase is certainly as old as 1561, and was due to these beggars pretending that they were patients discharged from the Abraham ward at Bedlam. The genuine Bedlamite was allowed to roam the country on his discharge, soliciting alms, provided he wore a badge. This humane privilege was grossly abused, and thus gave rise to the slang phrase 'to sham Abraham'.

349 This is the only time in the novel that Cawthorne uses this name, and these characters' sudden appearance presents something of a puzzle. Cawthorne may have intended that readers imagine Dick as an African-American or West Indian. There are a number of Islanders with such backgrounds: two of George Meredith's associates were 'men of colour': the carpenter and whaler George Brown and John 'Black Jack' Williams. Several lines on, however, Cawthorne refers to 'the two blacks, man and woman', which suggests that Dick is an Indigenous man. Whatever Cawthorne's intention, it is reasonable to suspect that there may have been other chapters to the novel that were not included in the 1865–66 serial version, possibly because Cawthorne wrote more than could be included in a year's publication of serial numbers. These missing chapters may explain the sudden appearance of Black Dick and his companion.

350 Coastal saltbush, *Atriplex cinerea*, very common along South Australian coasts.

351 Given Cawthorne describes the whaleboat running before a sou'westerly from Troubridge Shoals up the gulf, it seems that this 'lake' is meant to represent the Port River. See John Jones, 'Port Adelaide River, Its First Reported Discovery' (*Proceedings of the Royal Geographical Society of Australasia, South Australian Branch*, vol. 22, 1923: 73–5).

Chapter the Last

352 Given the context, the knoll in question must be clearly visible from the sea, suggesting that Haycock's Hill at Carrickalinga is the most likely site.

353 Elsewhere Cawthorne gives this word as *katta*, Kaurna, 'an implement for digging, etc' (Foster 1991: 81).

354 This is an interesting detail, suggesting that Cawthorne's version of Meredith's murder draws on what Maggerlede or 'Bumblefoot' Sal had told Alexander Tolmer in 1844, in that she records this detail about the attack while Meredith was reading the Bible. Cawthorne may have heard this detail either from Nat Thomas, George Bates or from Sal herself, the latter well known to Cawthorne's father.

355 While there are specific references in Psalms to Syria (for example, Psalm 60 refers to David's conquests there), Cawthorne probably has the lamentational verses in mind, those that refer to penitence, distress and sorrow, given his character has just lost his ship. Psalm 23 needs no commentary. See http://mb-soft. com/believe/txs/psalms.htm, accessed 20 December 2002.

356 In 'Literarium Diarium', his diary entry dated 12 July 1843, Cawthorne recorded a detailed description of Gooroongabeer ('Captain Jack'), a young Kaurna man preparing for battle: 'He began first by mixing some red ochre and fat and then making stripes like ribs all across his chest and belly, then he called his wife who made similar stripes across his back and legs. Then he made long perpendicular stripes on his thighs and rings on his arms. After this he oiled his back part and [he] [the] front [part well]. He commenced decorating his face by striping it with red and white, the first in oblique lines as well as the [second] varied white dots which made him look more like a ghost and a devil combined together than a human being . . . his lubra (wife) took a bunch of feathers and interwove them in his back hair so that it hung loose on the back part of his neck. Then a finer and smaller bunch of cockatoo feathers bound on a neat little stick was stuck perpendicularly into his hair in the front part . . . After this the 'Wowwoodteyadla' . . . was entwined with the front hair . . . the 'Moodlata', a nosestick, was stuck through the cartilage of the nostrils . . . the 'yoodna' tied round his loins . . . the 'Taara' or net band about 5 feet long was [carried round] the lower part of the belly and tightened . . . His body was fully ornamented to his satisfaction and he gave a glance at the bystanders expressive of vanity.' (Foster 1991: 13–14). Cawthorne arranged for Gooroongabeer to pose for George French Angas: his painting survives.

357 In his 'Sketch of the Aborigines of South Australia', Cawthorne records *kari- wappa* as 'a tuft of feathers' (Foster 1991: 81).

358 In his 'Sketch of the Aborigines of South Australia', Cawthorne records the Kaurna name for red ochre as *karkoo* (Foster 1991: 46). A Kaurna source for ochre is still recorded on contemporary suburban maps of Adelaide: Puturang, or Red Ochre Cove, near Moana, a Tjilbruke Dreaming site, a men's place.

359 A club, from the Dharuk *wadi* for stick or club, the word entering English in the late eighteenth century collected from the people of the Sydney region.

360 Nat Thomas, Cawthorne's model for Old Sam, was known to the Kaurna. Bull records an episode in 1837, when Thomas had been employed by the overseer of stock of the South Australian Company to help search for two mares that had

escaped from pastures at the mouth of the Sturt River. Thomas took the search party south to the mouth of the Onkaparinga River, where he knew were some native wells. There they were surprised by a large party of Aboriginal people. Thomas told his companions they were 'Onkaparinga and Encounter Bay blacks' come to the Onkaparinga estuary on the full moon to fish and for ceremonies, further explaining that 'the black woman whom he had on the island belong to one of these tribes, and he was aware that they were not pleased at her absence. He understood a few of their words, but thought it better for him to keep as much out of sight as possible' (Bull 1884: 33).

361   The Kaurna people, traditional owners of the Adelaide Plains. Cawthorne defines the territory of the 'Adelaide tribe, which probably never exceeded 300 souls' as 'a tract of country bounded by the hills near Willunga in the South, by Cox's Creek in the East, and the Gawler River in the North, and the Sea in the West – or a tract of country of about 100 square miles, which covered gives 3 souls to one square mile (Foster 1991: 90).

362   'serve him out' – give a *quid pro quo*. This is the French *server*, to do an ill turn to one (Brewer, E. Cobham. '[serve him out]' *Dictionary of Phrase and Fable*, Philadelphia: Henry Altemus, 1898; Bartleby.com, 2000. www.bartleby.com/81/, accessed 26 May 2002).

363   Cawthorne's directions are not that precise, but given that Nat Thomas showed him where Meredith was buried, this reference to the site of his grave can be considered reliable – Sal had shown Thomas where the spot was wheich enabled he and his fellow-Islanders to find and bury the body. The most obvious candidate for the 'conical hill' is what is now known as Haycock Hill in Carrikalinga. The river is now known as the Bangala River, while Carrikalinga Creek is a little to the north. The name Yankalilla is now given to a creek that has cut the gorge cuts through which the main road from Normanville to Cape Jervis now passes. People travelling to Kangaroo Island will pass by all these places.

364   Cawthorne deploys here a commonly deployed trope about Aboriginal people from the last half of the nineteenth century, representing them as in the twilight of their lives. Here, in a neat touch, Old Sam and the Islanders are also associated with that previous day, with a glorious new dawn looming with the coming of the settlers in 1836. Henry James Johnstone's 1880 painting *Evening Shadows* uses this trope. It is one of the best-known paintings in the Art Gallery of South Australia. Johnstone painted it in London in 1880, and it was the first painting to be purchased by the Art Gallery – it was donated to the Gallery in 1881. The Aboriginal figures were added later: the first version had no human figures.

W.A. Cawthorne's Watercolours

Aspiring to develop his artistic ambitions and live the life of the *litterateur*, William Cawthorne tried to teach himself to paint in watercolour and prepare images for possible lithographic reproduction. He took some classes with the painter S.T. Gill. When George French Angas visited South Australia in 1844, Cawthorne helped him with introductions to Kaurna men and women whom Angas wished to paint. He presented Angas with some of his own drawings and sketches which Angas then used as sources for some of his paintings. Cawthorne continued sketching and painting for several decades, with the result that in December 1855 he advertised an exhibition of some two hundred items 'Illustrative of Colonial Scenery' at his Academy in Victoria Square, Adelaide (*Register*, 18 December 1855). He records in his diary that no one came to buy. It seems he only sold a handful of watercolours in his lifetime, with the consequence that after his death his family donated most of the surviving paintings and drawings to the State Library of New South Wales, where they are held today. While Cawthorne's watercolours are often clumsy and amateurish, they form a remarkable visual archive of colonial life and scenes, and there are several that are of great historical importance. See The State Library of New South Wales website for this remarkable archive. Some few of Cawthorne's watercolours are reproduced in the following pages.

Unidentified coastline
attributed to William Anderson Cawthorne, ca. 1841–1897
Mitchell Library, State Library of New South Wales

Second Valley
attributed to William Anderson Cawthorne, ca. 1843–1875
Mitchell Library, State Library of New South Wales

Possibly a corroboree
William Anderson Cawthorne

Mitchell Library, State Library of New South Wales

Fishing from rocks
William Anderson Cawthorne
Mitchell Library, State Library of New South Wales

Beach scene
William Anderson Cawthorne
Mitchell Library, State Library of New South Wales

Bushing – under Mt Jagged – S.A. early morning 1857
William Anderson Cawthorne
Mitchell Library, State Library of New South Wales

Entrance to Murray
William Anderson Cawthorne, ca. 1841–1897
Mitchell Library, State Library of New South Wales

Mt Torrens, K.I.
William Anderson Cawthorne, ca. 1841–1897
Mitchell Library, State Library of New South Wales

Coast scenery, Spencers Gulf
William Anderson Cawthorne
Mitchell Library, State Library of New South Wales

Aborigines holding a corroboree
William Anderson Cawthorne
Mitchell Library, State Library of New South Wales

Fishing
William Anderson Cawthorne
Mitchell Library, State Library of New South Wales

[Kuree Paltee] (Corroboree)
William Anderson Cawthorne, ca. 1894–1895
Mitchell Library, State Library of New South Wales

[Kuree Paltee] (Corroboree)

William Anderson Cawthorne, ca. 1894–1895

Mitchell Library, State Library of New South Wales

View from the Bluff

William Anderson Cawthorne

Mitchell Library, State Library of New South Wales

'beyond the pale'

William Cawthorne's
The Kangaroo Islanders

William Cawthorne's
The Kangaroo Islanders

On 8 April 1802, Nicolas Baudin and Matthew Flinders had their well-known encounter five miles off the main in what is now known as Encounter Bay. Between then and the winter of 1836, when the *Duke of York* disembarked the first boatload of settlers at the Bay of Shoals to set up the South Australian colony, a fascinating interregnum prevailed along the southern coast. This was a twilight time in a contact zone between the Indigenous and non-Indigenous worlds. For thirty years dozens of vessels and hundreds of sealers and whalers sailed the coastline of southern Australia, using both French and British charts to find and exploit the bounty of the south coast: fur seals, and later whales. In the process the littoral and the offshore islands became far better known than the mysterious interior. While some gangs came ashore on the islands to spend just a season or two sealing and bay whaling, other individuals and small parties settled down for longer periods. Many lived with Indigenous women from either 'New Holland' or Van Diemen's Land, building houses, clearing land, gardening, running stock and raising families. Numbers of them settled down for good, living 'beyond the pale'[1] on the edges of the British Empire.

On their arrival in 1836 the South Australian colonists were fascinated with these men whom they called the Islanders.[2] While they were seen variously as runaway convicts, pirates, wreckers, savages, wild men, natural men and Robinson Crusoes, now and again one or two observers noticed that the Islander lifestyles, experiences and histories offered a further radical model for settlement in the Antipodes at a time when theories about systematic colonisation were very much in vogue.

The first literary representation of the 'Hemprors of Kangaroo Island' and of this fascinating period of Australian history is William Cawthorne's historical novel *The Islanders*, which was probably written in 1854. It first appeared in serial form in the *Illustrated Melbourne Post* over 1865–66 and much later in book form as *The Kangaroo Islanders* in 1926, more than two decades after Cawthorne had died. It ran some two decades before the publishing boom in the 1880s and 1890s, when the majority of the South Australian 'foundation memoirs' and colonial histories first appeared, and fifty years before the first book on Kangaroo Island was published.[3] Today there is an archive of dozens of books about the Islanders, including four novels: Vernon Williams *The Straitsmen: A romance* (1929); Robert Drewe's *The Savage Crows* (1976); Ann Clancy's *Rebel Girl* (1999); and Sarah Hay's *Skins* (2002).[4]

In the mid-nineteenth century Australian colonies, those writers interested in local subjects mostly turned to Bush experience for inspiration. Cawthorne himself published an early essay in 1848 on this matter, arguing for a magazine devoted to encouraging the writing of Australian literature:

We may be deemed enthusiastic, but we cannot resist asking – Are there no new associations in colonial life? Does the far-off dweller in his rude log hut, the hutkeeper, the lonely overseer, the rude bushman, the splitter, the out-station, the stealthy savage, the overlander – are they all lifeless realities? Unconnected, tame concomitants, emotionless? When on the weary journey in the backwoods of Australia, as the twinkling light of some unexpected settler comes flickering through the gloom of night, can we – as we pause at the sight – be uninfluenced with the hopes, the fears, the difficulties, the struggles of this early and solitary pioneer? Is there a heart so callous to all that age looks back to with delight, and which pre-eminently forms the poetry of life? That poetry, the foundation of all nationality, and the mystic union of millions. The cold dialectician may easily fathom the false philosophy of the sentiment, and smile with ineffable contempt at the baseless passion, the pseudo-yearnings of imagination; but if there be one object over which we may legitimately indulge our sentimental-isms, it is that of the Australian settler – the emigrant.[5]

When Cawthorne came to attempt fiction some six years after writing this essay, it was not in 'the backwoods of Australia' that he indulged his sentimentalisms, but along the littoral, the southern coast of Australia. In this sense *The Kangaroo Islanders* is a unique work for its representations of Australia's maritime heritage in a period when, as Cawthorne himself observes, most writers were beginning to turn their faces inland for the 'new associations of colonial life'. There is a great deal in this novel about the sea, from details about coastal trading in seal skins and salt, to descriptions of ship handling, to fine descriptive seascapes. This is a typical passage from early in the work, no doubt based on Cawthorne's own observations while crossing Backstairs Passage in a whaleboat on a summer's morning:

It was early morn, and such a morn as only Australia can boast, a clear, pellucid morn with not a cloud to mar the sky, not the faintest mist, nor any visible thing to blemish the unrivalled beauty of the early day. Looking up into the heavens the eye could perceive unfathomable depths; gazing upon the land, could realise its uttermost distances; and, scanning the sea beneath, could see as in a looking glass. There, at the very bottom, on a floor of pure white sand, the hungry shark was rising and falling or pausing as he watched the huge ship darkening his pathway. There, again, was the ill-shapen 'stingerree,' flapping its huge sides, as a bird does its wings when, hastening on some furtive expedition, it is driven like a small cloud across the expanse of heaven, or with marvellous deception covering itself with the sand until invisible to all eyes. There were the voracious schnapper in countless numbers, moving rapidly along in all the glory of purple and gold in their search for new marine pastures. The supernatural clearness of the atmosphere caused the neighbouring highlands, the distant capes, and the range of mountains in the vicinity of what is now called Cape Jervis, to appear singularly close. On the black rocks, black as ink, that lined some parts of the bay, sat a mass of wild sea fowl, contrastingly white. A little higher up, on another ledge of jutting rocks sat another group of white birds, and higher still a third. In the calm morning, though so far off, their solemn chattering, their spiteful pecking, their clamorous disputing, could be distinctly heard, tipping, tripping, and modulating with the gentle swell of the sea. Anon one of them would rise in order to visit some more favourite spot, and, clattering and spattering upon the water with outstretched wings, would leave behind, straight as the flight of an arrow, an agitated pathway, gradually melting to the finest line; or one would slyly pounce upon an unwary fish, and enjoy the whole relish without a squabble with his brethren as to the lion's share. High in the air could be seen a line of birds, with very long necks and very short bodies, but with flight even and swift. They were black swans making a beeline across the straits to the lakes and islands of the Lower Murray. Over the island could be seen several hundreds of unwieldy pelican flying in their peculiar way, and marking on the blue expanse as far as the eye could follow, the singular outline of the letter 'W.' They were winging their way to the seat of the primeval haunts of their race – the inland lagoons of the island (pp. 6–7).

Given that this is a novel about seamen, there are also many nine-teenth-century nautical expressions in this novel. Cawthorne notes in his diary that when he arrived on the *Amelia* in South Australia in May 1841 he 'was a black skinned sailor boy full of the sayings and habits of the boatmen'.[6] A decade or so later, when he came to write his novel, he was able to make good use of those sayings, no doubt helped along by his father's knowledge and experience, once Captain Cawthorne rejoined his wife and son in Adelaide in 1845 after half a decade at sea. As a result one of the small pleasures on offer in *The Kangaroo Islanders* is its display of colourful nautical slang and quotations from various chanteys. Given that so few colonial Australian novels refer to mari-time experience, this feature is memorable. One or two examples will suffice. At one point a character is described as a 'son of a gun'. This is a British naval expression for an illegitimate child, originating on the West Indies station. On some ships on blockade duty women were allowed on board; if children were born (the father unknown), then the entry 'son of a gun' would be made in the ship's log. At another point one of the ship's company is lost in the scrub and later rescued; this is how he is addressed by one of the Islanders after he is found, in Cawthorne's approximation of working-class and regional dialectal English in the style of Dickens and, earlier, of Sir Walter Scott:

'And here, you bale away cold water on his nob; we'll soon set yer up all a-taunt-o; but I hopes yer will be werry pertickler arter this how yer goes toddling about in this garden o' ours, which is summet like oursels, werry poorty in some places, and werry ugly in t'other.' (p. 39)

Websters Dictionary helps us discover that the expression 'all a-taunt-o' means 'fully rigged, as a vessel; with all sails set; set on end or set right. Origin: French, *Autant* as much (as possible)'.[7] The novel has many such examples.

In Chapter 13 of *The Kangaroo Islanders*, Cawthorne claims that his novel 'is a narrative of fact to a very large extent'. Where did a young Adelaide teacher and *littérateur* discover the colourful histories of the Islanders? Who told this 'townie' stories about Kangaroo Island when it was the *Ultima Thule* of the British Empire, in the period between Matthew Flinders's charting of the coastline in 1802 and the arrival of the first boatloads of settlers in Nepean Bay in 1836? Cawthorne's *The Kangaroo Islanders* is an important source of information about Australia's maritime history in general and sealing history in particular because it draws on stories collected from several of the old sealers whom Cawthorne met on Kangaroo Island during several visits during the 1850s. *The Kangaroo Islanders* does allude to historical episodes, if only in passing and in sketchy detail, because his sources were not only oral accounts collected from some of the people involved or their associates, but also because his informants may not have been willing to divulge too-detailed versions of some of the stories that they might have told. As late as 1844 the South Australian police were still interested in George Meredith's killing – and even arresting suspects – the murder occurring just months before the arrival of the colonists and which is represented in Cawthorne's novel.

There are a number of points of detail in *The Kangaroo Islanders* that suggest that Cawthorne did have access to reasonably specific information about people and events from Islander informants. Although he invents names for the majority of his Islander characters, he does use three names – 'Georgy,' 'Worley' and 'Pork[e]y' – suggesting the historical characters George 'Fireball' Bates, 'Governor'

Henry Wallen and [?] Pirkey, the first two of whom at least are well known. He records that most of his characters had sea-going backgrounds while others had been convicts. He mentions Sydney as a port of origin, and represents in some detail the business of sealing, Australia's first export industry. He describes the Islanders trading salt, seal, wallaby and kangaroo skins with the masters of the 'hookers', the small coastal vessels from Sydney, Port Dalrymple or Hobart Town that visited Kangaroo Island at regular intervals. He describes at length a 'menagerie' inland from Creek (Antechamber) Bay, where a group of Islanders, their Indigenous women and children lived like Robinson Crusoes and assorted Fridays. Making much of Islander clothing and diet, Cawthorne notes the quaintness of their unique lifestyle, which he suggests owes as much if not more to Indigenous as to European ways. He suggests that the Indigenous women lived in separate wurleys, that they maintained many 'traditional' Indigenous hunting methods, that they spoke in language and preserved a number of other traditional beliefs and practices, bringing up their children as Indigenous.

Cawthorne names one Indigenous man – Conday – and five Indigenous women in his novel: Bet, Bumblefoot, Brown Sal, Pussy and Suky, all of whom are historical characters either from Tasmania or from 'the main' – Bumblefoot (or Maggerlede) was Trukanini's tribal sister. He notes that the Tasmanian or Palawa women preferred the company of other Tasmanians, insisting that the Palawa were more highly skilled hunters than their 'New Holland' sisters. He very briefly alludes to at least one Indigenous man working as a sealer on Kangaroo Island.

Cawthorne also represents some of the more unedifying practices of the Islanders. He uses the word 'slave' twice to describe the relationships between men and women, which were often marked by violence. Cawthorne also records quite a number of details about the women's active involvement in sealing and wallaby snaring, reinforcing the perception that they played crucial roles in adapting traditional Indigenous hunting practices to the demands of their 'lords o' creation'. There is also a lively representation of a 'Sabine expedition', a raid on the coastline near present-day Rapid Bay in which Kaurna women are abducted. The reference to the capture of a woman known to the Islanders as 'Puss' on an earlier raid is significant. The murder of Captain [George] Meredith is the culminating episode of the novel, given with sufficient detail to suggest Cawthorne must have heard a little of the story, perhaps even from one of the group of Islanders who found Meredith's body in late 1836.

One or two of these details are of considerable significance for the record we have of the Islanders and their lives. An obvious example is the reference to their cropping the ears of the Indigenous women they lived with as a form of punishment, which is mentioned in Chapter 12 in an exchange between a couple of the Islanders – one of them Old Sam, based loosely on Nathaniel ('Nat') Walles Thomas. Here it is clearly suggested that the men are very aware of the need to keep the women subjugated, under control, and also aware that the women still preserve a secret and inaccessible world of 'women's business' that the men cannot easily enter, the gateway to which was knowledge of 'Hobart-Town' language, 'caterwauling' or singing in language.

> 'I say, Porky, the women smell a rat, aye! whose a been and split? this caterwauling means summut.'
>
> 'Give 'em a tarnation hiding all around,' suggested another, 'that'l keep 'em quiet while we's away; or slit their ears?'
>
> 'Yes,' said Porky, 'that might do some good; letting blood is fust rate. I know's it mysell; when I gets drunk, and gets knocked about, it's the bleeding that does me good; I feels all the better arter.'

The name Porky is of interest.[8] This may refer to a 'runaway whaler' called Pirkey, a man known to Mary Seymour, the daughter of Nat Thomas and Old Bet, who told her doctor Herbert Basedow that (in the 1820s and early 1830s?) Pirkey was living on Kangaroo Island with a number of Aboriginal women who had been stolen from Cape Jervis. 'Quite a number of children are said to have been brought to the world as a result of this importation, but according to Mrs. Seymour, they either died from natural causes or were knocked on the head directly they were born.'[9] There are few published references to Pirkey/Porky; he is not named by 'the Conciliator' George Augustus Robinson, whose records, kept while Protector of Aborigines in Van Diemen's Land, remain the most comprehensive account of the sealers. Neither does Pirkey's name appear in any of the shipping lists.

Philip Clarke suggests that Porky is another name for Henry Wallen, which does not seem likely, given Cawthorne also has a character named 'Governor' Worley.[10] It is just as likely that Porky is based on Henry 'Fireball' Bates, whom Cawthorne probably met in Hog Bay on one of his visits, and who is still remembered for running pigs there.

The ear cropping. There is no doubt that Cawthorne here records in shadowy outline something of the violence used to keep the Indigenous women in subjugation to the Islanders. In fact he may refer to a particular episode, details of which have survived in other places. An Indigenous woman named Charlotte was one of George Robinson's sources for information about the sealers on Kangaroo Island: as Tasmanian Protector of Aborigines he gives her various names as KAL. LOON.GOO, COW.WER.PITE.YER, WIN.DEER.RER and Sarah. Robinson recorded the following information after speaking with Kalloongoo after she joined the Aboriginal Settlement 1 June 1837:

> Interrogated the woman who arrived last night from Woody Island; result as follows (1) KAL.LOON.GOO, (2) COW. WERTITE.YER, (3) WIN.DEER.RER alias Sarah an aboriginal female of New Holland, the point opposite to Kangaroo Island, the west point of Port Lincoln. Was forcibly taken from her country by a sealer named James Allan who in company with another sealer Bill Johnson (this man was drowned subsequent to my visit to Port Phillip) conveyed her across to Kangaroo Island . . . Said the sealers beat the black women plenty; they cut a piece of flesh off a woman's buttock; cut off a boy's ear, Emue's boy. This woman is now on Woody Island with Abyssinia Jack. The boy died in consequence of his wounds. They cut them with broad sealer's knives. Said they tied them up and beat them and beat them with ropes. Bill Dutton beat her plenty. Said the sealers got drunk plenty and women get drunk too. Said the country where she came from was called BAT.BUN.GER.YANG.GAL.LALE.LAR. It is situate at the west point of St. Vincents Gulf. Said that Emue's brother was her husband. It is on the sea coast; there is a long sandy beach with three rivers. MAN.NUNE.GAR is the name of the country where she was born. Kangaroo Island is called DIRK.I.YER.TUN.GER. YER.TER; WAT.ER.KER.TER, an island.[11]

Rob Amery has established that Robinson is in error: Kalloongoo was a woman from the BAT.BUN.GER (Rapid Bay) district, not from Port Lincoln.[12] Robinson reports elsewhere the story told to him by John ('Abyssinia Jack') Anderson[13] that another sealer named James Allen had tied a Van Diemen's Land woman called Lar.roon.er to a tree 'at American Wharf Lagoon' (American River? American Beach?). He then slashed her buttocks with his sealer's knife and cut off part of her ear. Anderson also reported to Robinson that Nat Thomas had cut off the ears of a seven-year-old 'New Holland' boy, cutting so close to the head that a piece of the cheek was also removed. After lingering for several weeks the lad died.[14] This story emerges in fragmentary form in Kalloongoo's account quoted above. Robinson reports such details about the brutality of the sealers with considerable relish. He was, after all, charged by the Van Diemen's Land Lieutenant-Governor George Arthur to establish contacts with the surviving Palawa people and to settle them at the Wybaleena settlement on Flinders Island, so any evidence he might collect of the barbarity and inhumanity of the sealers gave his task an added moral imperative.[15]

Cawthorne uses some other interesting names for his sealers, some of whom are named in other sources, one or two not. The 1865–66 serial version of the novel refers to a sealer named 'Shaw' for the first reference, 'Straw' thereafter. William Shaw was an early visitor to Kangaroo Island, sailing in 1816 on the *Rosetta*, which took 2000 skins and 50 tons of salt back to Sydney for Jonathan Griffiths.[16] Perhaps Cawthorne heard the name from one of his informants.

While some of the characters named in the novel are known to history, others are not. The novel refers at length to the marooning of a sealer named 'Grip Hard' on the Althorpe Islands in Investigator Strait. The story is given in sufficient detail to suggest that Cawthorne heard it from one of his Islander informants. While the quirkiness of the name might suggest that this novel is the only published reference to this individual, including a yarn about his fate, it is tempting to speculate that Cawthorne might have heard a fragment of the well-known story about a sealer named 'Antonio', also collected by John Moore Davis direct from 'Sally' and published for the first time in 1878. She appears in *The Kangaroo Islanders* as 'Brown Sal', Suky's companion, the two women who kill 'Flash Tom' for marooning 'Grip

Hard' on the Althorpes. Well known on Kangaroo Island after settlement, 'Brown' or 'Little' Sal was a Nauo woman abducted by sealers from the Port Lincoln area, possibly even in a raid led by associates of George Meredith in 1834. She then spent time on islands off the west coast of South Australia, where she lived with Bill Bryan[t] on St Peter's and Flinders Islands before eventually moving to Kangaroo Island some time after Bryan's death in 1845 and after spending some time with John ('Black Jack') Anderson at King George's Sound.[17] One of the three women who wandered the scrub of Kangaroo Island with their dogs in the 1860s and 1870s, she died in 1877. Cawthorne's character's name 'Grip Hard' immediately recalls the Antonio story, often told on Kangaroo Island:

> Sally told me of an instance where a mulatto, named Antonio, who used to babble in his cups rather strangely of some tragic occurrences, was disposed of. Being a powerful and determined fellow, they were afraid to quarrel with him, and therefore determined to get rid of him the first opportunity. On one of their cruises, they came upon a seal-rookery, which could only be approached by descending the rocks from above – a great height, and a considerable part of which the man employed would have to be lowered down by a rope, and then drawn up again. Antonio volunteered to perform the perilous task; descended in safety, killed a number of fur-seals, skinned them, and sent up their skins, and then, at a given signal, began to ascend by the rope. His treacherous companions, after pulling him up some distance, stopped, and then William began to revile him for what he had said during his maudlin moments, and after taunting him for some time – while thus hovering on the brink of eternity – with the doom they had assigned him – in order, as they said, to keep his tongue quiet – they cut the rope, and the wretched man fell some hundreds of feet into the boiling abyss beneath.[18]

Another character who appears in the novel on page 99 is called 'Black Dick'; the name is used only once, perhaps intending that readers imagine Dick as an African-American or West Indian. There were a number of Islanders with such backgrounds: two of George Meredith's associates were 'men of colour': the carpenter and whaler George Brown and John 'Black Jack' Williams, and Maggerlede was abducted from Bruny Island by John 'Black' Baker. Several lines on, however, Cawthorne refers to 'the two blacks, man and woman', which suggests that Dick is a sealer of Indigenous background living on Kangaroo Island before settlement. Elsewhere in the novel he refers to a boy living with the sealer 'Flash Tom'. While the evidence is very slight, this is a significant moment, suggesting that, while we are very familiar with the involvement of Indigenous women in the sealing industry, there is much less evidence of the participation of Aboriginal men.[19] In passing, it is reasonable to suspect that there may have been other chapters to the novel that were not included in the 1865–66 serial version, possibly because Cawthorne wrote more than could be included in a year's publication of serial numbers. Missing chapters may explain the sudden appearance of the enigmatic Black Dick and his companion.

The plot of *The Kangaroo Islanders* represents the murder of a man named 'Captain Meredith' at Yankalilla. This detail is of considerable historical interest, referring to a real character and a series of events that, in spite of Cawthorne's subtitle of 1823, actually occurred in South Australian waters in the mid-1830s, and possibly as late as 1836. In the novel 'Captain Meredith' (his first name not given) is represented as a melancholy, introverted and fastidious master of an unnamed sealing and trading vessel. He sails to Kangaroo Island from Sydney to buy skins and load salt. Most of his crew desert to join the Islanders, and after the ship is wrecked on Troubridge Shoals the remaining crew sail south for Kangaroo Island in a whaleboat. They anchor off Yankalilla and Meredith goes ashore to read his Bible. There, on a conical hill near a river, while deep in Psalms, Meredith is inexplicably murdered by two Kaurna men whom he has never met before. They strike him down with a *kutta*, a digging stick, having mistaken him for an Islander who had recently raided their country on a 'Sabine expedition', abducting women.

Has Cawthorne's version of 'poor Meredith's' murder any historical basis? The writer was certainly familiar with some of the details of the Meredith story; he had been shown the murder site at Yankalilla by Nat Thomas on his 1852 Christmas trip to Kangaroo Island (Thomas was one of the group of Islanders who had found Meredith's body and buried it).[20] The novel is just one of several published versions of this killing which, although it occurred before settlement, came to resonate in colonial imaginations in the first decades of the colony. The murders of Captain Collet Barker at the Murray Mouth in 1831 and George Meredith at Yankalilla in 1836 were seen as defining moments in race relations by many South Australians. The shadow of both events lay over the early years of race relations in the colony in South Australia; these murders were interpreted as telling examples of the inexplicably violent and unpredictable behaviour of Indigenous people. These days we know that the brutality of the sealers on their raids of mainland communities may well have given Indigenous people motives for both murders, but at the time little was known (or understood) about why Indigenous people had acted as they did. In the early years in colonial South Australia stories circulated about these murders, told partly as a response to what was perceived as the brutality and savagery of the Aborigines, told to justify the appropriation of Aboriginal lands as an inevitable consequence of the arrival of European civilisation.

Versions of Meredith's murder can be found in a significant number of the travel books and histories that constitute the early attempts at history-making in South Australia. Here is William Leigh's meeting with one of the alleged perpetrators of 'poor' Meredith's' murder from an 1839 publication:

> One day, while dissecting a young seal at Kangaroo Island, a black woman came up at the time, and stood gazing, with apparent wonder, at my operation. I continued the dissection, and offered her the blubber. This established a friendly feeling between us, and she became very communicative. I remarked that her countenance was as expressive and pleasing as any I had met with. A friend came up at the time, and when she had departed, informed me that the woman, in whom I had felt so much interest, was no other than the murderer of poor Meredith. I stared at this information, and regretted I had not examined her cranium'.[21]

Although Leigh does not name this woman, she is Maggerlede, Trukinini's tribal sister, appearing in Cawthorne's novel as 'Bumblefoot' and well known on Kangaroo Island as 'Old Sal': she had been taken there for the first time after her abduction from Bruny Island off the east coast of Tasmania in 1825 or 1828 by 'a man of colour', John 'Black' Baker.[22] Leigh goes on to tell quite a story about George Meredith, given in sufficient detail to suggest that he had met individuals on Kangaroo Island who knew him and his story. A young man of twenty-one or twenty-two and unlucky in business, Meredith had fled society and settled for some time on Kangaroo Island, later moving to Yankylilly,[23] where according to Leigh he had built a hut and established good relationships with the Aboriginal people of the district. He had both a boy and a woman living with him, and after disciplining the youth for not saying grace over his food, he was then murdered with an axe by the woman in his hut while reading his prayer book. The boy and the woman then stole his whaleboat. After some time his associates on Kangaroo Island came to search for him, located his body (the prayer book still clutched in his hand) and buried him. The whaleboat was later found wrecked at Encounter Bay, the rudder discovered in the possession of Aboriginal people camped inland.[24]

Leigh's version of events was published in 1839. Perhaps the most intriguing of the various versions of the George Meredith story was collected by Kangaroo Island resident H.C. Barrett, who wrote to Norman Tindale at the South Australian Museum recounting a story told to him by J.P. Gell, who had known Maggerlede as an old woman in the 1860s or 1870s and from whom he had collected an account of Meredith's murder. Meredith is remembered as 'Marion' and Maggerlede as Sal: she told Gell that the Captain was a Bible-reading man who was killed near Second Valley by the blacks, who crept on him as he was sitting on the beach reading the Bible. She had escaped by swimming out to sea. Gell recorded that Sal used to weep when telling the story, and that she still remembered the Lord's Prayer, which 'Marion' had taught her.[25] Again there are certain details repeated: 'Marion' reading his Bible; his murder on a beach at a mainland site 'near Second Valley'; Sal's involvement.

There was obviously quite a strong tradition on Kangaroo Island that remembered Meredith as 'Marion'. Roland Snelling, a son of Henry Snelling who distributed rations to the Indigenous women on the island and after whom the beach is named, wrote to the Adelaide paper the *News* with another tiny vignette about Meredith and Maggerlede:

There was another black woman named Big Sal. She was brought over from the mainland by whalers also. She was a fine-looking, big black. But she was bumble-footed. She lost two of her toes through getting burned while drunk. She lived with a man named Marion, who had a large whaling boat . . . I was about 13 years old when they disappeared from Middle River. They always called my dad 'The Governor'.[26]

It is evident from such accounts that versions of the story about the Meredith murder were circulating not just on Kangaroo Island but also on the mainland: the fact that several published accounts exist says something about the significance of the event in the colony and the shadow it cast. An anonymous 1880 newspaper version was written by a member of a party that had travelled to Kangaroo Island. The party included such distinguished company as Commissioner of Crown Lands T. Playford, Surveyor-General G.W. Goyder and historian J.P Stow, strongly suggesting that the Meredith story was told especially when visiting the island.[27]

Two of the best-known early histories of South Australia are Alexander Tolmer's *Reminiscences of an Adventurous and Chequered Career at Home and at the Antipodes* (1882) and John Wrathal Bull's *Early Experiences of Life in South Australia and an Extended Colonial History* (1884); each mentions Meredith's murder in detail sufficient to indicate that numbers of colonial South Australians possessed relatively detailed versions of the story.

Tolmer was South Australia's most famous colonial policeman. In 1844 he led a police party to Kangaroo Island to round up escaped prisoners, and while there arrested Sal and her friend Suke as suspects for Meredith's murder. The woman he knew as 'Sal' was Maggerlede.[28] Tolmer wrote three versions of the Meredith story: two newspaper accounts in 1844 and 1866, and the extended description in his 1882 *Reminiscences*.[29] Tolmer insists that Meredith was the son of a wealthy Tasmanian settler; that he was an 'outcast through profligacy and crime'; that he was murdered with a tomahawk while reading his Bible on board his boat in Yankalilla Bay, the motive theft. His killers were said to be 'Encounter Bay' men, one named as 'Encounter Bay Bob'. Bob's real name was Tammuruwe Nankere or Parru Paicha; he was a well-known figure in Adelaide in the early years of the colony and known to Cawthorne.

Bull's 1884 history is also based on sealers' testimony and that of 'a Tasmanian black woman, called Sal, who had lost one of her feet when young by sleeping with them too near the fire' – Maggerlede again. She seems to have told her version of the Meredith story to anyone who would listen. Bull identifies Meredith's killers as two young men abducted from 'the mainland', precisely where is not given. He claims Meredith was eating porridge by his campfire when he was attacked, but he does not mention the murder weapon.

Who was George Meredith? He was born in 1806, the eldest son of the Tasmanian landowner and former Royal Marine officer George Meredith[30] (1777–1856), best-known before his arrival in Van Diemen's land for removing Napoleon's 'Cap of Liberty' in 1801 from the top of Pompey's Pillar in Alexandria, Egypt. Meredith Senior was then a young lieutenant on HMS *Hinde*.[31]

In 1821 the Meredith family settled as free settlers at Great Swan Port on the east coast of Van Diemen's Land, on what is now called the Meredith River in the Oyster Bay area.[32] There George Meredith established a pastoral empire and became involved in shipbuilding, coastal trading, sealing and bay whaling. In later life the 'King of Swan Port' became a powerful member of the Tasmanian establishment, sitting in the Legislative Council.

The celebrated colonial travel writer and novelist Louisa Anne Meredith was the murdered man's cousin. His brother Charles married her on 18 April 1839: if George had lived Louisa would have been his sister-in-law. Their eldest son was named George Campbell Meredith, but whether after the father or the deceased brother is not clear.[33] From the pages of several of Louisa's writings emerges a shadowy figure: George as his brother Charles remembered him in sanitised family reminiscence. There is the young man on the point of emigrating to Australia copying engravings of Aborigines; a kind young man; the author of a play in which his cousin Louisa had a small part; a student at Dr Lindsay's school at Bow; the young man sleeping on the floor of the cabin to toughen himself up for life in the Bush. George comes into sharper focus after arriving in Tasmania.

Louisa Anne Meredith describes events that took place in 1824, when George was eighteen and Charles thirteen. The two brothers were overlanding sheep to Hobart under very difficult conditions without proper food or shelter. George had taken up a land grant of 1500 acres at Anson's Creek, seventy miles from his father's station and the two brothers walked there to take possession. Louisa Anne Meredith records her husband's memories of the experience:

> Our entire joint equipment consisted of one knapsack, in which we carried a little flour, tea, and sugar; and we had a tin 'billy,' or small can, to boil our tea in; and one single-barrelled flint-lock gun. Two kangaroo dogs accompanied us, whose game was to be our food.[34]

The brothers are described enduring the vicissitudes of Bush life: Charles nearly drowned crossing a flooded creek; George became violently ill; both managed to cope.

Louisa Meredith also gives one or two glimpses of the Meredith family's involvement in the tanning, sealing and bay-whaling industries.[35] Between 1824 and 1832 the Meredith brothers worked in several of the family businesses, including pastoral activities. George Meredith Senior won a lucrative government contract to supply the convict settlement on Maria Island, and in 1826 he applied successfully for a lease for exclusive rights to seal on Isle du Phoques, the first such commercial agreement between the Crown and a settler. Meredith also set up a tannery to process the seal skins.[36] The Meredith family was also involved in shipbuilding, at least in part in response to the fallout from a bitter dispute between Meredith and Lieutenant-Governor George Arthur when the latter attempted to frustrate the family's many business enterprises.

In 1826 George Meredith Sr began building the *Black Swan*, a 50-ton 'colonial' schooner at Great Swanport to service the family's growing sealing and bay-whaling ventures. She was launched in 1829 and went sealing out of Swanport. In February 1830 she ran up on Prime Seal Island, to the west of Flinders Island in the Furneaux Group in Bass Strait: Charles was certainly aboard when she ran aground.[37] Several of his anecdotes about the wreck were recorded by his wife Louisa Anne Meredith:

I have heard Mr. Meredith recount his great delight at having once, some years ago, killed nine [seagulls] with one shot, when he had been shipwrecked on an island in Bass's Straits, and had lived for some days on a miserable sort of porridge or burgoo, made of flour recovered from the wreck, and so damaged by salt water it would not bake, mixed with water so strongly impregnated with alum that it could scarcely be drunk. After this diet, meat, even though that of a sea-bird, became valuable, and the nine gulls were a most precious acquisition; but being shot at dusk, they were put aside until dawn, to be prepared for breakfast; and then, woeful to relate, all that remained of them were two legs, the rest having been devoured during the night by rats.[38]

The *Black Swan* was repaired, refloated and then resumed sealing.[39]

An examination of the Meredith family correspondence preserved in libraries and archives in both Tasmania and South Australia suggests that, while the younger brother Charles was involved in the Meredith family sealing and bay-whaling enterprises, George was managing several land grants on the east coast, one adjacent to his father's at Great Swan Port on Oyster Bay. A letter dated 17 June 1829 describes what appears to be a contented landowner requesting his stepmother arrange to have him sent some spirits, spades, bags, two cakes of Windsor soap, two or three quills, two pounds of tobacco, some chain, boards and some 'trowsers', suggesting he had convicts assigned to him.[40]

Some time in 1832 or 1833 George had a violent quarrel with his father, details about which are very sketchy; it seems that not only did the family maintain a silence about the matter, but any letters making direct reference in the Meredith family papers may have been culled. Nevertheless, one or two fragments of information have survived. Louisa Anne Twamley (she would marry her cousin George's brother Charles in 1839) wrote to George Meredith Sr on 18 May 1833:

I have received from George a very long and truly interesting letter, which has given us more information than all the other letters (except <u>your own</u>) yet arrived from Tasmania; I cannot express to you how much it gratified me, more especially from the <u>inexplicable</u> and <u>mysterious</u> silence respecting him, which is so strictly maintained by yourself and other members of your family, you have give [sic] <u>distinct hints</u> which at such a distance are, pardon my freedom, ill-advised, as they lead to endless and distressing conjecture – He mentions his intended voyage to New Zealand, and Mr. Watson in a letter to myself mentions his own, Mr. W's regret at the 'circumstances which compel him to quit his adopted country' – you may imagine we feel a great anxiety respecting his real fate, and sincerely hope to receive more satis-factory and decisive intelligence.[41]

Whatever the 'circumstances' that caused the disagreement, George had obviously put his side of the story to friends and relatives back in Britain. In October 1832 he sold his East Coast properties to a Mr Orr for £2500, seemingly without his father's permission.[42] It may be that George wanted to go sealing and bay-whaling rather than living the life of the squatter: nearly a year later he writes home to his stepmother from the family's bay-whaling station on Maria Island, mentioning correspondence he has had with his father, along with the fact that they had taken four whales and had run short of casks, which hardly gives the impression of a prodigal son.[43] However, three years later, in an intriguing aside in a letter dated 13 February 1835 to their father, his brother Charles mentions his brother's 'infatuation' and the on-going necessity for the family to keep details about the matter from 'the Govt.' and out of the press, implying a dispute of a rather more complicated kind.[44] An undated memoir obviously written after 1853 when his half-brother John (born fourteen years after George) returned from South Australia to buy out the family properties at Cambria is in the Tasmanian Archives, entitled 'Answers re. George Meredith' and obviously intended for his children. In response to question #14, 'What do I recollect of George ——', the following is given, after an anecdote about visiting him at another Meredith property:

The only other time I remember seeing him was in the Parlour at Belmont, when he came to see our Father and there was a sad disagreement between them but I have no recollection what it was about – [45]

What (or whom?) was George infatuated with, sufficient to cause a row with his domineering father? Whatever it was, something happened between August and October 1833 that prompted George to commandeer the family's 25-ton *Defiance* (from Maria Island?) and set off for Sydney. Alexander Tolmer's account describing Meredith the 'outcast through profligacy and crime'[46] suggests a sexual misdemeanor of some kind, and given his later behaviour, perhaps he was involved with an Indigenous woman.

Whatever his reasons for leaving Van Diemen's land, George Meredith sailed to Sydney sometime around September 1833, seemingly intent on leaving for New Zealand for good. However, *Defiance* was wrecked in October 1833 (all hands saved), either fifteen miles south of Twofold Bay, Eden, New South Wales, or in Bass Strait near Howe Island.[47] Given Meredith's associate James Manning's later testimony before the Court in Albany, Western Australia, the last-named seems more likely, in that the latter reports the loss of the vessel at 'Cape Howe Island', as does a *Sydney Gazette* account:

> We are concerned to hear that the *Defiance* of this port [Sydney] belonging to Mr. Chapman, of Darling Harbour, was wrecked in Bass's Straits, near Howe Island some weeks ago. The captain, it appears was engaged on a sealing trip, and having anchored under the lee of a light ridge, took to his boat with six men, to proceed and engage some hands at a certain place some distance off. In the meantime a severe gale blew from the sea and drove the schooner from her anchorage upon the beach where she became a wreck. The greater part of the cargo will be saved, but still the loss of the vessel is severe. It ought, however, to operate as a caution to those 'penny wise and pound foolish' gentlemen, who enter into such speculation without protecting themselves by insurance.[48]

The vessel was salvaged: the *Blackbird* returned to Sydney 2 November 1833 with 'part of the wreck'. No doubt the 'Mr. Chapman, of Darling Harbour' was Meredith's business partner who had put up the money to pay for the trade goods that the *Defiance* was carrying. This fact, and the location of the wreck, suggest that Meredith may have changed his mind about New Zealand and instead equipped a ship to trade with the sealers of the southern coast, which is how he is described in Manning's Declaration and again how he is represented in Cawthorne's novel.[49]

George Meredith then joined the *Independent*, another Meredith family sealing vessel, in Bass Strait in late (October?) 1833. The *Independent* was skippered by an American named James 'Little' West; in later years she would be well known as a trader along Tasmania's east coast between Great Swan Port and Hobart Town.[50] Then Meredith and his associates were directly involved in an episode that would have resonating consequences and long-term repercussions, abducting four (and possibly as many as nine) Aboriginal women and several young men from Point Nepean just inside the heads at Port Phillip – one possibly a Bunurong man named Yonki Yonka – and shooting several other Bunurong men in the process.[51]

Details about Meredith's raid were well known to the early settlers of the Port Phillip district (or Bearpurt, as Melbourne was then known); eventually they came to the attention of the authorities in both Hobart and Sydney. On behalf of the Port Phillip Association, John H. Wedge wrote to Van Diemen's Land Colonial Secretary John Montagu on 15 March 1836 reporting that a 'flagrant outrage' had been committed upon the Aborigines some eighteen months earlier and four women abducted, and that the settlers in the new colony at Port Phillip were well aware that, unless measures were taken to protect 'the Natives', a spirit of hostility would be created against the settlers, 'which in all probability will lead to a state of warfare between them and the Aborigines, which will only terminate when the black man will cease to exist'.[52] J.H. Wedge then wrote to John Montagu requesting that the Commandant of the Flinders Island Aboriginal Settlement George Robinson be instructed to locate the four women abducted from Point Nepean on the Bass Strait islands and restore them to their families as an act of justice.[53] Wedge obviously considered that relationships between the settlers and the Aborigines in the new settlements around Port Phillip would be improved if the women were returned.[54] Given the antipathy between George Meredith Sr and Lieutenant-Governor Arthur, it is hardly surprising that Arthur ordered Robinson to find out what he could about the episode.

It is likely that Lieutenant-Governor Arthur first heard details about what George Meredith Jr had been up to in late September 1836, when the *Duke of York* arrived in Hobart after disembarking the first shipload of settlers at Kangaroo Island. Robinson certainly visited the ship, learning 'particulars of the death of G. Meredith junior on the main opposite Kangaroo Island'; it seems such details were not reported in the Hobart Town papers.[55] Just a day or two later, Robinson records that:

> The two Port Philip [sic] natives with Mr Fawkner met me in Macquarie Street [Hobart] and informed me that the sealers had taken away their wives and that they were now with them the sealers in the straits.[56]

J.P. Fawkner had brought three of the Port Phillip men to Tasmania (one had returned home before Robinson met him) to help put the Port Phillip Association case to Governor Arthur that 'the Commandant of Flinders Island . . . [should be instructed to] take measures for restoring these women to their families'. The two men with Fawkner were Derimut (Derrahmert) and Betmenjee (Baitbainger), both of whom were obviously considered something of a curiosity in Hobart in 1836, in that Benjamin Law took casts of both their faces, and the artist Benjamin Duterrau painted Derimut's portrait.[57] The pressure seems to have worked: Robinson's journal entry of 17 November 1836 records that he and Wedge had seen the Colonial Secretary and he was ordered to Port Phillip.[58] Robinson was then instructed to sail to Port Phillip to 'emancipate the New Holland females', but first he had to 'get the men in order to coin the women', that is, persuade relatives of the abducted women to accompany him to the islands of Bass Strait to convince the women to return to Port Phillip.

George Robinson's journal records several references to the Point Nepean raid, the first recorded even before he began to gather material for his report for Lieutenant-Governor Arthur dated 12 January 1837.[59] The journal entry dated 9 May 1836 notes that he not only had heard about Meredith's murder while visiting Hobart Town, but that the authorities and also the sealing fraternity were well aware of what Meredith Jr had been up to:

> Saw the Colonial Secretary [in Hobart] . . . [the sealer] Proctor informed me that the New Holland women was [sic] brought to the islands by George Meredith, that Munro has one, Baily has one and the other sealer the last. George Meredith was speared by the natives on the coast of New Holland, no doubt in retaliation for the injuries he has done to them. This was a just retribution. Many aggressions had been committed by the Merediths on the natives at Oyster Bay [in Tasmania].[60]

Robinson's sympathies obviously lay with Arthur.

Robinson arrived at Port Phillip on 26 December 1836, recording details supplied by 'Matilda the VDL native woman' as they sailed past the site of the raid, Matilda's knowledge clearly indicating how much was known in the sealing community about the episode:

> Point Nepean is on the eastern side of the entrance [to Port Phillip]. Matilda . . . pointed out the spot a few miles down the harbour at Point Nepean where she said George Meredith and his crew of sealers stole the native women. The men's names were Brown, Mr West the master of the schooner, a man named Billy.[61] Said the schooner anchored off, the sealers went on shore. Said there was plenty of forest boomer kangaroo at the point. Said they deceived the people; gammoned them. Said the native men upset the boat and the men were all wet and fell into the water. Said there was plenty of black fellows, some on the Port Phillip side, some outside, sea coast. Said the sealers were afraid of the Port Phillip natives. Said they employed her to entice them. George Meredith stole the, I think she said, four women, took them in the schooner first to Kings Island and then to Hunter and Clarks and Gun Carriage Islands, and then sold them to the sealers there. I am informed that [Jimmy] Munro bought one.[62]

A couple of days later Matilda told Robinson that 'the sealers did not shoot the blacks, nor did the blacks spear the whites; both parties were afraid to commence hostilities; but said the sealers tied the women's hands with rope and put them in the boat'.[63]

Using William Buckley as interpreter, Robinson began his

investigation. He met 'DERREMART' again, noting he had venereal disease, and J.P. Fawkner, who told him that John Batman had opposed his taking the Port Phillip men to Hobart.

Robinson reports that the 'father of Melbourne' was also suffering from venereal disease, 'his nose eat off . . . with a handkerchief held up to his face'.[64] He interviewed one woman whose two daughters had been taken away on a vessel with two masts. He could not convince anyone to accompany him, blaming 'depraved whites' like Buckley and Batman for having persuaded the Port Phillip people that if they had accompanied Robinson to Bass Strait they might have been left on Flinders Island. He collected the names of the four abducted women, recording their names in his Settlement Journal:

> The mother of the two girls stolen from PP
> DOOG-BY-ER-UM-BORE-OKE
> One of the girl's names taken by the sealers
> NAY-NAR-GOR-ROKE –
> Another girl taken by the sealers
> BOR-RO-DANG-GER-GOR-ROKE
> DERREMART's wife who was taken by the sealers
> NAN-DER-GOR-ROKE[65]

As later geneaological work has revealed, many contemporary Indigenous people are descended from some of these women.[66] Robinson later collected a further account of the raid, which filled in some of the details about the abduction, and how only the best-looking women and girls were enticed aboard and restrained, and how, after sealing on King Island, they were taken to the Furneaux Islands and sold there.[67]

Robinson and his party left Port Phillip 6 January 1837 and sailed for Preservation Island, where he interviewed James Munro:

> Found on shore James Munro who had a New Holland woman a native of Port Phillip. She was ill in bed. Had an infant child by some of the sealers; had also a daughter about fourteen years of age that she had in her own country. This was an interesting girl and it grieved me to leave her in such hands for I felt persuaded she would be maltreated. Another daughter belonging to this

woman was living with Strognal on Gun Carriage by whom she had had two children; she was about sixteen years of age . . . There is positive proof that Munro bought the woman with whom he had been cohabiting and it is currently reported that he gave £7 for her. He denies having given a consideration for her and accounts for his having her by her being old or he said he supposed she should not have fallen to his share; but this is only evasive, there is positive proof that not only was a consideration given for this woman but for every other woman brought from Port Phillip by George Meredith the original importer.[68]

Robinson realised that he would not find it easy to persuade the abducted 'New Holland' women to leave the Bass Strait islands. He records how he spoke to Munro's woman, and found her 'prepared to resist all and every overture made to her. She was evidently under fear', he claimed, although when he then spoke with another of the women, who was living with Richard Maynard and was 'far advanced in pregnancy', she told Robinson 'she would see me b—— first'.[69] Maynard was also 'impertinent', telling Robinson that 'he knew she was taken from her own country by G Meredith but with that he had nothing to do.' The women stayed with the Straitsmen.

After selling the four women, George Meredith then either bought (or bartered for) a ten-oared sealing boat – and Maggerlede. One account says she was one of the women abducted from Point Nepean, which is unlikely, as in 1829 Robinson already knew her to be an associate of sealers and no doubt would have remembered and named her if he had heard her mentioned while investigating at Port Phillip.[70]

While the *Independent* went her way, Meredith sailed on in the ten-oared whale boat to Kangaroo Island, arriving February 1834.[71] On board were Maggerlede, James Manning, George Brown and a Dutch sailor named Jacob Seaman. Bull claims two young Aboriginal boys were also aboard, abducted in the raid from Point Nepean.

Meredith's gang settled at Western River on the north shore of Kangaroo Island, where they built a house and established a garden: Brown was an African-American ship's carpenter who later became a well-known tradesman in the new South Australian colony after a stint as a headsman at the Encounter Bay whale fishery. Two other 'men of colour', both African Americans, John ('Black Jack') Anderson and John Bathurst, joined the sealing gang at Western River in September 1834.[72] They made sealing trips to the nearby Althorpe Islands and joined forces with another sealing party camping on 'Long Island' (Thistle Island?).

Some of the party then raided the Port Lincoln district, again attempting to capture Indigenous women to work for them. The *Perth Gazette*, 3 October 1835 has James Manning's report of the raid that he gave to authorities in Western Australia:

> In November [1834], on Boston Island, the people in this latter boat caught five native women from the neighbourhood of Port Lincoln; they enticed two of their husbands into the boat, and carried them off to the island, where, in spite of all remonstrance on the part of Manning, they took the native men in Anderson's boat round a point a short distance off, there they shot them and knocked their brains out with clubs. Manning believes they still have the women in their possession, with the exception of Forbes, whose woman ran away from him shortly after they were taken to the island. Two of the women had infants at their breasts at the time their husbands were murdered; an old woman was compelled to take them away, and carried them into the bush. Another native endeavoured to swim to the island to recover his wife, but was drowned in the attempt.[73]

One of the women abducted on this raid would later be known on Kangaroo Island as Sal or 'Brown Sal': she was John Moore Davis's informant when he collected the Antonio story mentioned previously, and appears as a character in Cawthorne's *The Kangaroo Islanders*. It is not clear if Meredith himself was present on this raid; his associates were certainly involved, as Manning's report makes clear. In November 1834 Meredith and 'Black Jack' Anderson were also involved in a disagreement with Manning on 'a bird island' (the Althorpes?), during which loaded pistols were flourished, Meredith taking £4/10/– from Manning.[74]

Accompanied by Maggerlede and either one or two young

Indigenous men, Meredith then sailed a whaleboat to Yankalilla on the mainland, either on a sealing expedition or with the intention of settling there. By 1836 the sealing industry was in decline, and there would have been very few if any seals on the beaches of the Fleurieu Peninsula, aside from occasional visitors from the offshore rookeries. One report even has Meredith building a hut at Yankalilla and living in close contact with the southern Kaurna. This is unlikely, as relationships by 1836 between the sealers and Indigenous people were not at all cordial, most sealers living on the offshore islands and only occasionally visiting the mainland in armed parties.

There are four locations suggested for the site of Meredith's murder. An 1870s Kangaroo Island source gives the place as the Yankalilla Gorge, inland from Lady Bay; another states that he was murdered while on the deck of his vessel, which was anchored off what is now Normanville Beach; a third names Second Valley. Cawthorne's location in this novel describes a small conical hill near a creek, possibly Haycock Point at Carrickalinga. Given that the site where 'poor Meredith' was murdered and later buried was pointed out to him by Nat Thomas, one of the islanders who found his body, Haycock Point is the most probable site.

When was Meredith killed? While Cawthorne says in the late summer of 1823, his death must have occurred some time between November 1835, when Meredith was reported to be on a 'bird island' (the Althorpes?) and taking £4/10/- at gunpoint from his former associate James Manning,[75] and 22 April 1836, when his death was announced in the *Hobart Town Courier*. The wording is interesting: 'We have the pain to announce the premature death of Mr. Meredith, junior, son of George Meredith esq. of Oyster Bay who we learn was barbarously murdered by the savages on the north coast of New Holland while on a fishing expedition'.[76] It seems likely that the news had arrived in Hobart Town from Kangaroo Island, for Yankalilla is on the coast of 'New Holland' to the north of the island. A couple of weeks later, 9 May 1836, George Robinson recorded the death in his diary.[77] On balance late summer 1836 seems the most likely time for his death. It is interesting to note that when the serial version of Cawthorne's novel was running in the *Illustrated Melbourne Post*, 'Our Correspondent in Kangaroo Island' reported from Hog Bay to the

Adelaide paper, the *Observer*, that 'some of our old islanders' thought Cawthorne's novel a 'queer yarn . . . [and] not very complimentary to them. They suggest the dates should be altered.'[78] Obviously there were readers on Kangaroo Island with memories long enough to challenge the novel's title page date of 1823. It is a shame that the *Observer*'s correspondent in Hog Bay did not have more to say about other historical events represented in the novel.

What happened after Meredith's death? Concerned about his disappearance – and about the threat posed by mainland Aboriginal men having access to his whaleboat – the Islanders Nat Thomas, 'Governor' Henry Wallen, William Walker, Jacob Seaman and George 'Fireball' Bates sailed a whaleboat to Yankalilla during the winter of 1836, just months – perhaps even weeks – before the arrival of the *Duke of York*, the first of the South Australian Company ships to drop anchor in South Australian waters. They rescued Maggerlede and found and buried Meredith's body. There is some doubt about whether his whaleboat was recovered: one version has the wreckage at Encounter Bay and the rudder in the possession of Aboriginal people somewhere inland.

The murder weapon, a tomahawk, with his blood and hair still attached, was found between 9 and 15 September 1836 by Captain George Martin, of the South Australian Company vessel *John Pirie*. Martin had been exploring the shores of St Vincent's Gulf in a whaleboat owned by the sealer William Walker, one of the Islanders who had found and buried Meredith's body. It is likely that Walker took Martin to the place because the early colonists were fascinated by the circumstances surrounding Meredith's death. Martin then sailed with the *John Pirie* to Hobart Town, carrying not only Colonel William Light's report for the South Australian Company Commissioners about the proposed site for Adelaide but also the affidavit referred to in a *Register* piece of 28 September 1844, which confirmed the news of George Meredith's murder for his family in Tasmania.[79]

We will never know the full story about Meredith's death. It is reasonable to assume – given his past behaviour at both Point Nepean and Port Lincoln – that when he was murdered he was involved in some way with Indigenous people, perhaps even up to his old tricks of raiding the coast for women to sell to his associates. But the South Australian histories do not record any stories about the gentleman's son, George Meredith, as murderer and abductor of Indigenous women. Instead the major published accounts represent him as a melancholy wanderer, wantonly slain one morning by his Aboriginal companions while eating his porridge. Drawn no doubt to the oft-repeated detail about his murder occurring while he was reading the Bible, colonial writers allowed the irony of the detail to reinforce the prevailing view that Indigenous people could not be trusted, that they were so bewilderingly and inexplicably violent that after settlement the colonial government was entitled to take stern measures to ensure the safety of the colonists. Reports of Meredith's death played some part in reinforcing this perception. We wonder today if 'poor' Meredith's story would have been told so often if his full history had been better known.

The Kangaroo Islanders was written by a young schoolteacher who occasionally wrote to the Adelaide papers using the pseudonym '*Ami des Noirs*', the friend of the blacks.[80] He was an amateur ethnographer, a man who often speculated in his diary about applying for the position of Protector of Aborigines, a man who gave two of his children Kaurna names. It is hardly surprising then that Cawthorne should have been interested in representing the experiences of the Indigenous women taken to Kangaroo Island. His novel names five of them, and as a consequence is one of the earliest fictions that attempts to represent Indigenous people as individuals with remarkable skills and with complex and private belief systems, confidently dealing with the complicated processes of cross-cultural exchange brought about by their contact with the sealers.[81]

An early insight into the Islanders and their relationships with Indigenous women is that represented in W. H. Leigh's *Reconnoitering Voyages and Travels with Adventures in the New Colonies of South Australia* (1839), which includes the only known visual representation of a Kangaroo Islander camp.[82] Leigh makes much of the Robinson Crusoe archetype as a way of helping him make sense of the Islander lifestyle 'beyond the pale', characterised as it was for him by associations drawn from Defoe's famous narrative: the island setting; freedom from social restraints; Crusoe's animal skin clothing; exotic fare at table.

Cawthorne was also much taken by the Crusoe analogy: there

are eight references in his novel to Defoe's work. Such associations are immediate but superficial, as revealed in Leigh's famous drawing of a night scene on Kangaroo Island, in which it is difficult to pick Crusoe from Friday, European men from Indigenous women. Islander fashion and domestic realities meant that both men and women dressed in a hybrid assortment of Indigenous and non-Indigenous items of apparel, footwear and headgear, typically made from various animal skins and capped off with various items of 'slop clothing', sea-faring garb. While the finer points are not often made about who was responsible for the needlework in the camps, it is more than likely that Indigenous traditions for treating animals skins and preparing clothing suitable for colder climates were followed. Certainly Cawthorne makes much of the animal skin clothing of his characters in this novel. This is the first description in Chapter 4 of Old Sam, loosely based on Nat Thomas, which stresses not only the remoteness of Kangaroo Island but also the fact that men such as Sam might have been escaped convicts, living beyond the pale of Empire, not building a colony for the Crown, as Crusoe eventually manages on his island:

> This man was as singular a specimen of humanity of the Kangaroo Island species as could be found. His outward appearance was exceedingly strange. He was naturally a man of large build, and hairy, so much so, that it was at times difficult to distinguish his natural hair from the hair of the skins he wore as clothes; he was a veritable Esau; he was clad in leggings made of wallaby skins, a waistcoat of skins, and a cap of wild cat skins – he was his own tailor, and, of course, the fit was not nice to a shade – his arms and neck were bare; he had no underlinen, for the simple reason that the nearest shop was some 1,000 miles away, and then it might not be convenient if one could call and buy, with a peering constable watching one at every step, as if he had some suspicions of having once seen the gentleman purchaser. Hence it was better to wear skin clothes without linen than certain other clothes with linen, and absurdly marked with broad A's. Well, the fit was not the best, but the odour of the suit was marvellous. It was this that gave the Islanders their unenviable notoriety. Many years afterwards, before

a grave committee of Parliament, a gentleman was examined who
gave it in evidence 'that they stank like foxes'. (p. 24)

Recalling the Robinson Crusoe archetype, were the women submissive 'girl Fridays' who prostrated themselves before their masters, witnessing their own cultures beset by European ways and customs? There is a great deal of evidence to suggest that quite the reverse happened. Many of the abducted women may have begun as very unwilling participants in these early nineteenth century small business ventures, but the nature of that industry – and where it was practised – meant that Indigenous skills of many kinds, hunting methods, bushcraft, culinary knowledge and many other kinds of expertise, were very highly valued; they were, indeed, crucial to survival. Rather than Girl Friday becoming like her master on islands like Kangaroo Island, it seems that at least some of the Robinson Crusoes learned more from their Fridays than they were even able to remember from their own cultural backgrounds. Some of the fascination with the Islanders seems to have been prompted by their wildness, their living 'beyond the pale', their seeming rejection of those lifestyles offered by the British Empire, captured comically but effectively in Chapter 11, entitled 'A Kangaroo Island Dinner. – Baked Wild Dog – Roasted Iguano. – Ant Eggs. – Wakeries, etc.' in which Cawthorne makes much of the Kangaroo Island diet, manifestly based on Indigenous foodstuffs, still eaten by Kangaroo Islanders in the 1850s when the writer made his several trips across Backstairs Passage. Cawthorne's is one of the more benign representations of the Islanders, offering insights into a lifestyle that had evolved on a number of the islands along the southern coastline of Australia, a lifestyle very close in some respects to that enjoyed by many contemporary Australians on those same islands, suggestive of post-Romantic notions about the attractions of 'natural' or 'wild' living, which still have a deep appeal.

The Kangaroo Islanders also represents the most obvious and most dramatic form of transculturation, what has been called miscegenation, the most feared consequence of Englishmen living 'beyond the pale' and a taboo subject in most colonial fiction. There are two tiny fragments in this novel that show us the children of the sealers and their Indigenous women; although such moments are all too few in this novel, it is remarkable that they are there at all for a work written in 1854 in the shadow of the Indian Mutiny, a defining moment in race relations in the British Empire. It should be pointed out that many Indigenous Australians are descended from the originals of the children mentioned ever so briefly here, as Lester Irabinna Rigney reveals in his 'Foreword' to *Alas, for the Pelicans! Flinders, Baudin and Beyond*.[83]

The precise nature of the status of the relationships between the Islanders and Indigenous women (and some men and boys) is difficult to determine and remains controversial. There is an on-going debate about how to interpret the fact that numbers of the Indigenous women were forcibly removed by sealers and whalers, made to work and even traded as commodities, as the Meredith story has already revealed. Captain Robert Morgan records the following resonating anecdote that reveals much about at least one of the Islander's attitudes to his Indigenous companions. The captain of the *Duke of York*, the first South Australian Company vessel to make landfall in South Australia, Morgan accompanied Edward Stephens on a visit to 'Governor' Henry Wallen's and Robert Day's farm several miles upstream on the Three Wells (Cygnet) River: 'Mr. Stephens invited them [Wallen and Day] to come with their wives to see him on Sunday and have a religious service but says the men to introduce our wives was to be like introducing a dog to your presence'.[84] The remark is recorded *verbatim*, Morgan providing no context for understanding its significance. To put the best gloss on it is to note that Wallen may have intended his observation to describe a class as much as a racial divide.

A significant aspect of Cawthorne's novel is that he represents the relationships between the sealers and Indigenous women as sometimes more intricate than master–slave, representing instead associations that bound together the lives of Indigenous women and the sealers based on complicated processes of give and take.

Given Cawthorne knew and interviewed some of the old sealers (who were men in their fifties and sixties when he met them), and given he made several visits to Nat Thomas's remarkable establishment at Freshfields at Creek or Antechamber Bay, where he met a number of the surviving women and their children, he was in a unique position to make judgments about the kinds of relationships that brought and held together individuals like Nat Thomas and his wife Bet. Like the pastoral industries of the 1840s and after, the sealing and later the whaling industries offered some opportunities for Indigenous people through seasonal work to participate in the wider economic life of the various colonies. While Michael Pearson notes that, while the Two-Fold Bay whaling industry in later decades was to depend upon the labour of Indigenous people, it was the sealing industry in southern Australia that first considered Indigenous work as economically valuable, their skills essential.[85] The distances from Sydney or Hobart Town to their island homes were such as to require the Islanders to lead self-sufficient, subsistence lifestyles which were seasonally dependent upon Indigenous hunting, foraging and fishing skills that were crucial to their collective survival. Cawthorne's novel makes it very clear that the women's talents (and especially those of the Palawa) were highly regarded, suggesting that their status as mere slaves, sexual partners or chattels may have changed after the initial period when the seals were plentiful. After about 1810 some of the sealers began to settle down with Indigenous women on the various islands of the southern coastline. The demand for the women's special skills at seal, kangaroo and wallaby hunting and mutton-birding must have enhanced the sense in which at least some of them felt themselves to be partners with the men, which is certainly the way Old Sam's relationship with Bet is represented in *The Kangaroo Islanders*.

In *The Kangaroo Islanders* Cawthorne describes other behaviours of the Indigenous characters that have an ambivalent significance. On the one hand there is the kind of language used by the Islanders when addressing their Indigenous companions suggested by the epithet 'black crow' (p. 61), a pejorative used often enough in colonial Australia for Robert Drewe to allude to such practice in the title of his 1976 novel, *The Savage Crows*. On another occasion an un-named woman remembers her lost home, singing 'in a loud wail, a monotone of lamentations' (p. 70). When Bet tells Sally that the men intend to raid the mainland for more women, they curse the Islanders: 'May their kidney fat be taken! May the sorcerers turn them into trees, and may they be smitten with the sacred girdle and the tuft of eagle feathers!' (p. 71)[86] And when the men hear this song, they know the women 'smell a rat', that this 'caterwauling means summut', threatening them with violence if they do not desist (p. 71). Such moments in the novel hardly encourage readers to imagine these 'singular domestic arrangements' (p. 26) as based on love, affection, trust and mutual exchange, so later on when Suky and Brown Sal cut Flash Tom's throat it might seem that Cawthorne's views on relationships between the Islanders and their women were entirely negative, where the cultural and racial distinctions that separate Crusoe and his Friday yawn wide. But this murder is not presented as we might have expected, as a telling moment of self-defence or an act of resistance, for Suky is described as acting as she did because Long Tom had marooned 'Grip Hard' on the Althorpes, implying that she had a strong attachment to 'Grip Hard' and had taken revenge for her lover's death.

There are other complicated moments in the text. When Handspike is lost in the scrub, wandering delirious around the shores of Pelican Lagoon, Bumblefoot is sent to look for him. On the one hand her skills as bushwoman are well established, but on the other hand she does her master's bidding in leaving to search for the lost man, departing the camp 'like a hound'. When she finds him by tracking him down, she cares for the stricken man:

'Come long,' said Bumblefoot, 'boat bime-by.' Retracing her steps, she halted by the way, and from a little native well, supplied the mate with sweet, fresh water, sat him down in the shade, and kept applying grass pads soaked in cold water to his head. The mate recovered his consciousness, and thought that Bumblefoot, though a black gin, with a halt in her leg, kindly bestowed upon her by her white lord and husband, as pretty a creature he had ever seen. Holding on by her arm, she led him through a shady but devious footpath straight to the huts.

'Wal,' said Sam, 'yer look as if all the bounce was taken out of yer, anyhow, mister.'

'Cocoa-nut too tin, lauty sun knock 'im down,' said Bumblefoot by way of explanation (p. 38).

The representation of a skilled and caring woman is extended by her final joke at the mate's expense, that his skull is too thin for the Antipodean sun, which can be read as a confident assertion of her sense of being at home in a country where even a crippled woman can find a lost Englishman. This must be one of the earliest moments in Australian fiction when an Indigenous character is described as cracking a joke.

Betty Thomas, variously known as Polecat, Old Bet and Black Bet, is the best known of all the Indigenous women taken to Kangaroo Island: Rebe Taylor's *Unearthed: The Aboriginal Tasmanians on Kangaroo Island* (2002) tells the fascinating and moving story of Betty Thomas and her descendants.[87] Her daughter Mary is often described as the first child of a non-Indigenous parent born in South Australia.[88] Bet happens to be the Indigenous character represented in the greatest detail in *The Kangaroo Islanders*. In Chapter 13 she is seen initially as an object of sexual desire, the stereotypical Aboriginal woman of colonial fiction, but even here, while her attractiveness is suggested, her wildness is also recognised. Her curly hair is very typical of descriptions of Palawa women:

> 'I say, Bill,' said one, 'do yer twig that black gal among 'em?'
>
> 'No.'
>
> 'Why, the bowman in old Robinson Crusoe's boat. Don't yer see her black curly wool? Well, I'm danged if these coves is not rum 'uns; see how she handles that boat-hook as a nat'ral born sailor.'
>
> 'She's jolly fat, too, isn't she?' said the other, 'and blowed if she isn't purty; I likes the wild look o' hern eyes. What say yer, Jim, let us go ashore, and live as they do?'

A later passage in the same chapter is just as revealing. Here Bet is again seen as a skilled boatswoman, body surfer and diver for crayfish. It should be noted that Cawthorne reinforces what can be found in other sources, that the Palawa were very skilled in various forms of hunting. Of considerable interest in the text is this authorial aside about Bet, which suggests that her status in the Islander community was certainly not justifiably described as merely that of a chattel:

> Sam was proud of his wife, and she had so appropriately proved her high talent, in the Kangaroo Island sense, for to row, to fish, to swim, to fight, to endure, to devise, these were Kangaroo Island abilities, the proofs of genius, the steps of rank, the very LL.D.'s and M.A.'s of their social status. After all, of what merit are the graces

of civilisation? They are only relative. It is most unphilosophical to attribute merit to the polish of polite society, for beyond its sphere it is useless. Place a civilised lady on Kangaroo Island, and she be an absolute nonentity – nay, further, she would be a hindrance. The very thing that elevated her in the one case would be her curse in the other. No, Sam was right. Black Bet pulling the bow oar, was the talented, educated, and, in relation to her sisters, the refined lady of the peculiar society of her adopted home.

As this is a narrative of fact to a very large extent, it may be here mentioned that many years after, when her island home had become known to throngs of vessels that passed and re-passed from the colony of South Australia to Port Phillip, a vessel was wrecked, and the crew and passengers got on the shore, on a wild part of the coast. They were nearly famished for water, and this same Black Bet, now an old woman, became the means of their rescue, leading them to a native well, and guiding them to a place of safety.

'When I saw her figure,' feelingly remarked one of the passengers, 'coming over the sandhills, and we all rushed up to her, and she, in her quiet but still active manner led us to the native well, I could almost have worshipped her!'

Black Bet is dead now, and she lies in a spot in a small clearing of the scrub on the hillside that overlooks the very inlet of the great lagoon, where poor Handspike lost himself, and received the sun stroke that nearly killed him, as described in the early part of this tale (pp. 77–78).

It is useful to see how much of what we know about Bet is suggested in this passage. She was originally from Tasmania; her birth name and date have not survived, although it is believed she was born around the turn of the nineteenth century. Several stories survive of how she reached Kangaroo Island: one version has her arriving with Henry Wallen in 1819, while her daughter Mary Seymour told Herbert Basedow she was kidnapped by whalers (one of them Nat Thomas) and brought to the island in a whaleboat with other women in about 1828. She was with Thomas at Creek Bay for much of the 1830s: their three children were born in that decade. While Alexander Tolmer's 1844 letter to the *Southern Australian* does not name the 'native woman who catches wallaby' for Nat Thomas, the individual mentioned clearly is Bet, as their 'three very interesting little children' are mentioned (24 September 1844, 2c). Tolmer's 1882 book version of the same police expedition to Kangaroo Island again mentions 'old Bet', who is described as present at [William] 'Cooper's camp' in August 1844: she was obviously employed to run the wallaby snares at that time, clearly suggesting her economic independence and her value to the Islanders as a skilled worker. Tolmer also describes how she and 'Old Wauber' were also employed by the South Australian police to track down Sal and Suke, suspects in George Meredith's murder.

There is also evidence from Cawthorne's other writings that he recognised that Bet was something of a free spirit. While he does not record actually meeting her in his two Kangaroo Island travel pieces written in 1853 and 1859, he does mention her daughter Mary in the former. However, Cawthorne must have met Bet in his Christmas 1852–53 visit, or at least heard plenty of stories about her, because 'W.A.C.' wrote a letter to the *Register* about 'Old Bet' in which he presents the following fascinating impression of her powers of imagination, obviously drawn from meeting her or from anecdotes from 'Old Nat' Thomas: 'Old Bet . . . is a capital wallaby-hunter, a first-rate hand at the steer-oar of a whaleboat, a good sealer, and the best of bushmen or bush-women, but she has an imagination that surpasses belief'. Cawthorne then recounts several stories about Bet making various discoveries during her rambles (even finding gold) that later proved to be rather more prosaic than her stories might have suggested: she even found some planking from the wreck of the *Osmanli*. Her husband Nat Thomas is quoted as saying that 'Old Bet will spin yer yarns that ye never heard afore of'.[89]

Bet died at Antechamber Bay in 1878.[90] The approximate site of her grave near the Chapman River at Antechamber Bay is marked with a stone monument.[91] The 'Old Bet' who appears in *The Kangaroo Islanders* bears some similarity to these glimpses we have of her on the historical record.

Finally, a note about the ending to Cawthorne's *The Kangaroo Islanders*.

'We must go back, I s'pose,' said Sam. 'Yer all adrift here, so let's be off.' As the night closes over the scene, so our story draws to an end.

From the sandhills a native warrior is standing gazing o'er the ocean.

The sun throws a glare across wave and hill, and then sinks behind a wall of dense cloud and disappears within the deepest shades. Anon, and the sea also becomes swallowed up in advancing blackness.

A speck of white flickers in the thickening gloom – it is the last glimpse of Old Sam – and then it also vanishes for ever.

In the darkness, in the uncertainty, like their lives, wild and weird, so we leave them.

There, on their favourite element, over their vices, over their follies, their heroism and their barbarities, we draw the veil of night, and bid the 'Islanders' and their Island home farewell for ever.

Here Cawthorne uses a trope often exploited by colonial writers and painters in the last half of the nineteenth century, that Indigenous people are in the twilight of their lives. Here, in a neat touch, Old Sam and the Islanders are also associated with that previous day, with a glorious new dawn looming with the coming of the settlers in 1836.[92] However, the sun did not set on the memory of the Islanders. Cawthorne's own novel has played a role in maintaining a communal memory of the fact that the sealers were hated and feared in the mainland Indigenous communities from which their women had been taken or traded, representing the kind of behaviour that led directly to the murder of George Meredith, the culminating event of the novel.

A number of commentators have speculated that the reasons for some of the conflict in the early decades of the colony's history may well have been a consequence of the behaviour of some of the Islanders between 1802 and 1836, who lived 'beyond the pale' in both senses of the phrase. William Wentworth has left this powerful – and early – journal account of an episode in 1816 at King George's Sound in Western Australia while on route for Britain. The passengers had gone ashore to stretch their legs and met with some Aboriginal people of the district:

Just as the people were getting into the last boat, the natives, who had been sitting close to the party on shore during the whole day in the most peaceable manner, suddenly withdrew, and a few moments afterwards there was a general discharge of spears from the direction in which they had retired, although, from the thick brush which covers every part of the bay, none of the natives could be distinguished. Several of these spears passed very close to many of the boat's crew, and one in particular just grazed Mrs. Napper's bonnet. Our people immediately fired in the direction from which the spears had been thrown, but as it was nearly dark, it is not known whether their muskets did any execution. This attack had not been provoked in any way, and it was consequently accounted for on the theory of innate treachery. Comparing the conduct of the natives on the two occasions (1802 and 1816), it is reasonable to suppose that something had occurred in the interval to bring about such a change; and nothing was more likely to bring it about than a visit from the sealers of Kangaroo Island.[93]

In an article published in 1895 in the *Evening News*, 'G.B.B.' quotes Major Lockyer, the first commandant of the settlement at Albany, Western Australia, who in 1827 asserted that many mainland communities were:

> driven to it [violent resistance] by acts of cruelty committed on them by some gang or gangs of sealers . . . it is not to be wondered at that they should, as people in a state of nature, seek revenge . . .[94]

At the end of his journey down river in 1828 and very close to the mouth of the Murray, Captain Charles Sturt notes in his *Two Expeditions into the Interior of Southern Australia* that he and his party were threatened by a 'large body of natives . . . fully equipped for battle'. When Sturt raised his gun, the Ngarrindjeri men demonstrated they were 'perfectly aware of the weapon' when they 'dashed out of their hiding place and retreated'.[95] Reflecting later on the death of Captain Collet Barker in 1831, Sturt argues that 'cruelties exercised by the sealers towards the blacks along the south coast, may have instigated . . . [them] to take vengeance on the innocent as well as on the guilty'.[96] The most enduring legacy of the Islanders may well have been the role they played in the creation and maintenance of mistrust between Indigenous and non-Indigenous communities in southern Australia. *The Kangaroo Islanders* certainly makes much of this mistrust.

F.H. Bauer's impression of Cawthorne's stature as an historical novelist is a typical one:

> The 'yarn' brings together a couple of murders, several beatings and various other outrages, and stages them all on Kangaroo Island. Cawthorne's father was the first keeper of the Cape Willoughby lighthouse ... Cawthorne [Jr] had plenty of opportunity to talk with a number of the old sealers still resident on the island. Their original tales were probably well embroidered and Cawthorne mixes several of them together in a sort of *pot pourri*. It is to be regretted that Cawthorne, in his access to the old sealers, did not write a somewhat more factual account.[97]

A *pot pourri* it may be. Nevertheless, *The Kangaroo Islanders* reflects its disparate sources and betrays its origins in the kinds of yarns and reminiscences that men like Nat Thomas might have taken the chance of telling a young Adelaide schoolmaster while sailing across Backstairs Passage in a whaleboat, or while lumbering up to the Sturt Light at Cape Willoughby on the back of a bullock wagon. The novel reveals the Islanders, their controversial lifestyles and ambivalent histories in glimpses, fragments and vignettes, in stories half told, in narratives in shadowy detail, without endings, in a pungent mix.

Notes

for 'beyond the pale'

1   Cawthorne uses this expression in his novel on p. 9 to mean 'outside the limits', 'the other side of the fence'. The phrase 'fence paling' still preserves a little of this meaning. In Ireland 'the pale' refers to those territories over which the British had jurisdiction after 1547. Cawthorne is not alone in deploying the term about the Islanders or Straitsmen. See Stephen Murray-Smith's study of the Straitsmen of Bass Strait, 'Beyond the Pale: The Islander Community of Bass Strait in the 19th Century', *Tasmanian Historical Research Association*, vol. 20, no. 4, December 1973: 167–200.

2   This name for the inhabitants of Kangaroo Island, the 'Islanders', which Cawthorne used as title for his 1854 novel, is to be found in many places in the earliest written descriptions of the arrival of the colonists in South Australian in 1836. See, for example, a letter from William Giles to George Fife Angas, noting that the scrub on Kangaroo Island is very dense: 'I would not go a Mile into this dense mass of Underwood, on any account: the native women lead the Islanders through this bush for many miles, but no one else would venture into the Interior' (PRG 174/1/1377, State Library of South Australia).

3   E.H. Hallack, *Kangaroo Island: Adelaide sanatorium, with map and illustrations by 'a native'* (Adelaide: W.K. Thomas).

4   Vernon Williams, *The Straitsmen: A romance* (London: Cassell, 1929); Robert Drewe, *The Savage Crows* (Sydney: William Collins, 1976); Ann Clancy, *Rebel Girl* (Sydney: Pan Macmillan, 1999); Sarah Hay, *Skins* (Sydney: Allen and Unwin, 2002).

5   'Zyne' [William Anderson Cawthorne], 'Colonial Literature' (*The South Australian*, 16 May 1848: 3b). This essay anticipates similar pronouncements to be made in the decade ahead by writers and essayists like Catherine Helen Spence and Frederick Sinnett, both, incidentally, with strong South Australian connections.

6   William Cawthorne kept a log during the voyage: 'Log of the brig *Amelia*, kept

by W.A.C. on journey from Table Bay to Adelaide, March–May 1841' (Mitchell Library Acc. No. A434).

7   Charles Dickens used the term in *Bleak House* (1852–53), in Chapter 13, Esther's Narrative: 'The dear old Crippler!' said Mrs. Badger, shaking her head. 'She was a noble vessel. Trim, ship-shape, all a taunto, as Captain Swosser used to say. You must excuse me if I occasionally introduce a nautical expression; I was quite a sailor once.'

8   Cawthorne uses the spelling 'Pirkey' only once in *The Kangaroo Islanders*: elsewhere it is given as Porky.

9   Herbert Basedow, 'Relic of the lost Tasmanian race – obituary notice of Mary Seymour', Man, 81, 1914: 161.

10 See Philip A. Clarke, 'The Aboriginal Presence on Kangaroo Island, South Australia', *History in Portraits: Biographies of nineteenth century South Australian Aboriginal people* (eds Jane Simpson and Louise Hercus, Aboriginal history monograph 6, Sydney: Aboriginal History, 1998: 19).

11 Brian N.J. Plomley, ed. *Weep in Silence: A history of the Flinders Island Aboriginal settlement* (Hobart: Blubber Head Press, 1987: 445–6). This report demonstrates the complex inter-connections that bound together the various communities of Islanders from Bass Strait to Kangaroo Island and beyond: the same names keep appearing. Women were traded from sealer to sealer: Kalloongoo was even abducted from her first abductor. On 5 June 1836 Robinson wrote to the Colonial Secretary informing him that Kalloongoo wished to return to her country in South Australia, but there is no evidence that she ever came home.

12 Rob Amery, 'Kaurna in Tasmania: A case of mistaken identity', (*Aboriginal History*, vol. 20, 1996: 24–50). YANG.GAL.LALE.LAR is obviously present-day 'Yankalilla', while 'long sandy beach with three rivers' refers to the coastline around present-day Normanville: there are no 'rivers' at Port Lincoln.

13 This John Anderson is 'Abyssinia Jack', who was born in England, served in the Royal Navy at Trafalgar and arrived in Australia in 1813. He moved back to Woody Island in Bass Strait after living on Kangaroo Island for a number of years – he was there in 1826. G.A. Robinson records a number of his anecdotes about sealers and their lifestyles. He is remembered as a family man, who had his daughter Mary's banns published in 1842. Stephen Murray-Smith, 'Beyond the Pale: The Islander community of Bass Strait in the nineteenth century' (*Tasmanian Historical Research Association*, vol. 20, no. 4, 1973: 179). See Brian N.J. Plomley and Kristen Anne Henley, *The Sealers of Bass Strait and the Cape Barren Island Community* (Hobart: Blubber Head Press, 1990: 34–5).

14 N.J.B. Plomley, *Friendly Mission: The Tasmanian journals and papers of George Augustus Robinson 1829–1834* (Hobart: Tasmanian Historical Research Association, 1966: 327, 335, 360, 479, 1010, 1016). It may be that the boy in question

was Pra.re, the son of James Allen and Emue. Emue (or Emma) later lived with John Anderson; she may have been originally a Kaurna woman who knew Kalloongoo. Anderson handed Emma and her son over to Robinson on 29 March 1831, who interrogated her at length, recording a great deal of information about the women living with sealers on Kangaroo Island. In 1836 Emma was living with James Munro on a Bass Strait island where it seems she died shortly after.

15   This point has emerged as a significant one in recent debates about Tasmanian history. See Keith Windschuttle, *The Fabrication of Aboriginal History. Volume One Van Diemen's Land 1803–1847* (Sydney: Macleay Press, 2002).

16   John Stanley Cumpston, *Kangaroo Island 1800–1836* (3rd edn, Canberra: Roebuck Society Publication no. 1, 1986: 42–3).

17   Allan Peters, ed. *Recollections: Nathaniel Hailes' adventurous life in colonial South Australia* (Adelaide: Wakefield Press, 1998: 130).

18   John Moore Davis, 'Notes Relating to the Aborigines of Australia', Appendix E, R. Brough Smyth, *The Aborigines of Victoria* 2 vols (Melbourne: John Ferres, Government Printer, 1878: 1: 322).

19   While Indigenous women (and especially Palawa women) seemed to have been skilled sealers in pre-contact society, the evidence for the involvement of men is scanty. Quoting Ryan 1981, Kostoglou notes that Mannalargenna, a well-known individual from the north-east of Van Diemen's Land, made several sealing voyages. In 1813 when James Kelly took the *Brothers* sealing in Bass Strait there were two Aboriginal men aboard. George Augustus Robinson only refers to one or two in his dairies: a young 'North west of New Holland' boy named Praree lived and worked with John 'Abyssinia Jack' Anderson, but whether he was taken as a worker or as a sexual partner is not clear. See Parry Kostoglou, *Sealing in Tasmania: Historical research project: A report for the Parks and Wildlife Service* (Hobart: Department of Environment and Land Management, 1996: 38). Another Indigenous man is mentioned as a member of a sealing gang left on Solander Island for three years, living with his fellow castaways on 'terms of perfect amity and understanding'. See Thomas Dunbadin, *Sailing the World's Edge: Sea Stories from Old Sydney* (London: Newnes, [1937]: 119).

20   Cawthorne also mentions 'poor' Meredith's murder in a 1883 manuscript poem 'A Midnight Reverie in the Bush', which can be found in the Cawthorne Papers, PRG 489/11, State Library of South Australia. The lines are given on pages 234–5.

21   W.H. Leigh, *Reconnoitering Voyages and Travels with Adventures in the New Colonies of South Australia, During the Years 1836, 1837, 1838* (London: Smith, Elder & Co., 1839: 155).

22   See J.E. Calder, *Some Account of the Wars, Extirpation, Habits &c., of the Native Tribes of Tasmania* (Hobart Town, Henn and Co., 1875: 104), for Calder's version

collected from Truganini about the abduction of her sister from the southern end of Bruny Island. Plomley also gives Robinson's version, Plomley 1966: 82, 105–6, 1011. See also Plomley and Henley 1990: 36.

23 There is good evidence that Leigh heard Meredith's story from the Islanders, in that this is the old sealers' spelling of Yankalilla. The name survives because of their usage. Leigh is probably wrong in this detail: Meredith and his associates built a hut and established a garden at Middle River, Kangaroo Island.

24 Leigh 1839: 156–7.

25 Norman Tindale, 'Kangaroo Island loose notes', AA/338/1/32, South Australian Museum.

26 Norman Tindale, 'Kangaroo Island loose notes', AA/338/1/32, South Australian Museum, including this cutting from the *News*, 19 March 1932.

27 'A Week on Kangaroo Island', *Register*, 8 March 1880: 5f. This brief reference to Meredith is as follows: 'Meredith . . . met a violent death at the hands of the blacks on the mainland for having assisted in abducting the wife of a chief.'

28 Alexander Tolmer, *Reminiscences of an Adventurous and Chequered Career at Home and at the Antipodes* 2 vols (London: Sampson Low, Marston, Searle and Rivington, 1882). John Wrathal Bull *Early Experiences of Life in South Australia and an Extended Colonial History* (Adelaide: E.S. Wigg, 1884).

29 'A Bundle of Stories: No. 3 – The Old Settler's Story', *Register*, 4 May 1886: 3a.

30 As far as I can determine, the Tasmanian Merediths were not related to the British novelist George Meredith (1828–1909), although both families may have shared Welsh antecedents.

31 Karl von Stieglitz, *Pioneers of the East Coast from 1642: Swansea–Bicheno* (Hobart: OBM, 1978: 34–35).

32 These days the traveller can stay at Meredith House, 15 Noyes Street Swansea, with views over Great Oyster Bay and Freycinet Peninsular. Bookings can be made at http://babs.com.au/meredith.

33 See Vivienne Rae Ellis, *Louisa Anne Meredith* (Hobart: Blubber Head Press, 1979: 21, 25, 26, 27, 51, 55, 56–9, 122). See also Louisa Anne Meredith, *Tasmanian Friends and Foes Feathered, Furred and Finned* (Hobart: J. Walch & Sons, 1880) in which her deceased brother-in-law George is represented in a number of episodes. See pages 88, 91, 93–96 and 99.

34 Meredith 1880: 99.

35 Meredith 1880: 217, 230–1. See especially Chapters 36 and 37, describing the Meredith bay-whaling activities.

36 Parry Kostoglou, *Sealing in Tasmania: Historical research project: A report for the Parks and Wildlife Service* (Hobart: Parks and Wildlife Service, 1996: 73).

37 The island is named by Charles Meredith in a story told to his family about shooting Cape Barren Geese. 'Mrs. Charles Meredith' [Louisa Anne Meredith],

My Home in Tasmania: during a residence of nine years (London: John Murray, 1852: 114).

38 Meredith 1852: 113.

39 The wreck is mentioned in a number of sources. See John Stanley Cumpston, *Kangaroo Island 1800–1836* (3rd edn Canberra: Roebuck Society Publication no. 1, 1986: 131), citing reports in the *Hobart Town Courier*, 6 February 1830 and *Colonial Times* 12 March 1830. See also Ian Hawkins Nicholson, *Shipping Arrivals and Departures Tasmania. Volume 1, 1803–1833* (Canberra: Roebuck Publications, 1983: 116, 124, 157); and Ronald Parsons, *Tasmanian Ships Registered 1826–1850* (Magill, SA: The Author, 1980: 5). Parsons claims the vessel was wrecked on Kangaroo Island.

40 Letter dated 17 June 1829, George Meredith Jr to his stepmother Mary, G.4/23, University of Tasmania.

41 Letter from Louisa Anne Twamley to George Meredith Sr, 18 May 1833, (Royal Society 1854/A106, University of Tasmania Library).

42 The sale is mentioned in two letters: Letter, #310. George Meredith Sr to his wife Mary, 1 October 1832 (NS/123/1, Archives Office of Tasmania); and Letter, #316 George Meredith Sr to his wife Mary, 9 November 1832 (NS/123/1, Archives Office of Tasmania).

43 Letter from George Meredith Jr to Mary Meredith, Maria Island, 6 August 1833 (University of Tasmania Library).

44 Letter from Charles Meredith to George Meredith Sr (13 February 1835, G.4/29/1, University of Tasmania Library).

45 John Meredith, 'Answers re. George Meredith', n.d. (NS 615/20, Archives Office of Tasmania).

46 Tolmer 1882: xx.

47 Cumpston 1986: 131–2. Cumpston quotes confusing reports about the loss of the *Defiance* in the *Sydney Herald*, 24 October 1833, from the *Sydney Gazette* date not given, and the *Launceston Advertiser*, 15 August 1833. Three different wreck sites are given, and three different captains' names.

48 *The Sydney Gazette*, date not given, quoted Cumpston 1986: 132. Cumpston also does not provide the publication details for the 2 November 1833 account of the salvage of the *Defiance*.

49 James Manning's Declaration, 13 August 1835, Albany Court Records 13, 19 August, 7, 8, 9 September 1835, Battye Library, Perth, quoted Cumpston 1986: 131.

50 Plomley and Henley 1990: 69. The 40-ton *Independent* was built at Great Swan Port in 1830 and was a slow sailer, according to Meredith family history notes held in the Archives in Hobart. She was eventually wrecked on Bruny Island.

51 Diane Barwick notes that this date is 'independently confirmed by the Bunurong

man Yonki Yonka. On 6 June 1841 William Thomas noted in his journal that Yonki Yonka had rejoined the Bunurong after 'eight' years as a captive of the sealers. Yonki Yonka was obviously the unnamed Bunurong youth described in the diary of Thomas's colleague Dredge on 16 June 1841: he, another lad and 'nine' women, one of whom afterwards escaped, had been seen near Arthur's Seat (north of Point Nepean) about 'five' years before when a sealing crew induced them into a boat, forced them aboard ship and put to sea. This lad was taken to Preservation Island but later boarded a ship at Launceston hoping to get home. Instead he was taken to Western Australia, where he was hired as a stockkeeper; he purchased a fare to Adelaide with his savings and then worked his passage to Melbourne and then rejoined his relatives.' Diane Barwick, 'This most resolute lady: a biographical puzzle', *Metaphors of Interpretation: Essays in Honours of W.E.H. Stanner* (edited by Diane E. Barwick, Jeremy Beckett & Marie Reay, Canberra: Australian National University Press, 1985: 212). Thus Yonki Yonka *may* have been one of the young men accused of Meredith's murder.

52 *Historical Records of Victoria: Foundation Series. Volume One: Beginnings of Permanent Government*, edited by Pauline Jones (Melbourne: Victorian Government Printing Office, 1981: 34–5, 39). On 2 June 1836 John H. Wedge responded to New South Wales Police Magistrate George Stewart's request for the 'Names of individuals who perpetrated the outrage upon the Natives at Western Port about eighteen months ago?' with '————, since killed by the Natives on the South Coast of New Holland, in the vicinity of Spencer's Gulf' (*Journals and Printed Papers of the Parliament of Tasmania 1885*, vol. V, no. 44, 'Expedition from Van Diemen's land to Port Phillip in 1835': 15). In this collection of documents about the origins of Melbourne published by the Tasmanian Government in 1885, half a century later, George Meredith's name is not given as the perpetrator, no doubt in deference to the family. His brother Charles had died in 1880, just five years before this was published: he had been a distinguished member of Tasmania's Legislative Council. The family was obviously deeply ambivalent about his memory even fifty years on.

53 J.H. Wedge to the Colonial Secretary, 8 October 1836 (Mitchell Library A7064, quoted Plomley 1897: 656).

54 Robinson's Report on the sealers, dated 12 January 1837 (CSO 5/19/384, Tasmanian State Archives, cited Plomley: 1966: 938).

55 Plomley 1987: 385. While there is no reference to the *Duke of York* in the Meredith family papers, her sister ship *John Pirie* is mentioned, bringing further news of the circumstances of Meredith's death. The *John Pirie's* Captain Martin found the murder weapon at Yankalilla. John Bell, George Meredith Jr's brother-in-law, wrote to his father-in-law George Meredith Sr 28 October 1836 with news that

he had learned from 'Captain Martin of the Schooner John Pirie a confirmation of your Poor sons melancholy fate' (NS/123, Archives Office of Tasmania).

56 Plomley 1987: 385.

57 Plomley 1987: 655.

58 Plomley 1987: 395.

59 CSO 5/19/384, Tasmanian State Archives.

60 Plomley 1987: 353. No doubt the news travelled to Hobart Town on a sealing vessel returning from Kangaroo Island, in that the earliest published reference to the murder is in the *Hobart Town Courier*, 22 April 1826: 2d. The date is too early for the news to have been carried there on a South Australian Company vessel, the first of which, the *Duke of York*, arrived at Nepean Bay in July 1836.

61 Did these companions of Meredith's make it to Kangaroo Island? Ship's carpenter George Brown is named in some versions as not only accompanying him but also building the hut at Middle River: he was an African-American. Plomley and Henley name James 'Little' West as the American master of George Meredith's schooner *Independent*, who later lived at Kangaroo Island with TIN.NER. MUCK, a VDL woman. Perhaps he also pulled on one of those ten oars. It is not known who 'Billy' was. See Brian N.J. Plomley and Kristen Anne Henley, *The Sealers of Bass Strait and the Cape Barren Island Community* (Hobart: Blubber Head Press, 1990: 38, 39, 41, 54).

62 Plomley 1987: 405.

63 Plomley 1987: 406.

64 Plomley 1987: 410.

65 3 January 1837. Plomley 1987: 675. Barwick notes that the '—oke' termination suggests a Port Phillip origin.

66 See Barwick 1985, and B.C. Mollison *Tasmanian Aboriginal Genealogies. The Briggs Family Genealogy (to September 1976)* vol. 3, pt. 2 (Hobart: University of Tasmania Psychology Department, 1977). Some of this research is also available on the WWW. See http://www.parliament.vic.gov.au/windowintime/views/ showview.cfm?viewid=0, recording a speech by Carolyn Briggs, a descendant of DOOG-BY-ER-UM-BORE-OKE.

67 Plomley 1987: 677.

68 Plomley 1987: 414.

69 Plomley 1987: 415.

70 Plomley and Henley note that when John 'Black' Baker was arrested on a charge of having abducted three women (one of them Maggerlede), the three women 'seem to have been lodged at G.A. Robinson's house in Hobart at this time' (Plomley and Henley 1990: 36). Robinson would surely have remembered her five years later. See Plomley 1966: 83, 246, and especially the entry for 10 October 1829.

71 R.T. Sexton, *Shipping Arrivals and Departures South Australia 1627–1850: A guide for Genealogists and Maritime Historians* (Canberra: Roebuck Society, 1990: 25).

72 This is not John 'Abyssinia Jack' Anderson, who was English.

73 Quoted by H.P. Moore, 'Notes on the early settlers in South Australia prior to 1836', in *Proceedings of the Royal Geographical Society of Australasia, South Australian Branch*, Session 1923–24, vol. 25, 1925: 115.

74 Moore 1925: 115.

75 Cumpston 1980: 131, quoting an account in the *Perth Gazette*, 3 October 1835, the trial of John 'Black Jack' Anderson. This is a source for the story told in Sarah Hay's Australian/Vogel Winner *Skins* (2002).

76 *Hobart Town Courier*, 22 April 1836: 2d.

77 Plomley 1987: 353.

78 *Observer*, 3 June 1865, Suppl. 1g. It is likely that George 'Fireball' Bates had been chatting with the Hog Bay correspondent.

79 John Woodforde's diary records Captain George Martin of the *John Pirie* at Rapid Bay on 8 September 1836, sailing in a whaleboat on a tour of St Vincent's Gulf. Sexton records him leaving Nepean Bay 7 September 1836 on William Walker's whaleboat. Walker undoubtedly showed Martin the site at Yankalilla (the nearest landing to the north of Rapid Bay) where Meredith was murdered: Walker was paid £2 for his services. See R.T. Sexton, *Shipping Arrivals and Departures South Australia 1627–1850* (Ridgehaven, SA, Canberra: Gould Books, Roebuck Books, 1990: 29). See also Plomley 1987: 353.

80 See Cawthorne's letter to the *Observer*, 9 December 1843, expressing his concern at the wholescale clearing of wattle, given its seeds were a staple food for the Kaurna. He signs the letter 'Ami des Noirs'.

81 While there are just one or two references to Indigenous *men* in the sealing camps, there seem to have been a few boys present: after 1830 there are many more references to Aboriginal men playing leading roles either at bay-whaling stations or on blue-water whaling ships.

82 Chapter 13 describes an 'Expedition into the Interior' when Leigh and a friend set off to meet 'Governor Wallen', who is described as 'the august Robinson Crusoe (an excellent personification)' (126) on his '"Island home", his three wives, his two friends – man Fridays, his pigs, his some hundred and odd fowls' (124). In his journal Captain Robert Morgan from the immigrant ship *Duke of York*, also recorded meeting Wallen: 'I saw a man some what like when a boy I have seen Robinson cruso with long hair and beard a stick in his hand and verry little apperil' (Morgan's spelling, 2 August 1836, 'Journal of the *Duke of York*, 25 February 1836–10 February 1838', Mitchell Library A270: 36).

83 Lester Irabinna Rigney, 'Foreword', *Alas, for the Pelicans! Flinders, Baudin and*

Beyond, Essays and Poems, eds Anne Chittleborough, Gillian Dooley, Brenda Glover and Rick Hosking (Adelaide: Wakefield Press, 2002: ix–xiv).

84   Robert Morgan, Entry 2 August 1836, 'Journal of the *Duke of York*, 25 February 1836 – 10 February 1838' (Mitchell Library A270: 36).

85   Michael Pearson, 'Shore-based whaling at Twofold Bay: One hundred years of enterprise,' *Journal of the Royal Australian Historical Society*, vol. 71, no. 1, 1985: 19.

86   All these imprecations have meaning: see the appropriate footnotes in Chapter 12.

87   Rebe Taylor, *Unearthed: The Aboriginal Tasmanians of Kangaroo Island* (Adelaide: Wakefield Press, 2002).

88   While Mary Thomas may be remembered as the first child born in South Australia of a non-Indigenous parent whose birth is documented, it is very likely that there were children from earlier relationships who either did not survive until 1836 or who moved back to Bass Strait or even Van Diemen's Land with their parents. Plomley and Henley note that in 1836 Nancy Allen was described as 'native of Kangaroo Island': she was believed to have been born in 1822 (Plomley and Henley 1990: 26).

89   *Register*, 15 September 1856: 3d. Nearly a decade later in a public lecture delivered at the Temperance Hall, North Adelaide, on 15 April 1864, a lecture entitled 'Aborigines and their Customs', Cawthorne notes what he calls the 'anomaly of Tasmania possessing a race of natives that betray every evidence of their Papuan origin'. He attached a parenthesis to this sentence – (Old Bet) – and then goes on to comment on what seems to him to be the fact that the 'colour, the hair and the form [of the Tasmanian] are more closely allied to the Malay than to the African Negro'. She was obviously a woman in his thoughts. See Foster 1991: 88.

90   H.C. Berrett's 1932 letter to Norman Tindale contains an anecdote about Old Bet's death. Little Sal is Brown Sal, originally from Port Lincoln, while 'Old Sal' is Maggerelede. Suke is the third woman. Little Sal, Betty and Old Sal all appear in *The Kangaroo Islanders*: 'Previous to Old Sal's death when the four blacks were together, the Bells were told that there had been a row in the camp at Springy Water and that Little Sal hit Betty over the head with a stick. Betty died some time later as a result of this blow. Old Sal stated that she was buried at Springy Water near the wurlie where she died. Old Sal told this story herself to Mr. Bell of Stokes Bay. The three surviving blacks frequently visited Stokes Bay and were always well behaved'. (N.B. Tindale, *Journal of Anthropological Researches on Kangaroo Island, South Australia 1930–1974 and additions* AA 338/1/32, Adelaide Museum.) I am grateful to Keryn James for information about this letter.

91   The plaque on the memorial reads: 'EARLY SETTLERS IN THIS AREA INCLUDED NAT THOMAS, WHO, WITH HIS TASMANIAN ABORIGINAL WIFE BETTY, ARRIVED ON KANGAROO ISLAND IN 1827 AND FARMED AT THE EASTERN END OF ANTECHAMBER BAY UNTIL 1878. THIS COUPLE HAD THREE CHILDREN, A SON AND 2

DAUGHTERS. THE ELDER DAUGHTER MARY, BORN IN MAY 1833, WAS THE FIRST DOCUMENTED CHILD OF A EUROPEAN BORN IN SOUTH AUSTRALIA. WHILE NOT ALWAYS WELL TREATED, THE ABORIGINAL COMPANIONS OF THE PRE 1836 SETTLERS MADE A SIGNIFICANT CONTRIBUTION TO THE EARLY DEVELOPMENT OF THE ISLAND. SEVERAL WERE BROUGHT FROM TASMANIA AND OTHERS MAINLY FROM NEARBY FLEURIEU PENINSULA. BETTY DIED IN 1878, AND WHILE THE ACTUAL SITE OF HER GRAVE IS UNKNOWN IT IS BELIEVED TO BE IN THIS VICINITY. KANGAROO ISLAND PIONEERS ASSOCIATION. DEPARTMENT OF STATE ABORIGINAL AFFAIRS.'

92 The most famous and most copied painting in the Art Gallery of South Australia, Henry James Johnstone's 1880 painting *Evening Shadows*, also uses this trope. Johnstone painted it in London in 1880, and it was the first painting acquired by the Art Gallery – it was donated to the Gallery in 1881. The Aboriginal figures were added later: the first version had no human figures.

93 W.C. Wentworth, quoted in G.B.B. 'The Pirates and Wreckers of Kangaroo Island' (*Evening News*, 28 September 1895: 8–9. Held in State Library of South Australia, D.5013 [T]).

94 Quoted in G.B.B. 'The Pirates and Wreckers of Kangaroo Island' (*Evening News*, 28 September 1895: 3. Held in State Library of South Australia, D.5013 [T]).

95 Charles Sturt, *Two Expeditions into the Interior of Southern Australia*, vol. 2 (London: Smith, Elder and Co. 1833: 244).

96 Sturt 1833: vol. 2: 166.

97 F.H. Bauer, 'The Regional Geography of Kangaroo Island, South Australia', diss. Australian National University, 1959: 303.

Bibliography

Australian Archives, Adelaide
'Sturt Light Journal', 1853–60. D26/1 1–2 1853–60.

State Records of South Australia, Adelaide
BRG 42 Series 37 Special List. Letters Received by the Colonial Manager.

GRG 51/1, Trinity Board Minutes, 1852–58.

GRG 51/14.

GRG 51/26.

GRG 35/1.

GRG 24/4. Colonial Secretary's Office. 1836–1842. *Letters received by Colonial Secretary.*

GRG 24/6. Colonial Secretary's Office. 1842–1845. Letters received by Governor, Colonial Secretary etc.

Moorhouse, Matthew. 1843. *Annual report of the Aborigines Department of the year ending 30th September 1843.* South Australian Public Record Office. GRG 24/6/1843/1234.

Moorhouse, Matthew. nd. Letter book (Protector of Aborigines Out Letter Book 21 May 1840 – 6 January 1857).

South Australian Government Publications
Legislative Council, Select Committee. 1860. *Report on the Aborigines.* Vol. Paper 167 Adelaide: South Australian Government Printer.

The South Australian Government Gazette

British Government Publications
South Australian Colonization Commissioners. 1836. *First Annual Report of the South Australian Colonization Commissioners.* House of Commons Sessional Papers 39/426.

South Australian Colonization Commissioners. 1841. *Fifth Annual Report of the South Australian Colonization Commissioners*. British Parliamentary Papers: Papers relating to Colonisation and other Affairs in Australia, 1842–44.

Mortlock Library of South Australiana, Adelaide

Angas Papers, PRG 174.

Brown, John 'Diary'. PRG 1002/2.

Facsimiles of letters and papers relating to the foundation of the colony. 2 volumes. PRG 1002/1.

Cawthorne Papers, PRG 489.

Cawthorne, William Anderson. 1856. ms. 'Lines . . . Loss of *Golbourn* . . . July 1856'. A/558/A4.

Cawthorne, William Anderson. ms. A558/A4.

Dutton, C.C. 1839. 'Diary.' D5935(L).

Finniss, Boyle Travers. 'Extracts from the reminiscences of the Hon. Boyle Travers Finniss.' ms. PRG 527/1.

Hutchinson, Y.B. 'Journal'. PRG 1013/1.

'*John Pirie* Logbook'. BRG 42–79.

Pullen, W.J.S. 'Papers'. PRG 303.

'*Sarah and Elizabeth* Logbook'. BRG42–81.

South Australian Company, BRG 42–28. Letters to Colonial Manager.

South Australian Company, BRG 42–34. Kangaroo Island Correspondence.

South Australian Company, BRG 42–9. Letters from Colonial Manager.

Stevenson, G. Journal kept on the *Buffalo*. ms. In Angas Papers, PRG 174.

Taplin, George. 1859–79. 'Journals.' ms.

Underwood, E. 'Reminisences 1840–47'. XXX 392.

Woodforde, John. 1836. 'Abstract of a voyage to South Australia in the Surveying Brig "Rapid" – Cap. Light – Written by John Woodforde, M.R.S. & L.A.H., Surgeon of Surveying party, August 19th 1836'. ms. PRG 502/1/2.

Zilm, H.A. n.d. 'The Narrindjeri tribe.' ms.

South Australian Museum

Berrett, H.C., 1932, Letter from Berrett to Norman Tindale, recounting information related to him by George P.T. Bell. Norman B. Tindale. 'Kangaroo Island Journal 1930–74,' AA 338/1/32.

Kartinyeri, Doreen, M. 1990. 'The Wilson family genealogies.' ms.

Mollison, B.C. 1976. 'The Tasmanian Aborigines: Tasmanian Aboriginal genealogies, with an appendix on Kangaroo Island.' University of Tasmania. ms.

Tindale, Norman B. 1936–65. 'Tasmania and the part Aborigines of the Bass Strait Islands and Kangaroo Island.' ms.

Genealogy Society, Unley
Cemetery Index
Lunatic Asylum Index
Adelaide Hospital Index
Mental Hospital Index
Lone Grave File

Mitchell Library, Sydney

Cawthorne, William Anderson. 'Literarium Diarium.' 1 January 1844 –
    28 August 1844. A104 (MF CY 363).
Cawthorne, William Anderson. 'Literarium Diarium.' 22 October 1842 –
    31 December 1843. A103 (MF CY 214).
Cawthorne, William Anderson 'Literarium Diarium.' 29 August 1844 –
    12 April 1846. A105 (MF CY 363).
Cawthorne, William Anderson 1841. 'Log of the brig Amelia, kept by W.A.C. on
    journey from Table Bay to Adelaide, March–May 1841.' A434.
Cawthorne, William Anderson. 'Diary 1846–1848.' B229.
Cawthorne, William Anderson. 'Diary 1849–1860.' B230.
Morgan, Robert. 1836–8. 'Journal of the *Duke of York*, 25 February 1836 –
    10 February 1838', A270.

Newspaper Articles

Advertiser
Australian
Chronicle
Church Chronicle
Colonial Argus
Hobart Town Gazette
Illustrated Melbourne Post
Islander
Lantern
Observer
Perth Gazette
Quilp
Register
Southern Australian
Sydney Gazette

[Cawthorne, William Anderson]. 1848. *South Australian*, 15 December, 2a.
[Cawthorne, William Anderson]. 1853. 'Journal of a trip to Kangaroo Island.'
    Observer, 15 January: 3d.

[Cawthorne, William Anderson]. 1856. 'Notes of a ten Days' Tour to the Murray and the North.' *Observer*, 29 March: 3a–d.

[Cawthorne, William Anderson]. 1848. *Register*, 16 December: 4b.

[Cawthorne, William Anderson]. 1867. 'Native Warriors.' *Illustrated Adelaide Post*, 23 April.

[Cawthorne, William Anderson]. 1868. 'Natives Catching Turtle.' *Illustrated Adelaide Post*, 12 August.

[Cawthorne, William Anderson]. 1868. 'Natives Killing Parrots.' *Illustrated Adelaide Post*, 23 January.

[Cawthorne, William Anderson]. 1869. 'Stalking Pelicans.' *Illustrated Adelaide Post*, 26 February.

[Cawthorne, William Anderson]. 1891. 'Goodwood Plotters.' *Quilp*, 19 February: 10.

'A Boy's Recollections.' *Advertiser*, 27 December 1886: 6f.

'A bundle of stories. By the Criticised Traveller.' *Register*, 27 April 1866: 4c.

'A bundle of stories. No. 2. The Whaler's Story.' *Register*, 25 April 1866: 2g.

'A bundle of stories. No. 3. The Old Settler's Story.' *Register*, 4 May 1866: 3a.

'A Colonist of 1836.' 'The Natives.' *Register*, 3 October 1840: 2c–d.

'A lifetime in music.' *Advertiser*, 17 November 1916: 9c.

'A Lord of the Soil.' *Lantern*, 20 August 1887: 19.

'A Native'. 'A Trip to Kangaroo Island.' *Observer*, 1 April 1905: 39a–c.

'A Pioneer of Yelkie. Interesting Early History. Memories of Mr. R.T. Sweetman.' *Register*, 3 March 1928: 19e–h.

'A Week on Kangaroo Island.' *Register*, 8 March 1880: 5f.

'A Week on Kangaroo Island.' *Register*, 8 March 1880: 5f.

'Aborigines of Tasmania.' *Register*, 6 April 1869: 2h.

'About early Kangaroo Island.' *Chronicle*, 2 March 1933: 46.

'Ami des Noirs' [William Anderson Cawthorne]. *Observer*, 9 December 1843.

'Amor Patriae.' [William Anderson Cawthorne].'Rebellion a Proper Subject for Colonial Enterprise.' *South Australian*, 21 July: 3a–b 1848.

'An Official Trip to Kangaroo Island.' *Advertiser*, 20 March 1880, suppl.: 1a–c.

'An old chapter in Colonial History.' *Register*, 25 January 1888: 6d.

'Australian Aborigine – Kangaroo Island today.' *News*, 19 March 1932.

'Before the Whites Came: Living Words of Dead Language.' *Mail*, 14 May 1921: 3e.

'Boston Bay.' *Register*, 8 July 1837: 2–3.

'Common Sense'. [Cawthorne, William Anderson]. 'The All England Eleven.' *Express*, 22 February 1864: 22.

'Common Sense'. [Cawthorne, William Anderson]. 'Two Thousand Five Hundred Pounds.' *Express*, 11 January 1864: 22.

'Coroner's Inquest upon the earliest South Australian settler.' *Register*, 30 April 1856: 3d.

'Death of George Bates. A Kangaroo Islander of the Old Time.' *Register*, 9 September 1895: 7d.

'Death of George Bates.' *Observer*, 14 September 1895: xx.

'Discovery of human remains on Kangaroo Island.' *Register*, 6 April 1866: 3a.

'Extraordinary Case.' *Southern Australian*, 24 September 1844: 2e.

'Government Gazette – Abstract of Census Returns. *Southern Australian*, 12 April 1844: 2.

'Kangaroo Island Salt.' *Observer*, 8 July 1848: 6.

'Kangaroo Island week recalls strange chapter of history.' *Observer*, 9 November 1929: 16c.

'Kangaroo Island. Some Early History.' *Observer*, 21 December 1918: 11a.

'Kangaroo Island.' *Observer*, 25 September 1844: 5–6.

'Kangaroo Island.' *Southern Australian*, 24 September 1844: 2c–d.

'Kangaroo Island.' *Register*, 25 September 1844: 3c–d.

'Kangaroo Island's Anniversary.' *Advertiser*, 27 July 1933: 8c.

'Kangaroo Island's lucky escape.' *Advertiser*, 17 June 1909: 6g.

'Lost on Kangaroo Island. An Incident of the Pioneer Days.' *Observer*, 20 May 1899.

'Mr. Tolmer's trip to Kangaroo Island.' *Register*, 17 November 1856: 2g.

'Mrs. Mary Seymour.' *Observer*, 13 September 1913: 41b.

'Native Fights.' *Register*, 24 April 1844.

'Nepean Bay.' *Observer*, 26 May 1860: 8b.

'Now where lies Little Sal?' *News*, 16 March 1932: 11d.

'Official visit to Kangaroo Island.' *Register*, 21 May 1874: 5a.

'Old Blue Jacket'. 'Letting the dead bury their dead.' *Register*, 12 September 1846: 2d.

'Old George Bates.' *Advertiser*, 27 December 1886: 6c–f.

'Old George Bates.' *Chronicle*, 1 January 1887: 6c.

'On Kangaroo Island, and the Runaways in the Straits,' *Hobart Town Gazette*, 10 June 1826.

'Proceedings of the Police at Kangaroo Island.' *Southern Australian*, 27 September 1844: 3.

'Proposed Volunteer Band.' *Observer*, 17 September 1860: 3c.

'Reminiscences of the early residents.' *Advertiser*, 23 May 1899: 6e.

'Robert Wallen.' *Chronicle*, 9 March 1933: 44b.

'Running Commentary on Men and Things.' *Observer*, 15 July 1843: 20.

'Some early history. First landings on Kangaroo Island.' *Register*, 10 November 1927: 10c.

'The "King" of Kangaroo Island.' *Register*, 10 October 1894: 5b.

'The body of Wallen.' *Register*, 9 May 1856: 2e.

'The early days. Who found Kangaroo Island?' *Advertiser*, 24 June 1909: 9g.

'The First Police Constable.' *Advertiser*, 27 December 1886: 6f.

'The firstborn on Kangaroo Island.' *Observer*, 9 September 1905: 38a.

'The first-born on the Island.' *Register*, 8 April 1905: 7e.

'The funeral of George Bates.' *Register*, 14 September 1895: 5e.

'The hermit of Kangaroo Island.' *Register*, 31 August 1895: 5d.

'The land commissioner at Kangaroo Island.' *Chronicle*, 10 March 1888: 6f.

'The last Aboriginal.' *Register*, 7 August 1871: 5c.

'The last of George Bates.' *Register*, 12 September 1895: 5b.

'The last of the Tasmanians.' 1 April 1905.

'The late George Bates.' *Register*, 10 September 1895: 5b.

'The late George Bates.' *Register*, 11 September 1895: 5a.

'The late George Bates.' *Register*, 7 November 1895: 5b.

'The late George Bates.' *Register*, 9 September 1895: 4g.

'The late George Bates's funeral.' *Register*, 13 September 1895: 5a.

 'The Late Mr. W.A. Cawthorne.' *Observer*, 2 October 1897: 35d.

'The Murder of Mr Meredith.' *Register*, 28 September 1844: 3b.

'The Native Corroboree.' *Register*, 16 March 1844.

'The oldest inhabitant.' *Chronicle*, 10 March 1888: 7a.

'The oldest South Australian Colonist.' *Register*, 4 January 1890: 5b.

'The oldest South Australian settler.' *Register*, 15 January 1890: 5a.

'The Pirates and Wreckers of Kangaroo Island' *Evening News*, 28 September 1895.

'The very first.' *Advertiser*, 3 August 1936: 14e.

'The Writer of Kupirri' [Cawthorne, William Anderson]. 1858. 'Rev. Mr. Gardner V. "Kupirri."' *Register*, 4 November: 3g.

'Thinks he can find Little Sal?' *News*, 17 March 1932: 6d.

'Thinks he can find Sal. Will look soon.' *News*, 17 March 1932.

'Trinity Church Sunday–School.' *Register*, 12 April 1862: 3e.

'Trooper Dan.'. 'Strange Tales from South Australia's Past. The Abo Girl's Revenge.' *Mail*, 7 February 1831: 19d–g.

'Useful life closed. The death of Mr. Charles Cawthorne.' *Register*, 27 June 1925: 9c.

'Very first white inhabitants on Kangaroo Island.' *Advertiser*, 1 September 1936: 5a.

'Victoria-Square Academy.' *Register*, 16 November 1858: 3b.

'Whitefellow'. 'Aboriginal Place Names.' *Register*, 3 March 1928: 16f.

'Yarns of Olden Times.' *Observer*, 17 April 1880: 658a.

Bates, George. 'Lines from an old pioneer.' *Register*, 8 December 1886: 6h.

Blackett, John. 'Kangaroo Island. Its Historical Associations.' *Register*, 28 December 1918: 7e.

Blackett, John. 'Kangaroo Island. Its Historical Associations.' *Register*, 30 December 1918: 6g.

Blackett, John. 'Kangaroo Island. Its Historical Associations.' *Register*, 1 January 1919: 4g.

Blackett, John. 'Kangaroo Island. Its Historical Associations.' *Register*, 2 January 1919: 4g.

Blackett, John. 'The Foundation of South Australia.' *Advertiser*, 28 December 1929: 13g.

C.[awthorne], W.[illiam] A.[nderson] 1856. 'Gold at Kangaroo Island.' *Register*, 15 September: 3d.

C.[awthorne], W.[illiam] A.[nderson] 1859. 'A Christmas Trip.' *Register*, 15 January: 3b.

C.[awthorne], W.[illiam] A.[nderson] 1859. 'A Christmas Trip.' *Register*, 28 January: 3b.

C.[awthorne], W.[illiam] A.[nderson] 1859. 'A Christmas Trip.' *Register*, 9 February: 3b–c.

C.[awthorne], W.[illiam] A.[nderson] 1859. 'Proposed Normal School.' *Register*, 3 February: 3d.

Driscoll, H.J. 'Early history of Kangaroo Island.' *Mail*, 28 March 1914: 17c.

Driscoll, H.J. 'Early history of Kangaroo Island.' *Mail*, 4 April 1914: 19g.

Driscoll, H.J. 'Early history of Kangaroo Island.' *Mail*, 23 May 1914: 21e.

Driscoll, H.J. 'Early history of Kangaroo Island.' *Mail*, 12 September 1914: 8g.

Farmer, Frank. 'Piracy and villainy in state's early history.' *Mail*, 11 April 1925: 1b.

Fairweather, Winnie. 'A Trooper of the early days.' *Observer*, 23 February 1924: 58c.

Fenner, Charles. 'A curious human document. Kangaroo Island relic.' *Register*, 7 April 1928: 5d.

Fisher, Robert. 'Journal of an Excursion into the Interior of Kangaroo Island. November 1836.' *Register*, 8 July 1837: 3.

Hooper, J.C. 'A Swim of 11 Miles.' *Register*, 17 February 1931: 6c.

Hutchinson, Biram. 'Ascent of Mount Lofty.' *Register*, 8 July 1837: 3.

Islander, 6 June 1984

Leak, John A. 'Aborigines of Australia.' *Register*, 7 August 1871: 6e.

Leak, John A. 'Aborigines of Tasmania.' *Observer*, 12 August 1871: 10d.

Lindsay, A.F. 'A Companion of Governor Hindmarsh.' *Advertiser*, 27 December 1886: 5f–g.

Lowrie, James. 'Sturt Light.' *Register*, 26 July 1853: 3b.

M., A. 'Reminiscences of Kangaroo Island settlement.' *Register*, 27 July 1886: 6d.

Mildred, Hiram. 'With Colonel Light.' *Advertiser*, 27 December 1886: 5g–6a.

Mildred, Hiram. 'The pioneer colonists.' *Register*, 19 August 1886: 6d.

Nantes, Charles. 'Human remains on Kangaroo Island.' *Register*, 1 May 1866: 3b.

Penny, Richard. 'The natives.' *Register*, 21 November 1840: 5a.

S.S. 'The infancy of South Australian settlement. Our pioneer ship. – a narrative of 1836.' *Register*, 27 July 1886: 6d.

Saunders, A.T. 'Notes and Queries.' *Register*, 30 September 1924: 9g.

Saunders, A.T. d.' *Observer*, 16 February 1929: 11c.

Smith, John H. 'Not So.' *Advertiser*, 13 January 1995: 12a.

Stuart, C.W. 'An Old Police Inspector.' *Advertiser*, 27 December 1886: 6g–b.

Tindale, Norman B. 'Hot on the Trail of Our Vanished Race.' *News*, 24 March 1932: 6c–d.

Tolmer, Alexander. 'Claim for Gold Discovery in Kangaroo Island.' *Register*,
    15 September 1856: 3d.
Wheaton, Cyril. 'First service on Kangaroo Island.' *Advertiser*, 25 July 1936: 18g.
W., G.B. 'Yarns of the olden times.' *Observer*, 17 April 658a.
W., G.B. 'Yarns of the olden times.' *Observer*, 29 May 1880: 898b.
Willson, Thomas. 'Government treatment of our oldest colonists.' *Register*,
    21 February 1877: 5g.
Willson, Thomas. 'Tasmanian Aboriginals.' *Observer*, 7 October 1871: 7b.
Willson, Thomas. 'Tasmanian Aboriginals.' *Register*, 26 September 1871: 6f.
'Zyne' [William Anderson Cawthorne]. 1844. 'The Natives.' *Register*, 8 November.
'Zyne' [William Anderson Cawthorne]. 1847. 'Port Gawler.' *South Australian*,
    1 January: 6a.
'Zyne' [William Anderson Cawthorne]. 1848. 'Colonial Literature.' *South Australian*,
    16 May: 3b–d.

World Wide Web

http://alt-usage-english.org/excerpts/fxbyhook.html
http://babs.com.au/meredith
http://pd.sparknotes.com/conrad/heartofdarkness
http://uk.geocities.com/mmorris01uk/dance.htm
http://www.bbc.co.uk/radio4/history/romanway_recipes2.shtml
http://www.foundingdocs.gov.au/places/qld/qld3i.htm
http://www.glenans-ireland.com/Resources/dictionary.htm
http://www.jcu.edu.au/aff/history/southseas/refs/falc/0929.html
http://www.julianstockwin.com/glossary.htm
http://www.murray-river.net/regions/waikerie/waikerie.htm
www.bartleby.com/81/

Theses

Amery, Rob. 1998. 'Warrabarna Kaurna! Reclaiming Aboriginal languages from
    historical sources. Kaurna case study.' A thesis submitted for the degree of PhD,
    Department of Linguistics, University of Adelaide.
Barker, Elaine. 1989. 'Civilization in the Wilderness: The Homestead in the
    Australian Colonial Novel 1830–1860.' A thesis submitted for the degree of
    Master of Arts, Department of English, University of Adelaide.
Bauer, F.H. 1959. 'The Regional Geography of Kangaroo Island, South Australia.'
    A thesis submitted for the degree of PhD, Australian National University.
Clarke, Philip A. 1994. 'Contact, conflict, and regeneration: Aboriginal cultural
    geography of the Lower Murray, South Australia.' A thesis submitted for the
    degree of PhD, University of Adelaide.
De Leiuen, Cherrie 1998. 'The Power of Gender,' A thesis submitted for the degree
    of BA (Hons) in Archaeology, Flinders Univerisity.

Foster, Robert K.G. 1993. 'An Imaginary Dominion: the Representation and Treatment of Aborigines in South Australia.' A thesis submitted for the degree of PhD, Department of History, University of Adelaide.

Gibbs, Ron. 1959. 'Humanitarian theories and the Aboriginal inhabitants of South Australia to 1860.' A thesis submitted for the degree of BA (Hons), Department of History, University of Adelaide.

Hosking, William James. 1974. 'Whaling in South Australia 1837–1872.' A thesis submitted for the degree of BA (Hons), Department of History, Flinders University.

Hunt, Jennifer. 1971. 'Schools for Aboriginal children in the Adelaide district 1836–1852.' A thesis submitted for the degree of BA (Hons), Department of History, University of Adelaide.

James, Keryn. 2001. 'Wife or Slave: The kidnapped Aboriginal women workers and Australian sealing slavery on Kangaroo Island and Bass Strait Islands.' A thesis submitted for the degree of BA (Hons), Department of Archaeology, Flinders University.

Matthews, Lydia, 1999. 'The Cross-Cultural Hunter-Gatherers on Kangaroo Island.' A thesis submitted for the degree of BA (Hons), Department of Archaeology, Flinders University.

Staiff, Russell. 1995. 'Imagining Felicitania: the Visual Culture of Early South Australia.' A thesis submitted for the degree of PhD, University of Melbourne.

Staniforth, Mark. 1999. 'Dependent colonies: the importation of material culture and the establishment of a consumer society in Australia before 1850.' A thesis submitted for the degree of PhD, Department of Archaeology, Flinders University.

Taylor, Rebe, 1996. 'Sticking to the Land: A history of exclusion on Kangaroo Island, 1827–1996.' A thesis submitted for the degree of BA (Hons), Department of History, University of Melbourne.

Walsh, Phillipa. 1966. 'The problem of native policy in South Australia in the nineteenth century.' A thesis submitted for the degree of BA (Hons), Department of History, University of Adelaide.

Whitehead, Kay 1996. '"Women's Life–Work": Teachers in South Australia, 1836–1906.' A thesis submitted for the degree of PhD, Departments of Education and Women's Studies, University of Adelaide.

Published Works

Abbott, G.A. and N.B. Nairn. 1969. *Economic Growth of Australia 1788–1821*. Melbourne: Melbourne University Press.

Adams, J.W. 1902. *My early days in the colony*. Balaklava: E.J. Walker.

Adam-Smith, Patsy and John Powell. 1978. *Islands of Bass Strait*. Adelaide; Rigby.

Amery, Rob. 1996. 'Kaurna in Tasmania: a case of mistaken identity.' *Aboriginal History* 20: 24–50.

Amery, Rob. 1998. 'Sally and Harry: insights into early Kaurna contact history.'
*History in Portraits: Biographies of nineteenth century South Australian Aboriginal
people*. Eds Jane Simpson & Louise Hercus. Aboriginal History Monograph 6.
Sydney: Aboriginal History. 49–87.

Andrew, Marjorie and Shirley Clissold. 1986. *The diaries of John McConnell Black*,
Volume 1, Diaries One to Four. 1875–1886. Adelaide: Investigator Press.

Angas, George Fife. 1847. *Savage Life and Scenes in Australian and New Zealand*.
2 vols. London: Smith, Elder and Co.

Australian Dictionary of Biography. Vol. 7: 1891–1939, A – Ch Melbourne: Melbourne
University Press, 1979.

Aveling, M. 1987. 'Colonel Gawler hosts a dinner for the Aborigines.' *Australians:
a historical library. Volume 2: Australians, 1838*. Eds F. Crowley, A.D. Gilbert,
K.S. Inglis and P. Spearritt. Sydney: Fairfax, Syme and Weldon.

B[roadfoot], J. 1848. 'An unexpected visit to Flinders' Island in Bass's Straits.'
Chambers' Edinburgh Journal 90 (20 September 1848).

Backhouse, James. 1843. *A Narrative of a Visit to the Australian Colonies*. London:
Hamilton, Adams and Co.

Barrett, J.W. 1918. *The Twin Ideals*. 2 vols. London: Lewis and Co.

Barwick, Diane. 1985. "This most resolute lady': a Biographical Puzzle.' *Metaphors
of Interpretation: Essays in Honours of W.E.H. Stanner*. Eds Diane E. Barwick,
Jeremy Beckett & Marie Reay. Canberra: Australian National University Press.
185–239.

Basedow, Herbert. 1914. 'Relic of the lost Tasmanian race – obituary notice of Mary
Seymour.' *Man* 81: 161–162.

Bates, E.L. 1951. 'History of East End of Kangaroo Island.' *Kangaroo Island Past and
Present: Being a Short History of the Oldest Settlement in South Australia*. Adelaide:
Kingscote Country Women's Association: 22–36.

Bateson, C. 1972. *Australian Shipwrecks: including vessels wrecked en route to or from
Australia, and some strandings*. Vol. 1. Sydney: Reed.

Baudin, Nicolas. 1974. *The Journal of Post-Captain Nicolas Baudin, commander-
in-chief of the corvettes Géographe and Naturaliste – assigned by order of the
government to a voyage of discovery*. Trans. Christine Cornell. Adelaide: Libraries
Board of South Australia.

Begg, A. Charles and Neil C. Begg, eds. 1979. *The World of John Boultbee: including
an Account of Sealing in Australian and New Zealand*. Christchurch: Whitcoulls
Publishers.

Bell, Diane. 1998. *Ngarrindjeri wurruwarrin: a world that is, was, and will be*.
Melbourne: Spinifex Press.

Bennet, J.F. 1842. *The South Australian Almanack and General Directory for 1842*.
Adelaide: Robert Thomas & Co.

Bermingham, K. 1975. *The sixth eleven tales of Robe* Kingston: J.M. Banks.

Berndt, Ronald M. 1940. 'Some aspects of Jaraldi culture.' *Oceania* 11 part 2: 164–185.

Berndt, Ronald M. 1965. 'Law and order in Aboriginal Australia.' *Aboriginal Man in Australia*. Eds R.M. Berndt and C.H. Berndt. Sydney: Angus and Robertson, 167–206.

Berndt, Ronald M. and Catherine H. Berndt. 1951. *From black to white in South Australia*. 2 vols. Melbourne: Cheshire.

Berndt, Ronald M. and Catherine H. Berndt. 1993. *A world that was: the Yaraldi of the Murray River and the Lakes, South Australia*. Melbourne: Melbourne University Press at the Miegunyah Press.

Berry, R.J.A. 1907. 'A living descendant of an extinct (Tasmanian) race.' *Proceedings of the Royal Society of Victoria* 20: 1–20.

Birch, T.W. 1820. 'Mr T.W. Birch, Merchant: Evidence to the Bigge Enquiry.' *Historical Records of Australia*. Series III vol. III, 1921: 354–58.

Birmingham, Judy. 1992. *Wybalenna: The Archaeology of Cultural Accommodation in Nineteenth Century Tasmania*. Sydney: The Australian Society for Historical Archaeology Incorporated.

Black, John McConnell. 1920. 'Vocabularies of four South Australian languages, Adelaide, Narrunga, Kukata, and Narrinyeri with special reference to their speech sounds.' *Transactions of the Royal Society of South Australia* 44: 76–93.

Blacket, J. 1911. *History of South Australia*. Adelaide: Hussey and Gillingham.

Blackstone, William. 1765–69. *Commentaries of the Laws of England*. Volume IV: Of Public Wrongs, with an Introduction by Thomas A. Green, Chicago & London: The University of Chicago Press, 1979.

Bladen, F.M. ed. 1896. *Historical Records of New South Wales*. Vol. IV. Hunter and King. Sydney: Government Printer.

Blainey, Geoffrey. 1977. *The Tyranny of Distance: How Distance Shaped Australia's History*. Sydney: Macmillan.

Bloomfield, P. 1961. *Edward Gibbon Wakefield, builder of the British Commonwealth*. London: Longman.

Blyth, Stan. 1990. *The Britomart's Gold and Other Stories*. Prospect, Tas.: S. Blyth.

Bonnemains J, E. Forsyth, and B. Smith. 1998. *Baudin in Australian Waters: The Artwork of the French Voyage of Discovery to the Southern Lands 1800–1804: with a complete descriptive catalogue of drawings and paintings of Australian subjects by C.A. Lesueur and N.M. Petit from the Lesueur Collection at the Museum d'Histoire Naturelle, Le Havre, France*. Melbourne: Oxford University Press in association with the Australian Academy of the Humanities.

Bonwick, James. 1868. *John Batman, the Founder of Victoria*. Melbourne: Ferguson and Moore.

Bonwick, James. 1870. *The Last of the Tasmanians, or, the Black War of Van Diemen's Land*. London: Sampson Low, Son & Marston.

Bonwick, James. 1884. *The Lost Tasmanian Race*. London: Sampson Low, Marston, Searle and Rivington.

Bonwick, James. 1898. *The Daily Life and Origins of the Tasmanians*. 2nd edn. London: Low & Marston.

Bourke, Colin, Colin Johnson, and Isobel White. 1980. *Before the Invasion: Aboriginal Life to 1788*. Melbourne: Oxford University Press.

Bowden, K.M. 1964. *Captain James Kelly of Hobart Town*. Melbourne: Melbourne University Press.

Boyce, James. 1996. 'Journeying Home: A New Look at the British Invasion of Van Diemen's Land.' *Island* 66: 38–63.

Boys, Robert Douglass. 1959. *First Years at Port Phillip 1834–1842*. Melbourne: Robertson & Mullens.

Brice, Ian. 1997. 'Reluctant Schoolmaster in a Voluntarist Colony: William Cawthorne's Dairy 1842–1844.' *Journal of the Historical Society of South Australia* 25: 80–93.

Brock, Peggy and Tom Gara, 2017. *Colonialism and its Aftermath: a History of Aboriginal South Australia*. Adelaide: Wakefield Press.

Brock, Peggy, and Doreen Kartinyeri. 1989. *Poonindie: the rise and destruction of an Aboriginal agricultural community*. Adelaide: South Australian Government Printer and Aboriginal Heritage Branch.

Brown, Anthony J. 2000. *Ill-Starred Captains: Flinders and Baudin*. Adelaide: Crawford House Publishing.

Brown, T. 1919. 'Nullarbor Plain.' Proceedings of the Royal Geographical Society of Australasia (South Australian Branch) 18–19: 150.

Bruce, Robert. 1902. *Recollections of an Old Squatter*. Adelaide: W.K. Thomas and Co.

Buick, Ivy and Bev Willson. 1996. 'Growing up at the Salt Lake.' *Colours of Kangaroo Island: 100 Stories of the people and places that make up its history*. Penneshaw: Dudley Writers Group.

Bull, John Wrathall. 1884. *Early experiences of life in South Australia and an extended colonial history*. 2nd ed. Adelaide, London: E.S. Wigg & Son; Sampson Low, Marston, Searle & Rivington.

Bunce, Daniel. 1857. *Australasiatic reminiscences of twenty-three years' wanderings in Tasmania and the Australias*. Melbourne: J.T. Hendy.

Butlin, Noel. 1983. *Our Original Aggression: Aboriginal Populations of Southeastern Australia 1788–1850*. Sydney: Allen and Unwin.

Calder, J.E. 1875. *Some Account of the Wars, Extirpation, Habits &c., of the Native Tribes of Tasmania*. Hobart: Fullers Bookshop, 1972.

Cameron, J. 1879. *Yilki a place by the sea*. Victor Harbor: Yilki Uniting Church.

Cane, S.B. and Tom Gara. 1989. *Undiri: Aboriginal Association with the Nullarbor Plain*. Canberra: National Heritage Studies.

Cannon, M. 1990. *Who Killed the Koories?*. Melbourne: William Heinemann.

Carroll, J.R. 1989. *Harpoons to Harvest: The story of Charles and John Mills, Pioneers of Port Fairy*. Warrnambool: Warrnambool Institute Press.

Carroll, John, ed. 1986. *Intruders in the bush: the Australian quest for identity*. Melbourne: Oxford University Press.

Cassidy, J. 1988. 'The Significance of the Classification of a Colonial Acquisition: the Conquered/Settled Distinction.' *Australian Aboriginal Studies* 1: 2–17.

Castles, A.C. and M.C. Harris. 1987. *Lawmakers and Wayward Whigs: Government and law in South Australia 1836–1986*. Adelaide: Wakefield Press.

Cawthorne, William Anderson. 1858. *The Legend of Kuperree; or, The Red Kangaroo. An Abvoriginal Tradition of the Port Lincoln Tribe*. Adelaide: Alfred Cawthorne.

Cawthorne, William Anderson. 1865. 'Aborigines and their customs.' In *Sketch of the Aborigines of South Australia. References in the Cawthorne Papers*. Ed. Robert K. G. Foster. Adelaide: Aboriginal Heritage Branch, S.A. Department of Environment and Planning, 1991.

Cawthorne, William Anderson. 1865–6. *The Kangaroo Islanders: a story of South Australia before colonisation 1823*. Adelaide: Rigby, 1926.

Cawthorne, William Anderson. 1927. 'Rough Notes on the Manners and Customs of the Natives.' *Proceedings of the Royal Geographical Society of Australasia South Australian Branch Session 1925–6* 28: 47–77.

Chamberlain, S. 1989. *Sealing, Whaling, and Early Settlement of Victoria: An Anotated Bibliography of Historical Sources*. Victoria Archaeological Survey Occasional Report No. 29. Melbourne: Department of Conservation and Environment.

Chapman, Gifford Desmond. 1972. *Kangaroo Island Shipwrecks: an account of the ships and cutters wrecked around Kangaroo Island*. Canberra: Roebuck Society.

Chittleborough, Anne, Gillian Dooley, Brenda Glover and Rick Hosking, eds. 2002. *Alas, for the Pelicans! Flinders, Baudin and Beyond Essays and Poems*. Adelaide: Wakefield Press.

Christie, M.F. 1979. *Aborigines in Colonial Victoria 1835–86*. Sydney: Sydney University Press.

Clancy, Ann. 1999. *Rebel Girl*. Sydney: Pan Macmillan.

Clark, D.J. 1989. 'Aboriginal Responses to European Colonisation.' *Archaeological Ethics and the Treatment of the Dead: World Archaeological Congress*. Vermillion: University of South Dakota, 64–83.

Clark, I.D., ed. 1988. *The Port Phillip Journals of George Augustus Robinson: 8 March – 7 April 1842 and 18 March – 29 April 1843*. Clayton, Vic.: Monash Publications in Geography 34, Monash University.

Clark, I.D. 1990. *Aboriginal Languages and Clans: An Historical Atlas of Western and Central Victoria*. Clayton, Vic.: Monash Publications in Geography 37, Monash University.

Clarke, Philip A. 1991. 'Adelaide as an Aboriginal landscape.' *Aboriginal History* 15 1–2: 54–72.

Clarke, Philip A. 1991. 'Richard Penney as ethnographer.' *Journal of the Anthropological Society of South Australia* 29 1–2: 88–107.

Clarke, Philip A. 1995. 'Myth as history: the Ngurunderi mythology of the Lower Murray, South Australia.' *Records of the South Australian Museum* 28 2: 143–157.

Clarke, Philip A. 1996. 'Early European interaction with Aboriginal hunters and gatherers on Kangaroo Island, South Australia.' *Aboriginal History* 20: 51–81.

Clarke, Philip A. 1998. 'The Aboriginal Presence on Kangaroo Island, South Australia.' *History in Portraits: Biographies of nineteenth century South Australian Aboriginal people.* Eds. Jane Simpson and Louise Hercus. Aboriginal History Monograph 6. Sydney: Aboriginal History. 14–48.

Clarke, Philip A. 2001. 'The significance of whales to the Aboriginal people of southern South Australia.' *Records of the South Australian Museum* 34.1: 19–35.

Cleland, John B., and Norman B. Tindale. 1936. 'The natives of South Australia.' *The Centenary History of South Australia.* Ed. C. Fenner. Adelaide: Royal Geographical Society of Australasia, S.A. Branch. 16–29.

Cockburn, R. 1984. *What's in a name? Nomenclature of South Australia.* rev. ed. Adelaide: Ferguson.

Cole, Valda. 1984. *Western Port Chronology 1798–1839 Exploration to Settlement.* Hastings, Vic.: Shire of Hastings Historical Society.

Colwell, Max. 1969. *Whaling around Australia.* Adelaide: Rigby Limited.

Conrad, Joseph. 1902. *Heart of Darkness: an authoritative text, backgrounds and sources, criticism.* 3rd ed. Norton Critical Edition. New York: Norton, 1988.

Cooper, Harold M. 1952. *French exploration in South Australia 1802–1803.* Adelaide: Macdougall.

Cooper, Harold M. 1953. *The unknown coast. Being the explorations of Capt. Matthew Flinders, RN along the shores of South Australia 1802.* Adelaide: The Advertiser Printing Office.

Cooper, Harold M. 1954. 'Kangaroo Island's wild pigs: their possible origin.' *South Australian Naturalist* 28.5: 57–61.

Cooper, Harold M. 1955. *The Unknown Coast: a Supplement.* Adelaide: The Author.

Cooper, Harold M. 1957. *Australian Aboriginal words.* Adelaide: South Australian Museum.

Copland, Gordon. 2002. 'The Mysteries of Karta: Creation, Colonisers and Crusoes.' *Alas, for the Pelicans! Flinders, Baudin and Beyond Essays and Poems.* Eds. Anne Chittleborough, Gillian Dooley, Brenda Glover and Rick Hosking. Adelaide: Wakefield Press, 129–40.

Cowlishaw, G. 1979. *Black, White or Brindle: Race in Australia.* Melbourne: Cambridge University Press.

Creamer, H.F.M. 1977. 'Malaise and Beyond.' *The Moving Frontier: Aspects of Aboriginal-European Interaction.* Ed. P. Stanbury. Sydney: A.H. and A.W. Reed. 147–55.

Crowley, Frank. 1980. *A Documentary History of Australia Volume 1 Colonial Australia 1788–1840*. Sydney: Nelson.

Cumpston, John Stanley. 1973. *First visitors to Bass Strait*. 2nd ed. Canberra: Roebuck Society Publication no. 7.

Cumpston, John Stanley. 1977. *Shipping Arrivals and Departures Sydney, 1788–1825*. Canberra; Roebuck Society Publication no. 22.

Cumpston John Stanley. 1986. *Kangaroo Island 1800–1836*. 3rd ed. Canberra: Roebuck Society Publication no. 1.

Cunningham, Peter Miller. 1827. *Two years in New South Wales: a series of letters, comprising sketches of the actual state of society in that colony, of its peculiar advantages to emigrants: of its topography, natural history, etc*. London: Henry Coburn.

Curr, Edward M. 1886. *The Australian race: its origins, languages, customs, place of landing in Australia and the routes by which it spread itself over that continent*. Melbourne: Government Printer.

Daily, B., A.R. Milnes, C.R. Twidale, and Jennifer A. Bourne. 1979. 'Geology and Geomorphology.' *Natural History of Kangaroo Island*. Eds. M.J. Tyler, C.R. Twidale and J.K. Ling. Adelaide: Royal Society of South Australia.

Dakin, W.J. 1963. *Whaleman Adventurers*. Rev. Ed. Sydney: Angus and Robertson.

Darian-Smith, K. 1993. 'The white woman of Gippsland: a frontier myth.' *Captured lives. Australian captivity narratives*. Working paper in Australian Studies no. 86. London: Sir Robert Menzies Centre for Australian Studies, Institute of Commonwealth Studies, University of London.

Davidson, Graeme, John Hirst and Stuart Macintyre, eds. 1998. *The Oxford Companion to Australian History*. Melbourne: Oxford University Press.

Davies, Eliza. 1881. *The Story of an Earnest Life: A Woman's Adventures in Australia, and in Two Voyages Around the World*. Cincinnati: Central Book Concern.

Dawson, James. 1881. *Australian Aborigines: the languages and customs of several tribes of Aborigines in the Western District of Victoria, Australia*. Melbourne: George Robertson.

Debenham, Frank, ed. 1945. *The Voyage of Captain Bellingshausen to the Antarctic Seas 1819–1821*. Translated from the Russian. London: Hakluyt Society.

Defoe, Daniel. 1719. *Robinson Crusoe: an authoritative text, contexts, criticism*. 2nd ed. Ed. Michael Shinagel. Norton Critical Edition. New York: Norton, 1994.

Delano, Amaso. 1817. *A Narrative of a Voyage to New Holland and Van Diemen's Land*. Facs. Ed. Boston: A. Delano, 1817; Hobart: Cat & Fiddle Press, 1973.

Depasquale, Paul 1978. *A Critical History of South Australian Literature 1836–1930 with subjectively annotated bibliographies*. Warradale, S.A.: Pioneer Books.

De Vries, Susanna. 1995. *Strength of Spirit: Pioneering Women of Achievement from the First Fleet to Federation*. Alexandria, NSW: Millennium Books.

Diamond, M. 1988. *The Seahourse and the Wanderer: Ben Boyd in Australia*. Melbourne: Melbourne University Press.

Dickens, Charles 1852–3. *Bleak House.* Ed. Norman Page. Harmondsworth: Penguin Books, 1971.

Dickey, Brian, and Peter Howell. 1986. *South Australia's foundation: Select documents.* Adelaide: Wakefield Press.

Dineen, Ann, and Peter Mühlhaüsler. 1996. 'Nineteenth century language contact in South Australia.' *Atlas of languages of intercultural communication in the Pacific, Asia and the Americas.* Eds. S. A. Wurm, P. Mühlhaüsler and D. T. Tryon. 2:1. Berlin: Mouton de Gryuter. 83–99.

Donaldson, Ian, and Tamsin Donaldson, eds. 1985. *Seeing the first Australians.* Sydney: George Allen and Unwin.

Doome, U. 1874. 'A cruise in Bass's Straits.' *Illustrated Sydney News.* 28 February.

Draper, Neale. 1987. 'Context for the Kartan: A Preliminary Report on Excavations at Cape du Coudic Rockshelter, Kangaroo Island.' *Archaeology in Oceania.* 22.1: 1–8.

Draper, Neale. 1999. 'Land Use History: The History of Aboriginal land use on Kangaroo Island.' *A Biological Survey of Kangaroo Island, South Australia in November 1989 and 1990.* eds. A.C. Robinson & D.M. Armstrong. Biological Survey and Research Section, Heritage and Biodiversity Division, Department for Environment, Heritage and Aboriginal Affairs, South Australia. Adelaide: Endeavour Press: 33–48.

Draper, Neale. 1988. 'Stone tools and cultural landscapes: investigating the archaeology of Kangaroo Island.' *Proceedings of the Royal Geographical Society of Australasia, South Australian Branch* 88: 15–36.

Drewe, Robert. 1976. *The Savage Crows.* Sydney: William Collins.

Dunbadin, Thomas. [1937]. Sailing the World's Edge: Sea Stories from Old Sydney. London: Newnes.

Dunbadin, Thomas. 1965. 'Whalers, sealers and buccaneers.' *Journal of the Royal Historical Society* XI: 1–32.

Dunderdale, G. 1898. *The Book of the Bush.* London: Ward, Lock and Co.

Dutton, Geoffrey. 1960. *Founder of a city: the life of Colonel William Light.* Melbourne: Cheshire.

Dutton, Geoffrey. 1974. *White on Black: The Australian Aborigine Portrayed in Art.* Melbourne: Macmillan.

Dutton, Geoffrey. 1977. *Edward John Eyre: the Hero as Murderer.* Ringwood. Vic.: Penguin.

Dutton, Geoffrey and David Elder. 1991. *Colonel William Light – Founder of a City* Melbourne: Melbourne University Press.

Edwards, Robert. 1972. *The Kaurna People of the Adelaide Plains.* Adelaide: South Australian Museum.

Elder, B. 1988. *Blood on the wattle: Massacres and Maltreatment of Australian Aborigines Since 1788.* Frenchs Forest: Child and Associates.

Elkin, Adolphus P. 1931. 'The social organization of South Australian tribes.' *Oceania* 2 1: 44–73.

Ellis, R. *Men and Whales*. London: Robert Hale.

Ellis, Robert W. 1976. 'The Aboriginal inhabitants and their environment.' *Natural history of the Adelaide region*. Eds. C. R. Twidale, M. J. Tyler and B. P. Webb. Adelaide: Royal Society of South Australia.

Elwes, Robert. 1854. *A Sketcher's Tour around the World*. London: Hurst & Blackett.

Eyre, Edward J. 1845. *Journals of expeditions of discovery into Central Australia, and overland from Adelaide to King George's Sound in the Years 1840–41*. London: T. and W. Boone.

Fanning, Edmund. 1833. *Voyages round the World; with selected sketches of voyages to the South Seas, North and South Pacific Oceans, China, etc*. New York: Collins and Hannay.

Fanning, Edmund. 1924. *Voyages and Discoveries in the South Seas 1792-1832*. Salem: Marine Research Society.

Finlayson, W. 1903. 'Reminiscences by Pastor Finlayson.' *Proceedings of the Royal Geographical Society of Australasia, South Australian Branch* 6: 39–55.

Finney, C.M. 1984. *To sail beyond the sunset: Natural History of Australia 1699–1892*. Adelaide: Rigby.

Finnis, H.J. [1950]. *Early Settlers on Islands in Bass Strait*. Adelaide: Pioneers Association of South Australia.

Flinders, Matthew. 1814. *Voyage to Terra Australis*. Facs. ed. Adelaide: State Library of South Australia, 1989.

Flinders, Matthew. 2000. *Terra Australia: Matthew Flinders' Great Adventures in the Circumnavigation of Australia*. Ed. Tim Flannery Melbourne: Text Publishing.

Ford, Hugh. 1979. 'Birds.' *Natural History of Kangaroo Island*. Eds. M.J. Tyler, C.R. Twidale and J.K. Ling. Adelaide: Royal Society of South Australia.

Foster, Robert K.G. and Tom Gara. 1986. 'Aboriginal Culture in South Australia.' *The Flinders History of South Australia*. Ed. Eric Richards. Adelaide: Wakefield Press. 63–95.

Foster, Robert K.G. 1989. 'Feasts of the full-moon: the distribution of rations to Aborigines in South Australia 1836–1861.' *Aboriginal History* 13 1: 63–78.

Foster, Robert K.G. 1990a. 'The Aborigines' Location in Adelaide: South Australia's first "mission" to the Aborigines.' *Journal of the Anthropological Society of South Australia* Special Issue, 'Aboriginal Adelaide.' 28 1–2: 11–37.

Foster, Robert K.G. 1990b. 'Two early reports on the Aborigines of South Australia.' *Journal of the Anthropological Society of South Australia. Special Issue, 'Aboriginal Adelaide'* 28. 1–2: 38–63.

Foster, Robert K.G. ed. 1991. *Sketch of the Aborigines in South Australia: References in the Cawthorne Papers*. Adelaide: Aboriginal Heritage Branch, South Australian Department of Environment and Planning.

Foster, Robert K.G., and Thomas J. Gara. 1986. 'Aboriginal culture in South Australia.' *The Flinders history of South Australia. Social history.* Ed. Eric Richards. Adelaide: Wakefield Press. 63–95.

Foster, Robert K.G., Peter Mühlhaüsler, and Philip Clarke. 1998. "Give me back my name': The 'classification' of Aboriginal people in colonial South Australia.' *Papers in pidgin and creole linguistics* No. 5. Canberra: Pacific Linguistics: 35–59.

Foster, Robert K.G., Rick Hosking and Amanda Nettelbeck. 2001. *Fatal Collisions: The South Australian frontier and the violence of memory.* Adelaide: Wakefield Press.

Fox, Malcolm. 1988. 'Music Education in South Australia, 1836–1984.' *From Colonel Light to the Footlights: the Performing Arts in South Australia from 1836 to the Present.* Adelaide: Pagel Books.

Gara, Thomas J. 1986. 'Burial customs of the Kaurna.' *Journal of the Anthropological Society of South Australia* 24 8: 6–9.

Gara, Thomas J. 1990. 'Bibliography of the Kaurna.' *Journal of the Anthropological Society of South Australia* Special Issue, 'Aboriginal Adelaide.' 28 1–2: 143–164.

Gara, Thomas J. 1990. 'The life of Ivaritji ('Princess Amelia') of the Adelaide tribe.' *Journal of the Anthropological Society of South Australia* Special Issue, 'Aboriginal Adelaide.' 28 1–2: 64–104.

Gara, Thomas J. 1998. 'The life and times of Mullawirraburka ('King John') of the Adelaide Tribe.' *History in Portraits: Biographies of nineteenth century South Australian Aboriginal people.* Eds. Jane Simpson & Louise Hercus. Aboriginal History Monograph 6. Canberra: Aboriginal History: 88–132.

Gara, Thomas J., Robert K.G. Foster, and Steve Hemming, eds. 1990. *Aboriginal Adelaide. Journal of the Anthropological Society of South Australia* Special Issue, Vol. 28 1–2.

Gargett, Kathryn & Susan Marsden. 1996. *Adelaide: a brief history.* Adelaide: State History Centre.

Gell, John Philip. 1842. 'The Vocabulary of the Adelaide Tribe.' *Tasmanian Journal of Natural Science* 1: 109–124, reprinted in *Journal of the Anthropological Society of South Australia* 25:5 (1988): 3–15.

Gerber, Richard. 1959. 'The English Island Myth'. *Critical Quarterly* 1: 36–43.

Gibbs, Ronald M. 1960. 'Relations between the Aboriginal inhabitants and the first South Australian colonists.' *Proceedings of the Royal Geographical Society of Australasia, South Australian Branch* 61: 61–78.

Gibbs, Ronald M. 1969. *A history of South Australia.* Adelaide: Balara Books.

Gill, J.C.H. 1966. 'Genesis of the Australian Whaling Industry and its development up to 1850.' *Royal Historical Society of Queensland* 8:1: 218–245.

Gill, Thomas. 1906. 'Who discovered Lake Alexandrina?' *Proceedings of the Royal Geographical Society of Australasia, South Australian Branch* 8: 48–54.

Gill, Thomas. 1909. 'A cruise in the S.S. "Governor Musgrave".' *Proceedings of the Royal Geographical Society of Australasia, South Australian Branch* 10: 90–184.

Goodridge, Charles Medyett. 1839. *Narrative of a Voyage to the South Seas; and the Shipwreck of the* Princess of Wales *Cutter*. Exeter: W.C. Featherstone.

Gould, C. 1872. 'The islands in Bass's Strait.' *Papers and Proceedings of the Royal Society of Tasmania*. 1871: 57–67.

Green, Martin 1980. *Dreams of Adventure, Deeds of Empire*. London: Routledge.

Grey, George. 1841. *Journals of two expeditions of discovery in north-west and western Australia during the years 1837, 38, and 39, under the authority of Her Majesty's Government. Describing many newly discovered, important, and fertile districts, with observations on the moral and physical condition of the Aboriginal inhabitants, &c, &c*. London: T. and W. Boone.

Griffiths, Tom, and Alan Platt, eds. 1988. *The life and adventures of Edward Snell: the illustrated diary of an artist, engineer and adventurer in the Australian colonies 1849 to 1859*. North Ryde, Australia: Angus and Robertson and The Library Council of Victoria.

Groom, H. and J. Irvine. 1981. *The Kaurna: Aboriginal People of South Australia*. Largs Bay, SA: Tjintu Books.

Grossman, Anne Chotzinoff and Lisa Grossman Thomas. 1997. *Lobscouse and Spotted Dog Which It's a Gastronomic Companion to the Aubrey/Maturin Novels*. Foreword by Patrick O'Brian. New York: W.W. Norton & Company.

Hahn, Dirk Meinertz. 1964. 'Extracts from the reminiscences of Captain Dirk Meinertz Hahn, 1838–1839. Trans. F.J.C. Blaess and L.A. Triebel. *South Australiana* 3 2: 97–134.

Hailes, Nathaniel. 1998. *Recollections: Nathaniel Hailes' adventurous life in colonial South Australia*. Ed. Allan L. Peters, Adelaide: Wakefield Press.

Hainsworth, D.R. 1967a. 'Exploiting the Pacific Frontier: the New South Wales Sealing Industry 1800–1821.' *The Journal of Pacific History* 2: 59–76.

Hainsworth, D.R. 1967b. 'Iron men in wooden ships: the Sydney sealers 1800-1820.' *Labour History* 13: 19-25.

Hainsworth, D.R. 1981. *The Sydney Traders: Simeon Lord and his Contemporaries 1788–1821*. Melbourne: Melbourne University Press.

Hale, Matthew B. 1889. *The Aborigines of Australia: being an account of the institution for their education at Poonindie in South Australia*. London: SPCK.

Hallack, E.H. 1905. *Kangaroo Island: Adelaide sanatorium, with map and illustrations by 'a native.'* Adelaide: W.K.Thomas.

Hannabuss, Stuart 1984. 'Islands as metaphors.' *Universities Quarterly*, 38.1: 70–82.

Harrison, R. 1862. *Colonial sketches*. London: Hall, Virtue and Co.

Harrison, Robert Pogue. 1992. *Forests: The Shadow of Civilization*. Chicago & London: University of Chicago Press.

Hart, John. 1854. *Letters from Victorian Pioneers: being A Series of Papers on the Early Occupation of the Colony, the Aborigines, etc*. Ed. Thomas Bride, Melbourne: Public Library, 1898; Ed. C.E. Sayers. Melbourne: William Heinemann, 1969.

Hassell, Kathleen. 1966. *The relations between the settlers and Aborigines in South Australia, 1836–1860*. Adelaide: Libraries Board of South Australia.

Hawker, James C. 1899. *Early experiences in South Australia*. Adelaide: Wigg & Son. Adelaide: Libraries Board of South Australia, 1975.

Hemming, Steve. 1984. 'Conflict between the Aborigines and Europeans along the Murray River and the Darling to the Great South Bend (1830–1841).' *Journal of the Anthropological Society of South Australia*. 22.1: 3–21.

Hemming, Steve. 1985. 'The Mulgewongk, a Water Monster or "Bunyip" of the Lower Murray River region of South Australia,' *Journal of the Anthropological Society of South Australia* 23.1: 11–16.

Hemming, Steve. 1990. 'Kaurna' identity: a brief history.' *Journal of the Anthropological Society of South Australia* Special Issue, 'Aboriginal Adelaide.' 28 1–2: 126–142.

Henderson, Graeme. 1980. *Unfinished voyages: Western Australian shipwrecks, 1622–1850*. Nedlands, W.A.: University of Western Australia Press.

Hercus, L.A. and P.J. Sutton, eds. *This is What Happened: Historical Narratives by Aborigines*. Canberra: Australian Institute Of Aboriginal Studies.

Hiatt, B. 1978. 'Woman the Gatherer.' *Woman's Role in Aboriginal Society*. Ed. F. Gale. Australian Aboriginal Studies 36. Social Anthropology Series 6, 3rd ed. Canberra: Australian Institute Of Aboriginal Studies. 4–15.

Hiatt, Les R. 1996. *Arguments about Aborigines: Australia and the evolution of social anthropology*. Cambridge: Cambridge University Press.

Hill, D.L. and S.J. Hill. 1975. *Notes on the Narangga Tribe of Yorke Peninsula*. Adelaide: Lutheran Publishing House.

Hill, Ernestine. 1951. *My Love Must Wait: The Story of Matthew Flinders*. Sydney: Angus and Robertson.

Hill, Ernestine. 1954. 'Last of the Tasmanians.' *Australian Geographical Walkabout Magazine* 20: 7–20.

Historical Records of Australia, Series I. vol. iv. Melbourne: Library Committee of the Commonwealth Parliament, 1915.

Hoare, Benjamin. 1869. *Figures of fancy: a volume of new poems: The Maori, The Ambush and occasional pieces by Benjamin Hoare*. Adelaide: Platts and Co.

Hodge, B. and V. Mishra. 1991. *The Dark Side of the Dream: Australian Literature and the Postcolonial Mind*. Sydney: Allen and Unwin.

Hooton, Joy and Harry Heseltine. 1992. *Annals of Australian Literature*. 2nd ed. Melbourne: Oxford University Press.

Hope, J., R.J. Lampert, E. Edmondson, M.J. Smith and G.F. van Tets. 1977. 'Late Pleistocene Faunal Remains from Seton Rock Shelter, Kangaroo Island, South Australia.' *Journal of Biogeography* 4. 363–85.

Hope, Penelope. 1968. *The voyage of the* Africaine. Melbourne: Heinemann Educational Australia.

Hordern, Marsden. 1997. *King of the Australian Coast: The Work of Phillip Parker King in the Mermaid and Bathurst 1817–1822.* Melbourne: Melbourne University Press.

Horton, David. 1982. 'The Burning Question: Aborigines, Fire and Australian Ecosystems.' *Mankind* 13.3: 237–51.

Horton, David, ed. 1994. *The Encyclopaedia of Aboriginal Australia.* 2 vols. Canberra: Australian Institute of Aboriginal and Torres Strait Islander Studies.

Hosking, Rick. 2002. ''A sort of *pot pourri*': William Cawthorne's *The Kangaroo Islanders*'. *Alas, for the Pelicans! Flinders, Baudin and Beyond Essays and Poems.* Eds. Anne Chittleborough, Gillian Dooley, Brenda Glover and Rick Hosking. Adelaide: Wakefield Press, 142–58.

Hosking, Rick. 2002. 'Notes' to William Cawthorne: 'Journal of a Trip to Kangaroo Island.' *Alas, for the Pelicans! Flinders, Baudin and Beyond Essays and Poems.* Eds. Anne Chittleborough, Gillian Dooley, Brenda Glover and Rick Hosking. Adelaide: Wakefield Press, 168–72.

Houston, Carol, and Robert M. Ellis. 1976. *The Aboriginal inhabitants of the Adelaide Plains.* Adelaide: Aboriginal and Historic Relics Administration.

Howard, Mark. 1991. 'Archdeacon Thomas Reiby's 1862 missionary voyage to the islands of Bass Strait.' *Tasmanian Historical Research Association Papers & Proceedings* 38.2: 78–87.

Howitt, Alfred W. 1904. *The Native Tribes of South-East Australia* London: Macmillan. Facsimile Edition, Canberra: Aboriginal Studies Press, 1996.

Hugill, Stan. 1966. *Shanties from the Seven Seas: Shipboard work-songs and songs used as work-songs from the great days of sail.* London: Routledge & Kegan Paul.

Hussey, Henry. 1897. *More than half a century of colonial life and Christian experience: with notes of travel, lectures, publications etc.* Adelaide: Hussey and Gillingham. Facsimile ed: Adelaide: Libraries Board of South Australia.

Inns, Robert W., Peter F. Aitken, and John K. Ling. 1979. 'Mammals.' *Natural History of Kangaroo Island.* Eds. M.J. Tyler, C.R. Twidale & J.K. Long. Adelaide: Royal Society of South Australia.

Jackman, William. 1853. *The Australian captive, or, An authentic narrative of fifteen years in the life of William Jackman: in which among various other adventures, is included a forced residence of a year and a half among the cannibals of Nuyts' Land, on the coast of the Great Australian Bight: also including, with other appendices, Australia and its gold, from the latest and best authorities.* Auburn, U.S.A.: Derby & Miller.

Jaensch, Dean, ed. 1986. *The Flinders History of South Australia: Political History.* Adelaide: Wakefield Press.

James, Keryn. 2002. 'Wife or Slave?: Australian Sealing Slavery.' *Alas, for the Pelicans! Flinders, Baudin and Beyond Essays and Poems.* Eds. Anne Chittleborough, Gillian Dooley, Brenda Glover and Rick Hosking. Adelaide: Wakefield Press, 160–172.

James, Thomas Horton. [1839?]. *Six months in South Australia: with some account of Port Philip and Portland Bay, ... advice to emigrants, ... a monthly calendar of gardening and agriculture adapted to the climate and seasons*. London: J. Cross.

Jenkin, Graham. 1979. *Conquest of the Ngarrindjeri. The story of the Lower Murray Lakes tribes*. Adelaide: Rigby.

Jessop, William R.H. 1862. *Flindersland and Sturtland, the inside and outside of Australia*. London: Bentley.

Jetson, Tim. 1996. 'An island of contentment? A history of Preservation Island.' *Tasmanian Historical Research Association* 43.1: 29–46.

Jones, J. 1921. 'Port Adelaide River.' *Proceedings of the Royal Geographical Society of Australasia, South Australian Branch* 22: 73–75.

Jones, Pauline, ed. 1981. *Historical Records of Victoria: Foundation Series. Volume One: Beginnings of Permanent Government*. Melbourne: Victorian Government Printing Office.

Jones, Philip. 1988. 'Collections and curators: South Australian Museum anthropology from the 1860s to the 1920s.' *Journal of the Historical Society of South Australia* 16: 87–103.

Jose, Jim. 1990. 'Legislating for social purity, 1883–85: The Reverend Joseph Coles Kirby and the Social Purity Society.' *Journal of the Historical Society of South Australia* 18: 190.

Journals and Printed Papers of the Parliament of Tasmania 1885. Vol. V, no. 44, 'Expedition from Van Diemen's Land to Port Phillip in 1835'.

Keefe, K. 1988. 'Aboriginality: Resistance and Persistence.' *Australian Aboriginal Studies*. 1: 67–81.

Kelly, James. 1820. 'Examination of J. Kelly: Evidence to the Bigge Enquiry.' *Historical Records of Australia*. Series III vol. III, 1921: 485–66.

Kelly, James. 1920. 'First Discovery of Port Davey and Macquarie Harbour.' *Papers and Proceedings of the Royal Society of Tasmania*: 160–181.

Kerr, Joan, ed. 1984. *The Dictionary of Australian Artists*. Sydney: Power Institute of Fine Arts, University of Sydney.

King, Phillip Parker, 1827. *Narrative of a survey of the intertropical and western coasts of Australia, performed between the years 1818 and 1822 : with an appendix containing various subjects relating to hydrography and natural history*. London: Murray.

Kingscote Country Women's Association. 1957?. *Kangaroo Island. Past and present. Being a short history of the oldest settlement in South Australia*. Kingscote, Kangaroo Island: Kingscote Country Women's Association.

Kostoglou, Parry and Justin McCarthy. 1991. *Whaling and Sealing Sites in South Australia*. Australian Institute for Maritime Archaeology Special Publication No. 6. Adelaide: State Heritage Branch, Department of Environment and Planning.

Kostoglou, Parry. 1996. *Sealing in Tasmania: Historical Research Project. A Report for the Parks and Wildlife Service.* Hobart: Department of Environment and Land Management.

Kwan, Elizabeth. 1987. *Living in South Australia: A social history.* Netley, South Australia: South Australian Government Printer.

Lampert, R.J. 1981. *The Great Kartan Mystery.* Terra Australis 5. Research School of Pacific Studies. Canberra: Australian National University Press.

Lawrence, Susan and Mark Staniforth, eds. 1998. *The archaeology of whaling in Southern Australia and New Zealand.* Gundaroo, N.S.W.: Brolga Press for the Australasian Society for Historical Archaeology and the Australian Institute for Maritime Archaeology.

Le Lievre, C. 1925. *Memories of an old police officer.* Adelaide: W.K. Thomas.

Learmonth, Noel Fulford. 1983. The Portland Bay settlement: being the history of Portland, Victoria, from 1800 to 1851. Hawkesdale: Baulch Publications.

Leigh, W. H. 1839. *Reconnoitering voyages and travels with adventures in the new colonies of South Australia, during the years 1836, 1837, 1838.* London: Smith, Elder & Co.

Lendon, Alfred Austin. 1926. 'Kangaroo Island: The Tragedy of Dr Slater and Mr Osborne. A Story of Ninety Years Ago.' *Proceedings of the Royal Geographical Society of Australasia South Australian Branch* 26: 67–84.

Lendon, Alfred Austin. 1930. 'Dr Richard Penney (1840–1844.' Proceedings of the Royal Geographical Society of Australasia South Australian Branch 31: 20–32.

Lester, Shirley. 1984. 'The importance of a shipwreck: the *Sydney Cove (1797), Tasmanian Historical Research Association Papers and Proceedings* 31.3: 1–12.

Light, William 1837. *Supplement to the First Report of the Directors of the South Australian Company* London: William Johnstone.

Light, William. 1839. *William Light's brief journal and Australian diaries with an introduction and notes by David Elder.* Adelaide: Wakefield Press, 1984.

Light, William. 1962. *A brief journal of the proceedings of William Light: late Surveyor-General of the Province of South Australia.* Adelaide: Public Library of South Australia.

Lincoln, Margarette. 1997. 'Shipwreck narratives of the eighteenth and early nineteenth century: indicators of culture and identity.' *British Journal for Eighteenth-Century Studies* 20.2: 155–172.

Little, Barbara. 1969. 'The Sealing and Whaling Industry in Australia Before 1850.' *Australian Economic History Review* 9:2: 109–27.

Loxley, Diana 1990. *Problematic Shores: The Literature of Islands.* London: Macmillan.

Lucieer, Michiel. 1992. *'Sturt Light' to Cape Willoughby: South Australia's First Lighthouse.* Adelaide: Lighthouse Press.

MacKenzie, J.M. 1976. *Sealing, Sailing and Settling in South-Western Victoria.* Kilmore: Lowden Publishing.

Mackenzie, John 1984. *Propaganda and Empire: The Manipulation of British Popular Opinion*. Manchester: Manchester University Press.

Magarey, A.T. 1893. 'Smoke Signals of Australian Aborigines.' *Reports of the Australian Association for the Advancement of Science*. 5:498–513.

Mann, William. 1839. *Six years' residence in the Australian provinces, ending in 1839: exhibiting their capabilities of colonization, and containing the history, trade, population, extent, resources, &c. &c. of New South Wales, Van Diemen's Land, South Australia, and Port Philip: with an account of New Zealand*. London: Elder & Co.

Manning, Geoffrey 1990. *Manning's Place Names of South Australia*. Adelaide: the Author.

Marryat, C. 1863. 'Local Tour to the Lighthouse on the South Australian Coast by C. Marryat.' *The Church Chronicle, Diocese of Adelaide* March 20, 1863: x.

Mattingley, Christobel, and Ken Hampton, ed. 1988. *Survival in our own land: 'Aboriginal' experiences in 'South Australia' since 1836*. Adelaide: Wakefield Press.

Maurice, R.T. 1902. 'A trip to the western interior of South Australia.' *Proceedings of the Royal Geographical Society of Australasia (South Australian Branch)* 4–5: 41.

McGrath, Ann. 1990. 'The white man's looking glass: Aboriginal–Colonial gender relations at Port Jackson.' *Australian History Studies* 24 95: 189–207.

McLaren, John. 2002. 'Bass Straitsmen: A Study in Survival and Regeneration.' *Alas, for the Pelicans! Flinders, Baudin and Beyond Essays and Poems*. Eds. Anne Chittleborough, Gillian Dooley, Brenda Glover and Rick Hosking. Adelaide: Wakefield Press, 192–204.

McNab, R. 1913. *The old whaling days: a history of southern New Zealand from 1830–1840*. Auckland: Golden Press, 1975.

Meredith, Louisa Anne. 1852. *My Home in Tasmania during a residence of nine years*. London: John Murray.

Meredith, Louisa Anne. 1880. *Tasmanian Friends and Foes Feathered, Furred and Finned*. Hobart: J. Walch & Sons.

Meyer, Heinrich A.E. 1843. *Vocabulary of the language spoken by the aborigines of the southern and eastern portions of the settled districts of South Australia*. Adelaide: James Allen.

Meyer, Heinrich A.E. 1846. *Manners and customs of the Aborigines of the Encounter Bay tribe*. Adelaide: George Dehane.

Micco, Helen Mary. 1971. *King Island and the Sealing Trade 1802: A Translation of Chapters XXII and XXIII of the narrative of Francoius Péron in the official account of the Voyage of Discovery to the Southern Lands undertaken in the Corvettes Le Géographe, Le Naturaliste and the schooner Casuarina, during the years 1800 to 1804, under the command of Captain Nicolas Baudin*. Roebuck Society Publications No 3. Canberra: Roebuck Society Publications.

Milton, John. 1642. *The Poetical Works of John Milton*. Ed. H.C. Beeching. London: Oxford University Press, 1930.

Mollison, B.C. & Coral Everitt. 1977. *A Chronology of Events Affecting Tasmanian Aboriginal People since Contact by Whites*. Hobart: University of Tasmania.

Mollison, B.C. 1974. *A Synopsis of Data on Tasmanian Aborigines*. Second Edition. Vol. 1. Hobart: University of Tasmania.

Mollison, B.C. 1976. *The Tasmanian Aborigines: Tasmanian Aboriginal Genealogies, with an Appendix on Kangaroo Island*. Vol. 3 part 1. Hobart: University of Tasmania.

Mollison, B.C. & Coral Everitt. 1978. *The Tasmanian Aborigines and Their Genealogies*. Hobart: University of Tasmania.

Moncrieff, Virginia. prod. 2002. 'Blackfella, Whitefella,' *Four Corners*, Australian Broadcasting Commission, Channel 2, Adelaide. 26 August 2002.

Montgomery, James. 1828. *The Pelican Island, and Other Poems*. London: Longman, Rees, Orme, Brown, and Green.

Moore, H.P. 1925. 'Notes on the Early Settlers in South Australia Prior to 1836', *Proceedings of the Royal Geographical Society of Australasia South Australian Branch Session 1923–4* 25: 81–135.

Morphett, John. 1837. *South Australia; latest information from this colony, contained in a letter written by Mr Morphett, dated Nov. 25th, 1836* London: John Gliddon.

Morrell, B. Jr. 1832. *A narrative of four voyages to the South Sea, North and South Pacific Ocean, Chinese Sea, Ethiopic and Southern Atlantic Ocean, Indian and Antarctic Oceans from the years 1822 to 1831*. New York: J. and J. Harper.

Muir, Marcie. 1982. *A History of Australian Children's Book Illustration*. Melbourne: Oxford University Press.

Mulvaney, D.J. and J.P. White, eds. 1987. *Australians to 1788*. Australians: A Historical Library. Sydney: Fairfax, Syme and Weldon.

Mulvaney, John D. 1985. 'The Darwinian perspective.' *Seeing the first Australians*. Eds. I. Donaldson and T. Donaldson. Sydney: George Allen and Unwin: 68–75.

Murn, Molly 2019. *Heart of the Grass Tree*. Sydney: Vintage Books.

Murray, A. 1848. *The South Australian Almanack and Town and Country Directory for 1848*. Adelaide: Murray.

Murray, L.C. 1929. 'Notes on the Sealing Industry of Van Diemen's Land.' *Report of the Australian Association for the Advancement of Science*. 19: 274–81.

Murray, Tim. 1993. 'The childhood of William Lanne: contact archaeology and Aboriginality in Tasmania.' *Antiquity* 67: 504–19.

Murray-Smith, Stephen, ed. 1987. *Bass Strait: Australia's Last Frontier*. Rev. ed. Sydney: ABC.

Murray-Smith, Stephen. 1973. 'Beyond the Pale: The Islander Community of Bass Strait in the 19th Century.' *Tasmanian Historical Research Association* 20:4, December: 167–200.

Murray-Smith, Stephen. ed. 1979. *Mission to the Islands: The Missionary Voyages in Bass Strait of Canon Marcus Brownrigg, 1872–1885*. Hobart: Cat & Fiddle Press.

Musgrave, T. 1865. *Castaways on Auckland Isles: a narrative of the wreck of the Grafton.* Melbourne: Dwight.

Nance, Christopher. 1979. 'Two South Australian Writers.' *Tradition: Journal of the History Teachers Association* 20: 19–22.

Napier, Charles J. 1835. *Colonization; particularly in South Australia, with some remarks on Small Farms and Over-Population.* New York: Augustus M. Kelly, 1969.

Newland, Simpson. 1893. *Paving the Way: A Romance of the Australian Bush.* London: Gay & Bird.

Newland, Simpson. 1926. *Memoirs of Simpson Newland.* Adelaide: F.W. Preece.

Nicholls, M. ed. 1977. *The diary of the Reverend Robert Knopwood 1803–1838.* Hobart: Tasmanian Historical Association.

Nicholson, Ian Hawkins. 1963. *Shipping Arrivals and Departures Sydney Vol, II 1826 to 1840 Parts I, II and III.* Canberra: Roebuck Books.

Norman, F.I. 1989. '"A horrible road to travel"—the diary of Captain Donald Sinclair at Macquarie Island, December 1877–January 1878.' *Tasmanian Historical Research Association Papers & Proceedings* 36.1: 33–51.

Norman, L. 1946. *Sea Wolves and bandits: Sealing, Whaling, Smuggling and Piracy, Wild men of Van Diemen's Land, Bushrangers and bandits, Wrecks and Wreckings.* Hobart: Walch.

Nunn, Jean M. 1989. *This Southern Land: Kangaroo Island.* Kingswood, SA: the Author.

O'Brien, M. 1990. *The Legend of the Seven Sisters.* Canberra: Aboriginal Studies Press.

O'May, D.G. 1974. 'Sailing Traders of Southern Tasmania.' *Australian and New Zealand Sail Traders.* Ed. Garry J. Kerr. Blackwood, SA: Lynton Publications.

O'May, Harry. n.d. *Sealers of Bass Strait.* Hobart: Government printer.

O'May, Harry. n.d. *Wooden Hookers of Hobart Town.* Hobart: L.G. Shea.

O'May, Harry. n.d. *Hobart River Craft.* Hobart: Government Printer.

Ostercock, Alan. 1973. *Time: on Kangaroo Island.* Adelaide: The Author.

Pasco, Crawford. 1897. *A Roving Commission: Naval Reminiscences.* Melbourne: George Robertson.

Pearson, Michael. 1983. 'The Technology of Whaling in Australian waters in the Nineteenth century.' *Australian Journal of Historical Archaeology* 1: 40–54.

Pearson, Michael. 1985. 'Shore-Based Whaling at Twofold Bay: One Hundred Years of Enterprise.' *Australian Journal of Historical Archaeology* 71 1: 3–27.

Peet, T.H. 1901. 'Letter.' *Proceedings of the Royal Geographical Society of Australasia (South Australian Branch)* 4: 80–81.

Peron, Francois. 1816. 'Historical Perspective: Kangaroo Island–1803.' Translated into English from Voyages de découverte aux Terres Australes.' *Natural History of Kangaroo Island.* Eds. J. M. Tyler, C. R. Twidale and J. K. Ling. Adelaide: Royal Society of South Australia, 1979.

Pike, Douglas, *et al.* 1962. *The Australian Dictionary of Biography*, Vol. 7 1891–1939 A—Ch, Melbourne: Melbourne University Press.

Pike, Douglas. 1967. *Paradise of Dissent: South Australia 1829–1857.* 2*nd* ed. Carlton, Vic.: Melbourne University Press.

Plomley, Brian N.J. 1976. *A word–list of the Tasmanian Aboriginal languages.* Launceston: The author.

Plomley, Brian N.J. and Kristen Anne Henley. 1990. *The Sealers of Bass Strait and the Cape Barren Island Community*. Hobart: Blubber Head Press.

Plomley, Brian N.J. ed. 1966. *Friendly mission: The Tasmanian journals and papers of George Augustus Robinson 1829–1834*. Hobart: Tasmanian Historical Research Association.

Plomley, Brian N.J. ed. 1971. *Friendly Mission: The Tasmanian Journals and Papers of George Augustus Robinson 1829–1834: A Supplement*. Hobart: Tasmanian Historical Research Association.

Plomley, Brian N.J. ed. 1987. *Weep in silence: A history of the Flinders Island Aboriginal settlement*. Hobart: Blubber Head Press.

Pope, Alan. 1989. *Resistance and retaliation: Aboriginal–European relations in early colonial South Australia*. Bridgewater: Heritage Action.

Pratt, Mary Louise. 1992. *Imperial Eyes: Travel Writing and Transculturation*. London and New York: Routledge.

Presland, G. ed. 1980. 'The Journals of G.A. Robinson: May to August 1841.' *Journal of the Victorian Archaeological Survey* II.

Presland, G. 1985. *The land of the Kulin: Discovering the Lost Landscape and the First People of Port Phillip*. Fitzroy, Vic.: McPhee Gribble.

Presland, G. 1989. 'The Journals of George Augustus Robinson.' *La Trobe Library Journal* 11.43: 9–12.

Prest, Wilfred, Kerrie Round and Carol Fort, eds. 2001. *The Wakefield Companion to South Australian History*. Adelaide: Wakefield Press.

Pretty, G.L. 1986. 'The Prehistory of South Australia.' *The Flinders History of South Australia*. Ed. Eric Richards. Adelaide: Wakefield Press. 33–62.

Price, Grenfell A. 1924. *The Foundation and Settlement of South Australia 1829–1845*. Adelaide: Preece.

Price, Grenfell A. 1926. 'The Work of Captain Collet Barker in South Australia.' *Proceedings of the Royal Geographical Society of Australasia South Australian Branch* 26: 52–67.

Pulteney Grammar School Magazine, 1953.

Radford, Ron and Jane Hylton. 1995. *Australian Colonial Art, 1800–1900*. Adelaide: Art Gallery of South Australia.

Rae-Ellis, Vivienne. 1979. *Louisa Anne Meredith: A Tigress in Exile*. Hobart: Blubber Head Press.

Rae-Ellis, Vivienne. 1981. *Trucanini. Queen or traitor?* Canberra: Australian Institute of Aboriginal Studies.

Rae-Ellis, Vivienne. 1988. *Black Robinson: Protector of Aborigines*. Carlton, Vic.: University of Melbourne Press.

Randell, William Beavis. 1985. *Journal of voyage to South Australia*. Gumeracha, S.A.: Gould Books.

Rawson, G. 1950. *Matthew Flinders' narrative of his voyage in the schooner* Francis. London: Golden Cockerel Press.

Ray, W.R. 1973. *Pulteney Grammar School, 1847–1872: A Record*. Adelaide: The Council of Governors of Pulteney Grammar School.

Redwood, R. 1950. *Forgotten islands of the South Pacific*. Wellington: Reed.

Reser, J.P. 1977. 'The Dwelling as Motif in Aboriginal Bark Painting.' *Form in Indigenous Art: Schematisation in the Art of Aboriginal Australia and Prehistoric Europe*. Ed P.J. Ucko. Prehistory and Material Culture Series 13. Canberra: AIAS; New Jersey: Humanities Press; London: Gerald Duckworth and Co. 210–19.

Reynolds, Henry. 1981. *The Other Side of the Frontier: An Interpretation of the Aboriginal Response to the Invasion and Settlement of Australia*. Townsville, Queensland: Department of History, James Cook University.

Reynolds, Henry. 1987. *The law of the land*. Ringwood, Victoria: Penguin Books Australia.

Reynolds, Henry. 1989. *Dispossession: Black Australians and White Invaders*. Sydney: Allen and Unwin.

Reynolds, Henry. 1990. *With the White People: the Crucial Role of Aborigines in the Exploration and Development of Australia*. Ringwood, Victoria: Penguin Books Australia.

Reynolds, Henry. 1992. *The law of the land*. 2nd ed. Ringwood, Victoria: Penguin Books Australia.

Richards, Eric, ed. 1986. *The Flinders History of South Australia: Social History*. Adelaide: Wakefield Press.

Rigney, Lester-Irabinna. 2002. 'Foreword.' *Alas, for the Pelicans! Flinders, Baudin and Beyond Essays and Poems*. Eds. Anne Chittleborough, Gillian Dooley, Brenda Glover and Rick Hosking. Adelaide: Wakefield Press, ix–xv.

Robinson, A.C. 1999. 'European History.' *A Biological Survey of Kangaroo Island, South Australia in November 1989 and 1990*. Eds. A.C. Robinson and D.M. Armstrong. Biological Survey and Research Section, Heritage and Biodiversity Division, Department for Environment, Heritage and Aboriginal Affairs, South Australia. Adelaide: Endeavour Press: 49–55.

Roe, Michael., ed. 1967. *The Journal and Letters of Captain Charles Bishop on the North-West Coast of America, in the Pacific and in New South Wales 1794–1799*. Cambridge: The Hakluyt Society.

Ross, J.O.C. 1987. *William Stewart, sealing captain, trader and speculator*. Roebuck Society Publication no.37. Canberra: Roebuck Society.

Roth, H. Ling. 1899. *The Aborigines of Tasmania*. Hobart: Fullers, 1968.

Ruediger, Wynnis J. 1980. *Border's Land: Kangaroo Island 1802–1836*. Adelaide: Lutheran Publishing House.

Ryan, Lyndall. 1972. 'The Extinction of the Tasmanian Aborigines: Myth and Reality.' *Tasmanian Historical Research Association* 19: 2, June: 61–77.

Ryan, Lyndall. 1981. *The Aboriginal Tasmanians*. St Lucia: University of Queensland Press.

Ryan, Lyndall. 1987. 'Trucanini.' *200 Australian Women*. St Lucia: University of Queensland Press.

Ryan, Lyndall. 1997. 'The struggle for Trukanini 1830–1997,' *Tasmanian Historical Research Association Papers and Proceedings* 44.3: 153–173.

Sadler, James. 1933. *Some annals of Adelaide*. Adelaide: Hassell Press.

Salter, Harold. 1991. *Bass Strait Ketches*. Hobart: St David's Park Publishing.

Sanders, C.S. ed. 1955. *The Settlement of George Sanders and his Family at Echunga Creek, 1839–40, from the Journal of Jane Sanders*. Adelaide: the Pioneers' Association of South Australia.

Savill, Vanda. 1980. *'Tha' she blows': old ships, old salts and old days of sealing and whaling*. Hamilton, Vic.: The Author.

Schaffer, K. 1993. 'Captivity narratives and the idea of 'nation." *Captured lives. Australian captivity narratives*. Ed.Kate Darien-Smith. Working paper in Australian Studies no. 86. Sir Robert Menzies Centre for Australian Studies, Institute of Commonwealth Studies, University of London.

Schürmann, Edwin A. 1987. *I'd rather dig potatoes: Clamor Schürmann and the Aborigines of South Australia 1838–1853*. Adelaide: Lutheran Publishing House.

Scott, Theodore. 1839. *Description of South Australia with sketches of New South Wales, Port Lincoln, Port Philip and New Zealand*. Glasgow: Duncan Campbell.

Seaman, Keith. 1990. 'The Press and the Aborigines: South Australia's first thirty years.' *Journal of the Historical Society of South Australia* 18: 28–36.

Serventy, D.L. 1987. 'Mutton–birding.' *Bass Strait: Australia's Last Frontier*. Rev. ed. Sydney: ABC: 62–68.

Sexton, R.T. 1990. *Shipping Arrivals and Departures South Australia 1627–1850: A guide for Genealogists and Maritime Historians*. Roebuck Society Publications No. 42. Canberra: Roebuck Society.

Shillinglaw, J.J. ed. 1879. *Historical Records of Port Phillip: the first annals of the colony of Victoria*. Melbourne: Government Printer.

Simpson, Jane. 1992. 'Notes on a manuscript dictionary of Kaurna.' *The language game: papers in memory of Donald C. Laycock*. Eds. Tom Dutton *et al*. Canberra: Pacific Linguistics.

Simpson, Jane. 1996. 'Early language contact varieties in South Australia.' *Australian Journal of Linguistics* 16 2: 169–207.

Simpson, Jane. 1998. 'Introduction.' *History in Portraits: Biographies of nineteenth century South Australian Aboriginal people*. Eds. Jane Simpson & Louise Hercus. Aboriginal History Monograph 6. Sydney: Aboriginal History.

Simpson, Jane. 1998a. 'Personal names.' *History in Portraits: Biographies of nineteenth century South Australian Aboriginal people*. Eds. Jane Simpson & Louise Hercus. Aboriginal History Monograph 6. Sydney: Aboriginal History.

Skelton, Raleigh Ashlin. 1958. *Explorers' maps: chapters in the cartographic record of geographical discovery*. London: Routledge and Kegan Paul. 910.9 S627

Smith, Mrs. James S. 1880. *The Booandik tribe of South Australian Aborigines*. Australiana facsimile editions no.1. Adelaide: E.Spiller, Government Printer, for Libraries Board of South Australia, 1965.

Smyth, R. Brough. 1878. *The Aborigines of Victoria: with notes relating to the habits of natives of other parts of Australia and Tasmania*. Melbourne: Government Printer.

Sobel, Dava 1995. *Longitude: the True Story of a Lone Genius Who Solved the Greatest Scientific problem of His Time*. London: Fourth Estate.

South Australia in 1842, by someone who lived there nearly four years. London: C. Hailes, 1843.

South Australian Association. 1834. *South Australia. Outline of the plan of a proposed colony*. Facs. ed. Adelaide: Austaprint, 1978.

South Australian Department of Environment and Planning. 1991. *Heritage of Kangaroo Island*. Adelaide: Department of Environment and Planning.

Staniforth, Mark and Mike Nash 1998. *Chinese export porcelain from the wreck of the* Sydney Cove *(1797)*. Australian Institute for Maritime Archaeology, no. 12. Adelaide: Brolga Press for the Australian Institute for Maritime Archaeology.

Staniforth, Mark. 1996. 'Diet, disease and death at sea on the voyage to Australia, 1837–1839.' *International Journal of Maritime History* 8:2: 119–156.

Stanner, William E.H. 1965. 'Aboriginal territorial organisation, estate, range, domain and regime.' *Oceania* 36 1: 1–26.

Starke, J., ed. 1986. *Journal of a Rambler: the journal of John Boultbee*. Auckland: Oxford University Press.

Stephens, Edward. 1889. 'The Aborigines of Australia, being personal recollections of those tribes who once inhabited the Adelaide Plains of South Australia.' *Journal of the Proceedings of the Royal Society of New South Wales* 23: 476–503.

Steven, Margaret. 1965. *Merchant Campbell 1769–1846. A Study in Colonial Trade*. Oxford: Oxford University Press.

Stephens, John. 1839. *Land of promise*. London: Smith, Elder and Co.

Stevenson, George. 1930. Extracts from George Stevenson's journal: 'Description of the behaviour of natives at Holdfast Bay 1 January 1837.' *Proceedings of the Royal Geographical Society of Australasia, South Australian Branch* 30: 44–77.

Stewart, William. 1815. 'Letter to Colonial Secretary Capmbell, 28 September 1815.' *Historical Records of Australia* Series III vol. II, 1921: 575–76.

Street, Brian V. 1975. *The Savage in Literature*. London: Routledge & Kegan Paul.

Stuart, I. 1997. 'Sea Rats, Bandits and Roistering Buccaneers: What were the Bass Strait Sealers Really Like?' *Journal of the Royal Australian Historical Society* 831: 47–58.

Stuart, Lurline. 1979. *Nineteenth Century Australian Periodicals: An Annotated Bibliography*. Sydney: Hale & Iremonger.

Sturt, Charles. 1833. *Two expeditions into the interior of Southern Australia during the Years 1828, 1829, 1830, and 1831*. 2 vols. London: T. and W. Boone.

Sturt, Charles. 1849. *Narrative of an Expedition into Central Australia: Performed under the Authority of Her Majesty's Government during the years 1844, 1845 and 1846*. 2 vols. London: Smith, Elder and Co.

Summers, J. 1986. 'Colonial race relations.' *The Flinders History of South Australia. Social history*. Ed. E. Richards. Adelaide: Wakefield Press.

Supplement to the First Report of the Directors of the South Australian Company London: William Johnstone, 1837.

Sutherland, George. 1832. 'Report of a voyage from Sydney to Kangaroo Island.' Edward Gibbon Wakefield. *Plan of a company to be established for the purpose of founding a colony in Southern Australia: purchasing land therein*. London: Ridgway, 1832; Adelaide: Public Library of South Australia, 1962.

Sutton, Peter J. 1982. 'Personal power, kin classification and speech etiquette in Aboriginal Australia.' *The Flinders History of South Australia. Social history*. Ed. E. Richards. Adelaide: Wakefield Press: 283–311.

Taplin, George. 1874. 'The Narrinyeri.' *The native tribes of South Australia*. Ed. J. D. Woods. Adelaide: E.S.Wiggs.

Taplin, George. 1874. *The Narrinyeri, or Tribes of Aborigines Inhabiting the Country around the Lakes Alexandrina, Albert and Coorong, and the Lower Part of the River Murray*. Adelaide: Shawyer.

Taplin, George. 1879. *The folklore, manners and languages of South Australian Aborigines, Gathered from Inquiries Made by Authority of the South Australian Government*. Adelaide: Government Printer.

Taylor, Rebe, 2000. 'Savages or Saviours—the Australian Sealers and Aboriginal Survival.' *Journal of Australian Studies* 66: 73–84.

Taylor, Rebe. 2002. *Unearthed: the Aboriginal Tasmanians of Kangaroo Island*. Adelaide: Wakefield Press.

Teichelmann, Christian Gottlieb, and Clamor Wilhelm Schürmann. 1840. *Outlines of a grammar, vocabulary, and phraseology, of the aboriginal language of South Australia, spoken by the natives in and for some distance around Adelaide*. Adelaide: Published by the authors at the Native Location.

Teichelmann, Christian Gottlieb. 1841. *Aborigines of South Australia, Illustrative and explanatory note of the manners, customs, habits and superstitions of the natives of South Australia*. Adelaide: Committee of the SA Wesleyan Methodist Auxiliary Missionary Society.

The Official Civic Record of South Australia: Centenary Year, 1936. Adelaide: Universal Publicity Company, 1936.

Thomas, Mary. 1925. *The diaries and letters of Mary Thomas (1836–1866)*. Ed. E.K.Thomas. Adelaide: E.K.Thomas and Co.

Thomas, Sarah. 2002. *The Encounter, 1802: Art of the Flinders and Baudin Voyages.* Adelaide: Art Gallery of South Australia.

Tindale, Norman B. 1936. 'Notes on the natives of the southern portion of Yorke Peninsula, South Australia.' *Transactions of the Royal Society of South Australia* 60: 55–69.

Tindale, Norman B. 1937. 'Relationship of the Extinct Kangaroo Island culture with the cultures of Australia, Tasmania and Malaya.' *Records of the South Australian Museum*, 6: 39–60.

Tindale, Norman B. 1937. 'Tasmanian Aborigines on Kangaroo Island, South Australia.' *Records of the South Australian Museum* 6: 29–37.

Tindale, Norman B. 1937. 'Two legends of the Ngadjuri tribe from the middle north of South Australia.' *Transactions of the Royal Society of South Australia* 61: 149–153.

Tindale, Norman B. 1953. 'Growth of a People.' *Records of the Queen Victoria Museum* 2: 1–64.

Tindale, Norman B. 1974. *Aboriginal tribes of Australia: their terrain, environmental controls, distribution, limits and proper names.* Berkeley, Los Angeles, London: University of California Press.

Tindale, Norman B. 1987. 'The wanderings of Tjirbruke: a tale of the Kaurna people of Adelaide.' *Records of the South Australian Museum* 20: 5–13.

Tindale, Norman B., and B.G. Maegraith. 1931. 'Traces of an extinct Aboriginal population on Kangaroo Island.' *Records of the South Australian Museum* 4: 275–285.

Tolmer, Alexander 1882. *Reminiscences of an Adventurous and Chequered Career at Home and at the Antipodes.* 2 vols. London: Sampson Low, Marston, Searle, & Rivington.

Torrens, Robert and Samuel Stephens. 1986. 'New Colony of South Australia. To small farmers and others …' in Brian Dickey and Peter Howell, eds., *South Australia's Foundation: Select Documents.* Adelaide: Wakefield Press: 59–65.

Townrow, K. 1997. *An Archaeological Survey of Sealing and Whaling Sites in Victoria.* Melbourne: Heritage Victoria.

Tragenza, John. 1982. *George French Angas: Artist, Traveller and Naturalist 1882–1886.* Rev. ed. Adelaide: Art Gallery Board of South Australia.

von Stieglitz, Karl. 1978. *Pioneers of the East Coast from 1642: Swansea–Bicheno* Hobart: OBM.

Warneke, R.M. 1982. 'The distribution and abundance of seals in the Australian region, with summaries of biology and current research.' *Mammals in the Seas.* Food and Agriculture Organisation of the United Nations Fisheries Series, 5.4: 431–474.

Watts, Jane Isabella. 1890. *Family Life in South Australia fifty–three years ago.* Adelaide: W.K. Thomas.

Wells, Edith G. 1978. *Kangaroo Island South Australia: Cradle of a Colony*. Kingscote: Island Press.

Wells, H.G. 1898. *The War of the Worlds*. With an Afterword by Isaac Asimov. New York: Signet Classic, 1986.

West, I. 1987. *Pride against Prejudice: reminiscences of a Tasmanian Aborigine*. Rev. ed. Canberra: Australian Institute Of Aboriginal Studies.

West, J. 1852. *The History of Tasmania*. Ed. A.G.L. Shaw. Sydney: Angus and Robertson, in association with the Royal Australian Historical Society, 1971.

Whitehead, Kay. 1999. 'From youth to "greatest pedagogue": William Cawthorne and the construction of a teaching profession in mid–nineteenth century South Australia.' *History of Education* 28 4: 395–412.

Wilkinson, George Blakiston. 1848. *South Australia: its advantages and its resources, being a description of that colony and a manual of information for emigrants*. London: John Murray.

Williams, Vernon. 1929. *The Straitsmen: a Romance*. London: Cassell.

Wiltshire, J.G. 1973. *William Dutton and the sealing and whaling industries*. Portland: Portland Council.

Wood-Jones, Frederick. 1934. 'Tasmanians and Australians.' *Man* 66–67: 52–53.

Wyatt, William. 1879. 'Some Account of the Manners and Superstitions of the Adelaide and Encounter Bay Aboriginal Tribes.' *The Native Tribes of South Australia*. ed. J.D. Woods. Adelaide: E.S. Wigg & Son, Adelaide: Friends of the State Library of South Australia, 1997: 157–181.

Yelland, E.M. 1970. *Colonists, copper and corn*. Melbourne: Hawthorn Press.

Young, James M. c 1890s. *A tale of the early days of South Australia*. Burnside.

Acknowledgements

This edition was first prepared for a PhD at the University of Adelaide. I am very grateful to both the university and to Amanda Nettelbeck, with whom I first taught courses in the literature of contact at Flinders University and who is also a co-author of an earlier publication, *Fatal Collisions: The South Australian Frontier and the Violence of Memory* (Wakefield Press, 2001), winner of the 2002 John Tregenza Prize for South Australian History and shortlisted for the 2002 NSW Premier's Prize for Literature.

Sue Hosking, who shares my enthusiasms for Kangaroo Island, past and present: for hours of listening & discussion.

The late Syd Harrex who, as an almost-local, helped make connections between KI and Tasmania, his birthplace.

Rob Foster, another co-author of *Fatal Collisions*. He kindly made available to me a copy of his invaluable edition, Cawthorne's *Sketch of the Aborigines in South Australia: References in the Cawthorne Papers* (Adelaide: Aboriginal Heritage Branch, South Australian Department of Environment and Planning, 1991), together with other material that proved indispensable.

Kay Whitehead, who has written so well about Cawthorne the educator, and who made available her research papers.

The late Geoffrey Manning, for very kindly making available his invaluable South Australiana database.

Mrs Anne Marshall, Cawthorne's great-grand-daughter, for her kind assistance in making available family memorabilia and recollections.

Bob and Joan Huxtable for their help in arranging for copies of some of the materials held in the Penneshaw Maritime and Folk Museum to be made available to me.

Mary Northcott, of the National Parks and Wildlife Service based at Cape Willoughby, for making available files held at the lighthouse.

Keryn James, who kindly made available her 2001 Honours Thesis, *Wife or Slave*, from the Department of Archaeology, Flinders University, which helped me with many points of detail.

Rebe Taylor, author of *Unearthed: the Aboriginal Tasmanians of Kangaroo Island* (Adelaide: Wakefield Press, 2002), for long and animated discussions.

Colleagues at both Adelaide and Flinders universities for their interest and assistance: Phillip Butterss, Nick Jose, Anne Chittleborough, George Couvalis, Trevor Fennell, Brenda Glover, Steve Hemming, Peter Howell, Lyn Jacobs, Peter Mühlhaüsler, Christine Nicholls, Lester Irabinna Rigney, Mark Staniforth, Graham Tulloch and Gus Worby.

Librarians at the State Library of South Australia, State Records of South Australia, State Library of New South Wales (The Mitchell Library), the Barr Smith Library, Flinders Library, Tasmanian Archive & Heritage Office, the State Library of Tasmania and the National Library of Australia in Canberra, particularly Helen Harrison at the Mitchell Library and Gillian Dooley in Special Collections at Flinders.

To the people at Wakefield Press, for their long-standing commitment to South Australian research: Michael Bollen, Liz Nicholson, Michael Deves and Clinton Ellicott.

Irish South Australia: New histories and insights
Susan Arthure, Fidelma Breen, Stephanie James, Dymphna Lonergan
(eds)

The Last Protector: The illegal removal of Aboriginal
children from their parents in South Australia
Cameron Raynes

Marra: The making of men
Nicholas Newland

Mary Lee: The life and times of a 'turbulent anarchist' and
her battle for women's rights
Denise George

Miss Marryat's Circle: A not so distant past
Cheryl Williss

One Common Enemy: The *Laconia* Incident:
A survivor's memoir
Jim Mcloughlin with David Gibb

Pendragon: The life of George Isaacs, colonial wordsmith
Anne Black

Pens and Bayonets: Letters from the Front by soldiers of
Yorke Peninsula during the Great War
Don Longo

Searching for the Spirit: Theosophy in Australia, 1879–1939
Jill Roe

South Australia on the Eve of War
Melanie Oppenheimer, Margaret Anderson, Mandy Paul (eds)

Turning Points: Chapters in South Australian history
Robert Foster, Paul Sendziuk (eds)

Yura and Udnyu: A history of the Adnyamathanha of the
North Flinders Ranges
Peggy Brock

Wakefield Press is an independent publishing and
distribution company based in Adelaide, South Australia.
We love good stories and publish beautiful books.
To see our full range of books, please visit our website at
www.wakefieldpress.com.au
where all titles are available for purchase.
To keep up with our latest releases, news and events,
subscribe to our monthly newsletter.

Find us!

Facebook: www.facebook.com/wakefield.press
Twitter: www.twitter.com/wakefieldpress
Instagram: www.instagram.com/wakefieldpress